THE
FINANCIAL TERRORIST

Also by this Author
One Step to Danger

THE
FINANCIAL TERRORIST

JOHN GUBERT

Copyright © 2010 John Gubert

The moral right of the author has been asserted.

Apart from any fair dealing for the purposes of research or private study, or criticism or review, as permitted under the Copyright, Designs and Patents Act 1988, this publication may only be reproduced, stored or transmitted, in any form or by any means, with the prior permission in writing of the publishers, or in the case of reprographic reproduction in accordance with the terms of licences issued by the Copyright Licensing Agency. Enquiries concerning reproduction outside those terms should be sent to the publishers.

Matador
5 Weir Road
Kibworth Beauchamp
Leicester LE8 0LQ, UK
Tel: (+44) 116 279 2299
Fax: (+44) 116 279 2277
Email: books@troubador.co.uk
Web: www.troubador.co.uk/matador

ISBN 978 1848763 272

British Library Cataloguing in Publication Data.
A catalogue record for this book is available from the British Library.

Ths is a work of fiction. Characters, companies and locations are either the product of the author's imagination or, in the case of locations, if real, used fictitiously, without any intent to describe their actual environment.

Typeset in 11pt Bembo by Troubador Publishing Ltd, Leicester, UK
Printed in Great Britain by the MPG Books Group, Bodmin and King's Lynn

Matador is an imprint of Troubador Publishing Ltd

*To my most wonderful supporters,
Anne and Charles.*

Prelude

The financial world lives on a dangerous roller-coaster with major names often crashing down from dizzy heights:

- In 1995, unauthorised trading in the Singapore offices of the reputed British bank, Barings, led to a loss of over US$1.5 billion and its sale for a dollar to a Dutch financial institution
- In 1996, the Japanese firm of Sumitomo lost US$2.6 billion as a result of unauthorised trading in copper by one of their employees
- In 2000, the hedge fund, Long Term Capital Management, was rescued by a group of banks after it suffered losses of over US$ 4.5 billion
- In 2007, the French Bank, Societe Generale, announced that unauthorised market transactions cost it over US$ 5 billion
- In 2007, the UK Bank, Northern Rock, needed two hundred billion dollars of UK government support to avoid bankruptcy
- In the year to March 2008, the US Investment Bank, Bear Stearns, saw its share value crash over 90% from US$18 billion to just US$ 0.25 billion as a result of a crisis of confidence. It was bought by US bank, J P Morgan Chase, with a US$ 30 billion support package from the New York Federal Reserve.

Some may claim that the events in this novel and the earlier "One Step To Danger" are far fetched.

Others would say they show amazing foresight about what could, and perhaps will, happen in the roller coaster world of finance.

John S Gubert

CHAPTER ONE

Rossi and Di Maglio; those names had hit the headlines over the years. The Rossi family had stunned financial markets around the world as they powered their way to untold wealth. The Di Maglio family were alleged to be Mafia aristocracy.

It had been business as usual at International Bank of Europe, or IBE as it was more commonly known, since its takeover by Rossi and Di Maglio. But, that was about to change. In the room were men and women with strange pasts, some shadowy, some sinister and some simply unconventional.

They would place lives at risk and people would die. Companies would fail or be destroyed. Markets would be manipulated. Scams would be run. Fraud would be a way of life. Some would win and some would lose. The amounts would be huge and the losers would be angry. Investors, speculators, governments and criminals would hit out.

The die was now cast. The stakes were high. The decision had been made. Rossi and Di Maglio were going high profile, high risk for high reward. The Financial Terrorist was preparing to strike.

Charles Rossi took in the impressive surroundings. The large polished table dominated the boardroom. From the walls, several serious faces pondered the gathering below. They belonged to former chairmen of the company. They had all been distinguished pillars of the establishment in their time, were men who had the ear of the great and the good of the land. Their austere portraits seemed to come to life, and frown as if they did not cherish the sight of the people around the august room where once they had presided in almost royal omnipotence.

Unusually, although there were some members of the board present, several of the attendees were definitely not on the board. The Chairman was not there. The Honourable James Johnson-St. John-James was the son and heir to the now senile Earl of Ember. His triple barrelled name emphasised his noble roots. Sir Brian Ffinch-Farquar was also absent. As indeed was Lord Dunkillin. They were three of the original directors who had been on the board at the time of the take-over. They remained and assured everyone who worried about those things that nothing had changed at IBE. That was not quite right, but they were not aware of some of the changes that had occurred and, perhaps more significantly, those that were being planned

Charles, as the new Chief Executive, had allowed the bank to continue on its former profitable path. IBE had, though, gained some new clients from his contacts. And, even more dramatically for some, a ladies' cloakroom with a baby's changing area had been installed on the top floor. That formerly strictly all male enclave housed the boardroom and the directors' offices. IBE had embraced equality, as only a Group obliged to do so can. For Jacqui Di Maglio, who smiled over at Charles, operated under her maiden name, although she was now Mrs Rossi. She was a director and, indeed, part owner of the holding company.

IBE had recently started dealing with a series of new clients in America. And Giovanni Petroni, who was in the room, was on the board of many of them.

They also undertook quite a bit of business with the secretive funds of their parent, and the reclusive Jack Ryder, who ran these and other funds, was also present. He had been accused of fraud some years before. It was claimed that he had embezzled a billion dollars from one of London's biggest international banks. But that had all since been disproved. And Jack was Charles' father, although Charles had since changed his name and the relationship was only known to a few.

Most people at IBE also did not know they did business with Di Maglio. Nobody called him by his first name, if he had one. He had a broad range of interests, and some had nominated Giovanni Petroni as their chairman. Di Maglio had an awkward habit of occasionally calling Petroni, councillor, and that fuelled further the rumours of his criminal links. When queried, he would say that all lawyers were known by that title in his house. The brave whispered that Petroni also was Mafia and Di Maglio's right hand man. But few dared to state that openly. And Di Maglio was in the room, standing apart from the others with Petroni by his side.

There were two final members of the group. One was John Stephens, a well-known foreign exchange trader, now employed by IBE. He had a somewhat hazy past, and indeed it had been no easy task getting the regulators to agree to his being the head of IBE's fast growing trading desk. He was, though, not on the board. His earlier role in the downfall of one of the larger US banks prevented that. He had been known as the man with the golden touch in London. Then he moved to New York, where he was said to have exceeded his authority. He had bet the wrong way, and his bank had lost a few billion dollars and its independence. Stephens always claimed that he was the unfortunate boss who had been the fall guy. He claimed events that led to the loss were not of his making. But a group of friends and associates knew how much he had made from the trades. And they knew that they had made more.

The other person was a girl in her mid to late twenties. She was called Maria Carter. Di Maglio had employed her at one time. She was a girl Friday. But she had a special touch. She killed on command. She was loyal for money. She was also bright. And she had the title of Personal Assistant to IBE's Chief Executive.

Charles Rossi looked around the room again. The hawk-like features of Giovanni never changed. He must have looked old and skeletal twenty years ago. He continued to do so. Then he noted the bull-like power build of Di Maglio. His black hair was slicked back from his low forehead. His dark eyes were smiling without malice, but also without warmth. He noted his father, tall and slim, with greying hair. Jack Ryder looked like an academic; a thoughtful man, who watched and noted everything, a thinker and a strategist.

Outside that group stood Stephens, looking shiftily from person to person, and drinking his coffee in isolation in one corner of the room. There was a man one would use but never trust. But Stephens knew his purpose. He would always obey for the right price, even if resentfully. Stephens would be lucky to see out the next year, even if he did as he was told, although for the moment he was unaware of this.

Charles smiled at the two women who were now talking together. Jacqui looked exotic in the extreme with her dark hair, hanging loose over her shoulders, framing her gentle face. Her eyes showed that she was a woman of steel. They were warm and lively, but determined as well. The soft face was capable of anger and menace if need be. Maria was a girl with the figure of a model, the face of an angel and the morals of a whore. But for Charles, her fierce loyalty to him as her paymaster was her principal required virtue.

Charles knocked on the table. "Ladies and Gentlemen, welcome. Please be seated for we have business to do. Let me organise the table."

He asked his father and Di Maglio to sit on either side of him. Jack Ryder took the right and Di Maglio the left. Giovanni immediately sat next to his boss, while Jacqui moved next to her father-in-law. Stephens and Maria sat opposite each other.

The group filled half the boardroom table. There was an air of expectation. Charles began to speak.

"Two and a half years ago, Jacqui and I created a holding company with Jack and Anne Marie Ryder."

He stopped and looked at some of the amused smiles at his failure to recognise his parents. But that was intentional, for Stephens would be unaware of the relationship and they all already knew that there was no value in giving information to Stephens unless he needed it. One of the first rules of survival was to share knowledge only on a need to know basis.

Charles continued, "It had two assets. Firstly, it owned a fund management company, which operated speculative investment companies, or hedge funds, as they are now known. That was worth around a billion dollars. Secondly, it was sitting on around four billion dollars of cash.

We now have three main assets. They are still the fund management company. It is worth around one and a half billion dollars. Then we have International Bank of Europe, commonly known as IBE, on whose premises we are today. It is one of the best known UK investment banks and must be worth around two billion against the billion we paid for it just over a couple of years ago. And, finally, we have just over three billion of cash.

Most people would be pleased with turning a five billion dollar enterprise into a six and a half billion one in eighteen months. But that's not good enough for us.

We now plan to make at least another five to ten billion in the next year, and we all need to work together to do that. For, in order to do that, our bank is going to have to go spectacularly bust. We are here today to agree my plans. They require input from you all. Needless to say the aim is for you also to share in the profits that result.

At the end of this meeting, any of you are free to leave the group. After that nobody can. I have agreed that with my partners and my father in law. Like the rest of you, though, they do not know the details of my plan. They only know that we are building up to the biggest financial coup of the century, perhaps even of all time.

I assume you will all tell me by the end of the meeting that you are with us, or, that you want to leave. If you go you will have to forget all that you heard here. One casual mention would be fatal. And I mean fatal. Indeed that rule will also apply to those who stay."

Charles looked at the faces around the table. There was no reaction from most of them. They knew the comment was directed at Stephens rather than them. Some knew enough of Charles' past to know that he could fulfil the threat, if need be. And others realised that Di Maglio would willingly offer his expertise in the matter if so requested.

Most of them knew how Charles had killed two Mafia hit men in the South of France. And they knew of the shootout in Paris, when the Russian Mafia had kidnapped Jacqui. They also knew about the two bloody attacks on the Russian Mafia in the South of France. And they remembered the last killing of Boris the Bear in Barbados.

Maria had also killed for them. Her list of victims included Jack Ryder's former associate, a man called Jim. He could have made life hard for them if he had survived; and Maria had ensured that he didn't. Di Maglio had killed and ordered more people killed than most. Giovanni referred to people as human capital and had them disposed of, as required, without hesitation.

The only person who did not know this world was Stephens but even he was a good enough judge of character to realise the truth. Jacqui also had not killed anyone, but she would and could if she had to.

Charles looked at them and smiled. He knew they'd all stay. Jacqui was fully aware of the plans. This was a charade especially for Stephens and for Maria. And both were needed for the plans to succeed. They had shown few scruples about right and wrong in the past; they would have to show even fewer in the future to ensure success.

Di Maglio looked at Charles, who noted there was pride in the glance. Charles shuddered at the thought. His father-in-law had proved to be a doting grandfather, but still a man to be wary of. Di Maglio ran his beloved drugs and prostitution Empire alongside his legal enterprises. He was the arch villain. The IBE plan was based on sophisticated financial manipulation; the Di Maglio operations were often just old fashioned thuggery. His days were coming to an end. Charles and Jacqui were part of the New World and they could not get him to realise that.

Charles smiled at them all. "Let me give you a short run-down of my plans and then I will take questions. If we floated IBE on the stock market, we could raise around two billion dollars for it. Last year it made profits of around two hundred and eighty million. That's not bad for a company of its size. I plan, though, to grow it substantially in the coming year. And it will first grow by acquisition.

The first acquisition should be the group of banks known as PAF or

Pan American Financial, owned by the Di Maglio family interests. Our friend Giovanni Petroni, who I plan to invite to join our board, is their chairman."

Both Giovanni and Di Maglio looked astonished by this announcement. It was the first time they had heard of the planned deal. They frowned and it sounded as if Di Maglio growled. But they said nothing.

Charles continued, "PAF is a group of eight regional banking groups in New York State through to California. Their attraction for IBE will be their ability to sell its securities products to their customers. In other words, we will create investments that they will buy. As there are over five million customers in PAF, we should be able to offload several billion of investments on them. More importantly, as we do, we will make money. I am expecting that many of the investments sold will be fraudulent; they will be empty shells. I'll look to my partner, Jack Ryder, for help in creating those. As many of you know he is quite an expert in that field. I estimate we could make several hundreds of millions of profits for the combined bank by charging fees when we sell the securities and also the odd billion for ourselves by creating the phoney ones."

Giovanni and Di Maglio nodded approvingly. Giovanni spoke, "And I guess you will buy PAF at a premium and so we make money up front."

"No. It will be a sweetheart deal, you will take shares in the company and not cash. You will get much more cash later when we float the enlarged bank in the market and you can sell your shares. It's actually simple. We sell clients investments and the bank gets the fees. We raise the profits of the bank. Investors see us as a growth stock. They pay over the odds for us, just before the whole can of worms opens."

Everybody around the table was nodding enthusiastically.

"And there will be more ways of increasing the bank's profits; we need to use these. I want Jack Ryder and John Stephens to arrange a series of trades by which we siphon money out of the bank. They both have experience at that. In the short term the bank will appear to make money from the trades but in reality it will all be pie in the sky and it will lose a packet.

We will sell the bank to the public at a high price. That way we should recoup our investment and more. And we can, at the same time, do quite a nice line in insider dealing through our funds. Especially as we will know that, soon after the sale of the bank to the public, it will be hit with trading and other losses; there will be a series of announcements and the share price will slump."

This time it was Jack Ryder and Stephens who nodded enthusiastically. This was their forte. They wanted to start talking about the arrangements immediately. Charles stopped them, "Let me finish the plans. I also want to lend to the maximum to a series of companies that will go bust spectacularly. We identified several targets some time ago and have been working on them. These companies are no hopers although they all have a reasonably long pedigree. They are the mongrels of the markets.

We have managed to place our current chairman and several other original directors of IBE, or their family members and friends, on the board of all of these companies. So they are going to be implicated. Our connection is not apparent, we have hidden it through the usual labyrinth of offshore companies. I've had to use the best lawyers in the world for this and they've earned their millions in fees. But nobody other than Jacqui and I know the precise linkages between the various companies.

The bank will lend several billion to these companies and they will all fall. It will appear that the money was lost on wildcat ventures. The money though will simply have been paid over to us, although no one will be able to prove that.

That will cramp the style of the establishment people on our board and their buddies in the market. It will also earn us a bundle in diverted cash."

Ryder intervened, "So you plan to make around a billion by selling fake investments to PAF's customer base? Then you reckon to sell the bank to the public? You could raise around five billion, if you manage to sell half the shares and the bank's profits soar as you described. Stephens and I should be able to make a couple of billion on the markets through fraudulent trading. And then the phoney loans will take out, say, another two or three billion. We should make another billion on insider trading. That makes just about twelve billion. IBE cost a billion. PAF must be worth a couple. As that will be lost money, it looks as if you are heading to make around nine billion. That's easily in the range you just mentioned.

I assume that the profits on the bank sale would be split with Di Maglio fairly evenly and so we are talking six or seven billion for us and two to three for them."

Giovanni shook his head, "We need a better deal for our side than that. I agree we split evenly the money from the bank sale. We should own around half the shares and you should own the other half. But we need more than you just said. I guess our cut on all the scams you are suggesting should be around forty per cent. As for the rest around this table, they should each be in for a few million performance bonus "

It was a fair deal and Charles nodded in agreement, "We have to sort out an agreement with you Giovanni but that's about the basis I had planned, although I think you are a bit high on your take on the scams."

Charles waited. Giovanni was silent. That meant he would take a lower cut. Charles and Jacqui glanced at each other; the split was more in their favour than they had expected. Charles looked at Di Maglio. He nodded too. Everybody smiled in agreement. This clearly meant a few million personally for Stephens, Giovanni and also Maria. Every one else had a finger in the Di Maglio Empire or the Rossi and Di Maglio holding company, which would get the bulk of the money. Greed triumphed over logic as the outsiders failed to notice that, ominously, the figures were getting to be worth more than their lives.

Charles interrupted the eager looks. "There is one extra deal. Once IBE's shares have slumped on the disastrous news, they will be the subject of a bid. The bid will be from Associated."

"How can you manage that?" gasped Ryder.

"It's simple really. We still have compromising papers on their chairman, Sir Piers, although he does not realise that. You don't all need to know the details or how we got them, but Jack, Jacqui and I know them. And they are dynamite."

Charles had no reason to reveal their contents to Di Maglio or Stephens. The papers showed that Sir Piers was involved in insider dealing at the time of the Associated take-over of their US bank. He had personally made five or six million from that deal. Charles also had some perfectly forged papers that showed he ordered a hit man to take out Jim, Jack Ryder's former colleague.

Maria giggled; she also knew of the papers and had been the killer in that incident. The tabloid press had gone to town on the case; it had been a fairly sordid murder. But then everything had been set up to make it look that way to ensure the stories were about the victim and not Jack Ryder. Maria was a perfectionist without any inhibitions when it came to the killing game.

"I'll offer Sir Piers his papers once and for all if he takes over IBE. I will play it as if I am contrite. I will worry about his moronic friends on our board, play concerned about our customers. The man's an idiot and will fall for that. In the end I reckon he'll pay a couple of billion for what's left of the bank. He'll have to act quickly, as otherwise it will have no customers left. But he will. It's the sort of deal that will appeal to him. Above all he wants his name kept clean. The fool could even get another title for his actions. He'll save a lot of people from embarrassment. And so the final sale of our stake will bring us in another billion or so.

That brings us up to around ten billion or so on your figures. Mine would be higher, but that depends on how well we manage to run the scams. There are more gullible investors and idiot bankers out there than you would expect. I'm sure that we can take them for a very bad ride! And the worst it is for them, the better it is for us!"

Charles stopped talking. Jack Ryder realised that he expected to make quite a bit more. Perhaps they would make another 50% or even more than that. They could really push the boat out on the fraudulent loans. Perhaps they would sell off more than half the shares in the initial public offering of IBE. But the bait was already good enough and they had no need to embellish it further.

Jack Ryder grinned. Di Maglio was beaming. Everyone else was too.

"We have a deal," said Di Maglio.

Ryder said, "You bet we do."

Giovanni asked, "Is it OK if I draft the agreements by tomorrow evening. I'll keep them simple."

Jacqui laughed and suggested, "There should be the usual penalty clauses for non performance."

That joke made Di Maglio roar with laughter and slap his thigh theatrically. He winked at Charles and pulled his hand across his throat. The others just sat there in open-mouthed agreement. They were again totting up their greedy vision of unlimited wealth.

"Are there any other questions?" Charles said, if only to ensure that they all snapped back to reality.

"Well, yes," replied Stephens. "What is the timing going to be?"

"The first thing is that we need an agreement. That should be simple. It will outline the role of each person. It would recognise that I call the shots for everything."

Charles waited, just in case there were any objections. Di Maglio, almost automatically, shook his head. He did not say anything. Nobody else reacted.

"I would ask Giovanni to sort that out. It has to identify the split. The one I had in mind is close to the one Giovanni suggested. We should keep that simple. Other than for the share sale and the profit from insider trading, fifty percent of all remaining profit goes to our holding company. Forty per cent goes to the Di Maglio organisation."

"What happens to the insider trading stuff?" queried Giovanni sharply.

"That goes to Rossi and Di Maglio. We fund it. We take the risk and the profit. That's our territory and it compensates us for all the business we will miss out whilst we work this deal."

"That's a hell of a bonus for you," growled Di Maglio.

"It is part of the deal and it's not negotiable. Anyway it would be hard to say what insider trading was deal related and Rossi and Di Maglio related. We could never agree a split."

Di Maglio looked angry for a moment. It was not a pleasant sight. Then he shrugged his shoulders, "As long as you hit your figures on the shared part, I'll buy it. But don't try anything fancy!"

Charles grinned, "Not with you guys watching. I know your punishment schedule."

That raised a wry smile, even from Di Maglio, although his eyes remained cold. He knew he would have no qualms about revenge on Charles or even Jacqui if he felt he was being cheated. And little did he know how much the plan was to cheat him and to what extent.

Charles allowed a short silence and then continued, "The remaining ten percent of the scam monies is split equally between Giovanni, John, Maria, our holding company and the Di Maglio organisation. That actually would mean that Giovanni, John and Maria will each get around a hundred million. Is everyone happy?"

This last comment was directed especially at Giovanni, Stephens and Maria, all of whom gasped in astonishment at the size of their cut.

Giovanni glanced over at Di Maglio, who nodded curtly, if unenthusiastically. Giovanni would need to be careful, Di Maglio did not want him to have two masters and Charles had just played him into the deal for much more than he would ever have considered.

Maria smiled, her eyes showing how excited and pleased she was at the prospect. She really was beautiful when she smiled like that. Charles couldn't recall having seen such a reaction before.

Stephens jumped in, a sneer on his face, "Why does Maria get a cut? She does nothing."

Charles turned round to him and Stephens shuddered as he noticed the look of fury on his face, "Don't ever question my judgement. I decide why. There are no travellers on this show. We need Maria, believe me."

"Sorry," said Stephens, backing off. "I was just curious."

"Then don't be. Just do as you are told and you can add a nice sum to the five million you made from your last scam. You're playing with the big boys now. So keep your eye on the ball."

Di Maglio came in at that point. His voice, as usual at times like this, was chilling. "If you don't keep your eye on the ball," he drawled, "you may find you have none to keep your eye on. So don't act stupid."

Charles grinned over at him, "I think we're on the same wave-length. But let me carry on. The first thing I want to do is to fabricate some investments for the American market. We need to make them simple. Otherwise they won't fly. How long do you need to put a package together?"

Jack Ryder thought for a moment for the question was targeted at him. The others waited expectantly. "You have five million customers in the US. You definitely need simple products.

We should do the same scam that we ran with Union Bank of Europe a couple of years ago. We can launch a series of funds, which PAF can push at their clients. The sales commission needs to be rich so the bank earns a bundle.

We make money by creating phoney investments for them to invest in. There are enough options there as that game has been running for years now. We can buy some genuine shares for the funds to invest in, but, before they buy them, we'll push up their stock prices. We make even more money for ourselves that way."

Giovanni chimed in, "If you can start up the funds within a week, I could have the sales literature around the banks within weeks."

"I'll need a few weeks to identify the shares they should invest in. They need to be ones whose prices we can manipulate. We also need to create the phoney securities the funds will buy. I'll be ready to roll on this one in about three or four weeks."

"What about the trading you wanted us to do?" Stephens demanded. He was starting to irritate with his impatience, he could be for the high jump quicker than had been planned. Maria and Charles exchanged knowing glances.

"Give me time. We'll come to that later," Charles said sharply. Stephens flushed. His eyes betrayed anger. Charles ignored that, although he now knew for certain that he would have to use him quickly and then dispose of him as soon as possible.

"Before we start to boost profits, we need to take over PAF. They are not as profitable as IBE despite their strong customer base. They haven't been run for profit."

Charles looked over at Di Maglio. He had not cared about profits on the banks. That was not why he ran them. He had needed something to help him launder the profits of his other illegal enterprises. That took his energy. But, over time, he had also built up a series of commercial relationships with banks outside his control and really had no need for his own. They were a legacy of the past when bankers used to be honest. These days, with tax and other havens all over the world, there was no shortage of corrupt bankers with dodgy values.

Charles said, "Both banks should be equal partners. You will own half of the combined bank. I want it to be just under half. We will own the balance and the majority. That way we still call the shots."

Di Maglio told Giovanni to get the deal done. The terms were irrelevant. He was looking for the big killing. The deal would be done as soon as the authorities allowed it. Charles guessed that it would be waved through and quickly. The idea of moving the banks out of Di Maglio's clutches would appeal to the regulators. They had never intimated it, but there was no way that they could not know of his ownership and involvement. But what could they do about it when any action against him could cause a panic among the banks' five million customers and among the customers of other banks as well? The regulators were in the business of calming markets, not exciting them. IBE could use its token directors from the great and the good to sway them. That would be easy despite Jacqui's involvement and Charles' slightly dubious past.

Charles now turned to Stephens. He was still visibly angry. But, once he saw his role was to be explained, he soon cheered up, "You and Jack Ryder must arrange for a whole series of deals that the bank will undertake and which will not appear accurately in their books. We will play around big time in the markets. We will cash in the gains; the bank will take the losses. You, John, will need to flee and take the can. You have done that before, it shouldn't be hard. You have no family or relations, and you will be fabulously rich as compensation for your pain! Does that make you happy?"

He nodded eagerly, "Will you give me a new identity? I'll need it."

"We're experts at that."

"You will work out the trades with Ryder, and you only trade if he agrees with all the details. Can you agree?"

"No problem. We should start planning next week."

"You can start to trade next week as well. You can do it for IBE. After a while, once both banks are put together, you will have more to play with."

He was now happy. "It's going to be fun," he said, "bloody good fun."

Again Maria and Charles exchanged glances. They thought that his use of the word bloody in this context was a bit unfortunate and wondered if he would fall off a tall building or in front of an express train. Maria could organise that.

Jack Ryder looked pleased, "We make fake trading profits for the bank. If we use state of the art products, we can fool any auditor. People with more integrity and much less skill than us have managed that in the past. But the bank will bleed cash in the end when it fails to get its money back. We'll have salted that away long before they realise it."

"But before that we go to the big deal," Charles said, "I want that to happen after the next profits are announced. I want us to make at least a billion of profit this year on the combined Group. I suspect that will mean we could sell half of our shares for around five billion. The company as a whole would be worth ten."

"The current combined profits are round five hundred million," said Giovanni. "I suspect we could get the value up to a bit more than ten billion if we manage to turn in over a billion profit in the year of the merger. We could add further to the profits by taking on larger loans for some of the Di Maglio companies. I'll arrange it and could see that some of those borrowers also go bust once the time is right."

"Excellent. We think alike. But don't be too greedy or it will look too suspicious. Together, though, we could make another billion."

Giovanni smiled, pleased to have a more direct role.

"What about the final scam?" Ryder asked.

"It's simple. You go for the ultimate inside trade. You sell shares you don't own in the bank. You know how to do that. There will be a lot of demand at the time of the sale to the public. Once you have a big enough position, spread widely so it is pretty invisible to the regulators, we'll put out a profit warning or something to dampen down the market. We then hit the shares.

There will be scandal after scandal. First, Stephens disappears and we find out about the trading losses. The share price will slump.

Then we'll announce the bad loans. The price slumps again.

We can then get the regulators looking at the investments we have been selling to the bank clients and they'll find that they are invested in some fairly dodgy and worthless stock. The shares will go into free fall.

As the shares slump, you buy back; and then I manufacture the bid. Hey presto we've made another fortune!"

"It'll work," said Ryder. "No problem. We've done similar things before."

Di Maglio spoke again, "You reckon you'll make ten billion over the next year or so. You're good. But what do you do next? You won't exactly smell of roses."

"I'll pretend to have been duped. I'll play the hard luck story. And I'll be back as I will still have the bulk of my wealth in Rossi and Di Maglio. It's only the bank that will fail. But we'll also weaken Associated by the deal. A lot of the business over there will leave the bank. And I believe Mr Di Maglio would agree to stop using them and he is their biggest depositor. When they are weak, we may be able to take them over. But that is not in the plans. That's an option for the future."

There were no other questions. Di Maglio said he had to leave. He needed to get back to the US. Giovanni would go with him. He'd call the next day. Stephens headed off, as did Maria. Jack Ryder, Jacqui and Charles were alone.

"Charles, that's brilliant." Jack Ryder glowed with pride at the ruthless simplicity of Charles' plan. "And it will work. I'll get back to Tropez now. I can get the afternoon flight. Tomorrow I'll start planning. I was getting tired of being a boring fund manager."

He was already deep in thought. He gave Jacqui an absent minded kiss, and shook Charles' hand, clapping him on the back, before heading out. Charles strolled over to the security monitors to see Di Maglio and Giovanni walking to their car in front of the bank. Stephens was in the car park and driving out in his BMW. Maria was getting into her Mercedes coupe. She smiled and waved to the monitor, blowing it a kiss as if to tell them she knew they would be there. Ryder came to the lobby and walked out of the building. He was lucky for a cab was passing. He hailed it and then left their field of vision.

Charles put an arm round Jacqui's shoulders, "We've never been here on a Sunday. It's strange with nobody around."

"You know you're quite sexy when you become authoritarian. It actually turns me on to see everyone hanging on to your every word. I've always loved power."

Charles put his arms around her waist. She was dressed in a dark short skirt and a white blouse. She looked great. He could smell her fragrance. He could taste her lips as he kissed her lightly.

He had taken off his jacket before the meeting. He pulled her closer.

"Uh, uh," she said. "Not here. We could be interrupted."

"No, we won't be." He moved his hands up her back, "There's only security around. They have strict instructions to keep clear of this floor until I tell them otherwise."

She laughed, "Did you plan this? I mean it's a bit crazy making love in the boardroom. I bet nobody else has. Shouldn't we turn the pictures around? It looks as if those old bores are watching."

"Those old bores would turn in their graves if they thought that someone was going to have nookie in their precious bank. There would be a series of fits if they knew it was in the boardroom."

"You're right. And you were good. I have an idea."

Charles waited. She moistened her lips and pulled herself away from him, kicking off her shoes at the same time. The next thing he knew, she had jumped onto one of the chairs and was sitting back on the long polished board table.

"Hey it's slippery," she called as she propelled herself along half its length. Her skirt rode up to her hips, revealing long shapely legs in sheer tights. She giggled as she rolled over and stretched her arms to either side of the table, hugging it and groaning, "I rather like the smell of the polish and the feel of the wood you know."

Charles went over to her. The boardroom had fine views of the City and the River. On one side it was overlooked by the sparkling great dome of St Paul's Church and on the other by the more pedestrian architecture of the Bank of England. God and Mammon must have been wondering what two people could plan to do on a twenty foot long shining oak table in a smart office block in the City. They both gave the impression of looking on through the eyes of the gargoyles and the other statues that stood guard on their roofs.

He helped her down from the table.

"We mustn't scratch it. The Honourable James is paranoid about its perfect sheen. He even took me to task for wearing sharp cufflinks the other day."

She giggled. Then a long passionate kiss was followed by a series of gasps and groans. Her hands moved round from his back and started to undress him.

"This gives those old men a reason to look angry at least," laughed Jacqui, glancing up at the sombre portraits.

He glanced up. He could take in the view of the Church over her shoulder. She could see the Bank of England over his.

Then they forgot about the Bank, the Church and the angry faces on the wall as they clung closer together. Suddenly he was startled, "Someone's around. Who in hell can it be? It can't be security. They're too good. The two on duty today are your father's old people. I had to have people who would keep quiet about the meeting."

Despite the sudden interruption to their lovemaking, Jacqui also was alert. She knew that you didn't fool around when there was danger. Still half undressed, Charles went over to the monitors. They showed the corridor outside the boardroom. He bounded quietly to the door at that side and swiftly turned the key in the lock. It shut with a click that he thought would have alerted anyone within earshot. But when he returned to the monitor, the two men were still approaching as if they were unaware of the disturbance they had caused.

Jacqui in the meantime had gathered up their clothes from the floor. She stood there waiting for Charles to react. The door handle turned noisily. Then they heard voices.

"They must have locked it. We'll have to go round the other side. If that's locked too, we'll just have to force the door. We need the tape that Wendy left there. It will be hard for her to get it tomorrow. It was dangerous enough setting it up there last week in the first place."

Jacqui signalled Charles to the other door and he quickly checked it was unlocked. It was opposite his office and now he headed there. Jacqui followed him. They left the door half open to be able to have sight of the boardroom. Without a word, they started getting dressed again.

"I've left my bra behind. It's by the table. I wonder what they'll make of that."

"It may give us time and distract them."

Charles moved over to his desk and removed the gun from its usual hiding place. He opened the drawer and took the spare one from the false bottom. He handed that to Jacqui.

"Heavier than you usually use. I'll lead. You can cover."

Charles moved over to get sight of the monitors and watched the corridor outside. He gazed at the two men, not recognising them. He looked at Jacqui. She shook her head. They were unfamiliar to her as well.

"They are not armed as far as I can see. That must mean they are local. Only a Brit would handle a job like this without a gun."

Charles nodded. She was right. He noted the name of Wendy. Who the hell was she? He knew no Wendy in the office. He needed to know who she was, if she had access to the boardroom, she could have access to other areas. As he had only called the meeting on Thursday, it meant she knew almost immediately. But how was that? He had to find out and get rid of her if necessary.

He peered round his office door, which was still ajar. The two men had their backs to him and were gazing at the bra in astonishment. He signalled to Jacqui to keep quiet.

Then a voice said, "One of the randy tarts they brought in has been at it. Jefferson mentioned one of them. He hates that little black haired job. He said she was an evil bitch."

The other laughed, "Well, he said Wendy's been keeping her eye on her too. Mind you, she must have her hands full as she's tracking the Rossis as well. It's lucky her boss hasn't got much of a job or she'd be working night and day."

"Come on. Let's get the tape," said the other. "I wish we could have used a bug but the old man said they might check the room for them. And tapes are at least invisible."

That at least explained the tape. They still did not know who Wendy was. She obviously worked at the bank and should be easy to trace. The two strangers moved over to the table. One ducked underneath it and produced a small recorder. He opened it and took out a tape. He slipped the tape in his pocket and then calmly walked over to a desk in the corner of the room. He opened a drawer and placed the recorder in it.

Charles still did not move. He needed to know how they got in and out. He couldn't let them out of the boardroom though and so he would have to get them to tell him. He needed the tape. He needed to know who they worked for. And he needed to know who Wendy was.

They casually walked towards his office. Charles kicked the door open and said, "Freeze."

They looked at him in horror. They had obviously recognised him. He still did not know them.

"I think you owe me an explanation. Why are you here?"

They remained silent.

"I am not sure if you know some of my methods. They may not be good for your health. Are you going to answer my question?"

There was still no answer.

Charles looked at them. They were both dressed in single-breasted office suits. They wore sober ties over white shirts. Their shoes had been well polished. Their hair was cut short. These were ex-policemen. They must be operating as private detectives. He walked into the room and told Jacqui to cover them. They gasped when they saw she also had a gun.

"Don't try anything funny. We're good at this." Charles doubted they would do anything. It was clear that they believed he would shoot. The sweat was beginning to leave a sheen on their foreheads, the pungent odour of fear was apparent as Charles moved closer.

He walked to the taller one and motioned him to step away from his partner. He moved up to him and searched him quickly. There was no gun. He went to his jacket pockets and took out a wallet. There was nothing else. He moved to the table, still keeping him covered. He opened the wallet. There was cash, credit cards and a photo, but nothing else. He noticed one of the cards. It showed he worked for a detective agency. It hardly looked inspiring with an address in an unfashionable area, more one for electronic shops and the like than detective agencies.

He walked back to him and searched him thoroughly. There was nothing else, just a bit of change in his pockets. He then smashed him over the head with the gun. The man's knees buckled and he groaned as his hands went to his head. But there were to be no more blows.

"That's a warning. If that happens when you do what you're told, imagine what happens if you don't. Lie on the floor; spread your arms and legs. Stay like that until you're told to move. And I mean stay like that."

Charles then turned to the second man. He was smaller than the first and more frightened. He had watched everything and was trembling with fear. After all, he was holding the tape.

Charles searched him. Once again he took a wallet. He took a mobile phone. And he took the tape. Otherwise there was nothing. The wallet revealed little. He picked up the tape.

"What's this?"

"It's for my dictating machine at home. I did some work. It's a report for clients. I am a private detective."

Jacqui moved towards him. Charles nodded. Her gun came in an arc, hitting him on the nose and cheek. It then swung back and slammed him from the other side. His face was bleeding badly. It looked as if his nose was broken.

"I think you misunderstood the rules he made. I hit you softly. Don't make him angry or you'll really get hurt." Charles followed through, "And when you get back home, you might find the family a bit upset. No kids like seeing their mother beaten up in front of them. They say it scars them for life."

The man glanced over at his wallet. He realised they knew his address. He saw they had seen the photo of his family. It was a nice family. But, if need be, he realised that Charles would have carried out his threat. He crumbled.

"It's a tape of your meeting. We came here to retrieve it."

"We knew that. If you want to get over this, you answer honestly three questions. First, how did you get past the guards?"

"We came through the side door from the little alley. It was unlocked and the security camera there has been rigged. It will just show the empty room. I don't know how it's done."

Charles did. That was easy to rig. They would need to step up security. He carried on.

"Who sent you?"

"Jefferson."

"Who's he?"

"Head of Security at Associated."

Charles was surprised but did not show it, "How are you getting the tape to him?"

"We'll deliver it at midday. He'll be waiting for us. He gives us the cash in return. He'll pay five thousand pounds. That's why we did it. It's well paid."

"Where will he be?"

He hesitated. Jacqui moved slightly. He shivered.

"He'll be by the Royal Exchange. That's just opposite the Bank of England."

Charles glanced at the clock. It was twenty to twelve.

"Who's Wendy?"

"I don't know a Wendy who's involved in this."

He did not even see Jacqui's hand move that time, but the pain on his damaged face must have been excruciating. He sobbed in agony this time.

"It's a girl called Wendy. She's Lord Dunkillin's secretary."

Charles now knew who he meant. A sour faced blonde who had been in the bank for about fifteen years. He knew she worked for them but, beyond that, he had nothing to do with her. He hadn't even recalled her name.

"I'm going to call the police. You will be charged with breaking and entering. You put up a fight and tried to escape. You had a gun and I managed to get it from you. I'll shoot Jacqui in the shoulder to make it look worse. I lost my temper and admit hitting you when you tried to kill my wife, but that's not going to cause me any harm."

The smaller man looked really scared. "Look we're freelancing. If this gets out, we'll lose our licences and our jobs. Can't you let us go? We'll say nothing."

"You'll talk. Who else knows you're here?"

"Nobody does. The family thinks I'm working. We don't tell them what or where. They know better than to ask."

Charles guessed this was right. He walked over to the phone and called security, "One of you, get up here. We have a problem."

He then called Maria, "Where are you?"

"I'm meeting a friend. I'm in Covent Garden."

"Come over here. We need you." Then a thought struck him, "Do you know Jefferson at Associated?"

"He's their Head of Security. We tried to recruit him in the early days. But he's straight, we failed."

"Would you recognise him?"

Charles could hear that Maria was now in the street. She must be heading to her car.

"You bet I would. I always remember people. He's a big man with reddish hair."

"He'll be by the Royal Exchange, opposite the Bank of England. Get rid of him. And I mean rid of him. He'll be there till twelve. He's waiting for some people."

She didn't ask why, she just said, "OK. I'll join you by ten past. "

The security man came in. He looked shocked. "Tie these people up. Watch them. And make sure that there are no signs they have been here. Tell your pal downstairs to check the side door into the alley and reset the camera. It's been rigged."

He nodded and was starting to tie up the men before they moved out. He had also drawn a gun from a leg holster. He could be trusted.

Charles and Jacqui both walked out. "Let's get to work and plug the leak. We need to find out more about Wendy, starting with where she lives."

CHAPTER TWO

Maria drove down Fleet Street and onto Ludgate Hill. The area was quiet, even for a Sunday. She quickly parked in her office space and walked briskly through Cheapside and to the Bank of England.

She was a trim figure in a body hugging miniskirt and a maxi coat. The coat was useful for it concealed her gun well. At the moment, though, she was leaving that well alone. All she gripped was a long stiletto. It was a sharp piece of strong, slim steel, silent, quick and lethal in the right hands.

She noticed him immediately. He was a big man with carrot-red hair. He was dressed in a long winter coat, his hands thrust in the pockets. He stooped slightly. And then he decided to sit down on the steps of the Royal Exchange. Once it had been an impressive building and one of the commercial hearts of the area. These days its cavernous rooms were full of boutiques and bars, although these were closed on Sunday. It looked dead that gloomy and cold spring day. And Jefferson wasn't going to improve on the sombre and funereal tone of this despondent symbol of past glories.

He looked at his watch and turned towards the Bank of England. He frowned, not out of concern, but perhaps more out of annoyance that his contacts had not kept to time. He didn't notice Maria as she eased herself behind him, swooping down and driving the knife into his heart in one quick movement. She did not need to check. She was already moving away as his head fell forward towards his lap. He remained there, hunched and immobile. He looked strange, but not strange enough. The few people around took no notice. Maria merely left and walked calmly towards the bank.

Meanwhile, Jacqui had been going through the personnel files on Wendy. She established she was really named Wendy Dale. She had been with her boss for twelve years, was thirty-four and unmarried. She had an address in Kilburn, though she most likely pretended it was in the adjacent and more fashionable Swiss Cottage.

"What do we do about her?" asked Jacqui.

"She has to go. Let's wait for Maria and then we'll decide how we go about it."

Jacqui nodded and noted the address. The file was returned, after she had wiped it clean of any fingerprints.

They went back to the boardroom. The two detectives were waiting nervously. The guard watched them casually yet carefully. He knew his job.

The one who had been hit by Jacqui whined, "Can we go? We'll keep quiet. We can't afford any trouble."

Charles ignored them, thought for a moment, then turned and left the room. Jacqui followed.

"Has your father got a hit squad in London? We need to get rid of those two but I don't want their bodies to be found. It would be too dangerous."

"He'd contract out in a place like this. He found the Brits too amateurish. He rated some individuals. But he didn't feel this was a place for a real operation."

"How do I find a disposal team for the two in there?"

"Why don't we just dump them somewhere and organise a hit before they get far?"

"What do you mean?"

She smiled, "We could use the two security guards if needed. Look, we steal a car for you. In this area that's quite easy. You and Maria take it. You change in to the usual garb, dark clothes and a cap. That gives you anonymity.

"We can load the detectives into the car we steal in our car park. Put them in the trunk and let's make sure there are traces of coke there so that it will stick to their clothes. There's some in the office. Stephens uses it.

"Get the guards to steal another car well away from here. Make a rendezvous with it. Drop the detectives off in a quiet area where nobody can see you getting them out of the car. You get away and then the others gun them down. As people appear, the guards move off and dump their car as soon as they can. They'll do that. It's a simple hit. They are quite good. And we'll give them a bonus."

"OK, and, if people are there, they will witness a gangland killing. The traces of drugs will reinforce that view. The men will have been working according to their families, but their company will deny that. It will make it look all the more suspicious and play into our hands. The men will have been seen alive miles from here and so nobody will be looking here. We can dump our stolen car well away from the murder scene and so it is unlikely to be associated with the attack. That's a good idea."

Jacqui thought, "There is a risk that Wendy Dale hears of the killings on the news. But, if we make sure the detectives have no papers, it will take time to identify them. The other risk is that Jefferson's body is found and the police issue a press release. But I doubt it. We haven't got many options anyway."

"I'll go and see the guard downstairs and set his part up. But how do we steal the cars?"

"That's easy. We'll lift one from the car park opposite. The guards can take theirs once they are ready and they should do it away from here. It's better to limit the time we have any of the cars and we don't want them to be associated."

Charles went downstairs to the guard and explained the plan, "I want you to think where we can meet up. And put your mate into the picture. We have a sub machine gun in the cache in the office. I'll get it for you nearer the time. Oh and there'll be ten grand each for you for the job."

The guard treated these unusual instructions as if they were absolutely normal. Charles sometimes thought that the heavies that Di Maglio had given him were far better than your run of the mill thug.

Charles glanced at the monitor and saw Maria approach. She strode up the steps, her eyes sparkling. He recognised that look. He had seen it when she killed before. It was a mixture of lust and satisfaction. She had explained it to him once. She said that, after a kill, one had an empty feeling and needed to make love to get over it. The last time one of them had killed, they had had sex, and the time before. Charles didn't expect to be in a supporting role this time with Jacqui around.

"Come upstairs," Charles told Maria. "We need to talk."

He turned to the guard, "When are you relieved?"

"Five. They usually arrive about a quarter of an hour before."

"Good. We plan to leave at half four. Think when and where you will meet us."

Maria and Charles walked to the lift. He brought her up to date. She looked at him quizzically. "It's lucky that you and Jacqui stayed behind to finish off some work. I thought you would have headed back home."

It was clear that she realised that he had not told the whole truth. He could see her mind buzzing and ignored it.

Jacqui, Maria and Charles sat together in the office. They ran through their plans. Maria agreed with them, "We have to clean up properly. If you clubbed the detective, was there any blood on the carpet or furniture? Has anyone checked?"

Jacqui nodded, "The guard cleaned up and has tidied up the detective's face. It isn't bleeding any more. There was some blood on the furniture but he cleaned that up. It should be OK."

Maria looked at her watch. "It's half one. Jacqui needs to get the car at about four. Then she drives it here and we put it in the car park. We stuff the two detectives in the boot. The car will have to be big enough to take them."

Jacqui agreed, "Assuming the guards leave by five, they should be on the road by half five. You should rendezvous around six. There won't be much traffic at this time of day. I wonder if they have worked out where you can meet."

Charles phoned down to the ground floor and asked the guard if he had any ideas. "I think the best place is Notting Hill. We can easily dump our car in the Paddington area and there are some good derelict places for the hit near by. With a bit of luck, if we leave the keys in their ignition, the cars will be stolen again and maybe even torched."

"I agree. We meet at Notting Hill. I will park by the junction of the Bayswater Road and Camden Hill. Then you lead me to one of the back streets to the north of the Road and I'll let the detectives out. You hit them once I have gone and as they walk away. The betting is that they'll head towards the underground either at Holland Park or Notting Hill, whichever is nearer.

You dump the car in Paddington and we'll do it well to the south. That way the chances of the two stolen cars being associated remains remote. We'll have stolen them from different places and will dump them in different areas. The main risk is my car is seen when we dump the detectives but I'll take care to be discreet. If necessary kill any bystander, after all it's unlikely in that type of area that it will be anything but a tramp.

I want no mobiles used. If anything goes wrong, fire two quick bursts of the gun in the air, we'll hear that. We shouldn't be seen together. And, afterwards, Maria and I have some other chores to do."

The guard once again agreed without question. He just said, "Don't forget the gun and enough spare ammunition. I assume it can't be traced. I plan to jettison it once the kill is done. I'd rather not carry it with me."

"Of course, it can't be traced. It's from Di Maglio," Charles snapped. "I'm not an amateur, you know."

He turned to Maria once he had put down the phone, "I need you to help me in Kilburn. There is always a possibility that Wendy Dale is out or with someone. We may have to waste two people. Or we may have to wait for her. And we need to be careful in case she hears something about Jefferson. It could be on the radio. We need to ensure that we are on alert at all times for all eventualities."

Jacqui agreed, "I'll head home after I have left the car. I'll wait for you there. I hate that part of it. I know you can't take any risk and call me to say how it's going. They'll scan the records for suspicious calls in the vicinities of the kills. They always do that. But I do hate the idea of total silence."

Maria made as if to protest. Jacqui shook her head, "Don't worry. I know the rules. And I know that they are important."

"Let me calm down our visitors. I'll tell them that we are going to negotiate with Jefferson, and that we will let them go, once his masters have agreed to lay off us. I'll put on the TV. They can watch the football or something."

Charles did that and the poor fools swallowed the story he spun them. They had no idea that they were in deep trouble and not going to see the next day. When he got back, he saw Maria had made coffee and brought some biscuits. He went over to Jacqui and kissed her on the back of her neck, "Shall we finish what we started?" he whispered.

"And what will you tell Maria?" she queried. "We can hardly ask her to wait in her office."

"Why can't we? I am sure she would."

"Look, there is only one thing that you can be sure of. She's not going to be jealous, but she may be upset. And you and she need to work as a team."

"Why wouldn't she be jealous?"

"God, men," replied Jacqui. "You've worked with her for two years and haven't realised. She's gay. She's a lesbian. She's lived with her pal, Claire, for the past seven years. You know the pretty blonde, who was on the boat with us in Barbados that Christmas after I was kidnapped by the Russian Mafia."

Charles looked astonished. They'd never discussed this before. He now realised why Jacqui was indifferent to him spending time with Maria. She suspected she was a lesbian. She thought she and Claire were lovers, although Claire was around less now she worked in New York. Charles also knew that Maria may have been gay but could be as heterosexual as the next girl could. They had slept together on several occasions, especially when Jacqui left for one of her trips to New York. But he obviously said nothing.

"Don't look so amazed," laughed Jacqui. "Do you think I'd leave you alone with her if that wasn't the case? I'm not stupid you know. And I'm very possessive."

At that moment, Maria came in and so the conversation stopped. She started busying herself. She, like Charles, had now changed into a black sweater and slacks. They checked with the guards, who had both changed into dark casual clothes. That was all they needed. They would wear baseball caps as well to make it difficult for people to identify the colour of their hair and their exact features.

"I'll drop my car back home," said Maria. "I'll be back in good time. I don't want anyone to know that I have been back here. It's better that everything looks as normal as possible."

Once she had left, Charles turned to Jacqui enquiringly, "No fear, this place is too busy. It's no longer out of bounds. Much as I'd love to, we'd better wait for another occasion. Besides, you need to psyche yourself up for the next steps. They're not going to be easy."

He must have looked disgruntled because she laughed and said, "I promise we'll come back and make love on the board table. I'll even wear a bowler hat if you want."

He smiled, "The question is where?" So they waited. Then just before four, Jacqui walked out and over to the car park. It took her a few minutes. She returned with a fairly standard saloon. She had taken one that was an innocuous blue. It was good. The boot would be large enough for their guests and the car was standard enough to avoid attention. Jacqui knew, instinctively, how to act in situations like this.

Nevertheless, Charles still asked her if she had avoided the security cameras. She nodded. Like the others, she had put on dark clothes. "I kept my back to the cameras and wore the cap, so they can't tell the colour of my hair. They won't be able to trace me. I found a cigarette in the street and left it near one of the cameras. That will put their forensics on a wild goose chase, if they notice the clue."

Jacqui then left. Maria and Charles headed upstairs to the detectives. "We are going to put you in the boot and drive you to the other side of London. Before we release you, we take delivery of some papers from Jefferson. We'll drop you in Notting Hill. You can say you were mugged, that'll explain the bruises on your face. Do you agree?"

They nodded eagerly. They were pretty dim, anyone could see the bruises were at least a few hours old. The story that had been suggested did not stack up. Or perhaps they kept quiet in the hope that Charles was stupid. "Why are you going to put us in the boot?" asked the tall one.

"We don't want anyone to see you. And make no noise or the deal is off and you'll regret it," said Maria. They agreed immediately and were taken downstairs.

The guard came and went over the instructions again. He reported to Charles, "We've erased all the videos in the security cameras and reset the system. It will look as if there was a failure. We'll restart it once you leave. That way it will only be discovered if anybody looks at the film for Sunday. They won't be able to establish why, but the system was off from midnight through to half four or so this afternoon."

"Well done, I'd overlooked that. I thought the tapes were just re-used."

"No. They are stored for a month and then re-used," he answered. "So if nobody is suspicious at the end of the day and they remain unchallenged for a month, then there will be no trace of what we have done. The only thing that we can't alter is the time clock."

"What about the boardroom?"

"It's clean as a whistle. Not even forensics could find anything there. There are a couple of scratches on the boardroom table though that we can't remove. You must have pushed your guns or something across the table."

Charles ignored that. There was no security camera in the boardroom and so they would never know what caused the scratches. He suspected it could have been the belt on Jacqui's skirt. She had, after all, propelled herself from one end of the table almost to the other.

Charles and Maria drove off and swung away from the bank towards the West End. The roads were quiet that Sunday evening and they reached Notting Hill in just over half an hour. They found a space at the bottom of Camden Hill and pulled in there. There was a muffled moan from the boot.

Maria got into the back seat and whispered to the detectives, "We are waiting for Jefferson. The meet is round the corner. As long as he does what he promised, we'll head over to Notting Hill then and find a quiet place to let you go. It shouldn't be long now."

She pretended to get out of the car. In reality, she closed the rear door and climbed back over to the front seat. They waited for the guards to appear. The guards reached the meeting point about twenty minutes later and headed slowly in front. Maria opened and slammed her car door and called to the men in the boot. "It's done. We now need to find a place to let you out without being noticed."

Charles followed the guard's car. It headed north and soon was in some pretty gloomy territory around Paddington Station. He did not know the area at all but it was well sign-posted to the West End and so he was relaxed they would have no difficulty finding their way back.

They drove up a small side street, full of empty, boarded up houses. It was waiting for the demolition men, an excellent place to dump the detectives in the back. Charles pulled his cap down further over his face and went to the boot.

"Out," he ordered. They obeyed promptly. They stood there stretching themselves and blinking nervously, "Now keep out of my life," he snarled, handing them a bag. "These are your wallets and things. Now go."

They did not look at the bag, which also contained a small packet of cocaine. There was not much there but enough to further raise the suspicions of the police. With the residue on their clothes, they would be labelled drug pushers.

Charles got back in the car and drove down the street. The detectives were walking quickly in the opposite direction. As he got to the corner, the guards' car pulled away from the kerb, driving back down towards the men.

Although they had turned into the next road, they heard the rattle of the machine gun as it mowed down the unfortunate detectives. Then there was silence. They did not say a word but drove on. They reached the park, it was late enough for there to be spaces there. They had no need to wipe down the car for they had worn gloves all the time, and they left it open with the key in the ignition. With a bit of luck it would be stolen again well before the police noticed it.

They went down the tube at Queensway, then they caught the train towards Kilburn, walking arm in arm for the last mile, so they would not appear on the station monitors. They looked like any other couple going for an early evening stroll. This was the last stage of the clean up. The fourth victim was hopefully the last.

Wendy Dale lived in a gloomy terraced house. Breaking in took a minute. Standard locks protected it and Maria took moments to pick them. There wasn't even a troublesome alarm for them to worry about. They had established she wasn't at home, they now had to wait.

In the kitchen was a calendar. Her social diary was hardly exciting if that was anything to go by. Her weekend appeared to have been spent in Oxford with a girl friend. She was a methodical woman. They established she would be on the seven thirty-train back. That meant they could expect her by nine unless she took a cab rather than the underground.

Maria and Charles went through the house. Upstairs there were three pocket-sized bedrooms. One was used as a workroom and study. They went through the papers. They could find nothing from Associated. Their name was also on none of the files.

The place was clean. She did not appear to be using it to store any material from the office. Charles turned to Maria, "Should we set the place alight once we have killed her?"

"There's nothing we need to destroy here. I'd prefer it to look like a break-in. We could take this jewel case, and she's bound to have some money on her when she returns. Otherwise, I can't see anything we would want to steal. Anyway, if we leave her here, she may lie there for a few days. That always helps in case someone thinks they saw something suspicious. The longer it takes to find her, the less reliable any witness will be."

"I need to question her in any case. If she starts to yell or anything, kill her quickly. We don't want the neighbours around."

The clock chimed nine and they waited expectantly. A taxi drew up. A couple got out. "Shit," muttered Maria. They went into the house next door. Charles and Maria breathed a sigh of relief.

Then they saw her. She must have caught the underground. She was walking up the street, carrying a small suitcase. She was on her own. She was medium height; slightly podgy with long tinted blond hair. With a bit of effort, she could have looked attractive. There was no elegance in the walk as she came to the house. It just mirrored the discomfort she felt as she wobbled on her too high heels in her too tight knee-length skirt.

She fumbled for the keys. Maria and Charles waited behind the lounge door. They wanted her away from the hallway. She was going to be shocked when she saw them waiting for her.

She closed the door and dropped the case in the hall. She went over to the phone and checked for messages. They listened carefully. The machine told her, "You have two messages." They heard a button click and an excited woman's voice called out. "There's a lovely new play on at the theatre. It's supposed to be great. Can we get together and see it. Please call, Wendy." Then a button clicked again. "Wendy. This is Jefferson. I've sent the two detectives into IBE. They'll get the tape. There was a meeting. They say that some big guns were there. We need to stop acting alone. I need to tell the boss what we've found. This could be big money for you. He's sworn he wants to see that bastard, Rossi, in jail. Call me when you get back."

Maria and Charles nodded as if on cue. "Hello Wendy," Maria said. "I think you've got some explaining to do before we call the police."

"Yes," Charles added grimly. "And you can tell us who Jefferson is. And why his boss wants to put me inside."

She was so astonished by their appearance that she didn't say a word. Charles took her by the arm and eased her into the lounge. She walked like an automaton. She was in total shock.

She then said, "How did you get in here?"

Maria answered. "I can pick a lock. Yours were easy. It's one of my skills. It allows me to disprove my reputation. You know the one that you credit me with in the office. See, I have other skills that don't require me just to lie on my back." That was delivered with a look of hatred.

This was getting them nowhere. Charles intervened, "Wendy, tell me what you have done. Tell me who this Jefferson is. And, if you co-operate, we will allow you to resign. That means you can get another job. If you don't co-operate, I'll fire you and hand you over to the police."

At that she started to sob. She cried real tears that made her mascara run into a blotchy black smudge. She looked awful. Her face was colourless. Her eyes were red. She was a picture of desolation.

Maria interrupted her cries, "It's too late to regret things now, you stupid fool. You'd do better to confess all to us. Who's Jefferson? Is that his Christian name? Is he your lover?"

Wendy gasped at this assertion. The bitch must have been a virgin. Nobody else would have been that shocked. "He's Mr Jefferson," she said, stressing the 'Mr'. He's head of security at Associated."

"What the hell are you playing around with him for? And why is that idiot Sir Piers, I suppose that's his boss, after my blood?"

"Mr Jefferson is my cousin," she said primly. "He said that you were crooked. I suspected you were too. I agreed to help him and told him of your meetings and things. There was nothing untoward until last week when I discovered you were having a secret meeting with your wife's Mafia father in the bank. And it was on a Sunday."

Charles feigned anger, "Why shouldn't I meet him at the bank? Him and others. That was Rossi and Di Maglio business. IBE is an investment.

The discussions were about other things. But, hell, I don't need to explain to you. Who else are you feeding information to?"

"Nobody. The only person who knew what I was doing was Mr Jefferson. Actually, his name is Hector. But he likes to be called Jefferson. That's his army experience. He's one of the Arbroath Jeffersons, you know."

This was said with some pride. Maria was having none of it. "Yeah, and Charles is one of the Corsican Rossis. My people are from the Bronx. Who gives anything? Have you been copying things at the office and selling them?"

"No," she spat indignantly, "How dare you? I work by high standards. I have nothing from the office here and I wouldn't take anything at all at any price. Don't judge me by your standards."

"Are you sure Jefferson hasn't told others?" asked Charles.

"No, I swore him to silence. He is a man of honour. He was a Major in the army."

"What were you going to get out of this? Were you trying to destroy the bank?"

Tears came to her eyes. Charles wondered what the bitch was going to come up with now. "I want it to be like the old days. Then I was proud to be in the bank. Now it has changed. A lot of the old people have gone. The board is different. And I know that one day you will get rid of my boss and the others from the old bank."

"Did Dunkillin ask you to do this?"

Once again she turned to him, this time in fury, "His name is the Lord Dunkillin. Respect him and his title. He knows nothing of this. But I am doing it for him and for the others who will bring the old bank back to its days of glory and honour."

"My God," interjected Maria. "You do talk a load of crap."

"Keep your American slang out of this conversation. I don't know what your role is in the bank. And I don't want to know."

"OK Wendy, cool off," replied Maria. "I'll let you into a secret. I'm not like you, I'm no repressed virgin. I've screwed the boss, and on more than one occasion. And I guess we'll do it again."

The women were hissing at each other. Maria was in control. She was just working on Wendy's distaste of her and everything she stood for to get her angry and to tell them all.

Charles intervened, "Hey, let's not argue. We need to resolve this. Look, I'll call the police. We better tell them also about Jefferson, the detectives and the others."

Wendy fell straight into the trap. "There are no others. The detectives were only there to get the tape. I opened the side door on Friday and also doctored the tape. Jefferson showed me how. It was easy. The recorder was voiced activated and the tape could last for hours. There is nobody else. We didn't even tell our families. The detectives didn't know where they were going or what the details were until they met Jefferson at Waterloo Station. Nobody knew as Jefferson arranged for them to be paid cash once the job was completed. He trusted Sir Piers enough to know he would get his expenses back."

"How were you going to go public? I heard what Jefferson said. Are you sure that you and Jefferson are the only ones who know?"

She nodded. Then she looked scared. It was something in Charles' look. She glanced back at Maria, she had now moved behind her. The moment Charles said, "Kill her" and the woman's mouth opened to scream, the knife plunged into her heart. It was a kitchen knife Maria had picked up on their tour of the house. She shoved the now lifeless body forward and it fell onto the carpet.

"Let's move," she said. "That was a dream."

"Get rid of the telephone tape. Take it. I don't want anyone to find out what Jefferson said."

Maria took the tape, and opened a drawer beneath the phone. Another recording tape was there. She removed that and put it in place of the original. "Miss Perfect kept a spare one. I should think everything here is in duplicate."

"Not the kitchen knives."

"True, but it's best to use something from the house in these cases. It makes it all look more like a robbery that went wrong."

"That reminds me." Charles opened the woman's handbag and took out a purse. He emptied its contents into his pocket. He also took her credit cards. That would allow them to send the police up another blind alley. They would get rid of them later.

"Leave the cards," said Maria. "They are not that easy to dispose of. We don't want to take anything that can be traced easily. The jewellery can be dumped in the River Thames on our way back. Cards float. We better also get to my place and check out the police messages."

Maria had a radio set up in her flat. They could monitor any action on the shooting in Paddington from there. They could also check if there was anything on Jefferson. Charles was fairly sure that the late Ms Dale would not be discovered for a couple of days yet.

There was rear door through the kitchen and they forced the lock with a gardening knife that was lying on the porch. It would now look like a break in. The wall around the garden was scaleable and, luckily for them, there was a small alleyway that skirted one side of it. That, they expected the police to assume, would be the way the intruder got into the house.

They left though the way they came. They walked down the street arm in arm. They stopped occasionally, away from any lights, for a brief kiss. Anybody would think they were just another couple making their way home from the pub or somewhere. They doubted if anyone was looking. Most of the curtains seemed drawn and many of the houses were in darkness. This was not a late night neighbourhood.

They walked on through Kilburn and into St John's Wood. They caught a train through to Baker Street, only there did they get a cab, just to Cheyne Walk by the Thames. Maria lived up the road from there in a mansion flat. They sauntered over to the river and stopped to look to see if there were any video cameras trained on the area. There were none. There was nobody around. The cars could not see Maria's hand as it slid behind Charles back and dropped the contents of the small jewellery case into the fast flowing water. That was followed by the case itself.

"You're sure it will sink?"

"I'm sure. It's heavy enough. I put some stones into the pockets. It'll take a long time to surface, and, even if it does, it won't be in one piece. The flap was open. It'll rot before long."

They walked on to the flat. They walked arm in arm, not so much as a disguise, but rather because they wanted to. Once again, Charles knew they would need to make love. Once again he felt the warmth from Maria's body flow through to him as they brushed against each other. Charles remembered the interruption of the morning and that increased his desire all the more. He thought of the four people who'd had to die, how stupid they were to get in the way. If they had stuck to their own business, they could have continued living. But it had been a matter of them or him. And, therefore, there had been no choice.

He noticed Maria move closer to him as they kissed. He realised they were stopping more often now. His hands moved round her body to her small firm breasts. And he felt her dig her hands into his buttocks as she pulled him close to her.

She opened the door of her flat, and he started to kiss her passionately. "No," she said. "First of all, we must complete the job."

She went over to the radio. It was in a den that she had constructed. A den rather than a study. It was her workroom. She could pick up nothing about the murders. "The police could have come and gone. Jefferson was around midday. The two others were at around half five. It's almost eleven now."

"Check out the news channel then."

They watched the news but there was little to note. There was a lot about politics and a bit about sport. Then the crime reporter came on.

"Police were called to Paddington today after two unidentified men were gunned down in a deserted street. They were walking towards London's Bayswater, when a gunman opened fire with an automatic from a passing car. Both men were hit several times and were dead on arrival at a nearby hospital. Police say they have reason to believe that this was a drugs related gangland assassination.

There was a further killing earlier today in London's worst ever day of violent crime. A security man from a City bank was knifed to death in front of the Royal Exchange. Police confirm that he was carrying a substantial sum of money. There are no known witnesses to the murder, but police are calling on anyone who was in the vicinity of the Royal Exchange around 12.30 or 12.45 this afternoon to come forward. The body was found shortly after the murder at 1.00 p.m. by a passer by.

A spokesman for the man's employers said that they had no idea why he was in the City on a Sunday. They could give no clues as to why he was carrying such a large sum of money. They said he was a loyal employee of six year's standing and an ex army officer."

"Nothing else," said Charles. That was good if they think Jefferson was killed around half twelve. You were there at twelve."

Maria nodded. "There were no amateur photographers around and I kept clear of the security cameras. I know their ranges. So we should be safe there. But why were the other two described as unidentified?"

"The bag didn't hold all the contents of their wallets. I kept it back."

"Where is it?"

"Jacqui took it with her. She was going to drop the stuff off in a wastepaper bin, but well away from the City. She'll drive somewhere out of our normal area for that. She said she'd put them in a bag first and make it look as if it were full of rubbish from a picnic. She'll be careful."

Maria nodded, "Is there anything else we need to do?"

Charles shook his head, "I think we have covered all trails. I'll need to get back home. I'll borrow your car. You can pick it up tomorrow. It'll be at home. If you need a cover, you came over to our area and left it there. You do that from time to time, so nobody would be surprised."

Maria smiled. "I usually only do that when I want to be naughty."

The next thing he knew were her arms around him, as she propelled him towards her large double bed. They fell on it together. They knew what they wanted. Charles' hand moved up under her dark sweater at the same time as her hands moved round from his hips. The room was lit by a pink glow from the light above the bed. They were both breathing fast, as if they had been running. It was a powerful need to have sex. It was not love. It was pure sex. They needed it after the tension of the afternoon. They needed it after the killings that he had ordered and she had carried out.

He kissed her, pushing his lips against her. They felt their teeth clash as he forced her mouth open with his tongue. They tasted each other. They felt each other's tongues moisten their lips.

After that, they tore off their clothes and pushed together in a frenzy that could only come at times like that. Charles thought of the frustration of the morning interruption, the excitement of the afternoon, the memory of Maria's body during the walk home. The result was not passion. It was not love. This, as it always was with Maria, was pure unadulterated sexual enjoyment.

She excited and was excited. Her sexuality was undoubted. She seemed to combine the best of both worlds in her bisexuality. Charles did not believe there were many like him. He was one of her rare men. The others were mainly by command when she needed to act the whore for her job. And that had never happened since she had started to work for Charles. It only arose when she was operating for Di Maglio.

Their urges had been satisfied. Their bodies had made their minds relax and forget. They lay together for some time before he gently moved away. "It's time to go sweetheart. It's back to reality."

She kissed him. "Thanks. That was good. Good for me and for you too. Come back whenever. You'll know when I need it as well."

He went to the bathroom and soon was washed and dressed. He prepared to leave. Maria had put on a towelling robe and was watching the news. She stood up as he returned, "It's the same story as before. I've rechecked the police radio bands and there is nothing on them. So it looks as if all has gone to plan. I'll see you in the morning at the office."

He took the keys and nodded. One short kiss. She still could sense him on her, and then he was gone.

Charles got home at just after one. Jacqui was awake. She got up and threw her arms around him. "Did it all go as planned? I heard about the Paddington shooting on the TV. They also covered the killing at the Royal Exchange."

"We got Wendy Dale. She was working alone. She's dead. Maria killed her with a kitchen knife. We made it look like breaking and entering. We dumped the cars. I left the one you stole near Hyde Park. With a bit of luck someone will take it for a joy ride and that will complicate things even more."

"But what did you do with the contents of the wallets?"

"I went for walk to St Katherine's docks. I was all alone at one point and so I threw them into the water. They sunk to the bottom. I then picked up the car and came home. I played with little Juliet. We went briefly to the park and fed the ducks. She's fast asleep now. Do you think we need to do anything tomorrow?"

"Yes. We need to start the ball rolling on the scam. I want to use our friend, Stephens, as quickly as possible. And then we need to dump him. He's bad news. But he will be useful as a fall guy. Maria will be glad to deal with him. She resented his attack on her this morning. She really went for Wendy this evening, I didn't know she knew she was telling everyone Maria was a little tart."

Jacqui laughed, "That would not have gone down well with our Maria. She doesn't like being treated like that, even as a joke."

Charles was only half listening. He had stripped and fallen into bed. He was now exhausted. He pulled Jacqui towards him, but, before he could think of anything else, he was fast asleep. He was still holding her in his arms the next morning when the alarm woke them with its strident call.

"Tonight," said Jacqui.

"Or perhaps in the boardroom, if it's free," he replied.

In a better mood than he expected, they cheerfully got dressed and headed to the office to meet the challenge ahead.

CHAPTER THREE

Maria walked into the office the next morning and whispered mischievously to Charles, "Sleep well last night? I did. I was exhausted after all that happened." Then she said, "Shouldn't we have a confab?"

Charles beckoned Jacqui. "What news?"

"No fresh news from Paddington or the Royal Exchange. The police seem to be going on the same tack. Two boys have been arrested with our stolen car. I suppose they were joy-riders. They were arrested in South London. That's good as it's well away from any of our incidents. Otherwise, I'll keep an ear open for any news on the late Wendy." She grinned and looked at her watch, muttering, "Poor timekeeping that girl. No standards."

There was plenty of day to day business at the bank that day. Maria called in during the afternoon.

"Nobody is concerned about Wendy. They are surprised. She would normally call in. They say she's not at home. Her phone's not answering. Obviously they don't know that she is at home but that it's not easy answering the phone with a great big kitchen knife in your back. I suspect they'll call the police tomorrow. It appears her parents are elderly and Dunkillin doesn't want to worry them."

Charles talked to Giovanni that afternoon and they went over the legal agreement. It all was simple. He was drawing up the necessary papers for the take-over of PAF as well.

"Shouldn't we really call it a merger?" he queried.

"No," replied Giovanni. "That will complicate things. Look, the regulators would prefer a take-over. I am going to pass the word that the Di Maglio family is quitting banking. The idea will be to make it look as if it is the first step in the boss's retirement plans. There are good reasons for us to intimate that, one or two things are getting hot over here."

"But Giovanni, he'll own a great chunk of the new company."

"No he won't. Little Juliet will own it. Di Maglio will gift it to his grandchild. I'm creating a trust, it will avoid tax. The idea of moving the bank into honest hands will mean that the regulators will want to kiss your ass. Trust me, it will be easy. You don't seem too bad yet, all you've done is speculate. At least that's what they think."

"What will he want in return? I know him well enough. He never gives without a purpose."

"He wants nothing. He may want help laundering stuff in the future. He'll make a lot from the scam and he has more money than he really needs. I guess you owe him a favour, but there is nothing in his mind at the moment."

Charles knew that sounded unlikely, but he accepted the explanation and asked, "When will the papers be ready?"

"I'll have finished them off for my side tomorrow. All will be ready for the sale. I'm using one of the big investment banks over here. You can advise yourself, we can't. You chose a law firm for the deal. Let's aim for a preliminary announcement next week."

"In that case I'll have to talk to the Bank of England. I'll have to bring in the board and especially the Honourable James. He'll have to come with me to the Bank of England. Why don't I call a special board meeting for Thursday? That way we can talk to the officials on Friday. But you'll have to cover several states. How will you do that?"

"We'll go in on Friday. We'll talk to them all and also the Fed and others here in New York. PAF's bosses are our people. They'll do what we want and when we want it."

"OK. I'll round up the lawyers and start the paperwork on this side. You can be at the meeting on a video link. I doubt you want to come back here to see me dragoon the nobility into line."

"I like it when they suck up to you, especially as they hate your guts. But I can watch it on TV. The atmosphere is not as cold that way."

Giovanni and Charles often joked. Indeed, Charles was closer to him than any of his own people, although he knew that Giovanni's first loyalty would always be to his father-in-law.

Charles then called his own father. He was working on creating the phoney investments to sell to PAF's unsuspecting clients. Jacqui was getting him all the information he needed. He was also looking to find some shares to ramp, just as they had in the old days.

"With five million suckers out there," Jack Ryder said, "We need to hit it big time. I reckon we can easily sell five billion of investments; after all, that's an average of a thousand dollars per client and that's peanuts if they have a half decent sales force. I would expect to start by putting about two billion of phoney investments into them and three billion of genuine ones. Many of the genuine ones we'll trade and ramp up, even before PAF's clients get them, and that should let us skim off around another billion or so for our own purposes. That's my latest calculation. So you may be able to up your take on the investment side to three billion.

By the way, I am also working with Stephens on some real slick stuff that will allow us to milk the bank. His deals are so complicated that I have a hard time coming to grips with them. Technically he's good. Personality wise, he even makes your father-in-law appear likeable."

Charles sounded nervous. "Don't touch anything you feel you don't understand. Don't trust him. Give him no discretion."

"I'd worked that one out. You didn't need to tell me. Oh, and by the way, Giovanni called and he gave me the names of some of the companies we can use. They have some special purpose Panamanian ones that are just ideal. This thing is really exciting."

"OK, let me leave that to you. Tell me how to do it but keep it simple. Find ways to get us to lend to them as well. But don't forget I have already some targets to lend to and have placed every Lord or Lady we could find on their boards. We mustn't overplay our hand or it will look too suspicious. But if you can get some of those new fangled investments going with Stephens, you know the ones that are really loans but don't appear to be loans. Then we can blame him for those as well when he takes the fall, and I want that to be sooner rather than later. He deserves to drop."

It was well after six when Jacqui appeared. "Aren't you ready? We have dinner with that City Guild. You know that charity do. Sir Brian is hosting our table, so we can expect some great yarns about hunting, shooting and fishing."

She kissed him. "Don't look so pissed off. It's for charity. You are doing your socialist bit and redistributing some of your ill-gotten gains."

Charles got up, straightened his tie and headed out. Maria was in her office and waved at him. "See you tomorrow," she called. "Enjoy yourself with the cream of the City intelligentsia. Those men have more dollars than brain cells!"

The car was waiting and they got into the back. Jacqui looked cool and elegant in a black cocktail dress. Her hair was pulled back and up. A plain gold choker, a gold watch, her wedding ring and single diamond engagement ring with matching earrings were tasteful additions to the simplicity of her outfit. She would turn heads and knew it as she smiled happily.

Charles could not match her for style, but was dressed in a hand tailored dark suit. It was perhaps a bit too fashionably cut for the conservative taste of the City. The average age of the gathering tonight was likely to be over fifty, a good twenty years more than either Jacqui or him. They would be greeted with the usual mixture of condescension and jealousy. How dare they be billionaires at their age? And there were doubts about their origins. That petulant outburst of Wendy Dale before her death was typical of the snobbery of some of the old class in the City.

They found Sir Brian quite easily in the crowd. Or, rather, they heard his booming voice and moved towards it in the bar. He was a small man with a substantial girth, half-hidden by a well-cut, double-breasted suit. He was on his third or fourth gin by the look of things, he was flushed and there was a thin sheen of perspiration on his face. He was of the old school, who abhorred the drunken antics of the 'Essex traders', as he called the foreign exchange boys. He believed his background meant he was immune to such behaviour. His view was that breeding meant you remained a gentleman even if drunk.

Jacqui looked at him with distaste. "It's going to be a bum pinching evening before the night is out. Keep me away from that revolting man, I'll hit him one day. I'd better not in such public place, though."

"Charles, Jacqui," Sir Brian brayed. "Come over and let me introduce you to some of the chums who'll be at our table tonight. This is Sebastian and Tara. They're in tin. This is Roderick. He's in sugar. And you know the memsahib. She's into my money." That was capped with a great guffaw, not only from the speaker but also from his sycophantic entourage.

Jacqui greeted his wifely apparition politely. She met the stares of the men with indifference, shook hands as appropriate. They accepted glasses of champagne, which was almost undrinkable. The waiters carefully covered the label with a white napkin. Its sweet and cloying taste indicated that this was no genuine champagne.

Jacqui pulled Charles aside. "Let's drift away. It'll be hard enough when we are on the same table. This lot are even denser than his usual crowd. They give hooray Henries a bad name. The one in sugar has his shirt sticking out of his flies and nobody seems to have noticed it, perhaps it's his normal way of dressing. Have you smelt his wife? I don't know when she bought that outfit. Either it's been in store or she's wearing mothballs instead of pearls."

They half turned and noticed Sir Piers Rupert-Jones from Associated. He was walking in with his wife, she was an attractive woman in her fifties. They had met before. She was pleasant. Charles whispered to Jacqui, "Let's talk to him. I want to see his reaction."

They walked over, "Sir Piers, Lady Rupert-Jones. How nice to see you again. How are you? Is business booming with you as well? We're having a whale of a time."

"Oh hello, Rossi," he said in a somewhat dismissive voice. "Mrs Rossi. How are you?"

"Very well, thanks," Jacqui replied. "Have you a table here?"

"No, we're joining some pals from my school, Eton. Where did you go to school, Rossi?"

This was a classic put down. He had asked the question many times before, usually waiting till there were more people around. His wife looked embarrassed.

"England. Jacqui was educated in America and Switzerland. I was at Oxford. Jacqui was at Vasseur. You didn't go to university did you? I thought that you came straight into your father's firm at sixteen?"

He reddened at these comments. He never realised that Charles and Jacqui were indifferent to his bluster and buffoonery, as indeed they were to all of his, happily declining, band of compatriots in the City.

Jacqui said, "I was sorry to hear about your employee being killed yesterday. I heard it on the news. He was in drugs or something, wasn't he?"

Sir Piers reddened, "No, he was not, Mrs Rossi. We do not know the cause of the tragedy. We believe it may have been an affair of the heart."

It was lucky that, at that point, he gave them a curt nod and turned away. Charles had just stopped himself smiling at that unfortunate turn of phrase. He knew where Maria would have placed her stiletto.

"He knows nothing. They don't know of the connection. The Dale woman spoke the truth. His man was acting on his own," Charles whispered to Jacqui. She nodded.

The dinner wended its weary way through indifferent food in palatial surroundings. The wine was served in generous portions and in all varieties. Indifferent red followed acidic white, to be capped by a sweet dessert wine. That, in turn, left space for port or brandy, or both. Charles and Jacqui left most of theirs untouched, although others drank plentifully. One suspected, for most, it would be a toss up between suffering the pain of an inevitable hangover against the relief of being anaesthetised against the boredom of the self congratulatory speeches that would presage the end of the interminable evening.

As they drove back, Charles turned to Jacqui, "Why do we have to go to such things?" As she started to reply, he said, "OK, I know we have to make believe we are part of that system. I only wish we could do it by proxy. Anyway, I'm tired. I need to get some sleep."

"And you have things to do tonight, don't you?" she whispered into his ear. And, at the same time, gave it a surreptitious lick, laughing as she felt him shiver at the touch of her tongue.

The next day was quite normal. Charles had more discussions with both Giovanni and his father. He arranged lawyers for the deal, and then he organised a board meeting for Thursday evening. The Hon. James shuffled into his office and queried the need for the meeting. "It is important," Charles said. "I am honour bound not to say anything till Thursday."

The Hon. James looked at him with disbelief. He was undoubtedly thinking that honour and the Rossi family were strange bedfellows, but Charles let it slide. Life was too short and he would take a fall in time. Maria came to him, "The police have found the body in Kilburn. They believe it's a simple break-in that went wrong. Dunkillin's in a state of shock, as are a lot of the girls. I might go and have a little cry with them. It could look good."

Charles went to Dunkillin and commiserated. He was genuinely upset. Charles queried if he knew her well. The old boy started to look a bit woeful. He then let it all out. It appeared the prim Miss Dale had a very close relationship with him. He wasn't worried about her, he was petrified that he could be implicated in a scandal. Charles looked suitably surprised.

"Perhaps you should go to the police and see that they treat everything with discretion," he suggested.

Dunkillin looked horrified at the idea. "I don't think so. Please don't say anything. "

"You didn't see her this week. You weren't round her place were you?"

He was now petrified. "No. Of course, I wasn't. I've never been there. She would come to my flat in Sloane Square. We were very discreet. She was so lovely. She had a wonderful figure, such a sweet face, lovely blond hair and a wonderful personality."

Charles' impression of Wendy was of a plump wench with a gloomy appearance and bleached blonde hair. She hadn't exactly seemed warm and cuddly during their one and only encounter of any substance. Still, he said nothing.

Maria was with Jacqui when he returned and told them of the discussion. "The dirty old man," exclaimed Maria. "And I thought she was an old maid. You have to watch the quiet ones. We could have sold her to your dad, Jacqui, if we had known."

"Hey," said Charles mockingly, "Stop speaking like that. We need a bit of decorum. Have you no feeling or do you have to continue to stick your knife in?"

They were both giggling and Charles saw this was going to develop badly. "Now, let's put on the old mournful look. Maria, check out any other gossip. Go over Dunkillin's office tonight for pictures or anything we can use, if we ever need to pressure him into something."

The next morning, Maria intercepted them as they walked into the office. "Come with the super sleuth and prepare yourself for a horrible sight."

She closed the office door and pushed down the engaged light. Then she opened her briefcase. She took out some photos. They were awful. Wendy was in the nude on a white rug in all her splendour, Wendy wearing a frilly short night-dress, and Wendy in a whole load of other poses, mainly nude or wearing strange underwear of the type available in cheap sex shops.

"Oh, that's really sad," said Jacqui. "The poor man's a weirdo."

"That may be. But they could come in use later. Did you find anything else?"

"No. I checked Sir Brian's office and the Honourable James'. They had nothing of interest. I had hoped that they might all be going hammer and tongs with her. That would have given us leverage on them all."

"That's not necessary," said Charles, "I already have a bit on the Honourable James and plenty on Sir Brian."

"Hey, come on and spill the beans. You never mentioned that before," cried Jacqui.

"I never thought it would interest you. Sir Brian frequents a strip bar down in Soho. He's known as the kinky knight. As for the Honourable James, I have nothing on him directly but a load of filth on his son. The boy's a total pervert and goes on sex holidays to Amsterdam. The Honourable James couldn't afford to have that published."

"I can't believe it," gasped Jacqui. "I mean it's not that they look normal. It's just they look so boring. Who would have thought that sex could play a part in any of their lives?"

"Don't be too dismissive. I think the Honourable James is straight. His wife's OK. It's just his son who's awful. Dunkillin has a bit on the side. That's hardly rare. It's only Sir Brian who's a bit strange. And with a wife like his, can you blame him?"

"You're right," said Maria. "I mean the poor man's married to a human gorilla. God, the bitch's ugly as sin, she has a better beard than many a man I've seen."

This debate on the wives of the old brigade continued for some time. In the end Charles called a halt, "I have to work and we have the board meeting to rubber stamp all that we have agreed. Then, tomorrow, we go to the Bank of England to get their blessing. On Saturday we want to announce that it's a marriage, made in heaven."

And, indeed, that is exactly how it all came about. The board meeting didn't last long. Charles timed it well enough for that. Evening boards are never popular, and, in any event, he made no attempt to allow anyone a drink. So the token great and the good were feeling fairly deprived. Worried that their immune systems would let them down without a top up, they agreed all that they were asked and then headed off to some happy hour in their clubs.

The meeting with the Bank of England also went well. They didn't actually say anything. They were agreeable though. There is one thing with the Central Bank in London, they are definitely not bureaucrats. And they enjoy the challenge of being the boss man in international banks. It all sounded good, and there was no cause for them to disagree with the words of enthusiasm from the Honourable James and Sir Brian. Charles kept in the background. The others were good enough at waffling about things they did not understand without any help from him.

The phrases tripped off their tongues. They would do a thorough check with help from the auditors. The lawyers were top notch. The synergies were strong. There was empathy between the boards. They used every platitude in the book. They knew nothing of PAF, and even defined the ten-minute board meeting on the subject as one where they had long, detailed and fruitful debate about the deal.

These were though not the only things they did. Maria, Jacqui and Charles were in all that weekend as well with their advisors. Then they announced the merger to the world.

In every state where PAF had offices, they would have to meet the regulators during the following two weeks. They had to get their approval but it was clear that was going to be easy. Di Maglio out of the banking system was like manna from heaven for those in charge. IBE was reputable, even if there was something dubious about its youthful owners.

Maria would keep track of events in London. She would be in contact with Charles at all times. That was nothing unusual. Maria was good at monitoring the bank and had done so before. She knew instinctively the smell of a problem even when she could not fully understand it. They had no qualms about being away.

Although they were in the bank all weekend, they never did manage to get time to check out the board table again. They were too busy organising things for the merger. Then they went through the phoney investments they were creating with Charles' father. They monitored the deals that Stephens had done, they looked over the companies to which they would lend and lose money, and they checked and re-checked the routes that the money they embezzled from IBE would take before it turned up at its different end destinations. Their plans were definitely complex. The good thing was that they would be difficult for any auditor or regulator to understand. And that made it easier to run their scams.

Jack Ryder was optimistic, "I think we'll make much more than you planned. I've run through some of the sums on the trades I'm setting up with Stephens. I think we'll end up clearing between two and three billion on them. I have thought of another few wrinkles to several of the deals. The great thing is that they are fail-proof."

By the time Sunday night came, they had everything ready. Charles and Jacqui relished the idea of being in the US. Jacqui snuggled up to him. "We can have some fun as well as working. It shouldn't be hard chatting up the local regulators, especially when they are overjoyed at the idea of my father getting out of their hair."

Charles and Jacqui left for the US. Charles had thought for one horrible moment that the Honourable James wanted to go along, but, in the end, he persuaded him that it was better that he ran things in London. Charles suspected that he was most deterred by his comment that they would need to fly coach internally, as most flights inside America are almost entirely one class.

They had discussed strategy with Giovanni. In the first week, their first stop would be Chicago and then they would go west, before flying back home via New York. The following week they would head to California before Washington, their final port of call. "We need to have a family meeting in California," said Giovanni. "Your father-in-law will be there. We want to talk about where we take his organisation in the future."

Charles didn't ask him for an explanation. He suspected this was the favour his father-in-law wanted for the gift of his banks to Juliet. He discussed the matter with Jacqui. "I can't believe that he's going to retire," she said. "And don't forget that you promised me that you will never run the illegal side. I don't want the prostitution, protection rackets or drugs Empire. We don't need them."

"Darling, I promised that I would never get involved with your father's sordid Empire. It caused us enough trouble with the Russians and others. I want nothing to do with it. I especially want you and Juliet to be well clear of it."

They whisked through the airport Fast Track and were soon happily ensconced in First Class seats for Chicago. They would be there in time for a late afternoon meeting with the local regulators.

They also arrived on time to be met by a Di Maglio limousine. Charles was given a gun. Jacqui got one too, a classical handbag size toy without too much shooting power. It was easier picking the weapons up in the US from a Di Maglio local agent rather than going through the rigmarole in London and carrying them through Heathrow. In any case, Charles no longer carried a gun as a matter of course in London, for he felt it was safe enough. But the US was different. Their guns were legal. The days of carrying illegal ones were gone. As indeed were the days when they forged their gun permits.

It was a typical wet and windy Chicago afternoon, but the regulators couldn't have been sunnier. They fell in love with Jacqui for a start. And then they fell for the rubbish that was fed to them. One of their first questions related to the future role of Di Maglio.

"My father has decided to cut back his business interests. He will not become a minority shareholder in our company, as he will place all the shares in trust for our daughter. And he will not have a board seat, nor will he be having any management responsibilities in Europe or the United States," said Jacqui

They turned to Giovanni who had accompanied them, "And what will your role be, Mr Petroni?"

"I have been asked to remain as US Chairman. That will ensure continuity. But my role will be strictly non-executive and we will be undertaking an executive search to identify a senior US banker to take on the role of Chief Executive of the operations over here."

Charles noted, "And I plan it so that Mr Petroni will be on the board of the main company as well. He understands the US business better than most." Charles also thought to himself that they would ensure that they employed a CEO, who was totally out of touch with technology, completely at sea in the dealing room and with little understanding of corporate lending. He realised that they would be spoilt for choice among the pre-retirement dinosaurs that graced the ranks of several major banks.

But he smiled and said, "We need a person of undoubted integrity and long experience. We value Mr Petroni's experience a great deal, and he is always urging us to ensure we have enough grey hairs on the board. Experience is so important to a young company with young management."

The time challenged senior regulator smiled contentedly from his side of the table, "Oh, but IBE is a bank with a lengthy history and great traditions. I wouldn't call you a young company."

Charles smiled back at him, "We try to uphold those traditions. But much of the management has changed since the take-over. We do have several people you may have met or heard of. There's our chairman, the Honourable James. Lord Dunkillin is with us still. And, as always, we have Sir Brian on board."

They didn't know them from Adam, but Charles could see visions of castles and moats flashing in front of their eyes. One can always look into an American meritocracy to find someone who would cherish the thought of meeting some ageing aristocrat.

The regulators kept on finding more reasons to want IBE to proceed with alacrity. In short, the meeting was over and done with quite quickly. Their journey had started and they moved west for the next two days before turning east again to see the New York Fed. They had thought that would be the main hurdle, but they had evidently got full reports from their friends in the provinces. All went like wildfire. IBE represented a clean slate. And they liked them. All they asked was to be kept in touch with progress, they were the main regulator as PAF's head office was in their state.

Charles explained that they would be in California the following Monday and then would cross back to Washington before briefing them again in New York on their final stop. The regulators promised they would give their agreement promptly. Once again, they could not contain their relief at seeing the Mafia out of the direct running of the banks.

In New York, they also saw some of the candidates to take on the top slot. They were a fine bunch of men. On average they had been bankers, man and boy. And, on average, they wanted a big office, a big expense account and as little work as possible. They did not realise how that suited

IBE. They would be wonderful fall guys. They would sign papers that they knew nothing about and it was possible that they would end up in court, or worse, when the game came to an end.

After several such meetings, Charles told Giovanni to choose one himself. "Get the Honourable James to vet them either in New York or in London. As long as they pass the idiot test and the mirror test, they'll do."

"I can guess the idiot test," he replied quizzically. "But what's the mirror test? Do they have to be good looking?"

"It's to check they're really alive. If the mirror clouds up, they're breathing. Then if you really want them, you can offer them the job."

Giovanni shook his head despairingly. Then he muttered, "Fucking Brits", grinned and slapped Charles on the back. He actually packed quite a hit for such a small man. "Well, see you in California. Have a good trip."

They called the office and checked out with Maria. All appeared to be going well. She made no mention of the killings. She did mention the funeral of the late Wendy, but they knew better than to talk about things like that on a telephone line.

"When do we head home? I miss Juliet," asked Jacqui looking at her watch.

"Look. I've just had an idea. Why should we head back to London for two days? We could all be together for longer. We're supposed to be in California for meetings on Tuesday with the regulators and then on Wednesday with your father. Why don't we get the nanny to fly Juliet out there and meet us? They could get out there by lunch tomorrow if they caught the nine o' clock flight. They can fly directly back from California and we'll join them a couple of days later."

Jacqui jumped to the phone and it was all arranged. "Put us up in Shutters on the Beach in Santa Monica. Get us a suite and an adjoining room for Juliet and the nanny." she called. "It's got good facilities for kids as well."

Charles also arranged an early morning flight out of New York. "Shall we go to Lola's?"

"No," she called back. "It's boring. I want a real meal. Why don't we go to the Trattoria del Arte and get decent pasta. I'm fed up of mock international, that's all you get on these business trips. By the way, the nanny is going to call me back and confirm if they can do the bookings. They'll get a flight, but I've told them to try to get first if possible. That way Juliet will sleep better and be in a good mood when she arrives."

"We could go to a club afterwards if you want."

She called back, "Why not? But we need to leave early if we want to get to LA before the others."

They then headed out for their pasta. Charles found it strange to have time on his hands in New York. His usual business trips were fairly standard; full agendas and fairly uneventful.

The last days had been tedious rather than troublesome. Going from regulator to regulator was hardly fun. It also was hardly fun interviewing some of New York's dimmest for the Chief Executive's job.

They changed into casual clothes. Jacqui wore a short skirt and a roll neck sweater under a calf length coat. Charles wore some black jeans and a white sweater as contrast to her all black. The sweater was loose enough to cover the gun that he had in his waistband.

The Trattoria was one of the best Italian restaurants in New York. The pastas and all that went with them were fresh. The tomatoes were incredible. They had a mound of the stuff and washed it down with Chianti. It was nearing ten when they finished. They sat together hand in hand and talked of Juliet. "And we better soon think of some brothers and sisters for her," said a quite broody Jacqui.

Charles let the comment pass. He knew that she would try to avoid being pregnant in the summer. She preferred to aim for the winter months, maternity wear is much more elegant then. She had noticed that when Juliet was born.

They carried on talking and drank their coffee. "Let's head down to Greenwich Village and take a look," suggested Charles.

"No. Let's head back. I have plans for you. I want to go home."

Charles wondered if he had misjudged her. Was she still broody? He decided not to ask. They walked out arm in arm and wandered over to the car under the umbrella of the attentive doorman. The driver was sitting in the front, he was the same Di Maglio driver who had accompanied them since they had arrived. That did not surprise them, though the poor man deserved some time off. They cuddled up to each other in the back of the stretched limo, there is a feeling of luxury in such cars. It was the sense of spaciousness. To top it off, Di Maglio's had genuine leather upholstery and every piece of wood gleamed.

The driver pulled up at traffic lights just by Carnegie Hall. Once, it had been a landmark building in this part of New York. Now it looked puny in comparison to some of the latter day giant and angular offerings that dominated the New York skyline. Their steel and glass shells allowed the architects to take flights of fancy and defy gravity through illogical shape. Charles was about to ask Jacqui what she thought of them, when he was jerked back from his musing by the rattle of gunfire. He hit the floor, grabbing Jacqui. That wasn't necessary as she was already there, her gun clear of her bag. Charles pulled out his and waited.

The sound of guns blasting and the pepper of bullets against the metal side of the car had ceased. There was a silence. He could hear no voices. There was no hooting of horns. Nothing moved for what seemed an age, but, in reality, it was only for a moment or two.

Charles yelled to the driver, "Drive. Get out of here." There was no sound. No movement. He raised his head. The driver was sitting and watching. He hadn't even ducked. It was as if he were waiting. And then Charles realised that he was. The door of the car was unlocked. It should have been locked the moment they got in. It had been unlocked to allow the gunmen access. A man ducked down, gun in hand. But, before he could register what was happening, Charles blasted him in the chest. The force of the bullets pushed him backward out of the car.

Jacqui slid forward and pulled the door shut. She rammed down the lock as Charles turned to the other side of the car and did the same. Once again there was silence. He smashed at the window between the driver and them. The glass must have been bullet proofed. It was definitely reinforced. Indeed, the whole car must have been made bullet proof, the shots had not penetrated the bodywork or shattered the windows.

The driver looked around. He was sneering. He was obviously part of the plot. They heard a click as the locks were released again. They realised that the driver had done that, and they hit the locks yet again, but this time they would not shut. The driver must have held down the switch in the front. Unless he released it, the locks could not be operated from their section.

"Stand by," Charles muttered. "They'll come again. Let's get out of the car. We're sitting ducks inside. We have more chance outside."

She nodded and he indicated the door on his side, "I'll go first and then give you cover. We try for the cars parked over there. I think the gunmen are all on your side."

There was another blast of gunfire. The car echoed with the sound of bullets thudding against it from quite close range. They seemed to come from the far side of the road. Charles felt fairly sure that his side was clear of gunmen. He pulled the door open and threw himself behind a parked car as bullets tore through the air in his direction. They hit cars parked at the side of the road. This time there was a crash of glass as window after window disintegrated with the impact of a hail of bullets.

Charles saw the door of the car edge open again and yelled "now" as he fired shots in the direction of the gunmen. The few shots hardly deterred them but it drew their fire away from Jacqui as she in turn hurled herself from the stationary car and joined Charles behind a parked van. Her hair was wet from the rain that was falling now as icy sleet. Her coat was dirty from the road. They hardly looked the smart couple they had been moments before on their departure from the glamorous restaurant.

"Your father's driver double-crossed us. I don't know who they are, but they had his help. He unlocked the doors. And he could have accelerated out of the trouble if he wanted."

"They don't want to kill us. I think they are trying to kidnap us," yelled Jacqui. "Otherwise, they would have just sprayed the inside of the car with bullets once they opened the door. They tried to get in. They were surprised by the fact that we were armed. And the gunmen avoided firing directly at us just now. We are worth more to them alive."

"Then let's keep them at bay. Shoot as they move forward only. The police will be here soon. Do you have spare ammunition?"

She shook her head. "I have one more clip. That's all. But we want the driver. If he gets out of the limo, shoot him, but not to kill. Just immobilise him. We need to question him."

Charles nodded. Two men with drawn guns were approaching their position. They were careful to keep under cover. They couldn't identify them. They were dressed in dark outfits and wore balaclavas. Charles saw a head poke out above a parked car and fired a warning shot. Whoever it was ducked. A burst of fire went over their heads and Jacqui fired back.

The sound of sirens broke the eerie silence of the last minute. The silence that had been disturbed only by the occasional movements from the gunmen, the shots they had fired at each other and screams from terrified passers-by. There was further movement at the side of the road and a car started up. Charles realised the gunmen were making their getaway. He looked at their limo, the door opened on the driver's side. A man jumped out and ran across the road towards the getaway car.

As Charles' shots rang out, the man screamed and fell face forward in the middle of the road. He was writhing in pain and clutching his leg. Then another burst of fire from the waiting car hit him and he was silent.

The car roared away as flashing lights came into view. "Put away the gun," Charles called to Jacqui. "Wait till the police arrive and they tell us to come out."

Two cars screamed past them in pursuit of the gunmen. Another screeched to a halt near them. Two policemen appeared from it, guns at the ready. They approached the body in the middle of the street. Charles got up and called out to them, "We were the ones attacked."

"Come out slowly and put your hands above your head."

"There are two us. There is me and my wife."

"Come over, one at a time. The man comes first."

Charles stepped forward, slowly with his hands up. Two policemen covered him. "I have a gun in my trouser belt. It's legal. My name is Charles Rossi. I am a banker here on business."

They took the gun and frisked him before signalling for him to relax. The same thing occurred with Jacqui. They hesitated about frisking her, and then decided against it. It may have been stupid but they seemed reluctant to frisk a woman. That could be useful sometime in the future, they both thought.

Charles went over to the driver. It was annoying that the man's accomplices had killed him. He needed to know who they were. He bent down. It was strange the driver wasn't bleeding that much. Charles realised he was still breathing. He bent down and pulled him onto his back. The policeman came over and ordered, "Leave him alone. That's evidence."

"The man's alive," Charles shouted. "We need an ambulance. He's an employee of my father-in-law. We need the best treatment. It will be paid for."

Jacqui appeared, in the meantime, to be speaking into her phone. "Are you calling your father?" asked Charles.

She nodded. "I know he's alive. We'll ensure he gets the best treatment. We also need to protect him until we know who tried to assassinate us. He could be a target."

That was obviously not the reason. They needed to know who he had worked for. The hit had obviously been planned. The bullet proof vest he was wearing had saved his life. And he had not told his accomplices about it. It was uncertain how the police would view the vest.

By now, the place was crawling with police. Charles went up to the officer in charge, "Look, we're freezing. It's pouring. We are based in the Pierre although we plan to fly to California tomorrow. We have meetings there next week."

The officer nodded, "We can interview you at the Pierre. But you can't take your car before the forensics people have been over it."

"It's my father-in-law's car. He lent it to us for our stay here."

The police returned the guns. Their licences had been checked in the interim. Suddenly, they were respectful. Whatever checks they had made, Charles and Jacqui were regarded as VIPs. Soon the ambulance arrived for the driver and Jacqui nodded to show it was her father's men.

Charles commandeered a stationary cab, one that seemed not to have been hit in the gunfire. He told the driver to take them the short distance to the hotel, giving him twenty dollars for his trouble.

As they walked into the hotel, Charles asked Jacqui, "What did your father say?"

"He will have guards on the driver night and day. The man has worked for him for a couple of years. He also wants us to fly in his executive jet to California tomorrow rather than take a scheduled flight. We will leave from La Guardia rather than JFK, and he will have a car pick us up. I know the driver in this case. It's his regular one. He wants us to use the jet internally for all trips. He is going to assign us new security. Our old friend, Claire, will be joining us. Strange, isn't it, we were talking of her the other day. He's put his organisation on red alert. He was shaken about the shooting."

At the Pierre, the doorman took a double take when he saw them. Charles and Jacqui were both pretty soaked and shivering. An anxious duty manager came up to them. Charles calmed him down and told him to show the police up to their suite when they came. "But give us fifteen minutes to shower and change," he asked.

They walked upstairs and stripped off. A hot shower and a fresh set of clothes later, they were fine. Jacqui was drying her hair when there was a knock on the door. A check on the spy hole established it was the detectives. Charles decided to be discreet and placed his gun on a table by the door before he opened it. They walked into the small suite with its sitting room adjoining the bedroom. The door between the rooms was half open and Jacqui sang out, "Charles, why don't you offer a drink. I'll need five minutes just to dry my hair."

He turned to the police. "Would you like coffee, tea or something more refreshing?" They both opted for coffee. He rang down. It would be with them in a matter of minutes. One could always guarantee good service, especially with a reservation through the legendary Di Maglio. The management must have been quaking in their boots.

They waited for Jacqui and the coffee. There was an awkward silence, then one of the detectives spoke. "While we're waiting for your wife, perhaps you could give us your details, and tell us how you came to be involved in this shoot-out?"

"My name is Charles Rossi. I am Chief Executive of the International Bank of Europe in the UK. My wife is a director of the bank. She is Jacqueline Rossi. Her family name was Di Maglio."

As usual in such company, there was an immediate exchange of looks at the sound of the legendary Mafia name.

"I am here to see US regulators. We are acquiring a US banking group. We were with the New York Federal Reserve Bank today, we went for a meal in mid town tonight and were heading back up to our hotel. Then the car was attacked at traffic lights."

"Do you both always carry guns?"

"In New York we do. You recognised the family name of my wife. I expected you to. That's why I mentioned it. Wouldn't you think it wise to carry guns? In any case we are allowed to. We carry them legally."

"Isn't it unusual for a banker and his wife to handle such a situation like professionals?"

"I have been trained in such things. I always thought it could come in useful. It did today. Jacqui has also been trained."

"Why was your driver wearing a bullet proof vest?"

"I asked myself the same question when I saw he'd survived a blast of a sub machine gun. Perhaps he feels uneasy north of 42nd Street. How should I know why he wore one? You should ask him?"

"Oh, we will, Mr Rossi, as soon as the doctors allow us."

At that moment, Jacqui came in. She must have realised that the conversation with the detectives was not going that well for she had changed. She was wearing a pair of body hugging jeans and a low cut sweater. They showed all the curves that they should. Her hair was loose and she had avoided much make-up beyond a splash of bright red lipstick. She looked very much like a walking invitation to bed. There were three men in the room and they all thought the same. Two were going to have to leave. And those two were not going to ask difficult questions. They were just keen to watch the body move.

The coffee briefly interrupted the more relaxed atmosphere. Jacqui served it, bending close to the detectives.

"How else can we help you?" she asked in a slightly huskier voice than normal. At the same time she lent forward. There were two sharp intakes of breath. Two men looked at her, totally captivated by the fluttering of her eyelashes. They were besotted by the way she was moistening her lips, looking open mouthed at the tip of her tongue peeping from between her crystal white teeth . They were longing for a glimpse of her breasts as she bent towards them. It was like watching fireflies around a light. It was incredible.

They hardly asked another question. Charles thought they were going to beg to let them stay just to carry on looking, but, in the end, they ambled over to the door. They had contacts for California, they had no further reason to stay. Charles closed the door behind them and, relieved, shot the bolt.

"You bitch," he said laughing. "The poor guys will be working all night feeling frazzled. They then go home and their wives will have a day job. You've condemned them to days of anguish."

She looked at him wide-eyed, "What about you?"

"I'm immune to temptation. I can withstand all your attempts at seduction. I decide, not you."

She laughed mockingly as she sat on the edge of the bed and wiggled herself out of her jeans. Keeping her eyes on Charles she gyrated out of her sweater. She bent down and her lips brushed against his. Her breath, so sweet and warm, breathed into his mouth. Her scent, softly sweet and exciting, wafted all over him. He took her in his arms. He felt her body. He shut his eyes. Her hair was on his face. Her lips and tongue were on his mouth. Her breasts were caressing his chest. Her thighs were folded against his. Their legs were intertwined.

Neither could take any more and they pulled themselves away. But it was only to tear off their clothes. Then they were together again. Their breath was coming faster and faster. Their minds were focused on the wonder of the moment as they slowly lay together on the bed and relived an experience they had known some thousand or so times. But, nevertheless, it was an experience that was unique and demanded only to be repeated in another form, in another mood, at another time.

CHAPTER FOUR

That morning, they packed quickly and headed off to La Guardia for Los Angeles International Airport, or LAX as it is more commonly called. The driver locked the doors the moment they were in the car, and smiling broadly at them alongside him was Claire. Charles looked at her. Claire whose gentle looks and ash blond hair hid the classical charms of a Di Maglio killing machine. She was a willowy figure in a black woollen dress, a protector from the past. Jacqui kissed her on both cheeks and Charles did, too.

"Well, I'll be looking after you both. And I'm longing to see the little one again. I got her a couple of presents, just for California. It's what every baby needs. There's a two piece bikini with a designer motif and matching sun hat and glasses. And there's a beauty case with genuine make up. They're all washable and non-allergic. You don't mind?"

"No, of course not," replied Jacqui laughing. "That's sweet of you to think of her."

They were chatting away. Charles half listened as they left Manhattan and sped through the grim streets of New York on that cold, wet morning. The few who were up that early on a Saturday looked universally miserable. The buildings changed and were now grimy reminders of the poorer side of the city. Life appeared to move lethargically outside the buzz of Manhattan. They moved to the freeways that cut between the buildings and created islands of tenements bathed in the smoky waste of the cars and trucks that were their main scenery. They could have been excused for wondering if they were in the richest country in the world or some lesser developed one.

Charles looked out for people walking in this concrete-clad, half-world. But he could find none. The only sign of movement came from the cars and trucks on freeways and streets; occasionally one could glimpse a shadow by a window in one of the tenements and imagine that was caused by a real person. The sidewalks appeared redundant in their emptiness. Life was a four wheeled affair travelling erratically in and out of the city.

They pulled into the gloom of La Guardia. Airports are never much fun. Flying is the ultimate American utility. The airports in New York are run without enthusiasm. Nobody seems to care and the passenger is just a passer-by using the pathways and escalators, stopping occasionally for fast food, the odd piece of shopping and the interminable queues to get through their chosen departure gate. La Guardia is pleasing from the air. Otherwise it is grim.

Charles turned to Claire. "Are you carrying a gun? We are. Do we go through a check?"

"No. You only do that when you use public airlines. We will be heading straight out to the jet by the hanger. I'm obviously armed too. We still do not know who attacked you. But we plan to find out if the driver wakes up today."

"How will you question him away from the police?"

"That's quite simple. We own the hospital. One of the doctors will take him to the theatre for an operation on his leg. He has a couple of bullets in it. Before we anaesthetise him, he will be questioned. Then, as he is brought back from surgery, he'll be dealt with. We can't have him spilling the beans to the cops about our interrogation. The shit deserves it anyway. He betrayed us. The penalty is clear."

She was right. If Di Maglio was not brutal in meting out punishments, then there would be anarchy among his men. Nobody could relax for one moment with those people around, but one had to employ such undesirables given the things they were used for. If you spared them, they would get back at you. You had to kill or be killed.

Di Maglio would execute the man without compunction. Charles and Jacqui, in reality, were no different; they were just in another market where there was less need for such action. But the security chief from Associated, the two detectives and the secretary had all been disposed of in a single day for similar reasons.

Charles recalled Di Maglio telling him once that they were alike; now he realised that was truer than he had thought. Though Charles dealt in money and Di Maglio in drugs, extortion and prostitution, they were both ruthless and would do all necessary to achieve their aims.

They were now at the plane. They got on and their luggage was loaded. That did not take long, as Jacqui was quick to point out. They had not bought clothes for California as they had planned to return home first. Charles expected that meant that Jacqui would head straight to Rodeo Drive and come back laden with new outfits. He didn't mind and, indeed, these days often accompanied her and let her buy things for him. Money was never an issue when you have billions in the bank, making close to ten million in interest each month.

The jet was comfortable. Claire knew her way around. They had coffee, fruit juice and croissants. She said they could have a full breakfast if they wished, but they declined. They went over papers sent from the office. There was little of importance and they got through that quickly. The phone rang and Claire answered. She handed it to Charles. It was Di Maglio, "The police interviewed the driver early this morning before we could get to him. He spun a strange yarn. He claims that he was given money by some Russians to help kidnap you two. And he says the Russians were after me as well. He claims they are Russian Mafia. And the strangest thing of all is that he says the gang is led by Rastinov."

"But that's impossible. I thought he was dead."

Di Maglio's voice was grim. "I did, too, but we have heard a couple of rumours recently. There have been some strange things happening around here. It could be true. We are investigating. But tell Claire to be really alert. I want to send extra guards. You'll need them in London as well. We'll talk about it when we meet."

Charles relayed what he had said to the girls. Jacqui went quite pale. She had seen more of Rastinov than the others. She had experienced the brutality of his men and had lost their first child due to him. Charles realised that the thought of him alive must traumatise her, and he had no doubt they would need to ensure that, if the brute were still alive, he really died next time. And that the next time had better be soon.

Charles had had one brief meeting with him and then thought he had seen him dead. Surely he could not have been mistaken? Surely it was Rastinov who died in the shoot-out at the Russian Mafia bunker in the South of France? He thought back to those horrific events. They had fought the Russian Mafia and killed the main leaders. They had identified them. If Rastinov were alive, he must have had a double or a double was now acting his part. That would be the only rationale. Charles thought back to the thick of the battle. It had been a bloodbath with so many victims. There would have been no time to double check. It was possible they could have been misled. It astounded him that could be the case. He had been an amateur at the time, but the Di Maglio men had accompanied him and they were experts. He couldn't believe that they would all have been deceived.

Jacqui interrupted this reverie, "What will we do?"

"Your father's people must kill Rastinov. There is no alternative. It looks as if we are heading for a bout of gang warfare again. We will have to be careful. We need to be armed at all times. And we should make sure that we have adequate protection for Juliet. I want you to concentrate on her safety, Claire. I'd quite like you to come back with us to London as well. I'll talk to Di Maglio about it. Would you agree?"

"I'd love to. Where would I live?"

"We may need to bring you and Maria to the house. It depends. I'll talk to Di Maglio and get his take."

Claire nodded, "He'll agree with you. It looks like the peace is over. Something has happened in the Russian Mafia. The deal we agreed two years ago appears dead. I guess that's why Di Maglio wanted you all to meet up in California."

The festive atmosphere had been dispelled. They were all serious now as they thought through the precautions they would need to take. This meant being armed day and night. It meant checking security at all times. Charles cursed the link between the evil world of Di Maglio and them. Then he calmed down. It couldn't be helped.

They started to lose height as the pilot brought them towards Los Angeles. The sight of the sea and a glimpse of the sun behind fluffy clouds helped dispel the gloom.

"Come on," joked Charles. "We've lived with Rastinov before and I suspect we'll have to again. This is the same world you used to live in, Jacqui. You never liked it but it didn't scare you."

"You're right. It's just that we had stopped thinking of the past. I had felt so safe. But you're right, we'll manage."

She was smiling again as they disembarked. "The London flight arrives in forty five minutes. Let's hang around for it and surprise Juliet."

They waited in the crowded arrival hall. Claire, who had disappeared for a moment, returned and told them to come with her. She had got the cases to the waiting driver and so he would take them to the car. They had now VIP treatment. That meant that they could get through to the passengers as they left the planes and before customs and immigration.

Juliet saw them the moment she came round the corner. The nanny put her down and she toddled towards them. She jumped into Jacqui's outstretched arms and they kissed each other happily. Then she saw Charles and the process was repeated. It was a sight that made many of the other passengers smile as they passed. A little girl and the chatter of baby talk for her parents. Then Claire came forward and gave Juliet a kiss.

They whisked through customs. Their case was the first out, emblazoned as it was with priority stickers. They grabbed it and headed out. A tall man in a chauffeur's outfit came up to Claire and said something. She nodded and he grabbed the case. They headed to the parking lot. Jacqui was carrying Juliet and the nanny was following.

"Charles," whispered Claire. "These places are dangerous. Keep an eye open. Keep hold of your gun. This place is moments from the freeway and then there are several options for anybody to take. We haven't got full security yet. Be careful."

"Is the driver armed?"

"Yes. But he's not the best. He is outstanding as a driver. He'll evade any pursuer. But he's not one for guerrilla combat. It really is up to you and me."

"Jacqui's armed as well. I know she's carrying Juliet, but once she's in the car we have another gun."

Claire was looking around from right to left. She glanced up as well. Car parks are places where it's easy to hide. She was incredibly nervous. Charles wondered whether she was not over sensitive.

"These guys managed to win over one of the Di Maglio drivers. That's not easy. The man knew he was dead meat if he was found out and caught. They can't kill him today but he'll not see the week out, you can bet at that. They must have spent a lot on persuading him. They got you in a good spot and at a good time. You must have been under surveillance. They'll know you were booked on a flight for LA, they may even know you've switched to a private jet if they have spies at the airports. They may know that Juliet's on this flight. And they can guess that we will not be on full security. Of course, I'm nervous, this is the best opportunity they'll have."

Charles' hand felt for his gun. He held it under his jacket. Claire was wearing a longish coat and he suspected she had an Uzi or something similar. The outline was clear. He realised that this was intentional, if they were to be ambushed the attackers would go for her first. They would know she was armed. That way the others would have a bit extra time. They would have that small extra chance to get away.

There was a noise to the left. A man darted forward. Charles pulled his gun clear of his jacket and Claire brought up her gun. The man was alone. He looked at them in panic. He bolted down the stairs. Charles shrugged his shoulders. Claire had already concealed her gun. He slipped his hand back under his jacket.

They were now near the car. The driver was about ten yards ahead of the rest of them. He activated the remote control. A roar filled the air.

Charles threw himself in front of Jacqui and Juliet and pulled them down to the ground. His body protected them from the force of the explosion. He felt the rush of air buffet him and smelt the acrid smoke.

The driver was blown backwards as he took almost the full force of the blast. The suitcase he was carrying flew through the air and landed a few feet away.

Claire threw herself down on the ground and rolled onto her back. She had drawn her gun again and was scouring the area for movement.

Charles checked out Jacqui and Juliet. They were fine.

The shocked nanny had been blown off her feet, was unhurt and just looking on in horror. She believed Charles to be a banker, and did not understand what was happening. The sight of his gun must have thrown her. The poor girl was just twelve hours out of London and apparently in the centre of a dangerous attempt on their lives.

Charles still had his gun drawn as he went over to the driver. He was still breathing. He was coming around. He seemed bruised and battered, but otherwise in one piece.

"Cover Jacqui and Juliet," yelled Claire. "Someone could try to snatch them."

Two men came running towards us. "Stop," yelled Claire. "Stop or I fire."

They stopped and shouted, "What's happening? We heard an explosion."

"Move away," shouted Claire.

The driver came to them, "Let's go? I'm OK. I can drive. I'm just all shaken up."

Charles thought he was concussed. The poor guy had lost his memory. The blazing wreck that risked setting alight the cars it had crashed into meant nothing to him.

"That wasn't our car," he yelled. He wasn't concussed. He had read Charles' thoughts.

"Then let's go. Check the car first. Look inside and underneath."

He nodded and went to a space several cars along from where the blast had occurred. He rolled on the floor and looked underneath. He looked through the windows. He opened each door. Then he jumped in and, waving Jacqui to take cover, backed out of the car space and towards the exit. He motioned to Jacqui to get to the car and she ran forward.

Charles did too, grabbing the case from the floor. Claire covered them from the rear. Jacqui bundled herself into the car and cuddled Juliet. She wouldn't have understood what had happened but she was trembling. Jacqui was holding her and keeping her quiet, it must have been the noise that frightened her more than anything else.

The nanny just stood transfixed. Charles yelled at her to get over to the car, pulling her that way when she did not react. She got in and sat in the rear seat, her eyes wide in horror and her mouth open in terror. Jacqui whispered something to her and she seemed to recover a bit.

Charles skirted the car. He looked at Juliet again. He noticed she clutched the little case of toys she had been holding. Charles jumped in the front of the car. That would let Claire cover the back. Her gun would be better at disabling any vehicle following them. She ran over and jumped into the car, which was already moving, slamming the door behind her.

"Open the window," she instructed the driver. And she pointed the gun out of it, monitoring the area. Charles had his drawn too and was monitoring the road ahead.

The driver punched a button on his mobile as the car gathered speed and screeched out of the car park and into the open. There was the sound of sirens approaching. The flashing lights would indicate the emergency services. There would be ambulances as well as the required police and fire-fighters. They suspected the latter were the ones needed most.

There was a voice from the mobile. The driver shouted back to it, "This is eight four zero seven. I am carrying VIPs. There has been an attempt on their lives in the airport car park area. I am heading for Santa Monica. Request an escort."

"This is Police Central. We read you. Identify VIPs"

"Charles Rossi, UK banker. Jacqueline Di Maglio, his wife. We also have their baby daughter, one nanny and one private bodyguard, female."

"We read you. We have them registered. You will be getting a motorcycle escort in around two minutes. Head on down the freeway. Retain radio contact. That is two drivers, both with an armed rider. "

The driver let the radiophone run. Charles said nothing. "Mummy, what was the bang?" a small voice in the rear of the car asked.

"Oh, just something old cars do sometimes, darling. Our cars never do that because we don't have old ones. Isn't it silly of people to let their car make such a big bang?"

Juliet appeared to agree. She then piped up, "Why is Auntie Claire playing with a gun? I thought only boys played with them."

"She likes to sometimes. She's playing with daddy. Look he has a gun too."

Once again that explanation was accepted. The conversation carried on like that while the driver sped towards Los Angeles. Cars around them hooted as they weaved between them at speed. Then they saw the flashing lights and sirens of two motorcycles. They drew up by the side of them and checked the occupants. They then drew ahead of them and sped along, lights flashing and sirens roaring as they cleared the traffic. The driver had put on his warning lights.

Claire sat by the open rear window, her gun on her lap but ever vigilant. Jacqui looked calm and was whispering and playing with a now totally unconcerned Juliet. The nanny was still in a state of shock, sitting bolt upright with her mouth half open. Charles turned to the driver, "Is the car bullet-proof?"

"That's what they tell me," quipped the driver.

Charles looked closer at him. He was a tall man. He was dusty and dirty from the blast, but one could see that he must normally look impeccable. His hair was carefully trimmed, he was clean and the creases were still visible in his trousers. He must be ex-military. "Where did you learn to drive?"

"Here in LA."

"You know what I mean. You're at over a hundred, you're relaxed and you are in total control on a crowded freeway."

"I was in the army. I learnt to do this type of driving there. I drove VIPs for the Government. Then I started working for Mr Di Maglio in California. The money's better than in the army and it's a lot less tedious. I organise all his car needs on the West Coast."

"You're good. What do you make of the explosion?"

"It wasn't very powerful. It was made to scare rather than to kill. I guess it was made for us. Someone saw me park. They wouldn't have booby-trapped this car as some pretty sophisticated devices protect it. I would have been aware of it the moment I pressed the remote control, although I always do a visual check as well as a precaution. I always activate the remote twenty yards or so from the car. If they have booby trapped it, you've a better chance of surviving at that distance."

"How did the remote set off the other car?"

The driver shook his head. "I don't think it did. I think that someone had set up the other car and blew it up as we approached. I think that it was chance that it happened around the time I activated the control. In fact I think it happened a few seconds after I had activated it. I remember hearing the beep of the car and the lights were already flashing on it."

Claire chimed in at this point, "I agree. Someone is trying to scare you. First of all there was the attack in New York. That was made to scare rather than to kill or hurt. Now we have had this. It's very bizarre."

"How do we get a police escort?" asked Charles. "I wouldn't have thought my father- in- law had that much influence with the West Coast authorities."

The driver laughed, "He has a lot of influence. They hardly want you hurt. We'll also have a police car waiting at the hotel."

Claire called out at that moment, "Helicopter overhead. It's not marked. Not police. Nor is it the TV people. Can we find a way of identifying it?"

The driver punched the button on his radiophone again, "This is us heading to Santa Monica under escort. We have unidentified helicopter approaching us. Please can you identify?"

A voice came back, "Understood. We are checking."

"It's coming closer and lower," called Claire. "I can't shoot at it. I wouldn't do much good with this thing and it would be dangerous. There are too many others around."

"Let's hope that your analysis is right. If it's the opposition, let's hope that they still only want to scare us."

The helicopter was coming in fast and swooping lower. A voice came over the radio.

"Helicopter identified as belonging to Zorba Import/Export of Seattle. No knowledge of principals. We have asked them to move off, but they have asked for proof of our authority. Stand by."

"That's a lot of help," Claire called out laconically. "The thing is almost on top of us."

The helicopter swooped down. A man was leaning out of it. He was armed with what looked like a rocket launcher. There was a flash and something roared by them. Minutes later it was weaving its way into the hills. Then in the distance they heard an explosion as it hit the side of the hill.

Charles muttered, "That was not a full force rocket. That was more a firework. We are still being stalked and they are still trying to frighten us. But hold on, it looks as if they are going to fire something else."

The driver was watching through the rear view mirror, waiting for the flash that would tell him it was time to act. As the rocket launcher fired, he swerved to the inside lane and onto the hard shoulder. He stamped down on the accelerator and the car leapt forward. The speedometer was at over a hundred and forty and, for the first time, they could feel the car bumping, weaving and grinding on the road. The rocket sped behind them and hit the protective barrier, exploding, showering the freeway with metal and causing cars to swerve as they got caught in the blast. They realised this was no firework. It was likely that there had been crashes, but they were too far ahead to be able to tell.

The helicopter zoomed towards them again. Jacqui called out, "There's a police helicopter coming the other way. It's going to intercept it."

At that moment, the pilot must have seen the police. He turned left and headed into the hills. The police helicopter was in full pursuit. Jacqui watched them carefully. Claire watched the road behind. Charles monitored the road ahead.

Jacqui called out, "They'll get away. They are faster than the police. They'll have a rendezvous in the hills. And blow up their helicopter. We'll do a check on Zorba, but I suspect I know who'll we able to trace the ownership to."

Charles nodded grimly. She was right. The owners would be linked to the Russian Mafia. He was also certain that they would trace the car that had exploded to them as well. They already had established the link between them and the attack in New York. He still, though, could not understand why they were so persistent and so open. The news of the attack would now be on the TV stations. The three of them had been in too public places. Charles wondered if it would affect the bid they were making for PAF.

The driver had drawn back onto the main carriageway and was holding his speed. The motorcyclists had clung to them like a glove. The riders had been aware of the events in the air but they had found it harder to manage their bikes at that speed than the driver in the car had. The convoy was, in any event, close to their turn off point now. They were now probably safe from further attack, but they couldn't be sure. Nobody relaxed.

The poor nanny was still in a state of shock. Charles realised she would not be with them at the end of the trip. He suspected he would need a girl from the Di Maglio operation until they had sorted everything out. They had sworn they would run separate empires. But there were some things one couldn't avoid. It looked like Maria and Claire would become part of the household. And it now looked as if they were going to have to take on a Mafia trained nanny. Such things existed. Quite simply the Di Maglio stable threw up a trained person for any walk of life. The Mafia had families. So they catered for them. They knew what was needed from cradle to grave. And feeling cynical, Charles wouldn't have put it past them to have their evil tentacles spreading out even beyond that.

They had left the freeway and soon the hotel loomed into view. They drew up in front of the main entrance just as a marked police car blocked off the approach road behind them. The outriders jumped off their machines and stood in front of the car. Claire got out. This time her coat concealed her gun. She was careful, though, and checked all around her. "It's all clear for the lobby."

The lobby was crowded and Charles didn't like it. He turned questioningly to Claire.

"You'll be covered. They won't try here. Not with police all around. We need to get in anyway."

Charles signalled to Jacqui to move and she hurried out with Juliet. The nanny followed as if in a trance. The driver was getting the cases. He shook his head at the porter who wanted to carry them. He did not want them out of his sight. Charles grabbed his briefcase and also Jacqui's, which he handed to Claire. The driver had the other cases. There were four. He had two under his arms and two by the handles. He would not be much good in a fight. Mind you, Claire had said that was not one of his strong points.

They must have seemed a strange sight. Nobody, luckily, thought of taking any photos. And the press were thankfully not around.

As the driver strode through the glass door, his upright figure and clean cut looks contrasted with the dust, dirt and grime on his uniform. Only his cap appeared to have escaped from the residue of the blast in the car park. His face was smeared with soot or dirt, or perhaps both.

Jacqui had dusted herself clean. Her hair was a bit dishevelled, but that could have passed as windblown. Her make up was delicate. A light red lipstick and gentle eye shadow contrasting the olive glow of her smooth, flawless skin. Her long, slim legs peeped out of her coat from time to time on black patent heels that made her look taller than she was.

Juliet had her arms around her mother's neck. Her dark long curls blended perfectly with those of Jacqui. Her skin was paler but still had the slight olive hint of her Italian ancestry. She was dressed in a red dress with a matching red bow in her hair. Her face was clean and glowing with innocence and interest as she looked around the lobby. She was evidently still upset, clinging to Jacqui rather than holding on to her.

The nanny was pale. Her clothes were still dusty from earlier. Her hair was all over the place, her eyes were blank. She was shaking like a leaf. When you have not experienced the works of the world according to Di Maglio, the first time comes as quite a shock.

Claire had also dusted herself down, although there were signs of dust and grime on the back of her coat. She had rolled onto her back to scan the car park for signs of trouble. Her hair was windswept. The long blond waves were a tangled mass, for she had been peering out of the back window for a good part of the journey. As a result her face was flushed from the wind. Her eyes sparkled from the excitement of the afternoon. Her lips were moist, her breath was coming out in sharp short bursts. It was strange. There was something vibrant about her. The thrill of the chase had a similar impact on Claire to the thrill of the kill for Maria.

Charles glanced at himself and self-consciously brushed down his clothes. He straightened his tie and smoothed down his hair. This all took a moment. Indeed, his inspection of his companions had all taken a matter of a minute. He was still standing in front of the hotel's revolving doors. The others were already half way into the lobby. A policeman was approaching, he seemed to feel something was wrong. Charles moved forward and into the hotel. Relieved, the policeman returned to his car and continued with his surveillance.

Charles caught up with the others and put a protective arm around Jacqui. Juliet looked at him and one little hand took hold of his. He smiled back at her and bent forward to kiss her on the head. This was crazy. They needed to distance ourselves from the Di Maglio world of crime. They had to protect Juliet. Jacqui and Charles' world was the non-violent area of finance. If it ever became violent for them, Charles swore he would leave it. And he meant it. He really meant it

The management rushed them into their rooms. The driver left, having told them that he would be on call whenever they needed him during their stay. The nanny was still traumatised. She and Claire unpacked the case that held Juliet's things.

Charles put on the cartoon channel, which grabbed Juliet's attention immediately. He pulled off his jacket and tie. Jacqui had hung up her coat.

They had a soft drink and all switched off from the violence of the street to watch an episode of 'Tom and Jerry'

Soon, Juliet was chortling at the antics of the cat and the mouse. Jacqui and Charles exchanged looks. This would help her forget. The troubled ride would fade into insignificance.

Claire returned. "The nanny's asleep. I slipped her a couple of pills when she had a drink. She thought it tasted weird but finished it all the same. I guess it will help her get over the shock. But you're going to need a new nanny. She asked if I knew if she could get a magazine called 'The Lady' here. She tells me that's where the aristocracy advertise for nannies in England. And she swears she will now only work with old money, so you're hardly going to make it."

Charles turned to Juliet, "Mummy and Daddy have got to make a couple of calls darling. Do you want to sit here and watch the television?"

"Can Auntie Claire sit with me?" said the little voice.

"I need her to help me. Can you sit alone? We'll just be over there at the table. We'll be near."

"Where's nanny?"

"She's asleep. She was tired after the journey."

Juliet nodded seriously, "I'll watch on my own. Can I come over if I want?"

Jacqui cuddled her and said, "Of course, you can. You know you always can." And the two smiled sweetly at each other and then lent forward and gave each other a kiss. Charles could sometimes see the mother in Jacqui taking over. Luckily, they were rich enough to handle both business and family. And, soon, they would be even richer. But first of all they needed to resolve their immediate local difficulties.

As they sat around the table, Charles turned to Claire. They had several things to resolve. "How is this going to be kept quiet, or, if it gets public, how do we sell it to the bank regulators? And finally, what the hell was the cause of all this mayhem?" He turned to Jacqui, "I suspect your father may know the answer to the last question."

It was with grim determination that Jacqui got on the phone. There was no way that she was going to allow her father to do anything that put Juliet at risk. He answered the phone himself.

"What happened?" he asked, when Jacqui said they had had some problems on the way in.

There was a furious response, punctuated by brusque comments from the other end of the phone. "What happened? Someone tried to blow us up. Of course we are all right. But we're trying to do some big deals here and your associates are not helping them. I will not have your foul business interests putting my daughter at risk. I don't care if you didn't tell them to attack us. They attacked us because of your business. So it's your fault... No, I won't stop yelling at you."

Charles gently took the phone from her. She let him and dropped her head into her hands. Claire went over to her and put her arm around her. It seemed to calm her. Charles took up the phone and told Di Maglio precisely what had happened. There were two leads to follow so far. Firstly, the driver in New York, and, secondly, the owners of this Zorba outfit.

Di Maglio said, "We can't get the driver. He's under night and day police guard. He won't talk to us."

"Does he know anything about your operations?"

"He knows nothing that can cause us any problems."

"Then I'd leave him well alone for the moment and depend on the police for information. Do you believe that Rastinov is still alive?" queried Charles.

"I have a horrible feeling he is. There has definitely been some fairly vicious infighting inside the Russian Mafia. They are causing us a lot of trouble. We can manage that."

Charles felt a slight panic as he wondered if the re-appearance of the Russian Mafia boss could impact his dealings with the regulators. He suspected Di Maglio could manage the news coverage, but asked all the same, "What about the publicity about the New York attack?"

"We'll manage that. You won't be mentioned by name. There has been news of the attack. It's been billed as a car hijack attempt and robbery. That way nobody really expects names. There is too great a danger of a copycat attempt and so the police refuse to release information about the innocent parties. Although I am astounded that anyone could see you as an innocent." Di Maglio laughed appreciatively at his joke.

Charles ignored him, "I guess that's all right. Can you also handle the attacks in LA? That will be both at the airport and at the freeway."

"Your names won't be released for the same reason. The police are already putting the news out that it was a spoof attack on a famous name by some publicity seekers. They have issued a statement about seeking the perpetrators who placed the public at serious risk of injury. They say they are following leads and expect to trace the attackers within days. Everyone will think it was an attack on some celebrity. You may feature in some of the tabloids but that's about as close you get to being one of them!" Again Di Maglio laughed at his joke.

But Charles wanted to be sure, "What about the car at the airport?" "That's not even rating much on the networks. It was an old car catching alight. The petrol tank exploded. It sounds pretty boring. The couple Claire scared off appear to think that she was police. I gather one wet himself with fright. Guys with wet pants don't fancy being interviewed. It doesn't look macho!" Again he roared with laughter.

"All right," agreed Charles, "So we can kill publicity. But we need bodyguards. I would like to bring Maria over but I need her for the business in London. We also will need a new nanny. Our current one is about two inches away from a nervous breakdown. Can you get me a better one?"

"I'll arrange one. Jacqui will approve. I know the right girl. She knows nothing about fighting or guns. But she's a member of a family and that means she knows how to handle such events. She's a nice girl, a trained nanny. She'd love to go with you to London. She won't spy on you. Don't worry."

Charles responded coldly, "You do read my thoughts well. But I need the right girl till you sort out your Russian associates."

His relationship with his father-in-law had always been quite cool. He felt at the moment that it was distinctly frosty, at least from his side.

"All right then. All I can do is try to get my people to track Zorba. I will be in LA on Tuesday. That way I can play with Juliet while you play with the regulators." Again Di Maglio laughed at his wit.

Charles was unimpressed. His thoughts were on protecting his family and he told Di Maglio, "We need better security. Claire will look after Juliet rather than us. I'll be armed at all times. But I'd like some better support. Can you send a couple of guards? I feel better with your people than with the local police."

Di Maglio was willing to help. They would have the required guards by morning. Then life could return more to normal. Charles breathed a sigh of relief. He turned to the others, "That's sorted out. He'll trace whatever he can. The good news is that we should get no publicity. But we are going to have to be careful. We have some big deals in the offing and I don't want anything to distract us. I suspect that this has something to do with the news he wanted to share with us when we have a family conference on Wednesday; it's definitely more than just the likelihood that Rastinov is alive."

Jacqui smiled back, albeit a bit wanly. "I'd like to pop into the shops. I really need some clothes. All I have is my work stuff. And they are New York rather than California. Could Claire and I go shopping? You could stay here with Juliet. I'll get a couple of casual things for you."

"That's fine. Will the nanny wake?"

"No chance," laughed Claire. "She'll be out till tomorrow. I fed her a pretty big dose. Let me use the bathroom in my room. It's just through the door there. Open your side of the connecting door and I'll open mine. We need to be able to get from one room to the other without moving outside. I won't use it unless needed. You two lovebirds can operate as normal."

She grinned pleasantly at both of them. Charles thought back to the time they were all together in Barbados. This was unlike that but, somehow, despite all the problems they had experienced, he started to feel in a holiday mood.

The two women were out for about ten minutes. They then met up, having tidied up and changed. "Let's go," called Jacqui with the enthusiasm she always showed when off on a shopping spree.

"If you buy lots, buy another case as well."

"Mummy, Mummy," called Juliet. "Buy me a present."

"Hey, why should you get a present?"

"I'm going to be a good girl while daddy looks after me."

"You better be," Charles said with mock anger as he ruffled her hair. She giggled and they sat cuddled together, watching another cartoon. One great thing about looking after a child is that one can watch cartoons to one's heart's content. And there was nothing more relaxing than that. As the door shut behind Jacqui and Claire, they sat down for a peaceful afternoon in front of the giant TV screen.

CHAPTER FIVE

Juliet soon got bored with the TV. She went to the make-up kit that Claire had given her. Then, in a good imitation of Jacqui making up, she started to play. First of all she put a towel over her shoulders. Then she put on the lipstick and other make-up. It ended up as no bad imitation of a make-up, a bit smudged in some places, but not at all bad for a little girl.

She then took up her doll and started to make her up. The attempt was not too good and the poor doll's face was soon smudged. Juliet looked at her father and shook her head. He looked in the bag and found the remover. She told him, "Mummy uses tissues with hers."

She trotted over to get a tissue from the bathroom, walking from the room to the main bedroom. The bathroom was off that room. Her scream jerked Charles to his feet. He was wearing a gun in his leg holster and had drawn it as he got up from the sofa. In a bound, he was in the bedroom and headed for the bathroom. She was there and alone, pointing at the bath and crying.

He could see nothing there and tried to get her to tell him what was wrong. She was crying so much that she couldn't speak. He looked carefully again and then saw what had shocked her. Crawling out of the plughole was a large insect. It was totally indifferent to the noise and just concentrating on escaping from wherever it came.

He slipped the gun back into his leg holster. Juliet had not appeared to notice it in any event. "It's only a sort of spider. It shouldn't be here. Shall I get rid of it?" he said. She nodded seriously, her eyes still full of tears. He took down the hand shower and flushed the beastie down the plughole.

"There Juliet, spider has gone. He won't come back. He wouldn't have hurt you. You're a big girl and he would have been scared of you. Now don't cry, we'll look after you. We always will."

She nodded and he took the tissue and wiped away her tears. "You've smudged your make-up."

"Shall I wipe it off like Mummy does after she's been crying?"

Charles automatically nodded, and she jumped up to get the make-up remover he had shown her earlier. He followed her into the room. Two things had shaken him. The first was the scream. The second was the comment on Jacqui. When did she cry? What was the cause?

Juliet came back. She was smiling now. She sat in front of the mirror again and removed the gunge with the same enthusiasm with which she had applied it. She then tackled the doll in similar fashion. Charles moved over and removed the bits that had been left behind from both of them.

"There" he said. "It's now as good as when Mummy removes her make up. When does she cry and smudge hers?"

"She says I mustn't tell."

"But she only means other people. You can tell me."

She looked serious again, "She cries when grandpa calls."

She meant Di Maglio. His father was known as gramps. "Oh come on Juliet, why would she cry if grandpa calls?"

"'He shouts at her. She cries."

At that moment there was a slight noise outside the door. His nerves were still on edge after her scream. He went over and looked through the spy hole, expecting it was Claire and Jacqui. It wasn't them. It was two women he didn't recognise. They had stopped in front of the door, and one was looking in her bag. She had obviously mislaid something and was searching through it.

They whispered to each other. People who whisper in hotel corridors are usually not supposed to be there. Charles glanced back to the lounge area. Juliet was happily playing pretend with her doll. He was alone with her. There was no way that he could hide her elsewhere. He needed to be able to see where she was. He took the gun from his leg holster and waited to see what happened.

He looked at them carefully. They were dressed in short skirts and wore low cut blouses. They had long hair, one a redhead and the other a blonde. They were in their twenties. Their coats were thrown over their shoulders. Their appearance and demeanour were out of place. He then realised, he had been stupid. They were hookers and they had managed to get past reception. He heard one of them say "604" as she read from a piece of paper she had fished out of her bag. That must be along the corridor. They were 611 and also had the rooms on either side of the suite. He breathed a sigh of relief, watching the two hookers move down the corridor. Then he heard a faint movement in the other room.

Only the nanny was there. She couldn't be up. Claire had told him that she had administered enough sedative to knock her out till the next morning. He moved carefully towards the connecting door. Juliet was still playing with her doll. He kept the gun away from her. There was no need for her to see it. Was the noise outside a decoy to allow someone to break into the other room? Or was he just getting paranoid?

He waited outside the room. The door led into the lounge area of their suite. He placed himself besides it so that anyone opening it would fail to see him from the adjacent room. He looked over to Juliet. She was still playing. She looked at him. He beckoned her to come over, putting his fingers to his lips. She looked puzzled and started to come over. Then the door by him opened. A woman came through and ran towards Juliet.

Juliet ran back away from Charles. She was scared. He held back in case there was someone else in the room. There was no movement, but he could not delay and so he went forward. "Put your hands in the air slowly. No sudden moves. Turn round."

She was a tall middle aged woman. She was dressed in dark trousers and a dark sweater. That was classical intruder garb. She wasn't scared, and he sensed she was not surprised. That meant she knew he was there, and that meant that she had an accomplice, or perhaps accomplices. He waited, sensing that only half the battle had taken place. Juliet was watching this scene quietly. She was obviously puzzled rather than frightened.

The tall woman stood still with her hands in the air and stared at the gun. He heard a rustle behind him. But he was too late. He felt a stab. He felt to the seat of his trousers and sensed the fluid being injected. He whirled round and grabbed at the syringe. That's what it was. He yanked it out and threw it down. His head was whirling. The room went round and round. The tall woman was laughing now, Charles saw two of her. There was a smaller woman nearer him. She grinned evilly. He fell to his knees. He fought against the drug. He needed to protect Juliet.

Then Juliet screamed. The tall woman had bent to pick her up. That allowed him to see through the haze that was forming in front of his eyes. He realised he had a gun in his hand. He tried to say something but couldn't. As Juliet screamed again, he sensed the tall woman had let go of her and jerked upright. She was holding her hand where Juliet had bitten her. Juliet was running towards the bedroom. He pulled himself to his knees again with one desperate burst of strength and pain and shot at the tall woman. There was another scream. This time it was from her as she stumbled back. He sensed he must have hit her, but did not know how badly as he could not see her for the haze. He swung round to the other woman who was moving towards him. Then the room went black and everything started whirling round. Then, there was darkness and silence.

They heard the scream of the child. They started as the gun blasted. They looked at each other as the second and unknown scream carried through the hall, Jacqui and Claire dropped their shopping bags and moved towards the suite. Jacqui had drawn her gun. Claire was checking the corridor for signs of anybody. Her gun was also in her hand. It was strange. No reaction from anywhere. Did people think it was a television on too loud? They registered, considered and then ignored the reasons. They needed to get to the suite.

Claire motioned to Jacqui to cover the door. She stood by the wall, facing the corridor, her gun at the ready. Claire went to the door of her own room just up the corridor and carefully pushed the electronic card into its slot. The door opened silently, the only reaction being a green light on the top of the lock. Claire moved into her room. She moved to the connecting door. It was a double door with locks in both rooms. On her side it was already open but the second door was closed. The door was solid and she couldn't see who or what was on the other side. She had to be quiet and she had to be fast. The only things that would play in her favour would be the element of surprise, and her ability to call on Jacqui for support once she was inside.

The door opened into the sitting room of the suite and there was no way they could fail to hear her coming. They would hear and see her, perhaps when she turned the handle to open the door, perhaps when she opened it. She thought through the room layout. Whoever had Charles and Juliet was unlikely to have placed them against the door. But there was a risk if she had to shoot her way in. She hoped that the door would not creak. Gently, she opened it an inch at a time. There was no sound from the sitting room but she could hear voices in the bedroom beyond. As she came through the door, she could make them out: "The bastard shot me," a woman's voice said. "They said he wouldn't shoot a woman. He shot me."

Then there was another voice. "Let's get out of here. I've trussed up the brat. We'll put a shawl round her and anyone will think she's asleep. All I have to do is hold her face in my shoulder."

"I need to stop this bleeding," said the other. I can't walk through the place like this. My clothes are covered in blood."

"Put your coat on. But get a towel from the bathroom and tie it over the wound. It'll have to be a face towel. Look I'll get your coat from next door so we can check it looks OK. The brat can't move, she won't bite you again. But we need to get away and fast, or the little bitch's mother will be back with the blonde bodyguard."

Claire realised that someone was coming to the sitting room. It was going to be the uninjured one. She was now sure that there were only two of them. She slipped silently to the ground and hid behind a sofa. The woman walked in past the sofa and didn't know what hit her as Claire, using the gun as a club, smashed it down on her head. Claire caught her as she fell and placed her on the ground. The sound of the blow had not travelled and that had been the only noise. Claire grabbed a tie back from the curtains and quickly hooked it over the woman's neck, tying the other end to her foot which she pulled behind her back. It took seconds to do. It also took Claire seconds to frisk her and remove the small handgun from its holster. The woman could yell when she came to. But by then it would not matter.

"What are you doing in there? We need to go," the other voice said. It was a whining and annoying sound. It was like the noise of an injured animal rather than a person. And at that moment Claire stepped into the bedroom, her gun pointed at the woman, who was sitting on the ground holding her shoulder. Juliet was well away, behind them on the sofa, immobilised and bound up in a shawl. She was out of the line of fire and too far away for the other woman to grab.

Claire covered the woman with her gun. "Jacqui," she called. The door lock clicked and Jacqui came in. She had bent down to a crouch and scoured the room with her gun leading the way. She quickly took in the scene. She started when she saw Juliet on the sofa and Charles lying immobile on the floor, but she knew that she must ignore them for the moment. The first job was to secure the place. The wounded woman moved forward just as Claire swung round her gun and crashed it into the side of her skull. The blow she had delivered to the woman in the sitting room was gentle in comparison. There she had been limited by space. Here she was able to use her full strength and take advantage of the space to add momentum to the force of the gun. The woman moaned and collapsed in a heap on the floor.

Claire signalled to the nanny's room. Jacqui went through the door and checked it out. She came back; all was clear. Claire went to the bathroom and came back with a small hand towel. Grabbing the smaller woman, she tied it round her mouth, pulling the mouth open and brutally fastening the ends as tightly as possible.

Jacqui, meanwhile, locked the connecting door to Claire's room before doing the same with that between the suite and the nanny's room. She then went to Juliet and untied her. The little girl fell into her mother's arms crying bitterly. "The nasty lady hurt me. Daddy shot her. Where's Daddy?"

Claire had moved over to Charles. She had taken in the syringe and noted he was breathing. His breaths were deep but regular.

She walked over to the smaller woman and took off the gag, "What was in the syringe?"

"It was nothing much. It's just a knock out drug. It'll wear off in an hour or so. Maybe less as he did not take a full dose."

"Good, let's hope you're right. In the meantime, as there's some stuff left in the syringe, we'll give your friend some. If she dies, you will too."

"I swear it won't harm him. It's just a drug."

"Daddy's having a sleep darling," Jacqui explained to Juliet. As Claire injected the unconscious woman on the floor, she said to Jacqui, "Why don't you go to the bedroom? I'll question this cow."

Juliet was asking, "What cow?" as Jacqui took her through to the bedroom. Moments later the television was on. The cartoon channel was again being used to distract.

Claire got to work on the frightened woman. She was dressed in a black skirt and blouse. They were professionals. Although she suspected she knew the answer, Claire wanted to hear for whom they worked. She looked at the woman and started to speak in a voice that would have made anyone shudder.

"There are three stages to what I can do to you. Stage one will begin now. I'll put the gag back on and then beat you over the head and then downwards. It'll be systematic and painful. I'll break some bones, the odd rib or too. I'll then take off the gag and give you a chance to talk.

If you won't, I put the gag back on and shoot you in the stomach. That's painful but it usually works. If it doesn't I wait till he comes round, take you up to the roof and give you one last chance.

If that doesn't work, you take a dive. It's your choice."

"What do you want?" said the woman.

"You're a professional. You know exactly what I want. I want information about your employer and your objective. You didn't shoot him. You could have. It would have been easier and safer. So why didn't you?"

"We were told to make sure he was left alive. We just had to get away with the kid."

"Carry on."

"We were to deliver her to two men who would be waiting for us outside the hotel. They would recognise us and use a password to identify themselves. We don't know who employed us. They were going to pay us well."

"That's crap. You know who they are. Tell us."

"I don't know."

"Then you're no use to us. And as you've annoyed us, we'll kill you."

This was delivered in the coldest of tones. At the same time, Claire raised her gun till it pointed directly at the woman's chest. The eyes widened in fear. They tried to meet Claire's and failed. Claire's finger moved slowly on the trigger.

"All right, all right," shouted the woman, her Slavonic accent becoming noticeable as fear took over. "I'll tell you. The man who employed us is called Rastinov. He's Russian Mafia."

"We know that much. But what is the reason? This is the fourth attempt in two days. You're trying to scare, not kill. It makes no sense."

"Di Maglio is rumoured to be selling out. We want his business and we want it at our price."

"What is your price?"

"We offer his family's safety. We want to show that they are not safe unless we let them be. That's why there was the attempt in New York. Also the two attempts this morning. We were not to harm the child and we would have kept her in hiding until Rastinov got the goods. Di Maglio dotes on his daughter and the kid. He would have crumbled."

"What are your links with Rastinov?"

"We work for him."

"What'll happen if you've failed?"

"He's not going to be pleased. He'll be really upset with Magya." She indicated the tall woman. "She's failed before."

"Won't he kill you?"

The woman looked surprised. "No, we knew the attempt was high risk. And Rossi responded quicker than we thought. We tried a decoy but it didn't really work."

"Di Maglio would be less gentle with failure," commented Claire. "And he taught me. So where's Rastinov?"

"I don't know. He moves around."

Claire looked carefully at the woman, then grabbed the towel and gagged her again. She pushed her to the floor and snarled, "Wait there till the banker comes round. Then we might let you go or we might kill you."

She then moved over to Charles and pulled him over to the sofa. He was not light but she managed to raise him. He looked as if he were asleep. She frisked him gently for any other weapons. She knew he would be groggy when he came to, and she didn't want him to start shooting by accident in that state.

The tall woman was still unconscious on the floor. Claire walked over and frisked her again. She already knew she didn't have a gun. She checked for handbags, but there were none. That was strange. She looked around for something with which to tie up the tall woman. She picked up a lamp and used the flex.

She opened the door into the nanny's room again. She put on the light. The place looked OK. Nevertheless, she moved carefully and checked cupboards and bathroom before double locking the door into the corridor. She had noticed the two shoulder bags on the floor. They must belong to the women, she did not recognise them.

She checked out the nanny. She realised she had been injected with some drug, simply from the fact that the bedclothes were pulled back. She picked up the bags and returned to the suite, pulling and locking the door behind her again. She hoped the nanny would not overdose between the two sets of drugs, but she had other priorities for the moment.

She went through the bags. There was another gun in one of them and nothing else of interest other than driving licences and credit cards. The names were identical on them all and Claire put them aside. They would help confirm the identities. She went over to the phone and dialled a number.

"Hi Roberto," she said. "It's Claire here. I need a clean up squad at Shutters in Santa Monica. There are two women. One shot in the shoulder. Both have headaches. We had a kidnap attempt. The nanny may have a drug overdose. Include a doctor in the team. Jacqui and Juliet are fine, Charles took a knock but will be all right. Otherwise, all's OK. We need extra security immediately. We can't wait till tomorrow. Pass the message on to Di Maglio now."

And with that, she put down the phone and turned to Charles. He was groaning slightly and seemed to be coming round. She put a hand on his forehead. It was quite cool. His eyes flickered open and she bent down and whispered, "Just relax. Everything's all right. Jacqui and Juliet are here." He seemed to register and lay there but his eyes were open. He was recovering.

She checked the corridor outside. Nobody was in sight. She still had her gun in her hand as a precaution. She opened the door and pulled the shopping bags they had left in the corridor inside the room. She carefully shut it behind her. Then, gingerly, she opened and examined each of them. There were clothes and a pair of shoes in them. She took out one after another. All was fine. Nobody had placed anything strange in them. The last bag held two boxes. She checked them out. One was a doll for Juliet, the other was a wardrobe for the doll. She placed them back in the bag. The pile of shopping was placed on the table. She screwed up the bags and threw them away.

The noise appeared to rouse Charles. He sat up slowly with a groan. Then, a bit unsteadily, he got to his feet.

"How do you feel?"

"I'm a bit groggy. Where's my gun?"

She handed it to him and he put it back in his leg holster. "Is Juliet all right? They were rough with her."

"She's next door with Jacqui. We should leave her there. I've sent for the clean up squad. They'll be here in about half an hour. They'll get rid of the women and clean up the bloodstains over there. The nanny needs checking out. I fed her tablets and these women stabbed a needle in her bum."

"Have you questioned them?"

"Yes. But they did not add much. It's Rastinov. And he wants the Di Maglio business. The price is your safety."

"Di Maglio won't accept that."

She nodded, "He can't. Those scum would just increase the price."

He lowered his voice, "How will they leave? Should it be by the window or the door?"

"I guess by the door. They're pretty low grade. I suspect that they were not expected to succeed. They're not worth a possible murder rap."

"They almost succeeded though. I screwed up."

"You're out of practice. But I goofed as well. We should have secured the doors. One person can't monitor a suite and two adjoining rooms. There were four doors to the corridor. That was too much. Sorry."

He smiled and moved towards her. He bent down and kissed her on the lips. "Don't worry. It's the outcome that counts. We're all right. We'll just have to increase security."

"I have that in hand already."

"Excellent." Charles now felt he was back in control. His head had cleared and, although shaky, he was thinking clearly. The drugs did not appear to have been too strong. He thought back to earlier. He remembered Juliet's words about her mother's crying. He had to find out about that. But first they had to move the women out.

He went into the room to check out Jacqui and Juliet. Amazingly, Juliet was asleep in the bed. She was still dressed. Jacqui was sitting by her side. She went over to him and put her arms around him. She rested her head on his shoulder.

"Are you all right?" she whispered. Her voice was soft and gentle.

"Yes, they stuck a needle into me, that's all. I'll need a blood test. But they can perhaps check out the syringe first."

She shuddered, "Don't even joke like that. Please."

They sat down on the edge of the bed and looked at Juliet. "We've got to make sure that she's well protected. We need to end this." Charles explained to Jacqui what Claire had told him.

He then took hold of her hands and looked into her eyes. Those big dark soulful eyes looked into his. "Jacqui, why do you cry when your father calls? It came up when I was playing with Juliet."

She looked sad, "He still wants us to be part of his Empire. He believes that you are the barrier. So he tries to turn me against you. He tells me that you play around with other women. He says he thinks you'll come over to his business once you tire of the world of finance. He thinks you'll work for him in any event."

"But how will that happen?"

"You'll be bored by finance and you'll need the excitement of his world. He also thinks you'll want the girls." Her lips were trembling. Her eyes were full of tears.

"But Jacqui, that's rubbish. I want you and I want Juliet. I want us to be super rich. And then we'll find our Shangri La."

She smiled through her tears. They had talked of finding an island, or at least a lonely beach before. They had talked of living quietly in mountain villages. But they never thought they really could.

"Look, when we talked about it before, we were not rich. If this all works we will have over ten billion dollars to our name. We can make money still but we can chose where we base ourselves. That doesn't mean we can't leave our island or mountain or whatever it is. We'll be able to do what we chose. We need a break. We'll have a break. And we should make a few more babies. Juliet needs brothers and sisters."

She smiled through her tears, "He taunts me about you. He says you'll tire of me. He says I'll always have to work for you."

"That's rubbish. We work together because you have a role in the business. We're partners. But above all, we're married and we're Juliet's parents. I can't ban your father. We've involved him in this deal. But if he tries to tie in the rest of his seedy business the deal will be off. We can find another target; PAF is just the easiest to arrange and has the advantage of being Mafia managed.

But please no tears. And while we're doing this deal, let's look for our island. Or would you prefer a mountain?"

"I want my beach. I want it on an island. Let's find somewhere in the West Indies. The islands are full of coves where we can be alone and away from him and his evil cronies." She smiled, "We'll find it."

There was a tap on the door. Jacqui jumped up and went to the bathroom. Charles opened the door to Claire.

"I have the squad here. They are cleaning the place. The doctor is with the nanny. She'll be OK, but she's going to have the king of headaches. He'll have her moved to the local hospital, so she'll be out of the way."

Jacqui came in and Claire continued, "He's also checked the syringe. It is clean. He has run a test on the stuff they injected into you. It was some sort of fast working anaesthetic. He wants just to take a blood test as a precaution. Then he'll patch up those scummy women and the others will dump them well away from here."

"What about security?"

"They are here. We have three guards night and day. They are professionals. They'll be good. Nobody will get past them. They'll operate in the corridor. They'll also put two guards downstairs in the lobby to watch people. And tomorrow we'll have a special nanny for Juliet. Tonight I'll guard her and sleep in her room."

Jacqui said, "She'll sleep in our bed tonight. I think she may have nightmares. She doesn't know you well enough, Claire. She'd be frightened if she woke up."

The cleaners were hard at work. They were all dressed in dark suits with white shirts and dark ties. Was black the standard colour of the shadowy world of crime? Everyone was in black. It was like a funeral although, for once in the shadowy world of Di Maglio, there was no corpse.

The doctor took a blood test from Charles. He ran some quick tests on it.

"Negative," he said. "You seem OK. The syringe was one of those disposable ones. It looks as if it was filled in the next room from a fresh bottle. There was one under the bed, together with another syringe. The blood on that is the same as the nanny's. In fact the only crossed blood I have found is yours on the woman over there."

"That tallies. I stuck the same syringe into her as they stuck in him," said Claire.

The women were standing there looking sullen. She turned to them, "Well ladies, prepare to meet your fate. I'm not telling you what'll happen to you but I can assure you that you're not going to have a fun weekend. As we know, you've friends waiting for you outside. So we won't harm you. But we are going to hand you over to the police. And they are going to charge you with breaking and entering, attempted kidnapping, assault and murder."

"We haven't killed anyone," wailed the smaller one.

"You killed the girl in the bed. She was given a massive overdose. Four syringes of anaesthetic."

That was untrue. The two women were now in a cold sweat. They thought they had been set up, that they were going to prison. They weren't. But it would be some time before they realised otherwise.

The woman protested, "We only gave her one. That just ensured she didn't wake up while we were there."

"Who's going to believe that? Take them away. Bye girls. Have a happy life."

When they'd left, Charles asked what was going to happen to them.

"We've a mock police truck outside. We'll put them in there and then find a place where they can escape. That way they'll be on the run for quite a while before they realise that they're not being sought. They'll be miserable and, in any event, they've bad headaches. Moreover, they have no money and no cards, as I've kept them. And I can't believe that Rastinov will be pleased. Who knows what he will do to them?"

The room had emptied. Claire and Jacqui unpacked their new clothes. "What do we do tonight?" asked Claire.

"We have to act as normal as possible for Juliet. We'll use the coffee shop and take her for a meal." He turned to Jacqui, "When do you think she'll wake?"

"I guess in an hour or so. That's time for us girls to get ready. I'll leave the bathroom door open and you leave the lounge one open as well. That way she'll come to one or another of us when she wakes up. Or we can go to her if she calls."

Peace descended and Charles sat down quietly with the TV on as accompaniment rather than for amusement. He thought back over their plans. By now his father and Stephens should have plotted out their full strategies. He needed to update himself on them. He picked up the phone and got through to his father. They chatted briefly. He decided not to tell him about recent events. "How is the plan progressing?" Charles asked.

"There are some investment funds in one of the US banks you are acquiring. They are good performers, which helps. But, most importantly, they are allowed to invest in almost anything. We'll use them; just change their management by placing our people in charge.

We have companies identified all around the place for them to invest in. We've created a new company. It looks as if it's broadly held but is in fact owned entirely by us. It's starting to build up stakes in a lot of the target companies that the US investment funds will invest in.

By the way, the company is based in the Cayman Islands; its parent is in the Dutch Antilles and our stakes are held through a couple of Swiss and Panamanian structures that lead in turn into a Liechtenstein company. I call that cosy and totally impenetrable.

We'll build up stakes slowly in our targets. I'm aiming at a total spend of between a billion and two billion dollars there. I expect to sell them on for double that. We'll easily cream off a billion or two that way. I'll use the normal procedures. The shares we target are good and some are undervalued; we'll just ramp up the prices so by the time the funds buy from us they pay us over the odds. And we also have those phoney investments in place and waiting to be sold to them too; those will be worthless at the end of the day.

All the bank has to do is sell a whole load of those funds to the poor punters to bring in enough cash so that they buy the stuff off us at our inflated prices. Then we pull the plugs on the different operations whenever it suits us."

"Good," responded Charles with some enthusiasm, "What about the deals with Stephens?"

His father sounded impressed, "I've been through everything he has planned. It's outstanding. There will be a series of deals in place, all highly complex. No auditor or regulator will have a chance of challenging the valuation. There will be nothing to compare. We expect them to make us at least a couple of billion clear. We could make more, but it will depend on the final scale we can get away with. He needs to be careful though.

If he's too greedy, it will get difficult to conceal the deals. But I'll make sure that doesn't happen, you can depend on me."

Charles was glad he'd asked his father to monitor Stephens. He reminded him, though, that he wanted to know what companies he was using. "I need details of the companies involved. I also have to identify others to whom we will lend, although we'll lend to some of those we use for Stephens' deals as well. We'll need to get together. But I want no meetings in London; I don't think IBE is that secure. We'll set up a meeting in Zurich or Liechtenstein for that. I don't want us to go for more than twenty companies. It gets difficult to control, otherwise. And, by the way, I want no more than two or three from the Di Maglio stable."

"But, I'm already planning on using six companies he's put into the play for me already."

"I know why I am saying this. Cut some out. You or I will manufacture new ones if need be. Is twenty enough?"

"Yes. I can easily make do with twenty. Why are you concerned about over dependence on Di Maglio?"

"I want us to be independent. I want to ensure he is always a minority player in any of our deals. He smells too bad at close up."

There was no response from his father on that point. Then he commented, "I want to start on the insider trading for our own account as well. Our activity will stimulate a market rise. So I'll do some deals that allow us to leverage on that. I'll use around half a billion dollars of our own capital for that. Then, before we pull the rugs on everything, I need to sell like hell to leverage on the inevitable falls that the series of defaults will create."

"Are you doing anything for the final hit on IBE?"

"I'll do some trading in the end and it will be big. But I need to be careful. I have some thoughts on how we do it. Let's talk about it when we meet. I'm a bit nervous about going into detail on the phone. I'm always scared about espionage, even if we both use the scramblers."

He was referring to the scrambling devices they had fitted to their phones after their social chat. These made their conversation unintelligible to any eavesdropper. But he was right. They had to be careful.

After they had said goodbye, Charles mentally checked through the list. The acquisition appeared likely to be rubber stamped. That could go through within a month or so, especially as there were no shareholder issues. Everyone was up for it, simply because Di Maglio had a pretty bad reputation. The investments to sell to the US clients were being prepared.

The sophisticated financial deals were being put in place and could start being rolled out as soon as wanted. They could also put the lending in place as soon as needed.

If they completed the bid in a month, they could think in terms of selling off the shares of the combined operation to the public about six to nine months later. That way they could put some good results for the first six months into the public arena and make an optimistic forecast for the next period. They would include the fees they earned on selling more investments, the fees charged on Stephens' deals as well as the interest on the phoney loans. People would buy it. They would be seen to be geniuses. Their past reputation for making money would limit the questions about the risk of such fast growth.

Once they had sold the shares to the unsuspecting public, they would remain strong on the back of the good results and the optimistic forecasts. Then the hit would come as the bank went into spectacular default. Its share price would nosedive.

In fact, it all meant that they had a fairly easy time ahead of them until around the summer. Nothing they were doing would stress them. Only then would they really be faced with the most difficult phase. By next Christmas or Easter at the latest they should be clear. Charles doubted, though, the Bank of England or any other regulator would ever agree that he should run a bank again. He doubted they'd let him run a coffee stall even. The great thing, though, was that would not matter. They would have money. And money would give them respectability. And there was more to financial manipulation than running banks. In any event, as Di Maglio proved, bad reputations are not inherited. So the Rossi dynasty could continue a couple of major scams a generation. That should ensure their wealth lasted!

At that point Jacqui walked back into the lounge. He sensed the smell of bath oil on her. It was a fresh, clean smell. She had tied a towel around her like a toga and sat down carelessly. It parted to well above her knees.

She yawned. "You know, I know what I'd like to do after all that excitement. The only thing is that we might wake up Juliet and I don't want to do that."

Claire had come in silently. "I should hope not. Hope I'm not intruding," she said with a big grin. "I left the stuff I bought here on the table. I unpacked it all to check nobody had messed around with it while it was outside."

Claire was dressed a bit more discreetly than Jacqui. Her long blond hair was just towel dried. She looked even softer and gentler without make-up. She was wearing a hotel robe that was belted tight. It was small on her, falling to a few inches above her knees.

"Let's all have a drink. We deserve one."

"Great idea," answered Claire as she dropped into an armchair. The robe shot up another few inches to reveal even more shapely leg and thigh. The belt also seemed to loosen in the movement. The top parted and revealed the outline of her breasts.

"I better make myself useful," joked Charles. "Or I'll get quite worked up. What do you want?"

He walked over to the fridge and looked inside. "Can you make me a virgin Mary?" asked Claire. Jacqui looked quizzically over at her. "Oh, all right, how about a champagne cocktail?"

"That'll suit me," said Jacqui. Charles had guessed she'd jump for that one. She always liked them.

"I wouldn't make good ones from the stuff here. I'll order some from room service."

He called down and asked for them to be served in large glasses. "I want them as a long drink rather than a cocktail. Can you get them up immediately?"

A few minutes later, they arrived. As he opened the door, he noted the guards on duty. They had two chairs by their door and were seated on them. They jumped up when they saw him. They were uniformed, which surprised him. He knew they were from Di Maglio, but hadn't realised he also owned a local security firm. He saw another guard over at the lift lobby as well.

The waiter deposited the drinks and looked at them inquisitively. Two under clad and beautiful women in a suite guarded by security men was perhaps not what he was expecting.

They drank and chatted. A little voice said, "Can I have a drink of milk?" Juliet came over to Jacqui and climbed onto her knee. Charles got her the drink. They'd had the fridge stocked for her as well.

She didn't mention the earlier incident. They didn't either. They all agreed to go downstairs and have a meal in the coffee shop. After all, they had missed lunch and it was well after six. The four of them went down. It was quite fun walking into the place and seeing everyone look at them. Charles carried Juliet, dressed in designer jeans and a blue silk shirt. She looked a mini version of Jacqui who was dressed in an almost identical outfit. Her long legs and slim figure suited jeans as much as they suited

Claire. All three of them had drawn their long hair back and tied it in a bow that matched their shirts. Charles looked quite sombre next to them.

Nobody bothered them and they had a quiet meal. They stayed till they saw Juliet was dozing off again. As they took her out, a strict matron turned to her companion and noted disapprovingly in a booming voice that, "The child should be in bed by now."

Claire smiled over at her, and returned the supercilious nod by delivering in the sweetest of soft voices, "And many years ago, if you'd been, maybe you'd be in a better mood today."

The evening had ended on a satisfactory note.

CHAPTER SIX

The next day was one of those idyllic days that happen from time to time in the Californian winter. It was a glorious warm sunny day. The slight chill in the air was hardly noticeable. Charles arranged a helicopter and the four of them headed off to Carmel. They agreed they did not need guards if there were three of them who would be armed.

They hired a beach buggy to be mobile. Claire made them stop at a hardware shop. She bought a pair of scissors. She then made them stop at a general store and bought four T-shirts with "I love California" on them. Then, one after another, they stripped off their jeans and she made them even trendier by cutting them down to shorts. They changed their shirts for a T-shirt. In sneakers, cut off jeans and T-shirts, they blended into the mass of people around them.

They wandered along the beach, tested the water and played beach ball with Juliet. They had got an enormous one from a stall. It was almost as big as Juliet and the wind carried it across the beach and, at times, into the chilly water. By the time they got to lunch, they were all whooping around like children.

The ball bounced into the water and started to float out to sea. Claire ignored the cold, dived into the water and soon rescued it. Her T-shirt clung to her body. Her hair wet from the sea. They all stood laughing. Then Jacqui turned to Charles, caught him off balance and toppled him into the water. He grabbed her hand and pulled her down into the gentle surf. They had a mock fight, indifferent to the effect of the sea. Juliet squealed with pleasure and jumped onto them before herself toppling off into the surf. There Claire swept her up and both of them did a dance in the waves.

They quickly dried off in the sun and the breeze before the chill of the ocean fully penetrated their clothes. Somewhat dishevelled, they returned to the buggy and drove off to one of the restaurants. The girls had carried tote bags with them and they maybe should have kept better watch over them for they held all their guns. But nobody had tampered with them. Somehow it did not matter. Today was about having fun.

They ordered fish with salad. Their clothes were now dry again. Their hair was frizzy from the sea. Their faces were glowing from the morning out. After lunch they all piled into the buggy and drove along the coast. They then went for a walk along another and more secluded beach, strolling along the sand and into the water. Juliet tired and sat on Charles' shoulders. She got even more exhausted and he held her in his arms, where she fell asleep. They sat down and stared out to sea. It was all peaceful.

The tall cliffs of Big Sur watched over them in the distance, behind the gentle curves of the sandy beach that snaked out into the horizon. The blue sea, sparkling in the sun, was a gentle flow until its final impatient dash to shore in a surf-flecked rush of angry white water. The seabirds walked along the water line, seeking impatiently the myriad of bugs uncovered by the force of the final wave. Overhead, from time to time, small flocks of seagulls scoured the oceans for larger morsels. An occasional yacht troubled the horizon. In the distance, a few other people wondered across the sandy beach. But they were far away and their group seemed cocooned from the intrusive world around them.

They told Claire about their dream of an island. She told them hers about a farm. She said she wanted it in the hills. She would breed horses, not for profit but as a hobby. She made Jacqui start as she said, "And I'll live there with my dream man and some kids; that is if I ever find one." She noticed Jacqui's reaction. "You think I'm gay, don't you? You think Maria's gay. We're not you know but it's a good cover."

"What do you mean?" asked Charles.

"The guys all think we're gay. We're good friends. But we're warm blooded heterosexuals. It's just that, in our business, we don't want to be the target of all those ghastly men. Look, don't split on us. It saves a lot of problems. Otherwise it's wall to wall seduction scenes whenever we're on a job. This way, we can even share a room with a man and they leave us alone."

Charles was as astonished as Jacqui. He'd thought Maria was bisexual and Claire occasionally so. Given that he had slept with both, that was not a hard assumption. But he'd no idea they were straight.

Jacqui was also surprised, "I didn't mind you were gay. But it never struck me otherwise. Hey, Charles, I'll have to be careful not to leave you with Maria so much. Look, the poor guy is dumbstruck. He now will have an inferiority complex. Maria will never have even made a pass at him."

Charles didn't even look at Claire. This was no time for confessions.

"I'm staggered. I'd never assumed anything else. Mind you, I can understand. I think you're right too. When you drop out of this job, you'll find the men responding like bees to honey. That'll be for both of you. Just take away the no entry signs and, before you know it, you'll have a selection to choose from."

Claire laughed, "Let's hope you're right. But don't say a word to the outside world. Tell nobody either about Maria or me. It's been great playing with Juliet. That's perhaps why I just opened up I guess. I got a touch of the maternal urges."

Soon afterwards, they walked off down the beach again. Juliet was on Charles' shoulders and the three of them arm in arm. The helicopter whisked them back to the hotel. They had room service before putting an exhausted Juliet to bed. And they stayed up together with a bottle of local sparkling wine rather than their preferred French brands. It was their way of telling California that they'd had a great day.

Too soon it was time for business. Claire was to look after Juliet. Jacqui and Charles dressed for the regulators. Gone were the cut off jeans and T shirts, Jacqui and Charles were both in blue and trying to look like respectable bankers. Once again, though, the relief at ridding themselves of Di Maglio as a bank owner made the regulators easy to handle. They would do all they could to expedite the bid. The approvals would come quickly. They were overjoyed that Di Maglio would no longer be on board, ecstatic that his stake would move to a trust fund for Juliet and enthusiastic about the advanced plans for a senior banker to head up the proposed new US interests of IBE. The sooner the better was their unequivocal message.

Charles and Jacqui also visited the Californian head office of the bank. It was a typical sleepy local bank with a good retail operation. As Charles noted to Jacqui after they had left, it was going to be easy to fleece. First, it had lots of customers. Secondly, it had a good reputation. And, most importantly, the local management loved the idea of expansion, especially if they got good bonuses for selling new products. They would have pliable people selling fraudulent products to gullible customers with the encouragement of mediocre management. The ideal set up for a scam.

The business over, they returned to the hotel. Security was manifestly tighter and it was far from unobtrusive. Di Maglio had arrived. He greeted Giovanni, who had been with them on their visits to the regulators. His reception was warm. His reaction to Charles was much cooler. Jacqui greeted him, but all could see that there was renewed friction there. Her natural feelings of daughterly affection and even her in-built dislike of her father's chosen profession were overshadowed by the fact that she was angry he had put her daughter at risk.

Giovanni advised him of progress, "They love the idea that you're exiting the banking business. They love Charles and Jacqui. They see them as squeaky-clean. Perhaps they feel they're a bit prone to speculation, but they see all the grey hairs surrounding them and believe that they have adopted the laws of the controlled side of the banking jungle."

Di Maglio laughed, "And they don't know that he's worse than me. He'll make a super fortune in the banking world. But once its doors are closed to him, he'll look for a new field and a new challenge."

"Daddy, he's not going into your business," retorted Jacqui. "And that's final."

"Oh, so you do rule the roost. I see you decide for him. Is that modern equality?"

"Mr Di Maglio, we have business to do. We will do it and you will get richer by a few billion. Then I will no longer be in banking and our business partnership will end. Have no doubt about it, Jacqui wasn't talking for me. She was saying what we both think. If you want to be welcome to spend time with us, respect that decision. Otherwise you may be a bit lonely."

Di Maglio glared at Charles but said nothing. That surprised him, "You said tomorrow we have some business to do. I suggest we leave it till then. But tomorrow we need time to discuss Rastinov. His actions are becoming bloody outrageous."

At that point Claire came back with Juliet. It was strange, it happened every time with Di Maglio. His hard features softened. His steely eyes became benevolent. His aggressive stance relaxed. He was the adoring grandfather. Juliet jumped down and kissed him. He went over to the table and picked up a large package, cheerfully wrapped in Mickey Mouse paper.

There was a scream of pleasure as the paper was ripped off. The parcel was opened and the pleasure turned to horror on the little girl's face. The horror turned to fear as she burst into uncontrollable sobs and ran for protection to Jacqui. Charles looked at the parcel. He stopped in shock. Inside it was the head of Magya. He covered it up. Di Maglio looked shocked. He controlled himself well.

"Who the fuck's that?" he queried.

"Her name was Magya. She was one of the women who came here yesterday," replied Charles.

He muttered, "The parcel had a small doll's house in it. Someone switched it. But where could that happen? How? I'm always under guard."

"Where did you buy it?"

"Near here. I went into a small toyshop. I bought it here. It was in my suite all afternoon. Then I picked it up tonight."

"Someone switched it. They're good if they can get close to you. We'll have to tighten security and establish how we tackle them. This has to stop."

"I don't like my present. The face looked like that nasty lady the other day."

Juliet's comment surprised them. Charles hadn't realised that she would not recognise it as a real head. That was all the better.

"Grandpa's sorry," he told her. "He bought you a doll's house and asked the shop to wrap it. They must have mixed it up with someone else's present. He'll go back there and get the right one tomorrow. Don't worry. Give him a kiss for the thought. You'll get the right present tomorrow."

The explanation satisfied her. She gave him a kiss. The atmosphere returned to normal; at least normal for an evening with Di Maglio. They had dinner in a pretty formal way. They talked about a variety of things. Di Maglio's brother, Aldo, joined them, but Di Maglio overshadowed him. Giovanni was quiet and thoughtful. Claire was withdrawn. Jacqui fussed over Juliet. It was hardly convivial. They were all relieved when it was over.

Di Maglio broke up the evening, saying that he would go to bed. He was tired. They all said "goodnight" and headed to their rooms.

As Claire was about to leave, Charles said, "Claire, if Jacqui agrees, I would like you and her to return with Juliet tomorrow night. I'll head out to Washington on my own and then back to London via New York. I don't like the way things are going with the Russians. We meet the new nanny for the first time tomorrow. The other one is still not up to travel. I don't want Juliet to be alone with someone new."

Jacqui and Claire both agreed. After Claire had gone and Jacqui had put Juliet to bed in their room, they sat together. Charles turned to Jacqui, a worried look on his face.

"There's something strange about the whole episode today. I can't quite put my finger on it. I can't see how they managed to swap the parcel. Professionals surround your father. There's no way someone could get by them. And his reaction was muted. It could be part because of Juliet, but I don't think that's the reason. What do you think?"

"You mean that the whole thing could be a set-up. But why would he do that?"

"Everything has been so strange. The attack in New York was stupid. The bomb here was useless. The helicopter on the motorway was risky and a waste of space. And the women who broke in timed everything so badly that it was unbelievable. Now we've had Magya's head. It doesn't add up."

"We'd better keep an eye on my father. Perhaps we need to do a solo; better, though, to do that after we've bought his banks. I think we can trust Claire to work for us. I think she's about to quit the business. She implied that when we talked on the beach. Once you talk of that type of future, you are about to leave the violence of her type of work. I've seen it before."

"Jacqui, can we trust Maria?"

"Trust her totally. The money you've promised her will be the bonus she's been looking for. She'll move on then. There's no point in her going back to my dad. And her role with us will be over."

"Can we trust anyone else?"

"I guess it's just each other."

Charles nodded, "We'll keep an eye on what happens tomorrow. I want to be sure that we follow up on anything strange. But we should be careful all the same. We could be wrong about it all. We need to act as if we are in the gravest danger."

The next day, they all met in the presidential suite taken for Di Maglio. It was a bizarre gathering.

Di Maglio sat at the head of the table. He was only medium height. He was a broadly built man. His hair was still black and Charles doubted he used any colouring. For a man in his late fifties, that wasn't bad. He didn't so much look at everyone, he glowered. His aim was to intimidate. He did that at all meetings. Charles suspected he alone was indifferent to his mood.

Giovanni sat next to him. He looked worried. He was uneasy. The owl-like eyes blinked nervously. The cadaverous face on the thin neck was more pallid than usual. The claw-like hands were knotting and un-knotting themselves. The shirt appeared to have expanded or the neck shrunk, and in the wide gap in front of the starched collar his prominent

Adam's apple bobbed about erratically. They had never seen him like that.

On the other side sat Aldo. He was rarely around now as he was semi retired. He was a softer version of Di Maglio. Taller, he was quite dapper. His hair receded and hung in grey strands over his ears. He was licking his lips and chewing at a half smoked cigar at the same time. He darted glances at Jacqui from time to time. He had a guilty look about him.

Then there were Jacqui and Charles. They were dressed casually in contrast to the rest. They looked fresher and healthier than them. Charles realised how out of place they appeared in this gathering. He saw clearly how right Jacqui was. They needed to get out of this environment as soon as they could. He told himself, there and then, their business dealings with Di Maglio would finish by the end of the next year.

Di Maglio opened the meeting, "We have two issues to discuss. The first was planned. The second relates to the Rastinov affair. They are linked, though. First of all, Giovanni will run you through my business interests so that you understand what I plan to do next."

Giovanni stood up and switched on a projector. He spoke to slides. The first slide started rather pompously with the words, "The Di Maglio Global Empire."

Giovanni cleared his throat and started speaking to the slides, "The interests can be split into two. On the one hand we have the core businesses and, on the other, the commercial interests.

The core businesses can be split three ways. They are drugs, prostitution and protection. Drugs have two arms and they are kept separate. There is drug procurement and drug distribution. The distribution is wholesale and global. We have no street business, that's all freelance. Prostitution is a single business. We operate the infrastructure for the prostitutes, including security and premises. That ranges from rooms in our hotels to apartments to clubs. The prostitutes are all freelance and pay us a proportion of their earnings. Protection is only operated in the States. We operate mainly through security firms; most are fronts. The business is fairly classical. It's just most of the methods that are different from legitimate providers.

The commercial interests can be split two ways. They are the related and the other businesses.

The related businesses are casinos, hotels and pharmaceuticals. The gambling and hotels provide opportunities for prostitution, enable us to launder money and give us business contacts. The pharmaceuticals give a cover for some of the drug procurement businesses although they have legal sides. There is also a research and hospital division under pharmaceuticals that lets us give medical care to our people if they need it away from the eyes of the authorities.

The other businesses are mainly financial services and you are acquiring those almost in their entirety. They are helpful but the regulation is tough and we could use trusted third parties for our needs. You can now buy a crooked banker fairly cheaply in several jurisdictions."

He looked around for questions. There were none, so he continued, "The businesses are all profitable. The core businesses have a limited amount of assets. These are mainly property. We value the property at around half a billion dollars. But they produce around a billion and a half dollars a year after immediate expenses. Those exclude the bribes we pay.

The related businesses have more assets. These are around a billion and a half dollars. But we earn around half a billion from them and so I guess they're worth around three or four billion if I were a seller. The other businesses, the banks, have a value of around a couple of billion on our agreed valuation and produce around three hundred million dollars before tax each year. They were investments to legitimise our money. We needed to pay tax somewhere. But we knew that the IRS wouldn't be able to tell the difference between us living on a couple of hundred million or a couple of billion.

In all, we have assets of around four billion earning over two billion before tax. I guess we pay a hundred million of tax at the most. Outside your proposed deal, Charles, we have two billion of assets earning a couple of billion each year. Not bad, eh? Obviously that excludes the private accounts of Mr Di Maglio in different banks; that's family money and not business assets."

Di Maglio intervened, "Now let me tell you what I want to do. The businesses are all run from a core central team of three, namely me, Giovanni and Aldo.

Beneath that we have five trusted lieutenants – they run drugs, prostitution, protection, the commercial interests outside banking and then there is a logistics guy who handles transport, guns and the like. Those five form the executive council, which Giovanni chairs, and also represents the banks.

Then we have about a hundred foot soldiers, ranging from girls like Claire through to enforcers. I need a successor. We are too old to keep this game in check without one. We don't want to retire yet, except for Giovanni. So my plan was that Charles should replace him when he has left banking."

"No deal," Charles said without hesitation. Di Maglio glared at him with unconcealed loathing.

"OK, I understand. That's why I decided to put the core business, that's drugs, prostitution and protection, for sale. I talked to a few contacts and they would pay me good money for it. Not as much as it's worth but still good. One offer is for two billion and then half the profits for twenty years. I doubt I can trust anyone that long.

There is another for three billion and then half a billion a year through me continuing to own the related businesses, that's the casinos, hotels and pharmaceutical operations. The buyer would pay more than I do at the moment for the services offered. That's the most attractive. It's from a Greek syndicate.

That was the one I was planning to take. I would cut my staff to twenty or thirty to manage the new businesses. I'd pay off the others with bonuses, but they could work for the new owners if they wished. I would have a big chunk of cash, especially when you delivered. And I would still have a good earner and something to do with my time.

Then we hit a problem."

He paused and took a drink of water, before looking Jacqui straight in the eyes. His forehead was glistening with perspiration. His face was flushed. His look was quite malevolent. Charles felt Jacqui tremble. But her face betrayed nothing.

They both looked around the table. All the others were uneasy. Aldo just studied the floor. Giovanni was looking fixedly at Di Maglio. None of them made eye contact with them. It was as if they were trying not to.

Di Maglio continued, "We were advised that the Russian Mafia wanted to buy out the business. We have had a working relationship with them for some years. You know all about that. They offered us the value of the assets or two billion and nothing else for all the businesses. And they said that the price of rejection was trouble.

We ignored that. Everybody talks tough in this business. Nothing happened for a bit. Then about two weeks ago there was an incident."

He looked around at them. He waited. He was playing with them, intentionally keeping them on edge.

"One of my supply planes was hijacked. It had also some of my top guys on board. They were all coming back from Columbia. They were all killed. The plane was destroyed. The drugs disappeared."

He stopped again. Then he continued, "And the next day I got a message from Rastinov to say he was in town. He hoped I'd liked the welcome back show he'd launched. Then we had the incidents with you. That's the threat. By the way he wants the banks as well."

"That's no problem," Charles said. "We can scupper that. If we give his identity to the regulators, they'll refuse ownership transfer."

Di Maglio, amazingly, hadn't considered that. He looked surprised and angry. He turned to Giovanni, who confirmed the comment. Charles was now really surprised. Giovanni was smart and would have known that too. He should have told it to Di Maglio. The fact that he hadn't most likely meant he hadn't known about that part of the deal. Why hadn't Di Maglio told him? Had they had a disagreement? What was Di Maglio hiding? Or had he just thrown that in to get Charles on board somehow?

He then said, "The only way out of an outright war with the Russians is to keep all the businesses in the family. The problems would go away if we were not selling. Our weakness is down to changing ownership."

"Rubbish!" said Jacqui vehemently. "The change of ownership is an excuse. We'd have trouble, irrespective. Rastinov wants the business. Either you manage him and his people as you did before, or you have trouble. That's your choice."

"I agree with Jacqui," Charles chimed in quickly. "This is nothing to do with the deal we are running, or your plans. This is a family issue about how to handle Rastinov. I'd go through with the deal with the Greeks and then attack him. You still have the people for that and, just like the last time in the South of France, you can buy good mercenaries."

Di Maglio glared at them both, "So you won't help the family?"

Jacqui came back, "The family don't need us. You sell to the Greeks. You pick up the three billion and the annual income from the retained operations. You'll make a few billion from our plans even after you have given the bank to Juliet. You must have billions stashed away elsewhere. You can sort the Russians out. This is hardly the worst problem you have ever faced."

He looked even angrier. Charles realised that he had to find out why the others were so stressed out. He turned to Aldo. He was the weakest. "What would you do?"

He mumbled, "I agree we should try to keep all in the family. Then it's a local problem. Otherwise, it's more difficult."

Charles stood up, "Gentlemen, I have lots to do. I can't help out in gang warfare. My speciality is finance. Do tell us what happens."

With that he moved to the door. Jacqui followed saying, "You'll come down to our suite later to see us won't you?"

Di Maglio didn't answer, he just glared. As Charles got to the door, he asked Giovanni when he would leave for Washington. "We should tell the pilot so he logs the flight."

"Giovanni will fly with me to New York," snarled Di Maglio. "He'll join you in Washington tomorrow morning. You two can catch a scheduled flight."

"Oh, I'm heading back to London tonight with Juliet. Charles will be on his own," announced Jacqui. "He'll arrange protection. So you can have your men back when we leave. But I'd like Claire to accompany Juliet, the nanny and me."

Di Maglio shrugged his shoulders and looked at her almost as icily as he had looked at Charles.

Outside Charles commented, "I doubt I improved relationships with your father."

"I agree. But he needed a clear message and he got one."

"There was something strange about the meeting. It was a game. What was the truth?"

"I don't know. He is not usually that inept. Perhaps it was a bad day. But we'll have to keep tabs on events. And I think we should step up the search for the island, it's too unpleasant in the cities."

The rest of the day was spent in the office. Maria offered to fly out and give support if needed, but that was declined. "Your role is to monitor the office. I'll be back on Friday morning. And I want you to join Claire and sort out the security arrangements. She and Jacqui will be back first thing. Jacqui will be in the bank office before lunch."

He talked to the Honourable James. Most of what he said was inconsequential, but one comment caught his attention. "There's a buzz in the market about our deals in America. It appears that someone on your side of the pond has been talking. They say that there is Mafia involvement in some of the West Coast banks. I had a chappie I know at the Bank of England call me about that."

"I've seen the Californian operation. And the accountants are going in now. From what I saw, it looks clean. It's mainly retail customers. They have checking accounts, personal loans, credit cards and some savings products. There's hardly any big lending other than to other banks. It doesn't look anything like a Mafia front to me."

"Oh, that's good. When will the audit boys have finished?"

"We have them in all the banks at the moment. We are also talking of taking on a senior US banker as the Chief Executive for the Americas. I have asked for guidance from the regulators. And, of course, I need you to vet him thoroughly. I've said that I depend on you and your peers from the old bank in these respects. You have the contacts and the skill to judge well in these cases."

Charles could almost sense the old fool preen himself. He would go back to his chappie at the Bank of England and bluster about having his finger on the pulse or his eye on the ball. And that was what they needed. He would be the man who pushed for the appointment of the Chief Executive in the US. That meant also that he would be the big fall guy when the losses piled up and his choice of chief executive had to take the can.

Jacqui and Juliet were, by then, packed and ready to go. They were with the new nanny, Claudia. She was a pretty little thing, although not terribly bright. She looked very Italian, darker than Jacqui, and she was a bit plump, but she had the advantage of youth. Charles thought that, by forty, she would be pretty large and pretty jaded. But she looked fine for the moment and Juliet seemed to get on well with her. The other nanny was to fly back over the weekend. Jacqui had talked with her and agreed to her request to quit. She had even given her a little bonus, for which she seemed quite grateful. They suspected that she would be looking for a quiet country house where excitement was talk of a new road or the odd scary mutt. She definitely wasn't right for their lifestyle.

Charles accompanied them to the airport. His plane was due about half an hour later. They had agreed to head off together to simplify security. Claire was with them. They had no other security now. Di Maglio had withdrawn it. There were no guards on the door. There were no outriders for the car and there was no special driver. They were in a people mover from the hotel. There were five of them, Jacqui, Juliet and Charles, along with the nanny and Claire. Claire took the back seat and Charles took the front. They would be the lookouts. Jacqui would just make sure that Juliet didn't feel something strange was happening.

They headed out to the airport. As always the roads were busy but they appeared to make good time. They could not believe that they were going to have a quiet time of it. Half way to the airport it looked as if that was going to be the case. They still kept vigilant. Claire had pulled her coat over her gun and looked out over the nearby cars. Charles sat and watched the cars they overtook. He checked the road-side for waiting cars. He monitored the feeder roads for unusual manoeuvres. The driver must have thought them a bit strange. Charles, next to him, sat there for the whole time with his hand in his jacket pocket, looking from one side to the other without making any comment.

They tracked the cars with suspicious looking drivers, and there were even more of those, but they all were false alarms. Soon they were turning into the airport and heading for the departure gates. Charles wanted to see everyone through to international departures before getting over to the domestic flights. They walked to the first class check-in. There was one person in front of them. The buzz of the airport lulled them a bit and Charles started when he heard his name.

"Mr Rossi, we have a letter for you," said a polite voice. He turned and saw a man in a chauffeur's uniform with a manila envelope.

"Who is it from?"

"I don't know. I was just asked to deliver this by the company. I haven't checked for the sender." And, then, seeing Juliet looking at them inquisitively, he passed the envelope into her eager hands.

Charles turned and grabbed the letter from her. In that moment the man disappeared somewhere in the crowd. Standing there with the letter in his hand, Charles wondered if it could it be a bomb. Was it another hoax? He was not going to wait to find out. He grabbed hold of a security man and said, "Someone dropped this. When I tried to return it, he seemed to panic and run. It looks suspicious."

"Let me have it. Abe, talk to this gentleman," he called to another guard as he hurried through a door out of the terminal.

The man addressed as Abe approached Charles, "What can I do?"

"It's nothing. I found an envelope. I was suspicious about it. I gave it to your colleague. I'm seeing my family off to England."

He was indifferent and said, "OK. Have a good flight." He didn't seem to register the possibility of a bomb. Their faith in airport security dropped another notch.

By this time, all were checked in. They headed to the departure area, and said goodbye. Juliet covered Charles' face with kisses. Then Jacqui clung to him for a moment, whispered "be careful" and then clung tighter, her body pressing against his as she kissed him. Claire gave him a brief peck on the cheek and he sensed her body, too, although it never touched him. He pecked the nanny on the cheek, and it felt just like that. He watched them through the checkpoint, waved one last time and then turned to go.

The security man, to whom he'd handed the envelope, was there. "Are you Mr Charles Rossi?"

"Yes."

"This was what was in the envelope". He produced a piece of cardboard and on it was written, 'Enjoy your last sight of your family.'

Charles breathed a sigh of horror. "My wife is on the BA flight to London. I'm on the Washington flight. I don't know if this is a sick joke or not. You'll have to check out the flights."

The security man signalled to two men standing near by. They were big, football player types. "These Gentlemen are FBI. They'd like a word with you."

"You don't understand, you'll have to search the planes and luggage. You saw the letter."

He nodded, "It'll be done. But this way please."

He led him down a corridor marked "staff only" at the side of the terminal. The two FBI men were following. "We need your details and we need to interview you about possible suspects."

Suddenly, one of the FBI men came close to him. He was pushed forward and the next thing he knew he was falling through a hole in the ground. Then it all went black. He came to and saw the three men peering down at him. "Trip, sir, did you?" asked the security man. Charles knew now that he wasn't one. But that didn't help.

He didn't answer. One of the supposed FBI men moved forward and kicked him in the ribs. "We got a message for your father-in-law. And it's going to be your head in a box. We'll do just as we did with Magya."

Charles started to stand up. They let him. That surprised him. They had him cornered and there were three of them. But if they planned to kill him, he could see no purpose in delaying. He wondered, or perhaps hoped, that he had got it wrong. His gun was still in the leg holster. He had put it there on getting from the car. It was still there, he hadn't been searched. It was his only chance if they planned to kill him. If they didn't, their joke would have backfired. As he pulled himself up, he drew the gun and pulled the trigger. He heard the click. He heard another click. They had searched him. The gun was empty.

He looked in their faces and saw the sneers of glee at his shock. But they had not noticed the iron bar he saw propped against the wall to his left. As he flung the gun down in mock anger, they started to laugh openly.

And, as they did, he grabbed the bar in both hands and swung it round with all his strength at head height.

It smashed into the first man's head with a sickening crack and he tumbled down. As it progressed to the next one, it had the same effect.

The third leapt back and drew a gun, but he was not quick enough. Charles raised the bar upwards again and slammed it between his legs. He screamed in pain and fell to the floor. His gun clattered across the room.

Charles quickly picked up his own gun, unloaded as it was, as well as the man's and headed off. First, though, he wiped the bar clean. There was no point in leaving unnecessary clues.

As he closed the door, one of the men on the floor was coming round. The one he'd hit last was still rolling over the floor, groaning. The third was still out cold. Charles wondered if the blow had killed him. It was possible.

He grabbed a chair and pushed it against the door that opened outwards. That would delay them for a moment.

He was in a room and the only exit appeared to be a ladder up to the next level. At the bottom of the ladder was his case. He must have fallen down that gap and dropped the case on the way. He could have been dragged into the side room afterwards. He now realised he had been out longer than he had thought. They had after all had time to check him out and empty the gun. He also realised now that his head hurt badly.

He climbed awkwardly up the ladder, carrying the case. There was a trap door and he now lowered that. It had a sliding bolt that he slammed shut. That would prevent anyone from following too soon.

He dusted himself down and ran his fingers through his hair. He found the corridor again and moments later he was back in the terminal. He looked for the sign to American Airlines' domestic flights and headed there. The whole incident had only taken a quarter of an hour by his watch. He breathed a sigh of relief. He would make his plane.

He also knew the whole thing was a hoax; something else to scare him. Otherwise, they would have just killed him whilst he lay unconscious. You don't hang around on a job like that.

He checked in and then went to the toilets to clean up. He wasn't in too bad a shape. His head ached and he was a bit bruised. He dumped the spare gun in a toilet cistern, reloaded his own and then went through security to hand it over. He sat in the holding area and waited for the plane. He didn't bother going to the executive lounge, he sat and wondered who knew they would be at the airport. This incident had been planned. But who could have planned it?

He thought carefully. The hotel knew they were leaving as he had booked the car. Di Maglio and his people knew. The airlines knew. All three could have been the source of the information.

He then thought back to their arrival. Someone had tracked the incoming car. They must have followed it in. The airline didn't know what car they were getting. Di Maglio knew. The hotel must have known as they had a place reserved for it.

Then he thought about the incidents on the motorway. That gave him no new leads.

Then there was the gift to Juliet from Di Maglio. He knew about it. Someone else knew who it was for. Anyone, though, could have guessed. Di Maglio was hardly likely to give a doll's house to one of his thugs.

Then there was the attack at the hotel. That also gave no leads, anyone could have been watching them.

He thought back to the incident in New York. It involved a Di Maglio driver and so far he had escaped the normal penalties.

Could Di Maglio be organising all this? Even for Charles, who had no great love for him, such an option appeared to be unrealistic. Jacqui infuriated her father but he genuinely loved her. And he had real affection for Juliet. Charles shook his head. He'd need to track the next almost inevitable attempt. Sooner or later there would be a clue.

The plane was called and he headed to the gate. He wondered if his attackers had escaped or not. He wasn't terribly worried about them. He personally couldn't have cared if they starved to death. He was just relieved to have seen the family back to the safety of England. And he would soon join them after the last stop in Washington.

On the plane, his neighbour was a computer addict. He sat around and worked or played all his way to Washington. Charles read the papers and the magazines they throw at passengers. He avoided the food, which on most US domestic flights is limited to say the least. He realised he had dozed off a bit when he heard a voice in the background tell them they had fifteen minutes to landing. He put together his papers and looked at the inky night sky around the US capital.

The journey to the hotel was uneventful. That was just as well as he had only a small amount of ammunition for the gun. Jacqui and Juliet would only arrive back around five a.m. his time. He decided to crash out and catch them when they arrived. He wanted to know that they had arrived safely.

He left a message for Giovanni. He suggested they met for breakfast in the coffee shop. He wanted to quiz him on his suspicions about Di Maglio. The message, however, said that he merely wanted to discuss strategy.

He watched the evening news, finally switching it off in frustration. The news was about alleged presidential misdemeanours. Since Nixon, US Presidents had tended to be pilloried for misdemeanours. The only exception had been Ronald Reagan. One could only guess they felt that he'd been pilloried enough for his acting in his youth.

He was asleep soon afterwards. He had put the alarm on for five so that he could call home at ten UK time. They would all be in mid flight now. Juliet would be sleeping, he supposed the others would be too. With that thought in mind, he slept till the alarm woke him from his uneasy sleep.

CHAPTER SEVEN

The moment Charles awoke, he turned over and grabbed the phone. He dialled the house and on the second ring Jacqui answered. Juliet had also picked up the extension.

"Did all go well?"

"I had two ice creams on the plane. And the captain sounded nice," said a solemn voice.

"That sounds fun. My pilot wasn't anything like that."

Jacqui came on the line again, "Did everything go smoothly your end?"

"Perfectly. There was a slight incident at the airport. Nothing I couldn't handle. It was another attempt to scare us. But I think they got more than they bargained for and came off a bit worse for wear."

Jacqui was unable to probe deeper as Juliet was still on the other phone, but Charles could hear the anxiety in her voice, "Do be careful. Just get the work done and then head off for home."

"That's what I plan. I am expecting to have breakfast with Giovanni. Then I'll head to the Washington Federal Reserve. After that, I prepare for the return trip via New York. When will you go to the office?"

"I'll go in after lunch. I've asked to be brought up to date on all that's outstanding. Then I can put in a full day tomorrow. I suppose you'll head straight in from the airport."

"That's best. We can then have a quiet weekend. Has Maria moved in?"

"She already had by the time I got back. She and Claire have taken the two master guest suites on the top floor. They say they have all they need. Maria had checked out all the security arrangements and was happy about them. She and I will go in together tomorrow. Claire will watch over Juliet. All's fine here, I only wish that you had better security."

"I'll be with Giovanni all morning. And the way to the airport here is hardly good territory for troublemakers."

She agreed and they carried on talking for a few minutes. It was just before six. Charles called down for coffee and headed to the bathroom.

He had showered before the coffee arrived. He was still towelling his hair as he walked over to the door as the bell rang and a quiet voice said 'room service'.

After carefully checking who was there, he opened the door and the waiter walked in. He placed the tray on the table. Charles tipped him the mandatory five dollars and shut the door behind him. He wished he could get some more bullets, he hated going around with an almost useless gun. Perhaps he could arrange something with Giovanni.

He watched the television news. If anything it was more tedious than the day before. For a moment he relaxed, enjoying the coffee and thinking through the issues and tasks facing him when he got back to London.

The next months would be laborious preparation. They would finalise the take-over, put in place the financial deals and then endure the long wait for the right moment to pull down the whole pack of cards.

Charles was directly involved in the first part of the process, although his only direct role in the scam itself was to organise the fake lending and ensure neither he nor Jacqui signed anything incriminating.

He knew that both Sir Brian and Lord Dunkillin rarely read routine documents in their signature books. This was especially the case after long lunches in their clubs. On one such day, Maria would, in Charles' absence, seek authorisation for some tedious but acceptable loans, and then get them to sign some other fairly incriminating documents. Charles knew exactly what those documents would contain and how he would be able to embellish them.

Maria knew well how to distract the two. They liked to feel her lean close to them and she would do this if they asked for explanations. The poor buffoons would not be thinking of the papers in front of them. They would be dreaming of stripping off Maria. She would have, if required, but definitely not of her own volition. So they would be duped and frustrated at the same time. Charles felt no sympathy and no remorse.

He went down to the breakfast room. Giovanni had arrived and was already at a table in the corner. He was drinking some infusion that looked herbal.

He looked more ghostly than Charles could remember. His body was bent, as if with fatigue and worry. His hands shook slightly as he greeted him. His lips were bloodless, while his eyes appeared bloodshot. Was he ill? Charles said nothing, but wondered if he could get him to talk about Di Maglio. If he was ill, it might be possible to get information.

Once Charles had sat down and ordered some more coffee, this time with toast, he started to talk, "Giovanni, I have three things on my agenda. The first is this morning's meeting. The second relates to the new Chief Executive. And the final one is about the Rastinov issue. Do you have anything else?"

He shook his head and waited. Charles asked, "How do we play the meeting today?"

"We say that we hope to progress to agreement in principle on the take-over by the end of the month. That's ten days and should be ample. I need to draw up some documents and that should be easy to achieve in that time."

Giovanni continued, "We tell them we wish to finalise the deal promptly. We say we will do the due diligence quickly with a target for completion by the end of next month. The good thing about that is that the auditors will have to admit that they rushed the whole process. That is why they will have overlooked a series of missing records in the books of the two largest banks outside New York."

"Those will be the ones in Texas and California. Why outside of New York? And what missing records?" Charles queried.

"The auditors are hotter on the east coast. We're more likely to have an easy ride with their provincial branches. In reality, they won't have missed anything, because the true records are there. I will ensure, though, that they disappear after their inspection. That way there will be a gap in both banks' records.

There will also be a series of loans written between those dates. The loans will be to non-existent companies and the funds will have been transferred to them. The companies will all be located in tax havens and we will salt the money away from them. That will imply that there was systematic fraud before the take-over as well after it. Nobody will be able to trace things back to the date when you took on the business; it will all have started before then and, in all likelihood, the regulators will insist that the auditors pay for the error and compensate IBE. It will muddy waters and should make us an extra billion. I felt I should pay my way."

"Giovanni, you're a genius. I like the idea. Go ahead with it. My father will help to make the money disappear into the ether of the banking system. He's an expert at that."

Giovanni was pleased by this compliment. He went on, "In so far as the regulators are concerned, we will say that we would like approval to complete the deal by next month. That gives us plenty of time to fix the books, produce a good set of results and an even better forecast when we later announce the public offering. That's the real reason for the timing; you need time to maximise the returns we will make. But we'll tell the regulators we wish to complete promptly to ensure that there is not too big a vacuum. We can mutter about the risks of delay. That stuff usually works with the Fed."

He drew breath, "I have also sorted out the Chief Executive. He is with one of the big banks, Eastern General Holdings or something, and really hasn't got a job. You know the role. He's a token presence on their management as a result of their acquisition of that New Hampshire outfit. He'll come over for a big office, a secretary with big boobs and a big salary. I guess we'll have to pay him a few million. You can get him to sign all the compromising papers you want when he joins. It saves you later. The Honourable James will love him. He's an old New England family, fortunately the slightly dimmer side of the dumber end of a long line of in-breeding."

"Should we tell that to the regulators?"

"We can in confidence. At least we tell them his name. Not about his intelligence. I'd prefer to tell his name just to the Fed in New York. That's his local and in reality they are the leader of the pack."

"That's excellent. I suppose we should leave in about an hour to be at the Fed here in Washington at nine. That gives us time for the difficult one, Giovanni. This Rastinov affair is very strange."

"Charles. You and I have worked together for a few years now. We work well together and we like each other. More importantly, we respect each other. I am a businessman, not a traditional Mafia man. Di Maglio is a Mafia man through and through. He will always live in an unbelievable world. He will always do everything to get his own way. He will stop at nothing. You are wary of him and you are right to be so, but you are too arrogant. You believe you can outplay him. Beware. That arrogance may make you blind."

"You're talking in riddles, Giovanni. Say what you mean."

"Charles. You are not listening. Have you seen Rastinov? Then you would recognise him, wouldn't you? Is he subtle? Why is he playing this game? Is this his normal style? Or has Rastinov changed?"

"Giovanni, can you assure me that Di Maglio is not behind the scares?"

"He definitely would not be. He wouldn't do that, especially to Juliet. That's the only person he will stop being Mafia for. He'd do it if it was just you and Jacqui, but Juliet was with you on all but one of the attacks."

"So you believe Rastinov may not be alive. You think the approach is too subtle for him. You think that there may be someone masquerading as Rastinov. I assume his aim is to get the Di Maglio Empire. But if it is someone else, then we need still to get to him and destroy him."

"That's right. Either you or Di Maglio, or both, have to destroy Rastinov or whoever it is and buy your freedom. Now I have said enough. But be careful. The phoney war could end and it could all get bloody."

Charles tried to continue the discussion but to no avail, Giovanni was tight lipped. Charles then explained to him the events at the airport. He was not over surprised. He promised that ammunition for the gun would be in the car when they left the regulators. They agreed to bring down their luggage and head straight for the airport once the meeting ended. As they were travelling together again, they had use of the Di Maglio executive cars and jet.

"And I will take you back to Kennedy after the New York meetings to see that you have no problems on the road," said Giovanni. "I have to look after you. You control my pension fund!"

And with that half-joke about the promised pay off, he got up. In the car to the regulators, he said nothing more about the earlier discussion. They arrived at the Federal Reserve. Once through the usual bureaucratic checks, they were quickly ushered into their meeting. As usual, they were seen as manna from heaven. The known Mafia involvement in the banks had caused serious concern. They were too small to be a national problem, but big enough to make the conservative guardians of the nation's banking service extremely nervous and, consequently, blind to the new risks they could face with the new owners.

They agreed that matters should be progressed quickly and that too many things could go wrong if there were a lengthy vacuum. Official approvals should not be hard. They would talk to their counterparts in other states to ensure that they moved smartly. Charles, now he was part of IBE, had not yet been tarnished. Anything had to be better than being owned by Di Maglio. Little did they realise that they would regret that naive approach. The IBE reputation would be in tatters within the year, and the authorities would discover that, in matters financial, there were many worse things than a Mafia connection.

The journey to the airport and into New York was uneventful. In the US the only comfortable way to fly is by private jet. The journey into New York itself was fast. The car whisked them through the grim indifference of outlying New York into the towering gullies of Manhattan and they headed south to Wall Street itself.

They stopped in Giovanni's office just off Broadway. It was near the soul-less headquarters of several of the US's most prestigious banks. Some were modern blocks of glass, with the odd ray of sunlight allowing them to catch a reflection of the ill planned styles of the neighbouring buildings, others were greyish mounds of ageing stone.

Wall Street itself is depressing. It is no wonder that many of the investment banks have moved to mid-town Manhattan. The downtown area is not conducive to original thought; the area is a mess of the old, the new and the ugly separated by fume filled arteries, the side streets overwhelmed by tired people, belching delivery vans and slow moving cars.

They had a pleasant meeting with the New York authorities. They must have had a good report on them from London for they had talked to the people there. The Honourable James had obviously blown his role and importance out of all proportion. The idea of a distinguished banker heading up the US businesses from New York enthralled. When they heard the name of the man in the frame, they smiled contentedly. Charles suspected they had a vision of gargantuan monthly lunches flashing in front of their eyes as they recognised the epicurean perfection of the provisional choice.

They ran them through the plans and agreed the consents that were needed. The authorities would work with them and their advisers to help in any way they could. It was staggering how gullible they were. The dream merger was perfect. Ownership by men of integrity and conservatism was better than those linked to corruption and crime. In reality, the poor fools again hadn't realised that corruption, fraud and embezzlement were replacing crime.

And Charles felt rather proud to be, alongside Jacqui, the main architect of that plan. Their wealth originated from his father's ingenuity. This, though, was their game. Jack Ryder had an important role in the whole matter, just as Jacqui and Charles had had in his original scheme. But it was a reversal of roles. This time, they called the shots.

Once they left the New York regulators, it was approaching four p.m. That left them three and a half hours till Charles' plane. They drove to mid-town and stopped off at the Pierre to allow Charles time for a snack so he could skip the food on the plane and try to snatch some sleep. He really needed to be in the office for all Friday, or he would have to go in for another weekend. And he had agreed with Jacqui that they would head into the country. They had a small cottage, buried in the heart of rural Sussex, between London and the sea. And they'd decided to try to have as many weekends as possible off before the game really started. Then, they would have little time for pleasure.

Giovanni again was silent on the whole issue of Di Maglio and Rastinov. Charles pumped him a few times but to no avail. In the end they just went through their different plans one after the other, fine tuning them here or there.

The auditors had finally drawn up an action plan. There were teams in each of the banks. They had top lawyers in London and New York working on the take-over itself.

They had employed a public relations firm with offices in all the major centres to produce good news about them. It was pushing their prowess as fund managers especially. And Jack Ryder was already buying into the investment funds of the US banks, to make it look as if the public were already responding to the take-over news and looking forward to even stronger performance from them.

The loans to the phoney companies were being set up. Giovanni was also organising, through long established and carefully placed officials in the main banking offices, the future disappearance of records and the generation of the non-existent loans. And Jack Ryder and Stephens were putting together the complex deals that would lose the unsuspecting banks further billions. Jack was also organising the companies and instruments for investment and building up stakes to sell on at a profit to the investment funds.

Charles was busy arranging a top-secret team to prepare the combined bank for its public flotation, where investors would buy the bulk of the shares from them just before the crash. And the dirty tricks department was already at work, ensuring that their so-called clean directors in London signed as many compromising papers as possible. They would all come in useful in good time.

They had also stolen some more papers from Associated with its chairman Sir Piers' signature on some of them. They had the dirt on him already from a previous incident, but you never knew whether you needed more. And Charles had an urge to engineer a link between Associated and the death of their Head of Security. He could not think of one immediately, and needed something that was foolproof. If he found anything more, then he could increase the pressure on Associated to ensure they did what he wanted. If they acquired IBE after its problems, that would make life easier for him and Jacqui. It could even pave their path back to the golden world of high finance.

A takeover would solve the problems caused by the bad debts and fraudulent trading. It would not sort out the investment fund scam and the resultant losses incurred by many of PAF's clients. If they had enough dirt on Associated and Sir Piers, perhaps they could do something there.

As for the shareholders, they would get something back from the takeover but they mattered less. They had less clout. Bad investment in shares, rather than through regulated investment funds, was a risk that would not get the sympathy vote if it went badly wrong.

Charles had a couple of other ideas on improving the profits from the scams but he did not feel like sharing them with Giovanni. Despite his warnings, they involved double crossing Di Maglio. And that was dangerous. Charles knew that Di Maglio would have him killed if he had the slightest inkling of his plans.

They checked and double checked their action plan. It all seemed to fit in well. The next month or two would be dedicated to the merger. Following that, they would put their plans into full swing, culminating with the sale of the bank to the public and its subsequent demise.

Charles felt good, "Within twelve months, we could have pulled it off and the follow through will be incredible. We could even cause a crash in markets. My father would enjoy that. Mind you, with our new wealth, I suspect that we'll be able to manipulate a few more in the future."

Giovanni shook his head. "Don't be too impetuous. Wait for the right opportunity and then strike. Learn to live the quiet periods as well as the exciting ones. Eliminate the risk of things going wrong. Otherwise, you'll lose as quickly as you win." He saw Charles smile. "Do take heed, Charles. That is sound advice."

Charles gently slapped him on the back. "Giovanni, I agree with you. I'm not laughing at you. Once this is all over, I'm going to retire for a year or so. And I'll keep myself occupied. But as a long term investor and not a financial terrorist, as that cretin Sir Piers once called me."

Giovanni looked at his watch. "It's time to take you to the airport. We want to see you through to the lounge. There you should be safe."

And he was right. Charles felt safe for the first time for a long time as he sat down in the lounge with half an hour to boarding. He disobeyed all advice and had a glass of claret. That was his alternative to a sleeping pill. As they raised the temperature in the cabin, the combination of the heat and the wine always made him sleepy. And he could think of no better way to spend a flight than asleep.

The air hostess asking if he would like some breakfast woke him up. She was a pleasant looking girl and she smiled genuinely as she remarked, "You slept like a baby. You must have been a good boy in New York. You had a clear conscience."

That sounded like an invitation to him. In any event he ignored it. He was no great supporter of unfettered promiscuity. Soon though were swooping down on Heathrow. It looked an uninviting place, as indeed any airport on a wet and windy morning tends to look. Charles had shaved and changed back into a suit. He'd shower at the office.

He moved along the interminable walkways and passport control. Then he went through customs and into the waiting area. He saw the bank driver at once, he was a security guard from the office. He recognised him immediately, alerted to the upgrade in security. Maria had done well. She'd been through everything. London felt much safer than California or New York, but that didn't mean that he should relax.

He had a shower in the private bathroom next to his office. With eyes shut, he felt the warm water refresh him as it splashed over him. It was the cold draught that alerted him to the fact that someone had come into the bathroom. Opening his eyes and blinking away the water, he peered through the steam. It was Maria.

"Maria, you are silly coming in here. Anyone could see you."

"No they couldn't. I went into your office and shut the door behind me. That's normal for a personal assistant. Anyway, I had no thought of stripping off and joining you. At least," she added with a mischievous grin, "not until you put the idea in my mind and showed you were in favour of it."

"Impossible girl," he shook his head at her suggestion. "I'll join you in the office. Now bugger off."

"Actually, I wanted to brief you on the problems we had here the other weekend. I prefer to do it here with the water running. That will prevent any bugs or listening devices picking up what we say.

"Dunkillin told the police about his affair. They accept he had nothing to do with the murder. In fact, they have a good description of two black youths who were seen running down the road in some panic at around half past midnight. The pathologist put the time of death at between twelve and three in the morning. As we know, we killed her at ten, it just proves you can't trust the experts. So far nothing has been found. The police are publicly continuing with their investigation, but I suspect they are pulling resources from it. They just keep hitting dead ends."

"Excellent. What about the security man?"

"The information we put out about drugs and things started to take hold and they made a connection between our late lamented head of security at Associated and the two detectives. Our friend was not too good at secret recruitment. He was recorded on their phone asking for the meeting at Waterloo. The idiot hadn't realised their office would record all calls and called them on its landline.

"The police believe the detectives killed him, although they haven't found the weapon and are struggling to establish a reason. That's not surprising as I disposed of the knife myself and the detectives had no cause to kill him. They regard it as murder but it's not a high priority for them. They think it has to be drugs related and they believe a pusher less is a good thing. The only thing they can't understand is why he had so much cash on him. Normally, if you kill someone, you would take their money. But they'll have to fathom a reason for that."

Charles interrupted, "I would suspect that Associated is also working hard to quieten things down. It can hardly do any good for their snowy white reputation. The thought of it," he added maliciously, "the old school tie linked with the criminal classes."

She thought that ironic, too, "Yes and especially as it appears our two detectives were hardly whiter than white. One had served time for assault. And the drugs they found on them didn't help. So the police are reacting similarly on their deaths. They are just open about them and say that it appears the two were caught up in drugs related gang warfare."

Charles felt sorry for their families and mentioned it. "Well, we can't start being contrite. It's dog eats dog. If we don't destroy them, they'll destroy us. We didn't ask them to butt in. It was their bloody fault." Maria's response may have been brutal, but they knew it was accurate.

"And," she continued, "they have only charged the boys who were caught joyriding in the stolen car with the theft of the vehicle. So they'll get away with a light sentence. And there appear to be no leads from the cars at all."

Charles switched off the shower and dried himself. "Now, before you tell me you've changed your mind about stripping off, go out and organise a decent continental breakfast for me. Then I need to go through all the routine stuff on my desk. And I want to run through some of the plans with Stephens and my father."

"And this afternoon," added Maria, "you and the Honourable James have a meeting with the Bank of England. And you have meetings with the two legal teams. The first is on the take-over and the second on the flotation. So you're going to be busy. I've arranged for you and Jacqui to have a salad in your office together. You will want to catch up on things."

He was soon at his desk and sorting papers. The great thing about being a chief executive is that you have lots of people to whom you can delegate all the routine tasks and anything else that you find tedious. Through his year or so at the bank, he hadn't found it difficult to move the paperwork. Ironically, he was seen as a good decision maker as a result. People love doing tasks for the chief executives. And they actually had some quite competent people in the middle ranks, as well as a cartload of absolute cretins at the top.

Jacqui walked into the office just before nine. She knew how to revitalise him. That day she wore a blue suit. Its cuffs and round collar were ribbed with gold braid. A diamond on a white gold chain was the only other adornment. Her hair was pulled away from her face. Her skirt stopped several inches above the knee and revealed her flawless legs clad in the sheerest of pale beige tights. Her heels were medium height and added a couple of inches to her five eight. As he got up, her perfume greeted him just before her lips. The mixture of the clean scent of her shampoo and the gentler jasmine odour of her perfume wafted over him seductively. He then felt the softness of her lips and, as his arms went around her, the gentle invitation of her whole body.

"I missed you," she whispered gently. "It's better that we're together when there's danger. It seems worse when we are apart."

He smiled at the comment. "From the last week or so, you could say it's pretty tricky when we are together as well."

"Let's get back to work, though. I'll see you for lunch. We can work out what we're doing over the weekend. I've been told of a great new pub that has got a lovely chef. That will suit your love of stodgy British food and roast." With that she swept out of the office and across to hers.

At eleven, Charles did the chief executive's statutory walk around the office. It helps to have been seen before making a big acquisition. He started at the ground floor, greeting the doormen and the branch staff. One floor up, they had the back offices. There they still moved masses of faxes even if the industry claimed to have become fully automated. A mass of telexes and other messages had to be fed into the computers to allow the deals to progress. The City was, in reality, a technology backwater, especially in the operations areas. He stopped and asked some of the staff about their work. He was one of the few directors who ever came down there, and that guaranteed him a sympathetic audience.

He worked his way up the building. Leaving the nether regions of the operational departments, he walked through the legal and audit departments. They were able to do all the day to day tasks. He would not use them for the take-over. They were stolid and honest, he doubted they would understand the way Americans worked. He preferred more malleable hired help for that task, partly because he paid them well for a purpose. And that purpose was to tell him what he wanted to hear, how to complete the take-over in the quickest possible time.

On the penultimate floor was the corporate finance department. His pass didn't work there. It was always infuriating how those arrogant sods hid behind the regulations to bar all and sundry from their hallowed overpaid halls; even their chief executive. The top floor housed the treasury department and here he felt more at home. This was where they traded in all financial products, including foreign exchange and derivatives.

The dealers were in full form with their coarse humour. "Why do Essex girls wear knickers?" called one. "To keep their ankles warm," came back a predictable shout. Charles laughed and cynically waved at them before heading to the glass box where Stephens lived.

He was on the phone but quickly ended the conversation. "How are your plans coming on?" asked Charles.

"There are a whole series of deals that we have put together with the companies you formed. They look as if we have taken in around twenty million of fees and are running positions that appear to be hugely profitable for us. In reality, we have even lent the companies the twenty million to pay us our fees and are running a genuine loss of some hundred million. We'll run up as many positions as we can over time, up to the maximum. Then, after the take-over, we can run some more through the American banks. Nobody understands these things. They are hugely complex and involve quite a lot of judgement in valuing them. The accounts people usually come to me for help with them and, even if they don't, the dealers will refer to me."

"What happens if you are away? I don't want these things discovered by chance."

"No problem. I have a computer model that prices the things. That's the only way to do it. They really are complicated. I am working on fixing

117

the model. It'll have a few files that it will ignore on my password but read on everybody else's. The files will over-ride their input and price how I want the price to go. Nobody can check the programmes as I have encrypted them and then ring fenced them with a security code. That way, even if someone had a question, they would have to come to me."

"Isn't it unusual to protect the files in that way?"

"Well yes. But I can always claim that I am doing it so that nobody accidentally corrupts a file. The auditors would find it a reasonable approach. They won't look at the programmes; they couldn't understand them unless they had a degree in quantum maths. And, if they had, the buggers wouldn't be auditors."

"I guess you're right. I won't ask what you have done to hide the real value. I'll just trust you." Stephens smirked. Charles looked coldly at him, "But only if you deliver the goods. There are two things you have to remember. First, you'll be seriously rich and totally free when this is all over. Second, if you stray one inch from my instructions, you'll regret it for what little would remain of your life."

The smirk had left his face. He was scared. Charles grinned, but it was not a warm grin, and said, "And there could always be another little bonus. We pay well for loyalty. Remember that as well."

Charles clapped his arm round his shoulder, if only as a matter of show for the watching dealers. He then walked away, sensing the frightened and resentful eyes on him. Stephens had given him an idea. He would go on a trip sooner rather than later. The phoney computer files would be put in use and they would not need him again. But, in the meantime, he needed him to peddle a few more crooked trades.

He walked back to the directors' offices and popped in to see the Honourable James. He said that the meeting with the Bank would be routine. He was planning to fly out to New York to see the candidate for Chief Executive over there.

"I've had some good reports on him," he said. "They say he's from one of the oldest East Coast families. That's old banking blood. He's had a distinguished career. Seems the sort of chap we should have on board. I'm seeing him and his wife for dinner. I find that's the best place for these sorts of chats. His wife is from Chile. She's from an old Spanish family. They go back a long way and are real nobility. Her great grandfather was the younger son and went to Latin America to look after the plantations they owned."

"Fantastic. That ties in with the impression I got from the regulators. They were all keen on him," Charles said aloud. 'What an idiot,' he thought to himself. 'He's looking to take on a top man in a major bank. He is really only interested in his blue blood and the fact that his wife is the right class. He believes the interview should be a chat at dinner. That will look good in any investigation.'

As he left, he smiled to himself. The irony hit him. Once again, poor Charles Rossi was going to be let down by his Chairman.

Back in the office, he touched base with his father. All was well and he was continuing in his careful identification of companies whose share price he could manipulate. This was his forte. He had no qualms about him. He talked to his mother as well. She was helping his father but, as usual, was keeping in the background. She would keep the books and also do some of the research on the companies they were acquiring.

They found companies with unmarketable shares and gradually built up stakes. Then when the time came, they really ramped up the share price before they got out at a massive profit. It was a tried and tested formula.

And some of the companies were the same ones as Stephens was trading with. Others were the ones that they would lend money to. All the funds would be siphoned off and the siphon, of course, always led back to them.

Jacqui came in around lunchtime and soon afterwards they were brought their salads. He told her about the incident at the airport and also about the discussion with Giovanni. She found it hard to make it out.

"It sounds as if Rastinov could really be dead and that someone is masquerading as him. I suspect that means there has been a revolt in the Russian Mafia. They were getting quite tame. We need to be careful. I wouldn't put it past my father to profit from the fact and he seems to be doing that by pretending that we can solve the problem by withdrawing the business from the market and running it. I doubt he invented the story about Rastinov, but I do think he's trying to use it to get his way. He could have been behind the attack on you. I'm less sure about his involvement in the others. Giovanni is right; both of us could be acceptable targets to him, but not Juliet."

Charles changed the subject. "Any luck on the island?"

"I have passed the word around. It's not that easy. There's a possible one near Mauritius. It would be our island and we would need to build on it. But I prefer something a bit more inhabited. I had thought of Mustique, but am not convinced. There are a couple of possibilities around St Lucia. Once we have a shortlist, we should go and check them out."

"That sounds fun. Do we leave for Sussex tonight?"

"Yes. But you need to leave here by six. Claire will leave this afternoon and take the car and luggage down with the nanny and Juliet. We've got to use the estate. There'll be a lot of us, you and me, Juliet, the nanny and Claire. Maria will come down and join us for lunch on Sunday. I've booked the pub I mentioned. The weather should hold but it'll be fairly chilly."

The cottage was a genuine one with thatched roof and all. It had a good-sized garden and a small gatehouse down the lane. The couple who had taken it acted as gardener and housekeeper. Jacqui would have told them of their arrival and the house would be aired and warm with the fridge well stocked.

They only had three bedrooms in the cottage. There were two largish ones and a small one. Then, downstairs, there was a lounge and a dining room. It was completed by a kitchen downstairs and a couple of bathrooms upstairs. It was simple but just perfect for them. The village people didn't know who they were. They thought they were City people. They thought they were well off. But otherwise they were quiet and kept to themselves. The couple who looked after the place must have given good reports on them. They got their house rent-free and were hardly demanded much in return, so the gratitude was merited.

They would go down by helicopter, picking it up from Battersea on the way from the office. That meant they should be in Sussex by seven at the latest. Charles looked forward to a quiet evening in front of the large open fire. It was their refuge. It was the only haven they had.

The afternoon meetings went well. The US regulators had obviously talked to their London counterparts. The different sets of lawyers were progressing well. Charles agreed with them what they would deliver over the next two weeks. By half past five, he had emptied his in tray, made his phone calls and wrapped up all his meetings.

Maria was still working as he left. "See you Sunday. Be a good girl."

"Dunkillin made a pass at me. Otherwise nobody's shown interest," she said in reply. "So it looks like a TV supper or a trembler for a dirty old man."

"What a choice," said Jacqui who had followed him, "I'd take the supper."

With that, they went to the garage where the driver waited. The roads from the City were not yet too overcrowded. They drove south of the Thames and into Battersea. There, the helicopter waited and by six fifteen they were soaring above the weekend rush and heading the forty miles to their retreat.

CHAPTER EIGHT

The helicopter swooped over the Sussex hills. They were dark and gloomy against a starless sky. The low, thick clouds had their dreary night hue and threw ominous shadows across the ground below. In the distance there was an expanse of sea. From there it looked calm with the occasional white horse on the horizon. But the wind that buffeted the helicopter told them that was an illusion. Close by, the sea would be turbulent and the cold water far from smooth.

As the helicopter landed in the field next to the house, the trees and bushes bent in its wake. The wind itself was strong enough to bend the trees the other way on the far end of the field. It would be a chilly walk to the cottage. And, for the first time, they noticed it was raining. It was gentle now but it could soon start pelting down. The clouds were menacing enough.

His mind flashed back to a time in the South of France. He remembered the cliff, the car with its two bodies and the flashes of lightening. He recalled the cruelty of nature that night as they had disposed of the two killers who had lain in wait for them. Their bodies had never been found. To the best of their knowledge, nor had the car. He shuddered as he looked at the trees again. Jacqui saw his look and gazed at the sky. She shuddered too. "It's like at the cliff near Ramatuelle," she said, reading his mind. He nodded.

"Let's run to the cottage. We need to be inside."

Charles jumped down from the helicopter and put his hands up. Jacqui allowed him to swing her down, briefly brushing her lips against his as she came level. They waved to the pilot and ran to the gate that led to the cottage. They winced as the rotors sent a blast of rain and a rush of wind at them as the pilot took off again for London. Then they ducked and hurried up the path.

They had hardly knocked when Claire opened the door and let them in. "It looks foul out there. The fire's going in the lounge. And you might just catch Juliet before she falls asleep."

They walked in and she was right. Juliet saw Jacqui and climbed on her lap. Minutes later she was slumbering, her head resting against Jacqui's chest. Charles looked at the two. Jacqui, her hair blown by the wind and her cheeks still pink from the cold outside, sat in the chair. The reflection from the fire illuminated her in its gentle glow. And, gradually, she seemed to breathe in unison with Juliet, whose colouring made her seem a miniature version of her mother.

She held Juliet gently and her looks, her body, everything about her softened. She lowered her head and gently kissed the child's hair. The child appeared to sense this through her sleep and cuddled closer to her mother. Charles wished he could capture that moment in more than his memories.

In the event, the spell was broken by the nanny's arrival. She failed to notice the peacefulness of that moment as she walked up to Jacqui and asked if she should take Juliet. Jacqui placed her fingers on her lips and shook her head. She wanted that feeling of closeness to last. The nanny suddenly realised that and left them in peace. Charles sat in his chair enjoying the moment and yet wishing his child were asleep on his knee.

They carried her upstairs and Jacqui changed her. She tucked her up in her cot. Her favourite toy, a panda, was placed near her. She looked angelic as she lay there asleep. Her dark hair and pale olive complexion nestled against the pure white pillow. The pink blanket reflected the rosy hue in her cheeks. Jacqui drew the curtains shut. If Juliet woke, the movement of the branches on the trees outside would frighten her otherwise.

Quickly changing into casual clothes, they went downstairs. Claire was curled up in one of the chairs reading a book. The nanny was in the kitchen and they asked if she wanted to sit with them. But she, too, was tired and indicated that she would go to bed. She would sleep on a camp bed in the same room as Juliet. That gave Claire the use of the other bedroom.

They were now alone with Claire. Jacqui sat on the sofa and cuddled up to Charles. They could hear the wind blowing more strongly outside and the windows resounded with the beating of the rain. "It'll be muddy tomorrow. Juliet will insist on going out and seeing the collie puppies on the farm. And she will also want to have a ride on the Shetland pony there."

"We've our boots and jackets and stuff. It'll do us good to get some fresh air and healthy rain and all. I hope Claire hasn't only brought those heels with her."

Claire was wearing a pair of quite alarming, spiky heels that evening, along with a pair of leggings and a fluffy violet sweater.

"Oh don't worry about me," she said. I'm going to commune with nature. I'll go out in my birthday suit if need be. Or if you are too conservative, I'll wear an anorak and green boots like you."

"My boots are blue. Juliet's are pink and Jacqui's are yellow. We're the psychedelic boot brigade! What colour's your jacket?"

"It's blue and I doubt it's too waterproof, but it's very fashionable."

"Claire," called out Jacqui. "It's like an anorak. How can it be fashionable? They are the very antithesis of anything fashionable. The only thing you can do is wear something tight and clinging underneath one. Then when you get to the pub and take it off, you look fashionable."

"And if the tight and clinging thing is really tight and clinging," came the response, "then the locals will get all excited. But it might be too cold not to wear something large and bulky under the thing."

"Wear two surplus layers," suggested Charles. "The top one should keep you dry. The second should keep you warm. And the third can keep all around you warm. That way you have all you need and you fulfil a social duty as well."

"Sexist pig," commented Claire, nevertheless with a smile of appreciation at the implied compliment.

Jacqui yawned. "If you're not careful, we'll make you sleep out in the yard to cool off."

"It's called a garden in this country."

"Oh, I know all about that in dozens of languages. In French I shouldn't say "I'm full" because it means I am pregnant. And there are hundreds of other expressions to avoid. But as long as you understand, it's no great shakes."

"I understand but I'm hungry. How about having a ploughman's?"

"What's a ploughman's?" asked Claire in surprise.

"It's a cheese plate. They call it that here."

"I got quite a shock," she said. "It sounded as if you'd become cannibals."

So they had their ploughman's and they each had a beer. Jacqui rarely drank that other than in the country. She said she could eat the wrong things there because they did so much exercise. In London she tended to favour healthy food.

Soon after that they headed off to bed. They knew that Juliet was likely to be up early the next day. Neither of them minded, they liked the anonymity and peacefulness of their refuge in the hills. This was the closest they had got to a mountain retreat. It was the nearest thing to their dream island. This idyllic cottage, nestling in the hills of the South Downs, was their refuge. It had no phone, no television. They had radios and, to be fair, they had mobiles. But, for the moment, they were all off duty.

The room was warm from the fire downstairs that heated the place well. Charles brushed his teeth alongside Jacqui. She was wearing a long white negligee. He pulled it down over her shoulders and kissed her gently on the back of her neck. He ran his tongue down her spine.

"Where did you learn that? It's quite erotic," she whispered. "But we'll have to be careful or everybody will hear us."

They moved towards the bed and held each other tight. He felt her warmth through the thin fabric. The belt of his dressing gown opened. Jacqui moved forward and kissed his chest. It was a long lingering kiss and the moistness of her lips glided over him.

His hands went round her face and lifted it up, gently tilting it back. He kissed her lips, then her eyes. He kissed her on the neck and the throat. He eased the nightdress down her shoulders. He kissed her again.

They moved to the bed and pulled away the sheet. The cool air suddenly hit them for the first time and they huddled under the covers. They clung against each other for warmth. They then moved closer for comfort. And finally they moved together for passion. It was a long, warm, wild and wonderful wave of love, which swept through him and into her. He revelled in the arching of her body, the crushing of her lips, the tight embrace of her thighs.

The outside world did not exist. The room wasn't there. For that one long glorious moment of sheer pleasure, they were alone. And as they sunk back into reality, they sensed the world around them come back to them again. They lay together, enjoying the aftershock of love. They allowed in again the noise of the wind and the rain, but it was distant and unimportant. They let the quietness of the rest of the house impose itself on them. They moved apart only to return to each other's arms and fall asleep together as only lovers can.

The rain beat against the windows in a fury, lashed by the wind. Somewhere, a window rattled in protest at the pounding that it received. The occasional cow raised its voice in protest at the elements. A fox called to its mate in an early search for food. The birds, which woke them so early on a normal summer's day, appeared to have long deserted the place in disgust at the unseasonable weather. They may well, if they had any sense, have headed for warmer shores. A dog barked in the distance, perhaps in apology to its master or mistress for taking them out at such an inclement time.

Then there was a patter of feet. Juliet climbed onto their bed and snuggled between them. She looked seriously at Jacqui and said, "You've got nothing on." Jacqui pretended she must have forgotten to put her nightdress on. "You often do that. Daddy does, too." They chattered away for a moment with her before Charles grabbed the bathroom. Washed, changed and shaved, he picked her up and took her downstairs.

They made breakfast and she chattered happily. Her hair was wild. Her cheeks were rosy. She was happy. Jacqui came down in jeans and a sweater. She looked fresh and relaxed. The country always had that effect on them.

Soon after, Claire appeared. "Your new nanny snores," she said to Juliet. "Either that or something's escaped from the farm. It sounds like a trombone. She's got strong lungs."

"Mummy and Daddy forgot to put anything on last night. When I came to see them they weren't wearing anything."

Jacqui blushed and then blushed even more when Claire said, "No clothes on. I hope they cuddled up to each other or they would have felt cold."

"They were cuddled up," replied the little girl. "But they often do that. Once, when I woke up at night and went to see them, Daddy was playing pretend fight with Mummy. And they didn't have anything on then. I told them off." This was said very seriously.

"Why did you tell them off?" inquired Claire inquisitively.

"Because Mummy's nice white nightie was on the floor. You know the one with the pretty coat that goes with it. And Daddy stepped on it when he got out of bed."

"Come on Juliet," said Jacqui. "I'm sure Auntie Claire wants her breakfast. Why don't we give you a bath and then get you dressed. Charles, why don't you make a coffee for Claire? And add salt instead of sugar if she doesn't stop grinning."

At that, Claire started giggling. "I'll get the coffee. Are we still going for a walk? It looks foul outside."

"Yes," called Juliet. "We're going to see the puppies and I want a ride on the pony."

"We can see the puppies but it may be too wet for the pony. We'll see when we get there."

Jacqui led Juliet upstairs and Charles settled down for another coffee.

"Children can be embarrassing. They blurt out the most amazing things."

"Charles. I was in the boat with you not that long ago. I know you and Jacqui aren't exactly celibate. That is unless you've become a different couple from the days in Barbados."

"They were good days. We'll get back to that sort of life again some day. It suits us."

"It suited us all. It's strange to think that in the next year or so, we could all retire."

"Don't forget. We need to make sure that we succeed and survive. I am still uneasy about the Rastinov affair. We need you and Maria to help us if there's ever trouble."

Claire smiled, "Don't worry. I daydream for a moment only. I'm armed at all times and on the alert. After eight years of this job, you develop a second sense. That'll take a bit of retirement to wear off."

Minutes later Juliet and Jacqui returned, "Well, should we go to the farm in the car or do we walk?"

"Let's get warmly dressed and walk. The wind has eased and it's only drizzling now. It'll do us good. It's only half a mile to the farm."

"What about the nanny?"

"She's awake. She'll be up by the time we return and she says she'll tidy up the place for us. She doesn't want to go out in the rain."

"She should," said Claire sardonically. "She needs the exercise. Otherwise she'll develop even bigger lungs with matching accessories."

With that they put on their boots and jackets. Well cocooned, they left the house and walked down the road and into the field. The field led to the lane that gave a shortcut to the farmhouse. Juliet skipped along between them. She sang a nursery rhyme to herself and soon Claire and Jacqui both joined in.

Charles vaulted the gate, swinging Juliet after him. Then Jacqui climbed over. She was half way over when they noticed the three men, just a few yards away. Some second sense told them they shouldn't be there. People don't walk down country lanes at weekends in suits. And one of them was wearing a suit. The others were casually dressed in jeans. And men going for a walk in a Sussex country lane do not look like hoods. They definitely don't look like Mafia thugs.

The man closest to them wore the suit. It was shiny by intent rather than wear. His long dark coat was open and his right hand was in his pocket. His greasy hair was slicked back. His eyes were cruel. His mouth was drawn into a grotesque sneer. He watched them and they watched him. It was a matter of seconds. Jacqui stood frozen at the top of the gate, one leg on one side and the other half way over. Claire was not yet aware of the scene. She was looking the other way and was on the other side of the gate. Juliet sensed something was wrong and her eyes widened in fear.

Charles hand moved to his gun and he started to draw it. The man's hand darted out of his pocket and they were looking down the barrel of a gun. But not for long as a shot from Claire roared out from behind them; the man in the suit staggered back. His gun was on the floor and his hands were clasped to his chest. Blood was flowing freely. He stumbled to his knees and then collapsed in a half conscious, moaning heap on the grass.

Jacqui screamed. Charles turned to pick up Juliet. He fell on his side, as he was pushed to the ground. A boot kicked him in the stomach. He bent double in pain. The other two men had quickly come up behind him, as he was distracted. Now they were retreating. Their guns pointed at them. One had grabbed Juliet who was struggling as she was pinioned under his arm. She called to them in terror and then started screaming, too. Claire jumped the fence and faced up to the men.

"One move from you and the child dies," shouted one of them.

Jacqui seemed to fall back off the gate. Charles thought she had fainted. He then realised that, out of view of the men, she was circling them. The hedgerow would give her cover and she would try to surprise them from behind. He recalled a stile about sixty or seventy yards up the lane. She would get over that. He hoped she was armed. They usually were, but her gun was rarely powerful enough for times like this

Claire pointed her weapon at the ground. Charles did the same. They knew they had to play for time. They had no option but to wait for Jacqui to appear. The man on the ground groaned. He tried to get up. There was so much blood on him. His clothes were sodden with it. The other two seemed indifferent to his plight. Charles suspected he was dying. They must have realised that, too. They had no further use for him.

Charles looked at them carefully. The one was big. He wasn't grossly fat, but he was getting that way. He was large. His head was square. His hair was cut in a style-less crew cut. He, too, was wearing jeans and a jacket that could not hide the fact that he was running fat. A large paunch stretched over his trousers under a dirty white vest that poked through a gap in his shirt. The bottom button was missing, and it looked as if the next could follow for it was under severe pressure from his excess girth. His face, though, was the most remarkable part of him. A square fat face. There were no eyebrows and no eyelashes. The eyes were too small for that large head. One ear was deformed. It must have been cut in a fight or something. And there was a deep red scar down the right hand side of his face.

Next to him, the smaller man was unremarkable. He was dressed in jeans and a sweater. He was slimmer, and even looked slight next to his grotesque companion. He had worried dark eyes and, from time to time, poked his nose with his free hand. The other pointed a gun at them both.

They backed off carefully. They kept them covered. Charles and Claire waited rather than move forward. They had to be patient. Jacqui was their best chance and the men appeared to have forgotten about her. Would she wait and ambush them? Or would she come down the lane? Charles hoped she would do the former. If she came down the lane, the dying man would see her and could still alert his accomplices. Juliet called out, "Daddy, Daddy." She looked at Charles in disbelief and distress when he did not come.

She called out again "Come Daddy, come. They're hurting." Once again he could do nothing except suffer the look of betrayal in the eyes of a child.

Then, Jacqui appeared. She had her gun at the ready. "Take the thin one," muttered Claire to Charles. "I can drop the other slob at this distance without hitting Juliet." They moved forward slowly as the men moved back.

There was a shout from the fat man, "Stop there. Don't move." The voice was guttural. It sounded foreign. They were definitely not English. Charles had no idea what nationality they or the dying man were. The voices seemed more Italian or southern European. The fat one could well have been a Russian. This could be Rastinov's people. But, Charles realised to his horror and fury, there was more chance they came from Di Maglio.

Jacqui was now about ten feet from the retreating men. Juliet could not see her. That was lucky, she may have given the game away. They ignored the fat man's instruction and moved forward without reducing the distance between the men and them.

The injured man was now behind them and Claire had kicked his gun well away from him in passing. But they were still around fifteen feet from the other men. That was still far enough for them to feel safe. But close enough for Charles and Claire to have a good chance when the moment arose.

Jacqui had now moved to within five feet of the men. They were still unaware of her presence as they stepped backwards, monitoring every move as Charles and Claire kept pace with them. They must have been thinking of a way to break the deadlock. The two found it difficult to retreat quickly. They didn't dare open fire for they stood an equal chance of being killed in the exchange. And they still appeared to have forgotten about Jacqui. That was amazingly stupid as she was now just behind them. She had placed herself behind the fat man holding Juliet. If she could grab Juliet, the others could finish the job off easily.

Her gun fired and Charles' roared at the same time. The fat man stumbled and dropped Juliet. His hand was on his heart. The other man stumbled and then shuddered under a stream of bullets. He lay still as Jacqui swooped up Juliet and moved her out of the line of fire. At that moment, Claire's gun opened up again and bullet after bullet found its mark in the fat man's chest before he collapsed in a heap.

Claire and Charles approached the two on the ground. He kicked the gun away from the thin man and bent down to feel for a pulse. "He's dead."

Claire knelt down. The fat man's gun was a few feet from him. As she checked for his pulse, his hand shot out and he grabbed her towards him. Claire jerked back. His other hand held a long and angry looking knife. It swept towards her. The roar of her gun ensured it never reached its target. The square head became shapeless at the impact of the bullet. The hand let go of Claire as the hulk fell, lifeless, onto the muddy field.

Jacqui was holding Juliet tight. The girl was still sobbing in panic as she clung to her. Jacqui was making soothing noises. She still held a gun in her hand. Juliet sat half on her arm. The other hand held her and stroked her head at the same time.

Claire covered the lane behind. Charles edged back to the gate and checked out the Italian looking man. He was dead. He checked his pockets, there was nothing to identify him. He looked down the lane. At that point it was straight for a good fifty yards. There was no other sign of life. It had started to rain harder. The blood was spreading into large watery red pools.

He picked up the gun. It would be dangerous to leave it. He returned to the other two bodies. "No papers. There's nothing to tell who they were," Claire said. She had picked up their guns and the knife from the fat man. They stood in the lane, Jacqui, Claire and Charles. They all held guns and looked first for anything else out of the ordinary. Then they checked if there were any chance witnesses as Juliet sobbed piteously in Jacqui's arms.

Claire said, "There's no way we can dispose of the bodies. Someone would find them. We can leave everything here and hope nobody saw us. Or we call the police."

"Claire, they know Charles and I have guns. We can be traced. Yours is legal too. We're going to have to call the police." He took out his mobile and dialled '999'.

A ring and then a voice said calmly, "Police, Fire or Ambulance."

"Police," he said in a resigned voice. The weekend was hardly going to be the break that they had hoped for.

"Police," said a voice with a strong Sussex accent. "What can we do?"

"There's been a shooting in Rose Wood Farm Lane. Three people are dead. There has also been an attempted kidnapping."

"Who are you?"

"I'm Charles Rossi from the Old Oak Cottage near Rose Wood Farm."

"Are you alone, Mr Rossi?"

"No I'm with my wife and little daughter. And a friend from America is here too."

"A car is on the way. Did you witness anything?"

"Yes. Three men were here and attempted to kidnap my daughter. There was a shootout and they are dead. We're all alive."

There was a silence at the other end of the line. You don't expect to be sipping your tea in a provincial police station and hear something like that. Emergency calls, at worst, are usually about the odd break-in.

A siren sounded in the distance. The officer on the phone added, "There's a car in your vicinity. They'll be with you soon. We'll have ambulances over there in ten minutes and more back-up."

The panda car drove up the lane and two policemen jumped out. They saw their guns and stopped in fright. Charles put his away and Claire did the same. Jacqui couldn't without letting go of Juliet. And that was impossible.

"It's all right," called Charles. "We're not going to attack anyone. Those are for self defence and are perfectly legal."

Without waiting for an answer, he made another call. This time it was to a lawyer. Jeremy Reynolds practised in the firm that bore his and his wife's maiden name. Reynolds and Rayburn were established solicitors and were based in Chancery Lane at the edge of the City. They were Charles' solicitors. They ran a genuine operation, Charles gave them half their business. They had the right contacts and that would be important now. They were also always available, that was part of the deal.

Reynolds would automatically get in touch with Commander Delaney at the Home Office. Delaney was father to Carrie, one of Charles' oldest friends. More important, he knew enough about Charles' shady background, or, as he said, enough to be useful and too little to put him inside. He was aware of Jacqui's past. He would realise that they should avoid publicity. It would be dangerous, there could always be copycat attempts.

The police started to take statements. Charles suggested they should do that back at the house. "The kid is in shock. We're all freezing and wet. I don't think we need to stand here. It is clear we have admitted to shooting these people in self-defence. So you know how they died. The question for you will be whether we have committed an offence or not."

One of the policemen, an Inspector, agreed. "We'll have forensics and CID here soon. They'll go over the area and take the bodies to the morgue. I should take your guns, but I believe you can show the permits at your house. So two of my men will go with you and check them out. I'm afraid we'll have to keep an eye on your house and ask you to stay indoors. I'll have to contact my senior officers."

Charles didn't want to tell him that his senior officers had most likely already been contacted. He wondered what the outcome would be. He was relatively relaxed that they wouldn't be charged, but he was more concerned that there should be no publicity.

They walked back to the cottage, accompanied by the two cops. Jacqui still cuddled Juliet. The nanny looked shocked when they arrived, but like all Mafia nannies, was calm and attentive. Jacqui said she would get the permits. She passed Juliet to Charles. He noticed she clung to him as eagerly as she did to Jacqui. He thought of her look of despair when he had not helped her earlier. That seemed forgotten, at least for the moment.

Jacqui and Claire returned with the papers and the police appeared satisfied.

"Please stay inside," said Jacqui, "we'll get you some coffee. There's no point in waiting in the rain."

Half an hour later another car drew up outside. Three plain clothed men stepped out. A uniformed driver remained at the wheel. It was obvious that the three were policemen. Their short hair and upright walk alone showed that. They were all in their late forties and early fifties. And the policemen in the house looked astonished that they should be there.

Claire let them in. A tall and distinguished looking one turned to them. "I'm the Deputy Chief Constable. I've been talking to the Home Office, the Commander, this morning. You must be Mr Rossi."

He turned to Jacqui and said, "Mrs Rossi." He looked at Claire and said, "Miss Claire Maine." He then continued, "We will need to have full details of the events that led up to the shooting. We have the outline. We will be able to identify where you crossed the field as the ground was so soft, and we'll have a fairly good story from there. The Home Office will advise us what story we should put out. I understand they are concerned that your identities are protected. When would it be convenient to interview you, Mr Rossi?"

"You can do it soon as you want to. Better to do it now while the events are fresh in our minds."

"My colleague, Chief Inspector Gay, will do the interviews. May we record you?"

Charles nodded, "I assume you will ask us to confirm the tapes are accurate once they're typed up."

He agreed. Then he took them one after another into the other room and asked about events. Two hours later the interviews had been completed and the police left, together.

The phone rang later that afternoon. It was Reynolds. "The Commander has just confirmed everything with the Home Secretary. The police will publicise the shooting of three men in the lane. They will say there was evidence that the men had recently come off a ferry at Newhaven. That's down the road from you, that's fairly credible. Usual cover story I'm afraid. They'll say it's to do with drugs. They'll say that some locals found the bodies. That way, if you were seen near the scene, you have cover."

"I assume they won't identify us."

"No way. As usual, we had advised the Commander about the incidents in the USA and the threat to Jacqui and Juliet. He is very concerned. He really has a soft spot for you all. Mind you he pretends it's all professional interest. You did yourself a good turn those years ago, saving his daughter's life."

Reynolds was referring to the fact that Carrie Delaney had been a drug addict until Charles managed to get her to a clinic for a detox. Her father hadn't been able to do that and they had become estranged. But after the clinic they'd got together again. Since then, she had married and had a child. The marriage hadn't worked. Her ex- husband hadn't liked it when he discovered he didn't know about bits of her sordid past. Mind you, not many people did.

"Are you going to tighten up security?" asked Reynolds.

"We've got Maria coming down later tomorrow. Claire's with us. Inside we can look after ourselves and we'll be careful outside. There's little more we can do."

Charles was fairly relaxed. Whoever was behind the incident would not try again soon. Not if they'd lost three men.

"Can you keep tabs on the investigation?" Charles asked Reynolds. "I would like to know who the men were. They had nothing to identify them."

"Don't worry. The police have already said they will want to check out any identities they establish with you. They also want to know if you can help with any connection."

Charles kept his thoughts about Di Maglio to himself. He wanted to test them out first on the others, but he would not do that until he had more information and then only if it confirmed his suspicions.

They kept the doors well locked and bolted that afternoon. It started to pour with rain, in any case, so there was no point in trying to go out. As the night drew in they checked all the windows were locked. The chances of an attempt to get at them in the house were remote, but they had learnt long ago that all precautions were good precautions.

Juliet seemed to have got over her shock. She played with the toys she had brought with her. She ran up to all of them at one time or another. She and the nanny seemed to get on well. Charles looked at the latter's chubby figure.

She had got over the surprise of their sudden return and, like all Mafia women, did not question the incident. They learn that, almost at birth. In cases like this, you get told what you need to know. And if you're not told, that means that you don't ask. Information is power in many walks of life. In the Mafia, it may be the difference between living and dying and, if you know too much, you can die.

Claire discussed the whole series of attacks once Juliet had gone to bed. "This is mad. I've never seen anything like this before. We've had the attack in New York. They tried to kill the driver although he was an accomplice. That was ruthless. The attack was inept. Then we had the bomb. That was meant to scare. Then there was the freeway attack. That was meant to scare. Then there was the kidnap attempt in the hotel. That was bizarre. The women failed and at least one was executed. Then there was the fiasco at the airport. Three against one and they screwed it up! Now we've had this. It was stupid, too. And three are now dead in an ambush against three, taken by surprise. It doesn't make sense."

"I don't get one thing," said Jacqui. "Their intelligence is first rate. They know the areas we frequent. They even knew today about the short cut we would take. They knew we were to go to the farm. They knew where we would join the lane. That's pretty good. And it's been good all the time. They must have an inside track."

"True," said Claire. "But they act in an inept fashion. The women in the hotel should have got out. A professional wouldn't hang around. The attack in New York could have been more effective. The guys today were third rate. It's almost as if they planned the attacks to fail."

"That's what I thought," Charles chimed in. "The kidnappers should have opened fire on us. They were on a loser once they let us draw our guns. A professional would have shot us, at least wounded us and asked questions later."

"Your father-in-law thinks it's the Russians," said Claire. "What if he's wrong? Who else could it be?"

"Nobody in the City," said Charles. "They have no experience in this sort of attack. In any event, there's no way they would have attacked in California and here."

"It could be someone associated with my father" suggested Jacqui. "Perhaps someone, who wants to reveal their hand later. Kidnap Juliet and use her as a ploy to get their own way."

"That's not too convincing. If he revealed himself and harmed Juliet, he'd be dead. If he let her go, he'd die too. If he's an insider, the act of betrayal justifies that according to the code."

"There are three people who know enough about the US and here to organise things," Charles said, thoughtfully. "Maria knew all our details and she knows this place."

"But she didn't organise the car in New York. I did, when my father offered to make it available," said Jacqui. "And we changed flights to California and didn't tell her."

"And you booked yourself for Washington," reminded Claire.

"Who else knew?" asked Jacqui.

"Giovanni knew."

"But he's never been here."

"Yes, but I mentioned to him we'd be spending the weekend here. I'm pretty sure I did. We chatted a bit in Washington and New York."

"Well, he is a suspect then," said Claire. "Who was the third?"

"Your father, Jacqui," said Charles hesitatingly. He had not wanted to bring this option up so early, but had no alternative. He didn't know how she'd react.

She started. Then she frowned. "He came here on one of his trips. He was leaving from Gatwick and we spent a day here before his flight. He knew everything else. He's a suspect too," she said.

"I could be a suspect," said Claire.

"You didn't know we were in New York until Di Maglio told you to guard us. Unless of course you were working for him and he had told you. And you didn't know where we were going today. You had no idea where the farm was. Maria's not been here before, so she could not have told you. And you have been too aggressive, lethally so, with our attackers to have been part of a plot, in all the clashes we've had. We'll count you out."

She nodded. "That's logical. So we have two suspects. They are Giovanni and Di Maglio. I don't believe it's either of them. But we have to be wary. I think we're looking at it the wrong way, we're missing something."

"Look. We're not going to find out tonight. The answer is to be vigilant. I doubt the police will be able to trace the gunmen. We better keep quiet in future about our movements."

"True," said Jacqui. "How about a night-cap and then let's go to bed

So after another glass of wine, they all headed off to bed under the protective thatch of their cottage, hidden in the normally peaceful South of England hills.

CHAPTER NINE

They both woke up with a start. The noise was strange. Charles glanced at his watch. Half past three. Someone was moving in the house, and they were trying to move as quietly as possible. That was not easy, the house was old and the floorboards creaked. Charles grabbed his clothes. Jacqui pulled on her jeans and a sweater.

They both took their guns. Old habits die hard. They were near their bed, that was their normal place. Exchanging worried looks, they crept out. The floorboards in their room were as creaky in the quiet of the night as the ones elsewhere in the house. If someone were there, they must have been heard.

As Charles eased along the hall, Jacqui glided carefully behind him. The noise was coming from downstairs. Someone was moving about down there. There was a creak from the guest bedroom where Claire was sleeping. Charles covered the door with his gun. It opened slowly to reveal Claire in a velvet track suit, bare feet, and tousled hair, gun in hand.

He pointed downstairs. She nodded. Jacqui indicated the third bedroom. The door was closed. They had looked in on the way to bed. They wouldn't have closed it, it was always slightly open. Jacqui moved towards the door. Claire moved to the other side. They didn't hear the knob turn. Jacqui threw the door open. Claire was covering the room with her gun.

"It's empty," gasped Jacqui, although she already knew. She looked at Charles in panic. Her hand went to her head. Then she pointed again downstairs. Charles and Claire were already one step ahead of her gesture and making their way down. The stairs creaked too much. Charles realised that, if someone was still there, there could be no element of surprise.

"Storm it," said Claire as if she had read his thoughts.

They ran down the remaining stairs and sprung into the lounge. Empty. They moved over to the dining room. Empty as well. Claire swooped into the kitchen. There was a rear door from there leading into the walled garden. They both were peering through. There was nothing visible. Claire opened the door. She crouched and studied the garden. The trees threw shadows across the lawn. The clouds covered the moon intermittently. There was no movement. Nobody was there.

They turned and moved to the front of the house. As they got back into the kitchen, there was a scream and then the crash of glass. There were shouts and then a gun fired. Then there was silence. Then a gun fired again. Once. Twice. Then there was the crashing of wood. Then there was nothing.

Charles tripped over her as he went through the lounge. He stopped and put a hand on her body. She was breathing. The hand felt hot and sticky, it was blood. Jacqui had been shot. He waited there for seconds until suddenly she spoke, "I've been hit. I'm all right. It's nothing bad. I didn't see them and they hit me. They've got Juliet. Get her back."

Claire called from the front of the house, "There're getting into a car. There are three of them. One's a woman."

Charles sprang towards her voice. The hall door had been shot down. Whoever had kidnapped Juliet had needed to shoot their way out. They had locked the door from the inside and they had had to shoot the lock.

Claire was running down the drive. Charles followed her. They had no shoes and the sharp gravel of the drive cut into their feet. He felt the cold whip through his open shirt. Claire was ahead of him. She vaulted the gate and ran out into the road. He was there seconds later.

A blue Mercedes was drawing away from them. They fired low. They hit the wheels and the left rear tyre. It blew and the car skidded at the shock. They could hear the grinding of the hubcap as it tore against the hard surface of the road. Claire motioned for him to take cover. She moved across the road and sought refuge by the hedgerow that marked the edge of the field. Charles kicked open the gate and took cover there.

A woman got out of the car. Charles peered in the darkness. It was a young girl. The plump dark features were familiar. It was the nanny. "The brat dies if you make any attempt to save her. We mean business," she called out.

Charles waited. They needed to know the odds. Claire would do nothing until she knew that. A man followed. He had a lifeless bundle under his arm. They recognised it as Juliet. They must have drugged her. He thought that would not have been too hard if the nanny was part of the conspiracy.

Another man got out of the front of the car. He carried an automatic of some sort and pointed it at them. "Try that again and the kid will die, before you. This is no longer to scare you. It's the real thing." He turned to the other man, "Change the wheel." All the while he kept them covered. It was no use. The man knew what he was doing. There was no way they would be able to storm them. The girl had now placed Juliet back in the car and she too was holding a gun. They could shoot the man changing the wheel but they would then be shot themselves.

Then the one behind the car shouted out, "Call the Police and we'll know. We track their radios. We'll kill the kid, dump her, torch the car and disappear. Follow us and we'll hurt the kid; really annoy us and we kill her, then you and then the blond."

Charles didn't reply but started walking back to the gate. "Hold it," shouted one of the men.

"I'm going back to my wife. She's been shot. I don't want her to bleed to death. You've won this round but you'll not win the next. I'll see you all dead first."

Claire stayed put. She was wary. Would they shoot at him? But he'd been through their games before. They'd shot Jacqui, it was true, but not to kill. Someone had been forced to fire at her to stop her. But they had aimed high. They'd hit her in the shoulder or the arm. They'd not aimed for the stomach or the heart. These guys wanted them alive.

He opened the gate and went in. He left it open and Claire darted after him. They ran up the drive. "Watch the door, while I check out Jacqui."

When Jacqui saw him, she sobbed, "Where's Juliet?"

"There's no way we can get her but we need to trail them. We tried to shoot out the tyres, but we only hit one. So they're going to use the spare. It'll take them a few minutes to change the wheel. We'll track them, but are you all right?"

She was pale and there were tears in her eyes. On the one hand she'd been shot and on the other she was facing up to the implications of the kidnap. He checked her out. The bullet wound was not as inconsequential as she'd made out. She'd lost a lot of blood.

He called over Claire, "They're not going to come back for us. Try to bandage Jacqui up quickly. I'll get the car keys and my papers, and things. We'll follow them in the estate. I guess it'll take four or five minutes for them to change the wheel."

He rushed upstairs and grabbed some clothes. There was a holdall in the bedroom and he stuffed it with some spare kit and ammunition. He grabbed his passport and wallet. They might head to the airport. Gatwick was only ten miles or so away.

He took out the mobile and dialled Maria. At the second ring, she answered. "We have problems," he said without a greeting. "Juliet's been kidnapped. Jacqui's been injured. Nothing serious but she needs a doctor. She got a bullet in the shoulder. Get here now. Come armed. It's the usual routine. Claire and I will get in touch. Don't contact Di Maglio until I tell you to."

She didn't query anything. She just said, "OK, be careful." He rang off and ran downstairs. The whole process had taken moments. He called to Claire to get clothes, papers and more ammunition. She ran upstairs at his instruction. He told Jacqui what he'd done.

"Wait for Maria. Don't let anyone else in. Keep the mobile operating and we'll contact you."

She nodded. He kissed her briefly and headed to the garden. He peered through the hedge. There were still voices there. They appeared to have changed the wheel and were lowering the car. They would still need to tighten the nuts. They weren't that good at this. They had given them time.

Claire appeared next to him. She had put on a pair of trainers like him. Otherwise, she had just stuffed things into a small bag. He passed her the keys. "Open the garage. Get into the car, but don't start the engine. You'll see them drive away. Start as soon as they are round the corner. They won't hear you then. But I don't want them to see us following them. Drive to the road without lights, in the meantime I'll cause a diversion."

Claire slipped away and he thought he heard her gently open the garage door. The people in the car made no sign of having noticed anything unusual. They had dumped their damaged tyre in the middle of the road and were throwing the tools into the boot. As they jumped in and started the engine, Charles moved forward. He waited till they were close to the bend and then fired at them. He aimed wide. His purpose was not to stop them. It was to make them think that the shots were the final act of despair of a loser.

In reality, there was no sense in stopping them. If he disabled their car, they could well hurt Juliet and perhaps just hijack his. He had been surprised they hadn't done that in the first place. Then he had realised why. They needed their own car. They must be catching the ferry to France. If they had pre-booked the tickets, they would have had to give details of their car. The last thing they would want would be an inquisitive official looking at Juliet. Not that they believed Charles would call the police. They expected that he would seek help from his contacts, whether Di Maglio or someone else. They, in turn, would alert the borders. Unless they got Juliet onto the boat quickly and smoothly, they would be in trouble.

Claire was turning into the road and Charles ran to the car, grabbing his bag, which he had thrown to the ground. He jumped in. "Go down the lane. It leads to the main London to Brighton road. I'm pretty sure they'll head south towards Brighton and then turn onto the road for Newhaven. There must be an early morning ferry. They'll be heading for France."

Claire drove through the pitch-black night down the lane. The clouds had thickened and the rain became more persistent. They still kept their lights off. They couldn't see any lights ahead of them. The road was winding. He still wanted to play safe. If they were seen, they would be lost.

He grabbed the phone and dialled a London number. A voice answered, "This is the Rossi residence."

"Is that you Douglas?"

"Yes Mr Charles." The voice was soft but precise. Douglas and his wife looked after the house in London. Douglas was butler, chauffeur, handyman, gardener and, in many ways, confidant. He knew little about their business dealings, indeed, they would have bored him. But he was aware of their personal affairs. He knew who Jacqui was. He knew Charles' background. And he knew all about Jack Ryder and his chequered past. He was totally loyal. There was a bond between them that assured that.

"We have a problem. Juliet's been kidnapped. We can't go to the police. If we do, they'll kill her, dump her body and disappear. We need to sort this out ourselves. Nobody must know about it. But I need a car. It has to be fast and it needs to be at Dieppe for the next ferry to leave Newhaven. I don't know when that is, but it's the next one to leave from now."

He answered the question. "There is bound to be one between five and six. The crossing takes three hours. With France an hour ahead that would mean you'll arrive around nine or ten. They time the early departure to allow people to make Paris for lunchtime. That tallies."

"I want you to get a helicopter and fly to Dieppe. Call Mackenzie and he'll fix you up. Hire a fast car there for us and a little folding motor bike for yourself. You should be able to get the bike into the car.

Park the car next to the port exit. Leave it open and put the keys under the visor. Leave it in a place where all the drivers from the ferry will pass. We'll find it. Look out for us. We'll be on foot.

And look out for a Mercedes. It's dark blue. It'll most likely have two men and a woman in it. The woman will be Juliet's nanny. Juliet will be in it but I doubt you'd see her. If we are not at the car yet, follow it on the bike. You'll only be able to keep up with it till it leaves the town. But you'll then know which road it took. We need to know that. If you have to follow it, call me on the mobile. Once we have made contact and I tell you, you can return the bike and head back to London in the helicopter. Hire both the car and the bike in a false name. You know where the spare papers are. Now, get going. But call the house in an hour. We may still have to abort if we got it wrong."

"I'll see you in Dieppe, or wherever, Mr Charles."

Claire was still driving down the lane while all this took place. She drove fast and well. He looked at her. Her blonde hair was damp and dishevelled. It fell over her shoulders and forward over her forehead. Her face was pale without make-up, but her flawless skin appeared to glow in the shadows of the night. The top of her track suit was undone, and, as she was leaning slightly forward to concentrate on the road, he could see the outline of her half-uncovered breasts. Her feet were bare in her trainers, which were muddy from the garden.

He glanced down at himself and wondered if they should tidy up before trying to get onto the ferry; otherwise, it would look as if they had suddenly taken flight for some reason. His jeans were muddy, his shirt was undone and he could feel the cold air. They looked too scruffy. They had no coats or jackets. In mid-winter they were dressed for the summer. And they would need to dump the car. The reason Charles had arranged for transport in Dieppe was simple. If the nanny saw the car, she could recognise it. There mightn't be many people on board the ferry at this time of year. It would be easier to conceal themselves as foot passengers. They would dump the car at the port.

He dialled again on the mobile. He got through to Maria, "Where are you?"

"I'm just heading out of London. I have a doctor with me. He'll do all the necessary. He's trustworthy. I should be down there in about half an hour or so now."

"Jacqui is alone in the house. Claire and I are chasing the kidnappers. Keep the lines open. We're going to need to have you around."

He then dialled again. This time he got the house. The phone rang two or three times. His heart stopped when nobody replied. Then he heard Jacqui's voice.

"How are you?"

"I'm a bit drowsy. It hurts. It's a burning sort of feeling. Where are you?"

"We're trying to track the kidnappers. I think they're heading for France. We've made arrangements. Maria will be with you in half an hour or so. She's coming with a doctor."

"I have locked myself in. The front door is damaged. I'm upstairs. I doubt anyone will intrude but I thought I better be careful as I'm not exactly on top form."

"Where are you? Can you see the front of the house?"

I am in the guest room. That gives me a view. I know I need to watch for Maria. I'll be OK."

"I'll keep you informed. Love you. Be careful."

There was a weak laugh. "Who's talking? You're the ones in real danger. Look after yourselves. And bring me back my baby." The last words were accompanied by a strangled sob that was painful to hear. The line went dead.

Claire called, "They're ahead. Or at least I think it's their taillights. They're just at the junction."

"That's the main road. See if they turn left. That leads to Brighton and then on to the port at Newhaven."

"Turning left."

"Give them space. Drive on sidelights once they are a good way ahead. There's hardly anybody on the road and so we'll be able to follow where they go. I know where they are likely to turn and that'll help."

They drove on. The sidelights were now on. They could see the car ahead. He suspected that they might be able to see them, but they would think that they were far behind as the lights would be quite dim. And there was no reason why they should suspect that the car was following them. They were on the main road and it was highly likely that anyone else on the road would be heading to the town.

As they approached Brighton, Charles told Claire to be careful. "They should turn left off the road. Follow a bit closer. I want to make sure they turn to Newhaven. There are a couple of small ports here and there is an outside chance that they have a boat waiting. I doubt it, though."

They watched and they turned left. Claire got as close as she dared and they saw them take the Newhaven road. Charles had guessed right. He glanced at his watch. It was approaching four. He pulled out the mobile and called directory inquiries. They put him through to the Ferry Company at the port. The ferry would leave at just before five. That was in under an hour. But they were now less than half an hour from the port.

He booked two passengers. He used their real names as they had to tally with their passports. They repeated Mr Charles Rossi and Miss Claire Maine. He turned down the suggestion that they should take a cabin. He guessed that the kidnappers would do that and couldn't risk being seen by them. Their only chance of snatching Juliet back was to do so by surprise. They couldn't risk a gunfight, that would be too dangerous. They had to ensure that any steps they took did not place Juliet at risk.

Charles called home and got Douglas's wife. "When he calls in for messages, tell him the Dieppe meeting is on. Tell him I'll be with Claire, the American girl. And get ready for Jacqui and Maria. They'll be back in a couple of hours or so. And Jacqui's been hurt. Nothing too serious but she'll need help."

They got to the port area and saw the Mercedes turning into the car holding area.

"I'll see you by the gates. Park in a side street and lock the car," Charles called to Claire as he opened his door. She stopped and he jumped out. He watched from the gates and saw the Mercedes stop and then head for the ferry before driving up the ramp into the car bay. He turned and saw Claire jogging towards him.

"Let's go. They're on board" he called. They collected their tickets and got through the cursory customs and passport checks. The boat was almost empty. At that time of the year you don't get that many holidaymakers. And the trucks tend to reduce in number over the weekends, especially on the early departures.

"We better go on deck. It'll be chilly but there are more places to hide. We could easily be spotted below decks. I'm afraid it's going to be a cold trip."

They climbed on deck. They found an area where they could escape by several routes and sat down. He turned to Claire; "You should put something warm on. Do you have anything?"

She shook her head. "Just a sweatshirt, which I threw in with some tights and wash things that came to hand into the bag. I didn't think of anything else. I was more interested in papers and ammunition. What about you?"

"I did the same. Just like you. And I grabbed papers and cash."

"I'm going to find it hard to put my tights and shirt on out here. Once the boat gets going, I'll sneak down to the Ladies and put them on. Can I huddle up to you? That's for warmth. It's for nothing else."

For the first time since they had left, he relaxed a bit. He grinned, "It's a bit nippy out here for the something else."

She put her arms round his waist and let him put his round her shoulders. They sat close together. It warmed them up a bit. It also, he thought, gave them some cover. People would think they were lovers. Mind you, they would have had to be pretty stupid ones to stay up on deck. As the ferry headed out to sea, the wind grew stronger and the thin rain was driven against them despite the bit of shelter they had in their semi-covered piece of deck.

Claire shivered against him. Her body felt icy as it pressed up against his. "Look Charles this is hopeless. We can't stay up here. I'll have a scout inside and see if there's a decent place to hide. I'll also try to see if I can find out more about the suspects. And they may sell some sweaters or something in the shop."

She disappeared, Charles waited. The cold wind blew into his face. It caught hold of the thin fabric of his shirt and tugged at it. It found gaps and, as it hit him, his body felt ice cold. The rain came in a continuous fine sheen. It left a film of moisture all over him. Then another. And then another. In the end he realised he would soon be soaked. He tried to get his mind off his damp, cold, misery. He felt a sudden depression sweep over him as he thought back over the last weeks. The last twenty-four hours had seen Juliet kidnapped and Jacqui shot. Now they were on the ferry tracking their quarry, when he should have been entirely focussed on the financial coup they were planning.

He was furious that the nanny had betrayed them. She must have, somehow, let the kidnappers in. Another Di Maglio winner, he thought bitterly. For the first time it struck him. The Di Maglio driver had betrayed them in New York. The Di Maglio nanny had betrayed them. Their Di Maglio car had been attacked in Los Angeles. Their hotel had been targeted there as well. Was Di Maglio really behind this? He shuddered at the thought. He was not the sort of person he wanted as a friend. He was the last sort of person he would have chosen as a father-in-law. But the worst thing of all would be to have him as an opponent. He was too good. It would be too dangerous.

In any case it was too unlikely. Nobody would have been allowed to shoot Jacqui. Not from his entourage. It was too dangerous. However good a shot they were, there was still a high chance of a mistake. An outsider, like the Russians, would take that chance. He didn't think Di Maglio or any of his people would. Not with Jacqui. And in any case, the incident would have traumatised Juliet. Despite all his faults, Di Maglio was genuinely fond of her. He would never put her through that.

Charles found it hard to fathom out what was happening. Who was doing this to them? The Di Maglio story about the Russians and his Empire rang false. They knew how he would react. They would only risk gang warfare if a madman led them. And the madman would have to be inept as well. It was true that Rastinov or some feral substitute could fit that bill. But it was doubtful Rastinov was really alive. Logically, Tobin still ran the Russian Mafia. He had succeeded Rastinov after they killed the mad Russian in the attack on his place in the South of France. Charles was sure they'd killed him. Yet Di Maglio would have them believe that he could still be alive. It made no sense, at all. Perhaps, Di Maglio was faced with a palace revolt. It could explain why he wanted Charles in. He needed a younger man to help him re-establish control. But if that were the case, Claire would have been aware that something was happening. She wasn't in the inner circle. But she'd worked for Di Maglio since she was eighteen. That was almost eight years. She was as close to the inner circle as anyone got. And it was clear she was as perplexed as they were as to the source of the attacks. Her reactions, when they were threatened, showed she was loyal to them. Equally important, she hadn't recognised any of the people used. She would have recognised anyone from the Di Maglio stable.

He shook his head and buried it into his hands. A gentle hand on his shoulder made him start for his gun, but the quiet voice of Claire pulled him together. "They are in a cabin. It's a first class one on the upper deck. I've got us one on another deck. It'll be nasty, as it is second class. Four bunks but nobody else in them. It'll let us keep warm and we can move upstairs before the boat docks. They won't move till they can go down to their car and that's around the same time as the foot passengers are called just as they get into the harbour."

"Is there any chance of snatching Juliet?"

"No. Not from their cabin. There's a steward on duty. And we've nowhere to go. We can't afford a shoot out. Your friend, the Commander, mightn't be able to help us here. I doubt we're in his jurisdiction."

They headed downstairs. She'd warmed up a bit but Charles was shivering. The air down there was fairly bad. The cabin was poky. It only had a wash stand. But it was at least warm.

"We need to dry off and dry our clothes," said Claire. She stripped off her shirt and fished inside her bag for a bra which she quickly put on.

Charles stripped off too and put on some dry underwear. He then took the thin hand towel and dried his hair as best he could. She took another and did the same thing. There was a radiator in the room and they placed their shirts on it. Their trousers were wet, but not wet through. Charles' shirt was worse than Claire's was. Hopefully it could dry in the couple of hours before they hit France.

They huddled together under a couple of coarse grey blankets. Gradually they got warmer. Claire dozed off in his arms. He was conscious of the contours of her body. In the half-light in the cabin, he watched her face relax. She looked softer. She felt gentler as her body relaxed too. Her thighs pressed against his. Her breasts nestled against his chest. Her head fell onto his shoulder. He tightened his arm around her, wanting to protect her as she slept.

Charles also must have slept for a bit for, suddenly, he realised that the boat was shuddering. It was slowing down. They must be approaching the harbour. Claire woke at the same time and glanced at her watch. It was almost eight, or nine in France.

"We better get on deck. We want to avoid them and get off quickly."

They dressed in moments. Their clothes were nearly dry. Claire had pulled on some thick tights, but they were still ridiculously lightly dressed for that time of the year. It was crazy that they had not taken thicker sweaters or a jacket at the house. In a rush, it was easy to forget the obvious.

They made their way carefully up to the deck area. The suspects were nowhere to be seen. Charles phoned the house and Douglas' wife answered, "Have you news from Jacqui?"

"They'll be here in about an hour. They were going to leave the cottage about now. Jacqui's fine but they felt she should rest a bit. There was no point in rushing back up. And Maria thought it safer in the daytime."

He called the cottage. There was no answer. He dialled Jacqui's mobile number. Again there was no answer. He dialled Maria's mobile number. It rang. No answer and he felt a surge of panic. Then Maria's voice came over.

"How's Jacqui?"

"Why don't you talk to her? She's feeling better."

Jacqui's voice came over. Anxious and weaker than usual. "Where are you? Have you got Juliet?"

"We're tracking Juliet. We know where she is. We're on the ferry from Newhaven and just approaching Dieppe. It's too dangerous to attack. We'll have to wait for a chance. Douglas is waiting in Dieppe with a fast car. We'll find them. The important thing is to snatch Juliet without a gunfight. We still can't tell who they are. But they'd prefer not to kill. The danger is that they may have to in a fight."

Jacqui didn't argue. "We mustn't tell the police. If pictures are flashed all over the place, we'd have the same risks. What about my father? "

"He's a suspect."

"Maria and I thought that."

"If he's behind it, he could be having us watched. I doubt he was doing that at the cottage. They thought it would be a quiet snatch as it was an inside job. But the London house may be under surveillance. Claire and I will need a cover story. Think of one before you ring him. But he mustn't know that we are tracking the kidnappers. Tell him we will need his help all the same. Do anything to stop him from getting suspicious."

"The cover story will be easy," replied Jacqui. "They actually left a note. They told you specifically to wait for a meeting. They have your mobile number. They'll call you. They said it hadn't to be me. That could be a ruse to keep me out of the way. They may want to meet and are afraid I would recognise them, if they work for my father."

"Let's be wary what we say to your father, until we know who's behind this. Tell him I'm with Claire and am using her as a driver and body guard. Also say she's here as I need someone to help if we get Juliet back. I couldn't just get her to sit in the car on her own as I drove home. Make it sound we expect it's a blackmail attempt. We better go to zero communication except in an emergency."

"Charles, I'll call in at the office. It'll not be possible to trace a call there through the switchboard. I'll call you through Claire. The switchboard won't recognise her."

"Jacqui, you're sure you're all right?"

"Yes. The doctor removed the bullet. It touched a bone in the shoulder and chipped it. He's cleaned it all up. He says the arm will be stiff for a bit. Otherwise, there's no problem. And he told me something else."

This was said in a softer voice. It was a bit tearful. Charles hesitated, "What else?"

She seemed even closer to tears now; "I'm pregnant again. That's why I keep getting all emotional. Do be careful. I want the baby. And I must have Juliet back."

"There's no danger from the shock?"

"No, the doctor's here. He says that I'm fine. He's given me nothing as he says that would be bad for the baby as he had to give a local to clean up my shoulder."

"I'm pleased. It's great. We'll be together soon. I promise. All three will be, or rather all four of us."

They talked for a minute or so more, but they were now fast approaching the harbour.

"I have to go, as we want to get off as soon as this boat docks. Be doubly careful."

Charles joined Claire who was sheltering away from the wind in an area of the deck that was half enclosed.

"They're all fine. They're on their way to the house in London. Jacqui's been seen to and there's no serious damage."

Claire said, "I asked someone where we got off and it appears it's through a door just below here. That means we'll have to wait. We need to stay here as there are hardly any foot passengers. The first class cabin passengers have to pass by the doorway on their way down to the car deck. There are only a few cars and trucks and they'll all be parked forward. So we need to be careful. We'll dart down at the last minute."

They docked in that slow and ponderous way of ferries, easing backwards and forwards and then edging against the dock. The Dieppe morning greeted them with mournful indifference. It exhibited all the joy of a cold, wet, windy and grey day on an off season morning during an off peak time. Nothing looked open and everyone seemed sullen. Men huddled in dark thick clothes with the only glow coming from the odd Gauloise stuck to an upper lip. Charles shivered. This felt like a bad omen. The town looked dead. The town even felt dead.

But as the boat docked, Claire jerked him from this gloom, "Time to go."

They headed downstairs into the boat's stale but warm air. The slightly overpowering smell of English cooked breakfasts came to greet them from the nearby cafeteria. A few tired looking people with battered cases waited at the door. Young couples with rucksacks were the only cheerful ones around. They pushed into the middle of this small group and crouched down for fear that the people they were hunting would appear.

The gangplank swung over and everyone shuffled down it. Nobody, other than them, was in a hurry. They got to the front immediately, but Charles warned Claire to slow down. If they were too rushed, Customs could be suspicious. They already looked a bit strange without coats. But officialdom was as indifferent to their presence or their welfare as the town's unwelcoming aspect had suggested. Soon, they were outside, and ahead were the station and the gateway to the ferry terminal.

They hurried over to where a large saloon car parked by the gate. Douglas greeted them. Charles jumped into the driving seat and Claire got in the other side. Douglas got into the back. He talked to them quickly, "The cars are just coming out, so I didn't have to trail them. There's a large bag on the back seat here. It has some things for you. I took anything that was dark and warm. I thought you may need some clothes. I bought Miss Claire a couple of Miss Jacqui's sweaters. I've added two more powerful guns and some ammunition in case you need it. And there is a couple of thousand dollars from the safe, as well as about a thousand euros. That's all we had. Anything else you need?"

"Douglas, you're wonderful. Go back to Newhaven and pick up the estate car. It's parked near the port. Here's the name of the street. Claire jotted it down. Look after Jacqui while I'm away and avoid contact except for emergencies."

He nodded and ducked away, picking up a motor bike from the verge near the car. He was a tall figure, but he seemed much smaller as he crouched over the bike. He blended well into the background in his dark outfit. He knew how to do that from his Special Forces days. Those were the days before he'd had to disappear. Jacqui and Charles knew why. His wife knew why. But nobody else did. In fact they didn't even know he was alive. And he wouldn't have been if it hadn't been for Charles. That was the root cause of his loyalty.

The blue Mercedes drove slowly from the port and followed the signs to the motorway. They pulled in behind it, following a couple of the other cars that had come off the boat. There was nothing suspicious in a line of cars heading that way.

"They seem to be heading for Paris. Why don't you try to get some rest and then we can change over drivers later? I'd get a sweater and keep warm. See also if you can get the heating going in the car. I don't know BMW's that well."

She did as asked. She turned round and pulled the bag left by Douglas towards her., picking out a sweater and putting it on. The warm air was comforting as Charles was still in shirt sleeves. He tracked the Mercedes, as did several of the other cars as they all headed in the direction of Paris.

"We're going to have to guess where they are heading. And we may need to change cars en route. I hope we have a chance. We can dump this one anywhere, it'll have been rented in a false name. We have more false identities in the bag. I asked Douglas to bring some. We always keep a few. You never know when they'll come in useful. We chopped and changed in the old days but then we were on the run. These days we're much more like good citizens."

Claire smiled and put her seat back. She was soon sleeping again. He let her. The road was boring and he concentrated on the Mercedes ahead as they moved towards the French capital. The dark gloomy dawn made way for an equally depressing day. Occasionally, the wipers cleaned off the mixture of drizzle, surface water and dirt from the road. For a few fleeting moments, it looked as if the cloud would break and allow them to see a bit of sky. But it obviously decided that was not appropriate and so, as they drove on, the gloom persisted.

The Mercedes eventually arrived at the outskirts of Paris. They kept a keen eye on the blue car, they could easily lose it here. By now, Claire had woken again. Charles was glancing at the petrol indicator. They were only a quarter full. The Mercedes would need to stop soon, it had not been refuelled since the cottage. He didn't want them to do that on the inner motorway. It would be difficult for them to do likewise in the same garage. They needed them to stop off on a motorway in one of those gargantuan filling stations, which afford anonymity.

He realised that he had one big advantage. They knew their car but the kidnappers didn't know theirs. And that was the way it had to be.

CHAPTER TEN

The Mercedes went round the inner motorway. It was hard to keep up with it. The driver didn't know the road well and kept getting into the wrong lanes. Then, suddenly, he would swerve out again. He would rejoin the road to a tumultuous crescendo of hooting from the irritated Parisians who were making their way round the diabolical concrete halo that encircled their capital city.

Charles kept in the centre lanes. If necessary he could dart off the road. But it would have looked too suspicious to keep on weaving in and out of the inside lane every time the car in front did. And he couldn't be sure that they weren't doing it to check whether they were being followed.

The road bent round Paris and indicated the West and then the South. As the sign said Lyon, the car appeared to keep in the right lane. They looked and nodded to each other. Sure enough, as they approached the Lyon turnoff, it indicated and took the approach road for the motorway South.

"Claire, have the Russians still got that place near Uzes in the South. You know their compound in the hills just outside Avignon?"

"The one you and Di Maglio razed to the ground a few years back?"

"That's right."

"The last time I heard they still had it. It was rebuilt after the attack. It is apparently totally different now. There's a modern compound and much more high tech security. Do you think that's where they're heading?

"If they go towards Lyon and then on beyond Valence, that's the likely destination. It would also prove that we're dealing with the Russian Mafia."

He thought for a moment. "Claire. There really are only two options. Firstly, these are Russians and there is some truth in the bizarre stories of Di Maglio. The whole truth is unlikely to be as he says. He always will twist a story to eke that bit extra advantage out of it for himself. The second option is that Di Maglio engineered this. Then the car is heading to Geneva to his place in the hills behind it. But we'll only know if that's the case as we go further south."

"Don't forget it may be a wild card. It could be a breakaway group from your father-in-law's people or the Russians for that matter. Don't you remember Boris the Bear in Barbados?"

Charles nodded grimly. Boris had been part of a breakaway group sent to assassinate Jacqui and him. He had caught up with Charles and had nearly succeeded in killing him. Charles had been lucky that they met in a confined space where Boris' incredible bulk had slowed him down. Charles remembered the knife Boris threw. It missed his head by a hairbreadth and had stuck four or five inches into a doorframe. And he had had to shoot Boris several times to stop him, even when fatally wounded, from coming forward to try to kill him with his bare hands. But Claire was right; one must always be alert.

"They're pulling into the motorway complex there," called Claire. They were about a hundred yards behind them and Charles immediately slowed down. That allowed the kidnappers to get further away and disappear round the bend in the road before they in turn swerved onto the slip road themselves. They saw them again immediately. They had stopped at one of the first pumps. Charles recognised the man who had changed the wheel. He was walking to the pump.

They stopped at a far pump, out of sight. It was the type you activate with a credit card. Claire had put on a top with a hood and she had covered her blond hair with it. She jumped out and operated the pump. Once they had filled up, the machine whirred away and regurgitated the card and a voucher. Claire grabbed them and Charles started the engine again. She took a sheet of paper roll and appeared to be working at removing dead flies from the windscreen. Her face was well hidden and Charles carefully looked away also towards the complex behind the pumps. He realised she wanted to get a view of the Mercedes as it passed in front of them.

He couldn't see when it would and so he simply looked away. The last thing he wanted was for Juliet to see him. She would give them away immediately. Claire jumped in and Charles saw the Mercedes was rejoining the carriageway. He pulled away. "What did you see?"

"They're all in there. Juliet is sitting in the back with the nanny. I think she's OK. The two men we saw are in the front. I got a good view of them again. I don't recognise them as Di Maglio people. But it came back to me who the girl is. Her name's Claudia Palomi. Her father is Giorgio. He's a Di Maglio hit man. That means that Di Maglio is most likely double-crossing us. I cannot believe she would betray him. She knows the rules and all these Mafia girls have strong family ties. There'd be blood money on her head from the moment she acted against his instructions; her family would try to kill her as a matter of honour. That is, if they got to her before Di Maglio killed them as a matter of course."

Charles knew she was right. "I can't believe she'd act against Di Maglio. She'd know the consequences."

Claire shrugged her shoulders. "It's unlikely. But it has happened before. The families are very protective about the daughters. She may have a lover. He may have persuaded her. She may think she can get away with it. But it's unlikely."

They were driving fast. Charles had been at the wheel for over five hours and was getting tired. They pulled in and quickly swapped places. Then Claire roared away until they could see the Mercedes again in the distance. The road to Lyon offered little distraction. The Mercedes didn't stop. Luckily, Douglas had left some chocolate and water in the car. The kidnappers, or quarry as Claire ominously insisted on calling them, must have had some food as well, for they never stopped.

Towards Lyon they pulled into another petrol station and Claire followed suit. They parked the car. They watched from the distance. The two men went into the restaurant.

"This could be our chance. The nanny's alone with Juliet," said Charles. Claire nodded. They left the car about two hundred yards away. Charles would have preferred to leave the engine running and the doors open, but that would have been asking for trouble. It would, though, have made for an easier getaway. Using the other parked cars as cover, they carefully approached the Mercedes.

Once they were about fifty yards away, the door opened and the nanny got out. She was carrying Juliet. They could see she was asleep or drugged in her arms. Charles was about to jump out and run to the woman. Claire pulled him down.

"What's wrong?"

"It's a hand-over. The kidnappers are in the diner but there's a man with them and I think he comes from the car parked next to the Mercedes. He'll be paying them off. The nanny will leave with the new guys. That way, the kidnappers don't know where Juliet is being taken.

"Look carefully and you'll see a black Citroen. And I recognise the driver. He's the one in the car now. He drives and enforces for your father-in-law. I can't see the other very clearly but this is not the time to do anything. Otherwise, there would be a shoot out. I'll keep watch. You go back to the car. Bring it closer when I signal. We'll need to know who to follow."

Charles did as she said. He was sweating. He'd thought they would be able to grab Juliet. Now everything was unclear. And more importantly, it seemed Di Maglio was their opponent. The man he feared most was the man they would have to beat.

He waited in the car. Claire crept closer. She was very close to the Mercedes. He didn't know what she was doing. But she then crept back. She signalled to him to come, retreating all the time. He approached her and she ducked into the car.

"Park here and wait," she said. "We need to allow the Citroen to go. The other car won't follow. I don't think it would have in any case, but I've made double sure of that."

"What did you do?"

"I slashed a tyre. They have no spare wheel. Even here, that's going to delay them enough. I want to follow the Citroen without the fear that we could be followed by the Mercedes."

"I'd still half like to grab the nanny and Juliet and risk a gunfight. I know we can't. It would be too dangerous. "

"She knows too much," said Claire. "I wouldn't be surprised if she doesn't disappear. But she can't disappear forever. And we know who she is. She won't see twenty."

They sat and waited in the car. Then the nanny moved away from the Mercedes, still holding an inert Juliet. She waved cheerfully at the men in the restaurant and got into the Citroen.

"Claire, they either really can't know that we're here, or that is outstanding acting."

She agreed as they watched the Citroen rise gently in the air as the strange hydraulics set into motion. It was about to depart. But this time, they were sure that it would head to Geneva and not the Russian's compound. This surely had to be an official Di Maglio operation.

They pulled out behind the Citroen. "The good thing is that they didn't notice us. So we start from scratch with the Di Maglio people here. The bad news is that they will leave the motorway if they head to the Geneva compound. What should we do?" asked Charles.

Claire responded thoughtfully, "There's no way we can track them to the Geneva compound. My guess is that they'll cut across country. We'll have to follow them as far as we can and then try to cut them off. If we can get ahead of them, we can double check where they are going. But, if they are heading to Geneva and they are Di Maglio people, there is no other place for them. The compound is the only really safe place around. I can't believe he would risk this operation elsewhere. I'm still trying to work out why it's happening like this."

"When we have time, Claire, we need to go through that. I also need to set up some business cover at the bank. There's a mega deal in progress. I can't let that go now. It's all gone beyond the point of no return."

They drove on down the motorway. They kept well back. The kidnap had been ham fisted and the people in the Mercedes must have been amateurs. Otherwise, they would have taken more precautions and would have checked to see if they were being followed.

Charles or Claire had done that repeatedly when they came to a long slip road leading off a motorway. Either they'd strayed on it with a keen eye on their rear mirror before cutting back, or they'd even exited the motorway on a couple of occasions. Both times, they had merely headed back on again and then sped up to get closer to the other car. But on no occasion was there a sign of someone following. That had given them comfort.

They weren't that surprised the Citroen wasn't taking such steps itself. It thought the Mercedes had left England unnoticed. They had their guard down.

"Could we attack them if they are so confident?" asked Charles.

"Normally we could. The risk is that we'd never be able to get Juliet away quickly. Anyway, we can't shoot up the car while she's still in it."

She was right and Charles knew it. It was frustrating being a hundred yards or so behind her and unable to do anything. They then got to the part of the motorway where there were several options. One was moving away from Geneva towards the South, another was to cut over to Switzerland. The Citroen turned to Switzerland.

"Let's drive on," said Claire. "We need to take the risk. They'll be watching carefully here for anyone following. We can't be seen at this point."

Charles agreed with a heavy heart. Juliet was getting further away now. Another sign said 'Geneva' and Claire told him to take it. She had a map in front of her and she directed him across the minor roads. They came to a main road and then a motorway.

"This way is definitely longer but it's the fastest I can think of. We need, though, to step on it. You'll have to risk being stopped by the police. Just put your foot down and go as fast as you can."

He put his foot down and the speedometer soon moved up from the steady hundred and twenty kilometres they'd been going earlier to a hundred and fifty and then a hundred and eighty. That was well over a hundred miles an hour and he thought it fast enough.

Claire muttered, "This is a motorway. You're not fast enough."

He pressed the accelerator down further and soon was edging over the two hundred mark. At that speed, even in the heavy and powerful BMW, he could feel the wheels lose partial contact with the road.

"If I go any faster, there's a risk that I'll become airborne."

"Stick to the road. These bits of tin make lousy planes," was her cryptic response.

They moved from motorway to main road and then through lanes onto other roads. The closer they got to Geneva, the better Claire knew the area. They would soon see the lake below. They were on a mountain road. Claire directed him over a path that was little better than a mountain track. He did seventy on the bumpy surface and was instructed to go faster. At a hundred he ignored her urgings.

"This cuts off a huge corner," she shouted over the noise of the car handling the ruts of the track. "Once we go down the other side, we'll be on the main road and about twenty miles away from the compound. A bit after that, there's a deserted barn overlooking the road. We have to stop there and hide the car. Anything closer and Di Maglio's surveillance equipment will pick us up."

They bounced from the path onto a main road and, for once, she told him to slow down. Then, suddenly, she shouted, "Stop at that path." When he did, she got out, swung open a gate and motioned him through. She closed the gate and jumped back in. "Up the track and to that barn." Half way up a pretty steep hill that he had to take in first gear was the barn she'd mentioned. The path skirted it and he turned right onto some waste ground at the front of the place. She nipped out again and ran to the wide doors that were secured by a bar. She unlatched them and the doors swung open. She darted in and checked the place out, gun in hand. She came back and gestured impatiently for him to get in. Once he had, she bolted the barn doors shut. The bolt on the outside was attached to one inside. One could lock it from both sides.

"We need to go up onto the ledge. There's a window there that looks over the road."

She started to climb a ladder and he followed. They sat on either side of the window and watched the road below. Minutes passed. They sat in silence. Charles felt tired after the hours of non-stop driving. Then he spotted the car in the distance.

"Someone's coming from over there. I can see them against the hills."

The car moved closer. It was black. It was a Citroen. It was the Citroen. Charles had a terrible urge to go down and shoot it to a halt. But he knew that wasn't practical. The helplessness was infuriating. Claire moved over, as the car passed. She placed her hand on his arm.

"We'll rescue her soon. But we need to plan it. And we need to be careful. At least we know where she is and who has her. The chances of her being harmed physically now are limited. We need, though, to get her out pronto. We need to talk and we need to get in touch with Jacqui."

"We can only do that tomorrow when she goes to the office. She said she'd be there. It's the safest place for us to talk. Elsewhere, we could be traced."

"Should we stay here the night?" asked Claire.

"I think it'd be safer. If we head off to a hotel nearby, there's a risk that we could be noticed. The car seats will go back. You can use that. And I'll sleep up here. The straw's not uncomfortable and it's actually dry."

"Why are you so coy all of a sudden? I don't mind if I stay here with you. In fact I'd prefer it. This isn't the most homely of places but it might be the best. It's better not to sleep in the car. If anyone comes in, they can't miss the car. We'd be better to shift our stuff up to this level and sleep here. That way we get a warning of intruders and a chance to get away. In the car we're sitting ducks."

So they shifted their bags up to the ledge and set up the guns in case they were disturbed. They were getting famished but agreed that there was no way they could go and find food. So they made do with the rest of the chocolate that Douglas had left in the car and some water.

"This is a pretty miserable way to spend a Sunday night, even in Switzerland," said Claire.

"I wonder how Juliet is," said Charles. "I wonder if we could get Jacqui in there to see her."

"How would you do that?"

"Get her to go there for sanctuary. She needs a doctor to see her arm. Her father can arrange that. She could give us an inside lead."

"Di Maglio would never show her Juliet."

"Perhaps not, but that doesn't mean she couldn't find her. It'll be easier as an inside job. And we could support her from the outside."

"Don't you need her in the bank?"

"You're right. I need Jacqui in the bank. Otherwise, I have nobody to trust there. Maria would be all right but I doubt she could get my instructions through to people there. But they'll all obey Jacqui."

It was not long before they decided to get some sleep. It had been a long day with the drive across France and down into Switzerland. Outside it was dark and gloomy. Occasionally, the moon would surface from behind a cloud, but not for long. The Swiss landscape was too uninviting for gazing out of the window for any length of time. The night was soundless. There seemed to be nobody in their world, not even animals. They gave up looking out on this wasteland.

Charles burrowed a hole in the hay and stripped off his trousers and the sweater. He grabbed the sweater again and used it as a pillow. His body soon warmed up the cocoon he had created and he started to drift off to sleep. Claire, meanwhile, was looking dreamily in the distance. He could see her profile framed by the window. From time to time she ran her hands through her blond hair and then let it fall again over her shoulders.

That was the last thing he noticed as he drifted off to sleep. Then he felt a cool hand stroke the back of his neck. At the same time he heard a bird singing outside. It was such a melodious sound. It dispelled his gloomy memories of the nightscape he had left behind. It was still dark but morning was approaching and there was a fresh and friendly breeze in the air.

He turned and realised that his burrow had been changed. Next to him in a communal straw enclave was Claire, her head resting on his sweater and just inches from him. He turned towards her and saw that she had still the healthy glow of sleep about her. Her face was smiling and her eyes were inviting.

The hands moved from his back to his chest and gently stroked him. The languid, wistful movement was soothing and exciting. The smell of her hair, the cleanliness of the hay and the perfume of her body blended together erotically. The warmth of her body and the moist caress of the hay burrow pushed them together. The tempting and timid glow of early morning light drifted over them. In that mixture of smell, heat and light their senses awoke as they drew together.

Their few bits of clothing interrupted this pleasure but did not reduce it. The gentle smoothness of her body came through the material. In any case they soon rid themselves of that inconvenience. Their bodies, now liberated, moved together. They relished in the feel of skin and hay.

He made love to her for the first time since a long ago day in

Barbados. Then her body had been warm and enquiring, friendly and comforting. Now it was still gentle and soft, but there was urgency, a keen desire and a longing that he had not sensed before. Her body arched as she sought him out. She drew up her legs to welcome him more. She clung to him as if she never wanted the new closeness to be over.

Her movements carried him to greater desire. Then it was over. Then there was quiet and peace bar the heaviness of their breath and the occasional rustle of the hay. Their sense of the world outside slowly returned. Their bodies regretfully parted. They were still together for they could not bear to separate so soon.

Her voice was as soft and gentle as she had been, "I should have met you long ago. We could have gone to my farm together. Now we can only make love every now and again." She became wistful, "And that will be every few years. For most of the time we will be friends, just family friends. Then, maybe, we'll be lovers again for a passing moment. This can't be more than that. It wouldn't last. It wouldn't work."

He sensed he knew what she meant, the beauty of the moment had struck him as much as her. He knew this was different. It could not be mimicked or equalled unless desire, situation and circumstance repeated themselves in a different environment with as little premeditation as had occurred that morning.

They dressed slowly. This was no normal affair. It would last in their minds for a long time. This was a fleeting insight into the intensity of passion, the strength of desire and the power of physical love. Dressed, they looked out at the milky sky. It was a pale colour, with long thin streaks of cloudy white brushing over it and falling to the earth. The sun, a slow burning ball of distant light, crept over the horizon. It made an imprint on the fields around, having moved slowly across the hills in its search for life. It seemed to burst into a momentary intensity, until, assured of its survival, it lapsed into a pleasured serenity with the world around it.

The spell needed to be broken. The moment had passed. They had to return to their task. They picked up their few possessions and moved to the car parked below. Charles opened the door to their refuge, gun in hand and careful in case any intruder was about. But all was quiet and peaceful as they drove back to the road and left the barn behind in the lonely solitude of their secret.

They drove down into Geneva and parked near the centre. They picked up their bags and selected a modest hotel where their slightly bedraggled appearance would not be out of character. Nor would the early hour of their arrival be a problem as long as they showed willing to pay for the privilege.

They went up to their room. The bed dominated it, more due to the size of the room than its own scale. But they had no intention of ruining the day by seeking out each other's bodies so soon after the uniqueness of their recent communion. They stripped off their clothing and headed for the bathroom where they showered with each other. It was the final rite in a celebration that had started with the hint of dawn. It refreshed their bodies and minds as they returned fully to the evil world of Di Maglio.

They breakfasted in their room for it was just after nine. They waited another hour and then called the office. Jacqui was at her phone and immediately asked about Juliet.

"We know where she is but we had no chance of rescuing her. We know who took her. We're in Geneva."

"Oh, my God. It was him. He did it. He would even harm his granddaughter to get his own way. This time he's gone too far. When we have her back, he leaves our life for good." Then, with a bitterness and brutality that shook them, she added, "And the only way we'll achieve that is when he's dead."

Ignoring her anger, Charles said, "We're finding it difficult to know how we can get through to Juliet. They don't know we're here."

She said, "I'm the only one who can get there and get her back. We have to swap places. One of us is needed here and the other has to get Juliet. You return. I'll meet up with Claire and we'll both go to the compound. I can use the injury as a cover. You can insist I take refuge. We'll use the baby as an excuse if he seems too suspicious, although I'd rather not tell him at the moment. But it's a good fallback. After all, Rastinov was the cause of that miscarriage I had in France; I could be petrified it would happen again. He'll fall for that as a story."

"All right. We considered that but felt it could be too dangerous. I hadn't thought of taking Claire as well as a further insider. I'll check the flights from Geneva. We can meet at Heathrow. You could catch the plane I arrive on."

He explained all to Claire. She smiled, "I thought she was being a bit broody. I had wondered if she were pregnant. She seemed dreamy at times. That was out of character. I wonder if I'll be, too."

"What do you mean?"

"I could be pregnant. It wasn't planned today. I don't go around sleeping with every man I meet. I didn't prepare for it. Don't be concerned, the chances are not too high. It's just possible. And I won't cause trouble."

She kissed him, "And Jacqui must never know. It's a bit like you and Maria. You don't sleep together without reason. You need each other at times. It makes you alive again for others. It takes away the sadness of events you'd rather never happened. Some people are like that. I am. Maria is. And you are. We know that. And we understand it. That's why we'll not let others into the secret. It would be wrong, they couldn't understand."

So with the thought of that bizarre and unwelcome possibility, Charles left Claire at Geneva's immaculate airport and joined Jacqui in the sterile alleyways of London's Heathrow. When he saw her, she was pale. Her arm was in a sling and her step was slower than usual.

"Don't look so worried. It hurts a bit and I lost quite a bit of blood. But it'll make everything more convincing. We should, though, make the call now."

"No. I have to let you arrive in Geneva first. We want you to join up with Claire before he sees you. Otherwise, your father could send someone. He'd then know that Claire was already there. We've also changed the car. We had to in case the old one had been noticed. Claire will have gone shopping and she'll have some clothes. So you two should pass scrutiny. In any event your father has no reason to doubt her loyalty."

They kissed and he felt a pang at her departure. He knew she was right. She had to go out on her own. "I'll join you at the weekend. That'll be normal. Just try to find Juliet this week and we can see if we can spring her later."

She nodded but Charles was not convinced. If the opportunity came, they would act. It was right they should. They would have no other option. But he needed the delusion that they would be in no danger. And so he stuck with his self-deception as they parted. She made her way to her departing flight and he headed to the car, to home and then the bank where preparations really did demand his attention.

The journey into London allowed him to reflect on the events ahead of him. They needed to move quickly on the take-over and build up some more of the loans with the different companies they had targeted. They could move money around the system without trace and without effort. They could ensure that the movements were authorised by people other than themselves. More important, they would be people who were unaware of the plot, but whose own accounts would benefit sufficiently from their actions to raise the required suspicions.

They would also get some of the complex trades in place. That would be done through Stephens and would be easy to place at his door. He also needed to check with his father that all was progressing to plan on his side. In the unpredictable world of finance, all seemed to be working in their favour. It was their personal world that was threatened. Di Maglio again was the cause, but this would be his last chance. And they needed to be careful, the stakes now were very high. One mistake would be disastrous.

Charles arrived at the bank to be greeted by the Honourable James. His face was flushed with excitement. He had taken a call from the Bank of England and they had indicated their keenness to help accelerate the take-over. It was obvious that they'd heard from the Americans. Everyone had swallowed their story; hook, line and sinker. The Honourable James was leaving for New York himself that very evening to see the resident idiot-elect, the new chief executive of their prospective US operations.

"He seems such a damn good chap," enthused the Honourable James in the voice he reserved for people of his own class. "We're going to meet over a drink and go on to dinner. He's sorted a place out for me at his club. Says it's much more comfortable than the hotels. Damn good chap. Good find. Sounds tops."

And with that gush of absolute irrelevance, their number one stool pigeon fussed back into his office to double check with his secretary his tickets, his cars, his reservations and all the other trivia that the unseasoned traveller finds indispensable for the smallest of inconsequential trips.

Charles then called Di Maglio. "Why didn't you come with Jacqui? She's not well," snarled Di Maglio.

"I took her to the airport," retorted Charles. "She had Claire in any case. We couldn't both be out of the office today. Too many things need to be done on the other deal. In any event, I need to be here for when the kidnappers reveal their hand. They said they'd contact me and I waited for them at the cottage, but there was nothing. The strange thing is that they didn't look Russian. They didn't look anything actually. And thanks for the nanny. She was a great find!"

"She didn't let you down. I know her and her family. She must have been kidnapped alongside Juliet. Don't give me your shit."

Charles was staggered that he'd try to pull that one off and responded in kind. "Your whole organisation's becoming a fucking disaster. Your driver screws up. Your nanny screws up. And you can't do anything about it. The cops get to the driver first and you become useless. The nanny fouled up. She was in cahoots with the kidnappers. She worked with them. And you make out otherwise to protect your inflated bloody ego."

Di Maglio swore violently. Charles was not surprised, the gist was clear. If Jacqui and Charles agreed to take on his Empire, then he could get it back on track. The fact that he was old and wanted to retire was the cause of all the troubles. And, if they would work with him, Di Maglio ranted on, "Then Rastinov will opt out. He would be scared of a united organisation. His strength is in our disarray. He's no fool even if he's a bastard. He'd let Juliet loose. Not even a man like him is going to harm her. They'd drop her somewhere and disappear. We need them to see us united and the organisation in firm ownership."

And he went on in the same vein, "The people I employ aren't angels. I don't go for boy scouts. Of course, the place gets scary if you say you're going. Everyone fights if they're not run through fear. Fear's what makes the organisation disciplined. Who's afraid of a guy who's about to quit?"

"Find Juliet," shouted Charles in the end. "Then we take over the bank. But nothing else is on my radar for the foreseeable future. That's enough."

He hoped that gave his father-in-law some hope they would cede in time. If Di Maglio relaxed, it improved Jacqui's chances. Charles wondered if she would find Juliet. She knew the compound well and would be able to see where security had changed. They would have hid Juliet somewhere on, or perhaps near, the compound. Di Maglio himself would have kept well away from her. He would have kept her away from his normal henchmen. It would spoil his plans if anyone knew he was holding her or ever realised he had had her kidnapped.

Charles spoke to Jacqui. They played out the charade they had started and that allowed him also to give an account of his discussion with her father. Then he turned his mind back to the scam. They met lawyers and the others you require when you make a take-over. Then he worked through details on some strategies with his father, who had good control over Stephens and all his complex trades. That relieved Charles, he found that area difficult to follow. This was where he needed his father's skills, honed as it was by years of study during his spare time in his former banking days.

The week progressed. The Honourable James was satisfied. The regulators were satisfied. Giovanni and Charles agreed all the documents.

The trust deed for the Di Maglio holding was drawn up. It was now in favour of all their children, whenever they were born. As the weekend approached, the kidnappers had still not sought contact. Charles headed for the late Friday flight to Geneva and the hope of finding little Juliet.

CHAPTER ELEVEN

A Di Maglio driver was waiting as Charles exited customs at Geneva. He had driven with him before. He was a thickset man with little charm and no conversation. Like many of the Di Maglio entourage, he was a lifer. He had graduated from pimping to the extortion rackets and now to his trusted position as driver. He would have two classical key loyalties. He would obey without question and he would kill without compunction.

Charles sometimes wondered how Jacqui had emerged unscathed from this dysfunctional background. Yet, that was a strange characteristic of many of the Mafia women. Jacqui, Claire or Maria were all basically soft, they could be ruthless to a point, but that was simply to achieve their goals. Claire and Maria would work for Di Maglio, but out of a desire for wealth. Once they had achieved that, would they throw away the skills they had honed in their temporary profession and revert to their truer and better natures.

Charles entered the house with his luggage. He had, in London, bought some rather expensive and highly sophisticated equipment. It would allow him to check out the house at night. He hoped it would let him find where they held Juliet. Jacqui and Claire hadn't been able to trace her so far. Otherwise, they would have somehow got him a message, if only to tell him to stay away.

He had talked to Jacqui each and every day. They had pretended to wait for news on Juliet but none had arrived. They continued to pretend they were worried about her whereabouts. In reality they were. But it was more about her exact whereabouts than anything else. And they firmly believed she would be unharmed. That calmed them down. But Di Maglio mustn't suspect that they knew more about his plot than they made out.

The house was quiet and Charles walked to the rooms that he knew were reserved for them. They were on the second floor in the so-called East Wing guest suite. There were four large rooms in that area. Each had its own bathroom and an even larger lounge area. He walked to theirs. It had the best view of distant mountains.

On a clear day one could make out the peak of Mont Blanc. Today was such a day.

A door to the corridor opened and Claire appeared. "Charles, Jacqui's with the doctor at the moment. She's in the pool area. He's making her do some exercises. It's just physio. She should be back in the next ten or fifteen minutes. The doctor was late and she didn't expect you so soon."

"I'll head over there," he said. "I'll just drop off my case."

He walked into the room and looked at Mont Blanc. He felt comforted by the familiar sight. Claire had followed him and motioned him towards the bathroom. He went there and switched on the shower and the taps.

"What is it?"

"We can't trace her. We haven't looked everywhere. We can't do that without raising suspicion. Your father-in-law acts well. He seems concerned. Jacqui is more worried than she made out. But she's holding up."

"What about you?" he gave her a questioning look.

"I'm fine. Look, I'm not due for another couple of days. I can only tell you then. The risks were not that high. There were risks. That's all. But I promise nobody will know who the father was. I'll find a way to cover up if I have to. There's nothing to be done about that for the moment. What are we going to do about Juliet?"

"I've bought some of the latest detection gear. It is electronic and has a range of up to three hundred yards or so. It is radar based and not detectable. It sends back signals of the contents of any room and has been programmed to tell the shape of an object and also define certain key ones."

"Which ones can it tell?"

"Things like a bed, cupboard or table. But it also identifies humans by weight and height and so on. We'll try it out tonight. It takes a shot of each room and then stores it in a mini computer. We'll go floor section by floor section. The shorter I keep the running time, the lower the risks of detection. Mind you, the claim is that it cannot be traced. It's just that time increases the risks of any possible detection."

"Let's hope it's better than our attempts at detection so far. Are you going to hide it? You'll have dinner downstairs tonight. Someone's bound to check out your luggage."

"True. I'll hide it easily though. It's only a small thing. All miniaturised."

The door opened and Jacqui walked in. Her arm was out of a sling and she looked much better now. They talked but were conscious that they might be bugged. Their distrust of her father had really plummeted to new depths. Although it would not be the first time he had bugged them, they had thought such fears would be in the past. Claire suggested they go for a walk. It was a pleasant enough night for that despite the cold.

Out in the open, walking along the still green lawns of the compound, they talked more openly.

"We've checked everywhere in the house other than the West wing. That part is too well guarded. It always has been. It's the nerve centre of his Empire. I don't think she's here. I think she's somewhere else."

"She's in the vicinity. Otherwise, they wouldn't have come here. I suspect he feels he can keep her safe here. He's got enough people. Perhaps we'll need to scan the houses around here. Tonight I'll do the West wing. We better also screen the attics. Are there any cellars?"

Claire nodded, "Yes, but I wandered round them the other night. There's nothing there but wine and stores."

"What about false walls or hidden mezzanines?

"I know the place too well," said Jacqui. "I would have noticed."

"They could have been there always."

She shook her head. "I played here as a kid. I was always alone. I explored every corner of the place other than the West wing. That's always been taboo. I can't believe there is anything I don't know."

"When will you need to return? If you stay here too long, he'll get suspicious."

"I could stretch it another week. But anything longer would be suspicious. Have you got to be back on Monday?"

"I have to meet the Honourable James on Sunday night. I need to fly out to New York on Monday morning. I'll fly back Tuesday."

There was a bench in the grounds in the shadow of a large pine tree. Jacqui sat down on it and looked wearily over the long expanse of well-trimmed and tended lawn. The borders were cut back and flowerless at this time of year. The trees had already long lost their leaves. The whole garden seemed to be mournful. She shook her head.

"Charles, tell me the state of play in the office. I need to think of something else. It'll clear my mind."

He sat down beside her. Claire decided to wander off to a pond nearby and watched the ducks swim around.

He recounted the latest news. "We've started lending to the phoney companies. I have about half a billion of loans to them and we have already passed all the money through the banking system and into our secret accounts. It will be totally untraceable. We've targeted six companies so far and in four cases we've had fun getting the signatures onto phoney instructions.

Lord Dunkillin signed off on two of them and then promptly transferred the money to the Dunkillin Trust in Liechtenstein. The money then vanishes from there. Ffinch Farquar signed a couple more. He pushed the money to a couple of the companies. His wife is on the board of them and she was asked to sign some papers. She's unwittingly siphoned off the money from the company to an account in another name in Cayman. She doesn't realise it but the account is in her name. It's disappeared from there too. Staff who didn't see anything strange about them did the others.

Giovanni also did around three quarters of a billion for us through the American arm to make sure the loans do not start with the purchase. That would be a bit too suspicious! But the good news is that the proceeds are also with us and not, as I had feared, in one of your father's secret accounts.

So we've made our first billion or so and the bank will assume it'll make about twenty to forty million a year in interest margin on the loans. The interest is payable annually and so, unless something happens to scare the credit guys, nobody will know it won't be paid until twelve months time. And that'll be far too late."

"What about Stephens and your father?"

"They've been writing these strange deals to a couple of shadow organisations we have. The way it's done, the bank has received several million of commissions. The deals look as if the bank has no problems as we are valuing the things incorrectly. They're crazy deals and in reality the bank is already losing around a hundred million on them. When we're ready, we'll crystallise those losses. The bank takes those and we get the profit in our accounts. But we've now trimmed our sights in this area back slightly and are targeting just two billion of shortfalls. That will only come about after we sell the bank to the public."

"When will that be? Have we a firm date in mind yet?"

"I'm trying to accelerate everything as much as I possibly can. The prospectus is being prepared. We want to complete the bid. That should be through in a couple of weeks. We'll wait for the six monthly figures in May. Then we'll float in late June and go bust in August at the earliest, maybe a couple of months later."

"What about the investment scam?"

"That's progressing well. My father's doing the usual job of accumulating the shares and making sure he doesn't move the market. For instance, we're buying a couple of shell companies. Both are quoted on strange little stock exchanges and are really worthless. With careful manipulation, we can change them into hot property and get their prices soaring. Once that happens, we'll get the US funds to buy them from us. As the companies cost us hardly anything to acquire, anything we sell for is almost entirely profit. It's all going like a dream."

"If only we had Juliet, everything would be perfect."

"Tonight we scan the house. Otherwise tomorrow we search the neighbourhood."

Jacqui shivered. "Come on, you're cold. Let's get you back inside. I'll have to meet your father. I suppose we'll have to have a nightcap with him. And he'll expect us for dinner tomorrow," said Charles.

"No. I said I needed a break. We'll go into Geneva. Claire's going to stay here. I need to be with you. I want to be alone."

Charles put his arm around her and hugged her gently. "We'll find her. And then we'll deal with your father."

She looked grimly at him. "And we will deal with him."

The three of them returned to the house. They went to the lounge where Di Maglio sat in splendid isolation. He did not look a happy man. The first thing he did was turn on Charles.

"What the fuck do you think you're doing in London when your kid's missing and your wife's shot? I've a good mind to keep Jacqui here and kick you out."

They thought instantly that Di Maglio must be suspicious. He obviously wanted to rile Charles. He needed to react but he had to keep control of himself. Charles turned to him in fury. The hatred was evident and it was not make believe. But he had control of his temper. There was no way that he was going to blow this one. "First of all, get one thing into your head. You don't own Jacqui. You don't own me. We asked for your help. We asked it in two ways. Jacqui needed peace and quiet. We thought she was safer here than in London. We asked you to find Juliet. We thought you were at least good for that, but no. You haven't found one thing."

"Look you," he yelled, but Charles cut him off.

"We'll leave tomorrow. Juliet is our concern. You forget this is your fault. You've put her at risk with your drugs, your extortion, your pimps and your prostitutes. You live with shit and contamination all about you. We don't need you. We can cut out the bank deal. I'll do that happily."

"You'll go ahead with that deal. After your crawling up to the regulators, they'd crucify us if you dropped out," roared Di Maglio.

"And why was I in London? But if you can't find Juliet, I'll call it off. I'll tell the world that she's been kidnapped. I'll say it's because of Mafia links to the banks. I'll say the Russian Mafia wants control of your US operations. You'll have a worthless asset on your hands. There'll be a run on the banks. Find Juliet or we reconsider the deal."

"I don't believe you. The rest of your scam then fails."

"No, the rest of the scam is deferred. I can wait. I can do it later. I'm young enough. I'm not a warped old man like you."

"You don't talk to me like that," Di Maglio bellowed. This time he had really lost it.

"You think how you talk to me. When you're civil, I'll be civil. When you're useful and get your scum to find Juliet, I'll be polite. But till then keep out of my life and we'll keep out of yours. We leave tomorrow. And we leave for good."

With that Charles stalked out and Jacqui followed in tow. They walked along the hall and up the stairs to their room. She was trembling. Charles whispered in her ear, "I had to do that. That will have frightened him. He needed to be thrown off balance. If we find Juliet here today we snatch her and leave anyway. If we don't, we need to scour the neighbourhood, as she could be close by. For that we need to go."

"When will you put the scanner over the house?"

"I need everyone to be in bed as otherwise it's difficult to operate. I would guess around one or two in the morning. I'll do it from the entrance to our room. If this place is bugged the bugs are more likely to be in the centre of the room and the lounge than elsewhere."

They got into bed and watched television until around one. There was a decent film on cable and that helped pass the time. Charles lent over and kissed Jacqui before picking up the case and walking over to the little lobby by the door. He sat on a chair there and unlocked the case. The bedroom light was on and that gave him enough light.

He would need to work in the dark to avoid the reflection of the light on the miniature screen. He carefully followed his notes as he set up the scanner. It was a delicate device and the latest in high tech. He had had it well explained. He pressed the on button and it worked.

"Clever guys these NASA engineers," he muttered to himself as he switched off the light and started to move the sensor around the house. He went through one floor at a time.

The ground floor was quiet. There was nobody around. The place was deserted. He moved up a flight to the floor below them. He found people but they were all adults. The machine identified their body mass and he carefully eliminated them. The floor completed, the machine checked the floor area against the floor below. It tallied. There were no secret rooms. He had missed nothing.

He sent the scanner again around the secret West Wing, for that section was only two storeys high. He had hoped they'd find signs of Juliet there, but no luck. There was a mass of electronic equipment in that part of the house and two people sitting at monitors. But otherwise it was empty and quiet.

He moved on to the third floor. The North Wing was Di Maglio's quarters. It also housed his people. Again he drew a blank. There were people there but no child. He moved to their Wing. He checked their room and could make out Jacqui in the bed and him on the scanner. He crossed the hall and realised he was in Claire's room. She seemed to be asleep. She was alone. He moved through the other two suites but they were both empty.

He moved up into the roof area but that was totally deserted. He sent the scanner outside and checked out the few outhouses and garages but there was no sign of Juliet. She had either been moved away since their arrival or she had never arrived at the house.

That could only mean that she was in a safe house in the neighbourhood. There was no doubt that they had followed the car to here. And there was no doubt that the car had contained Juliet.

He went back to the bed. Jacqui looked, but she already knew. She bit her lip as he shook his head. Her head leant on his shoulder.

"We scour the region tomorrow. We'll go for a drive in the morning. We can always take one of the cars here. It won't look strange after the row with your father. Let's leave early. We can skip breakfast and head off before they realise that we're going. I'd have liked to take Claire with us but that may look suspicious. She doesn't know about the row yet. It's useful if he trusts her."

They slept an uneasy sleep that night. Charles kept thinking of Juliet. And now the nagging doubts came to mind. Perhaps they had made a mistake after all? Perhaps they had failed to see something whilst they were in the barn? Perhaps Di Maglio was telling the truth and Juliet had been kidnapped by the Russians?

Then he thought of the strange effects. They had had no calls. Di

Maglio had had no calls. It was now more than a week. That was long. Usually, the calls would have come as they got really anxious. In the case of kidnapping a child, that would be two or three days.

Charles could not identify any Di Maglio activity. Normally, there would have been a meeting to review things. There would be reports on police activity. It was impossible that there was so little going on. And it was unlikely that he would keep any information from them if he really were looking for her.

In the end, Charles dozed off. Jacqui woke him. It was just after seven. They both got ready and made their way downstairs. The house was quiet. The kitchen was empty and Jacqui quickly made them a coffee. They drank it standing up. She knew where the car keys were and they took one for a Range Rover.

They headed out. A man appeared and Charles recognised him as a Di Maglio driver. He queried where they were going. "We're going for a drive," Jacqui said and walked past him. He headed back into the house. No doubt he would make a report to Di Maglio. He might wonder why Charles was carrying a large briefcase. It held work papers but they covered the miniature scanner.

Charles jumped into the driving seat and Jacqui sat next to him. The car roared into life and he headed for the outside gate. He pressed the remote control button on the dashboard and the gates opened wide. But, from ten yards away, he noticed that they were closing again. Someone had over-ridden the controls. He accelerated and squeezed the car through, with a grinding of the door on Jacqui's side as it skimmed the metal of the closing gates.

He turned left and headed down the narrow road that led to the main route for Geneva. There were no houses here. They turned left at the bottom of the lane. There the road widened but it was a winding section of road that cut between the wooded slopes of the hills. He turned a bend and almost hit a car coming in the opposite direction.

Neither of them had expected another car on the road at that time of the morning. They both swerved away from each other at the last moment. Charles hit the verge but the four-wheel drive took that in its stride and, after bumping once or twice, he pulled the car back onto the road. The other car had skidded and then also straightened out. It was disappearing round the corner.

As Charles thought that was close but no damage was done, Jacqui cried out, "It was the nanny."

Charles slammed on the brakes. "What do you mean?"

"I saw her in the car, in the passenger seat. It was the nanny. I recognised her. I don't know if she saw us."

Charles reversed onto the verge and spun the wheel round. He jammed his foot down on the accelerator and the car jerked forward. The road was too narrow and windy to allow fast speeds but he accelerated nevertheless. They had to catch up with the car before it got to the compound. Charles then remembered that there were some houses just beyond the place where they had turned left. He wondered if they were heading there.

The car screeched round the bend on the wrong side of the road. Charles pulled it back over again. Jacqui was looking pale in the seat next to him. She was holding onto her bag. Her knuckles were white.

"Get your gun ready. We may have to shoot out their tyres."

"Juliet could be in the car," she screamed back at him.

He had not thought that. All the same, she had her gun ready.

"Bend forward at the next straight stretch of road and get me mine. It's in the leg holster. My right leg."

There was no chance for her to do that just then for they were swerving left and right as they screeched round the bends on the road. They were betting their luck on two things. First, they hoped that nobody would be coming in the opposite direction at that time of morning. Second, they hoped the people in the other car hadn't recognised them and were driving normally. If that was the case, and they didn't hit someone coming the other way, they would catch them up in the next few minutes.

They hit a straight piece of road. Jacqui lent forward and pulled up Charles' trouser leg. She took the gun from its holster and wedged it under his thigh. He saw she had pushed herself back in her seat, her feet straining against the floorboards as he spun into the next bend.

"Ahead of us," she shouted. The car they had nearly hit was there. It was just thirty or forty yards ahead of them. It hadn't noticed them yet, or at least it hadn't reacted. They needed to get next to it to allow Jacqui a good look at the car. If Juliet wasn't in it, Charles would force it off the road. There was no way he could trail it without being noticed.

He accelerated again into a bend and then out of it. They were now just a few yards behind. He powered the engine forward as they got to the next bend. He was fully on the wrong side of the road. He was almost alongside the car. He saw two cyclists ahead and jammed the brakes, wrenching the wheel to pull the car behind his target. One of the cyclists was wobbling dangerously as they passed. He saw him fall off in his rear mirror. The other was just looking back at them in amazement.

They then went into another bend and again he pulled to the other side to overtake the car. The other car, alerted to the danger, was going as fast as it could on the winding road. Its rear wheels were swaying dangerously as they drew alongside again. This time they pulled next to it just as they both entered a blind bend. This time, though, luck was on their side and there was nobody coming the other way.

"Back's empty," yelled Jacqui. "Nanny and man are in the front. There's nobody else."

Charles saw the road on the far side went into a narrow ditch. There was a slope down to it as well. He pulled the Range Rover into the side of the car and forced it gradually off the road. The driver fought against him but his car was lighter and less stable. Charles saw his wheels were inches from the ditch and rammed him again. The car swerved over and then, in a cloud of dust, tipped to one side. The roof was held by the slope. The wheels on the far side were in the ditch. The ones on the near side were in the air.

Jacqui leapt out before Charles had stopped. She stumbled a bit and then ran over to the car. Her gun was at the ready. He jumped after her. There was no sign from the car other than a terrified sobbing of a girl.

Charles pulled open the door. The driver was unconscious. Blood was pouring from a cut on his head. He must have hit the windscreen. Charles lent over to him, ignoring the petrified girl other than to cover her with his gun. He went through the driver's pockets and took the gun that he had expected him to be carrying. He slipped it into his pocket. The girl stirred.

"Don't you dare move or I'll shoot," he snarled with all the anger and hatred that he felt towards her. Jacqui was right. The trembling girl in front of him was none other than their former nanny. He checked the front of the car and felt under the seats. There were no more guns.

"Climb out of the car," he ordered the girl. She knew better than to disobey. He undid the man's seat belt and pulled him out too. He checked him over again while Jacqui covered the girl. He would be all right once he came round. He'd hit his head, but that was all. Charles dragged him to their car and placed him in the rear seat, then took off his belt and tied his hands and one leg together with it to immobilise him. Jacqui was glaring at the girl and saying, "Tell me where Juliet is."

The girl shook her head, "I don't know. I don't know."

"Get her in our car," Charles said. "Let's get off the road and away from the car before anyone passes by."

Jacqui moved the girl to their car while Charles quickly cleaned off any prints he may have made. Door handle. Dashboard. Seat pockets. Storage boxes. Seat area. He kicked the door shut again and went back to the jeep. Then, as an afterthought, he went back. He opened the door with the rag he had used to get rid of the fingerprints. He took some matches that he had noticed by the driver's side.

Opening the petrol cap, he stuffed the rag into it and set it alight. It was burning and he ran the twenty yards to their car. Jacqui had realised what he was doing and the engine was running. He slammed the car into gear and drove on. Just as they rounded the bend, there was an explosion and he caught the flash in the rear mirror. Then the turn in the road obscured everything but a trail of smoke that rose from the destruction of the car.

He turned off the road on a small country path and followed it into some dense trees. He stopped. He ordered the girl out. The driver was groaning and he had overheard her asking him anxiously if he was all right. He guessed it was her father. He now had a way of getting her to talk.

He pulled out his gun and calmly shot the man in the leg. He chose the fleshy part. It didn't look nice but would cause no lasting damage. She screamed when her father cried out in terror and pain.

"Next time it will be his knee. Then his stomach. After that I'll target the other knee. I might then add another bullet to his collection. And I'll carry on doing it till you tell us where Juliet is.

"Once you've told us we all go there and, if she's not there, I kill him. If you double cross us, and there are others there who cause us trouble, I kill you both. I'm a good shot and so is Jacqui. So make your choices. Live, let him live or you both die. Choose. And fast."

She hesitated again. She was torn between fear of them and the consequences of any action she took. Charles aimed at the father again.

"Your child is safe. I wouldn't hurt her. She's in a house along the road. She's with my mother. She's well looked after," the nanny sobbed.

"OK. We pick her up. You know what'll happen if you cheat us. Get back in."

She scrambled back next to the injured man and Charles told her to direct them. He drove back onto the road and followed it past the bend they had taken from Di Maglio's place. She directed them to a house that was about a mile further on. There were no cars there. It looked peaceful.

Jacqui got out, gun in hand. "Leave this to me just in case my father's people are here." That was sensible as they would all recognise her.

Charles ducked out of view, but covered the groaning and bleeding man in the back with his gun. The girl looked on, crying.

Jacqui came back moments later. She was carrying Juliet. A crying woman was begging her to do something but she shook her off angrily.

"You sort yourself out. Get out of my way. If my father kills you and your family, that's your problem. We didn't ask you to get involved. Now get lost."

Juliet was clinging to her. She saw Charles. "Daddy, you came," she sobbed. The picture in the lane in Sussex flashed back to his mind. The look of disbelief on the little girl's face as she thought he wasn't going to help her.

"Of course, I did, sweetheart," he called to her. "Don't worry, Mummy and I won't ever let you down."

They told the ex nanny to get out. They told her and the woman to pull out the wounded man. "And give me my belt back while you're at it." The poor guy was still tied up. They pulled him out. They begged for mercy. They begged them to see that Di Maglio would be merciful. They were frightened. If they hadn't been, and if Juliet hadn't been there, Charles suspected he would have killed them.

As he started the car and it moved slowly forward, the ex nanny ran to them and begged one last time for help. Jacqui looked at her with disgust. "Never, ever come near me again. This will be nothing to what I'll do next time." And with that she shot the girl in her stomach. Charles drove off. Juliet didn't seem to notice. As the bullet hit the girl, she had clutched her stomach in astonishment. Juliet hadn't seen her fall on the ground in pain. They knew the wound would not be dangerous. Jacqui's gun would not cause a large wound. But it would be painful and Jacqui was right to give her the warning. More importantly, it was a warning to Di Maglio, just as the father's shooting had been.

"You have your passport?"

"Of course, I never leave it behind in a foreign country."

"We go to the airport?"

"I guess so. But don't go to Geneva. That's too dangerous. If my father has wind of this he'll try to cut us off."

"We can take the back streets to Geneva and then get a train. There's a regular service to Zurich or Milan. We can chose when we get there."

"Good idea. Let's move. They'll never think of the station. At least not immediately. They may wonder if we decided to take the car once they find we haven't appeared. But in the end it'll be found. I'll leave it in the centre."

They drove at break-neck speeds through the small roads to the outskirts of Geneva. Charles saw a taxi rank and pulled into a parking lot opposite. It was empty on a Sunday morning and he left the car on the ground floor. He picked up Juliet and his case. Jacqui got out.

"I'll leave the keys. With a bit of luck it'll be stolen and confuse your father more."

A taxi was available immediately and took them to the station. They checked the trains. One for Zurich left in a matter of minutes. They bought their tickets and then they were happily ensconced in the first class carriage and on their way there.

"The only risk we have is that the car is found too soon and they then know what we did next. The taxi rank nearby is the obvious place. We could be traced through the driver. But I'd be surprised if things moved that fast."

Jacqui shook her head. "Father will need to talk to his people. This is a turn he wouldn't have expected. He'll have no plans for it. He'll contact us, but he knows it's going to be tough. We know he kidnapped Juliet. We now know he must have been behind the incidents in the US. We know his people shot me. He must be getting worried. He'll think you may also carry out your threat about the bank."

"That places us in danger. Although he knows I am always careful, he may be frightened that I've left some papers somewhere safe. I did it before when we had the troubles in France."

They sat quietly and took turns to comfort Juliet. Jacqui questioned her gently. It was evident that she had been well treated. She had not seen Di Maglio. That didn't surprise them. She had been told they'd been called away on business. That was a tolerable excuse as they had left her before. But she had sensed something was wrong. She had evidently been worried rather than scared. She clung to whoever was holding her at the time.

They arrived in Zurich's main station a few hours later. They established there was an early afternoon flight and they caught it to Heathrow. Charles called Maria on her mobile and explained what had happened. "Di Maglio called already. He wanted you to phone him when you returned. I'll get Douglas to pick you up."

In the early evening they returned. They were back home. They felt safe.

"We don't call my father till later," said Jacqui. "Have you got to get together with the Honourable James?"

"I'll do it on the phone. But I have to head to the States tomorrow morning. We should contact Claire and get her back over here."

"That may be difficult. She works for my father. She's loyal to both of us. We'll play that by ear. Let's talk security with Maria. But, first, let's get Juliet to bed."

So she occupied herself with Juliet while Charles made arrangements for the States. All the time, he knew they were going to have tough times ahead. They had a new enemy. And nobody enjoyed that if the adversary was Di Maglio.

CHAPTER TWELVE

He picked up the phone again and dialled Di Maglio. He was put through to him immediately.

"You think I had something to do with the kidnap. I've been set up. I knew nothing about it. They wanted you to think it was me. I swear it must have been the Russians."

"What about the nanny and her parents?"

"We've dealt with them. They're dead. They betrayed me. They were offered money and new identities to help on the kidnap. They dealt only with middle men."

"You're capable of killing them if it suits your plans. But you could also make them disappear. I don't believe you. I don't trust you. I'll use none of your people. Prove yourself by clearing up this mess and keeping it away from me and my family."

"Can I speak to Jacqui?"

"She's with Juliet. Just do as I say. We're not in the mood to be sociable. We don't believe you. You're in this up to your neck. I can't totally understand your game plan but I know what your end game is. You want us to run your operations. You can't bear to think of them ending. You'll do anything for that. I've news for you. We'll take the banks but nothing else. So get off our backs and re-plan without us."

Charles put the phone down on him. That was not the safest of strategies. Di Maglio could react violently. But there was an outside chance that he'd come to his senses and rid them of his business and its problems. Charles went through what he'd done with Jacqui. She thought it was the only way.

"I'll not take his calls. Let's freeze him out. He doesn't yet know I'm pregnant. I didn't need to tell him in the end and so never did. Once he does he may come round easier. He likes being a grandfather. He's got that one bit of humanity left that a child seems to bring out."

With that cold dismissal of her father and the ready assessment of his warped nature, she came to Charles. Her arms went around his neck. Her body moved against his. She brushed warm and moist lips against him.

"Juliet's asleep. We should get an early night."

"I thought you were pregnant."

"I am. It's amazing I still am after the last week or so. But that doesn't mean that I am going to become celibate till next summer."

So they moved to their room. Juliet was fast asleep in the adjoining one. They switched on her alarm and shut their door to the world. Jacqui and Charles kissed each other for a long time. It was more than a week since they had last made love and they needed each other as only people who have been through such a trauma do.

She pressed herself against him and smiled, "If you think I'm going to send you away like this, you're mistaken."

She was wearing a long quilted dressing gown and he pulled it down her shoulders and kissed her neck. The bandage from the gunshot wound had been removed and there was now just a plaster. He kissed around it and gently ran his mouth over the bruises round the edges.

She lent forward and undid the buttons of his shirt. One by one they were opened. At each button he felt her hand move across his chest in a light circular motion that sent tremors of excitement through him. As she finally removed the shirt, she ran her fingers down his chest, this time grazing him with her nails in a way that made him shiver in pleasing anticipation.

She undid his belt and trousers, easing him out of the rest of his clothes in one smooth fast movement. She moved again towards him and kissed him on the chest before resting her head there as if to listen to his heart beating. She moved closer to him and they made their way under the sheet for warmth, comfort and solitude. They came together as they lay side by side. Their lips clung together. His arms clasped her back as she eagerly pushed against him; demanding and inquisitive; exciting and excitable.

They lay together for some time after. Gradually they felt their bodies slip into a mood of total contentment and relaxation. Gently, they slipped apart, but continued to hold each other. First they were in each other's arms, then hand in hand, and finally her head on his shoulder. Then, with one last, long, lingering kiss, they fell asleep. They were safe with each other. Harmony had returned.

The next day, the magic of the moment was still with them. They had experienced this so many times. The feelings changed. The moods were different. But the peril of their lifestyle pushed them to different peaks in their own lives and in their own physical longing. He would rather not have left. Maria would stay. Douglas would be there.

He had now also some special guards. He had arranged that with the Commander. They were not police but they were the Commander's own men. His job took him to areas where he used unusual methods. He, therefore, had some unconventional acquaintances for a policeman.

Charles left the house with Juliet and Jacqui waving at him from the window. He noticed the guards there, visible to a trained eye but not to the occasional passer-by or inquisitive glance. They were different from the usual Di Maglio people. These would be ex-members of the Special Air Services, the elite anti terrorist brigade of the British Forces. He was grateful for his friendship with Commander Delaney. He knew that Jacqui and Juliet would be safe, especially as Maria would also be with them.

The car sped to the airport and got him to his plane in plenty of time. He walked into the first class lounge and read the papers. The markets were quiet. Thankfully, there were no articles about anything related to their activities. That was excellent. It would have been the last thing they wanted. Suddenly a pair of hands covered his eyes; a perfume that he recognised immediately swept gently over him and a voice said softly, "Guess who?"

"Claire. What on earth are you doing here?"

"There was no point in staying in the compound. I didn't have a job when you upped and awayed. Tell me how you did it. How on earth did you find her? Di Maglio was furious. But I can tell you about that later."

Charles explained what happened. "Do you know what Di Maglio did to the people who held Juliet?"

"He was remarkably lenient. The father was beaten up for his stupidity. Otherwise they did nothing. The daughter had to see a doctor. Bullet in the stomach as punishment. Jacqui has a bit of the Mafia about her after all."

Charles noted again that Di Maglio had lied to him about these people. He had said he killed them. One more reason, if they needed it, for them never to believe a word that he said.

"But how exactly did Di Maglio react when he heard?"

"I was asleep still. It was about eight o' clock when he came storming into my room to see if I was there. He told me you had sneaked off with Jacqui. He thought I might have been involved. I played innocent. It was quite convincing. We then waited and about two hours later we got news of the car crash and the shooting. Somehow, the explosion had not been picked up on his monitors; it appears there were some faulty surveillance cameras in the area and that made him even madder. He went ape-shit with anger. He hadn't thought of sending extra cover to the house where Juliet was, as he thought he had it covered electronically. So he said he'd bluff it out with you."

"He tried, but it wasn't convincing."

"Anyway, I got up and was told to head back to New York. Di Maglio said he wasn't happy with my role. He said he didn't want me to work with you again. He said I was too close to you. That could lead me to betray his orders. He thought it better that I stayed clear of you all. He was giving me a warning. I'll need to be careful. So I put myself on this plane, as I knew you'd be on it. And here I am."

"Isn't that dangerous? What if he sees us together?"

"I'd be in trouble. I don't know what he'd do. In the old days he would have had me knee-capped or something as a minimum, perhaps even killed. But they have always been more lenient with women; they think women are weak. They'll say I was attracted to you and it was sex. That's always the usual reason for them. In any case, Di Maglio has softened up in recent years. I wouldn't be hurt much."

She shrugged her shoulders dismissively at the idea. Charles looked at her and smiled. He looked at the blond hair, the blue eyes, and the trim pleasant figure. He noticed, not for the first time, the slight breathlessness with which she talked. He wondered what she'd look like if she really were pregnant.

Somehow it was difficult to associate motherhood with her. He knew very little about her past. She always refused to talk about it. Jacqui thought she had started in the hotel side, but both Maria and Claire drew a veil over their earlier lives and how they got into Di Maglio's evil world.

"And how are you?"

"Well I got here early for the plane. The other thing hasn't happened yet. It was due yesterday. I'm usually quite regular. We'll have to wait."

They went over to the desk and arranged two seats side by side. The plane was then called almost immediately. On board they started talking again. Charles brought up the question of Di Maglio, despite her earlier casual dismissal of his reaction, for he was concerned at the likely reaction if she were found with him.

"Is Di Maglio going to cause you problems? Are you sure you're not running a big risk? We know he's aware we're all quite friendly. This conflict with him could turn out quite nasty."

"He knows I helped you follow the kidnappers. But that won't cause a problem. He didn't tell me what he was doing. I just tried to protect you all, but that was my role. He may wonder why I did not report in when we were on the road. There was no reason for a communications blackout. But I doubt he'll do anything about it. He'll be working out his next move. That's the sort of man he is."

"What will you do? What have you done for Di Maglio all these years? You've actually never told me how you got involved."

Charles knew he'd asked this before and been told that it was none of his business. But now he needed to know. After the night in the barn, it was imperative for him to know. This was not driven by idle curiosity. He wanted to understand how the past could affect the future. Claire appeared to realise this and revealed all.

"It's not hard to get involved. I was good at school. Good at sport. I could have gone on to university and got a degree. But I was bored. I wanted to travel the world. I became a second rate model. I had the height but my boobs were too big. They were into the anorexic look at the time. So I did what a lot of models that don't make it do. I became a really high-class hooker. And I was one of the best.

I always liked sex. I actually enjoyed making love to all those men and quite a few women too. I had about twenty regulars and then did the odd elite party. I did that for a bit and then met Di Maglio at a party. He said I was too bright for a hooker. He offered me a job. He said it would pay me more. He had me taught guns. I got to learn unarmed combat. And I became a controller."

"What's a controller?"

"I managed a group in Chicago. They were mainly pimps. I then moved to the hotel business and did a couple of years in Las Vegas. I then went to work in the Di Maglio headquarters as an enforcer. That's where I really got to know Maria. She was one too."

"What's the job of an enforcer? Are you still one?"

"No is the answer to the second question. An enforcer sorts out anyone who falls out of line. That can mean anything from talking to them through to getting rid of them permanently. The group was ruled with a rod of iron then. It was brutal. Actually the concrete boots were never my line. I tended to give the early warnings.

I then joined his elite. I became a sort of Girl Friday. We did anything that was needed. I once had to sleep with a President so that we could get leverage on him. I helped kidnap an oil magnate's wife. I took part in a raid on one of our rival gangs. And I tell you that made your jaunt in the

South of France a couple of years ago look like a primary school party."

"You even looked after us in Barbados that year," said Charles with a wry smile.

"That was a great assignment. It's strange. I've known you for three years or so. We went to bed together way back, and then the other day again. That's not bad for an ex-hooker. I really have reformed. And the irony is that I must have slept with hundreds of men in my time. Well I guess that's exaggerating. There weren't quite hundreds. I told you, that I tended to have regulars. I didn't just pick them up. I wasn't particularly careful but nothing ever went wrong. I wouldn't do it again. It's strange. I then sleep with you twice and every minute that goes by implies I could be pregnant."

"What'll you do about Di Maglio if you are?"

"I wouldn't be very much good to him would I? I'd have to quit. That wouldn't be a problem. Once he knew I was pregnant."

"And where will you go?"

"I'll buy my farm. I'll disappear off the face of this earth. It would be crazy for you to know about your son or daughter. I wouldn't have to marry. I'd find someone every year or so to sleep with. Just to remind me that I sometimes liked sex. I wasn't meant to be a whore. I wasn't meant to be a wife. I was meant to be a mistress."

"Can't I see you? We could have an annual reunion."

She smiled at him. There was sadness in her eyes. Her voice became a bit throaty. "No. It wouldn't work. It's not you and it's not me. I'll ride my horses. I'll watch things grow. But we need to stay apart. Or we'll destroy what we had. And we'll destroy what we have."

"You know, you're amazingly moral. You should have hung around for the right guy. You should never have become a hooker".

"But I did. And it was right for me. I've several million in the bank. I have earned it. I invested in good illegal businesses. Now I have clean cash and I can live on it for the rest of my life."

She lent over and kissed him. The seats were wide. A wide table separated them. It was far from comfortable and some heads turned. But they turned away when they ignored them. She then took his hand and kissed it, too.

She murmured, "I would have loved you. I would have been good to you. But I met you at the wrong time and in the wrong place. The spell will be broken now. You know my past. It will always worry you. It's too alien for you. You can't comprehend."

He knew she was right even if he didn't want to admit it. They talked on and off as the plane wended its way to New York. She was going home. He would be close by in the Pierre. They agreed to share a car.

"But I go home on my own. You go to your hotel."

He had started to realise that she was drawing a veil over their past. She was getting ready for the future. He needed to meet the Honourable James in any case and had no appetite for bumping into him with Claire. So they landed in New York. He hadn't thought of booking a car in advance. Nor had she. So they decided to take a cab. It made its way through the ugly drive from JFK and headed to the smart flats where Claire lived.

In the back of the cab, she turned towards him. She held his hand against her stomach. He left it there and gently caressed the firm flesh. She glanced out. He looked at her questioningly.

"We're being tracked," she said. "I've noticed that grey limousine twice. They keep on trying to keep just one car between them and us. They were near the taxi queue at the airport and they have followed us through ever since. I can't believe Di Maglio would try it again."

"We'll never get away from them in a cab."

"We need to take them to your hotel and then create a diversion, somehow. If they're just following us we should be all right. If they want to attack us or something we could have problems."

They thought how they would create a diversion. It was difficult when you can't trust the driver. They could pay him off quickly. And then run. But that was not going to fool professionals. And somehow they both suspected that this time Di Maglio would have used people he could trust. This time, he would have chosen people who would succeed. But what would they have to succeed at?

He thought through the options. Perhaps he wanted to frighten them? Perhaps he wanted to kill them? Perhaps he wanted to kidnap them? Would it be both of them or just one of them? Would they recognise Claire? Or would they assume she was just a hanger on?"

The car continued to track them. It moved closer as the traffic cleared. If they wanted to make a strike, they would do so soon. The road ahead was clear. They could attack, then take one of many turnoffs and disappear into the bowels of New York.

Claire was looking intently at the car and its occupants. She screwed up her eyes as she stared into the following car. She started all of a sudden. Her lip was trembling. She was looking worried.

"Are you armed?" she asked nervously.

He nodded. There was no way that he risked travelling without a gun. His permit helped him and the special treatment he had arranged with the Commander meant that he did not have to surrender the weapon even at the airport. She had had to leave her gun. She would have picked up one on her return home. She turned towards him.

"They're enforcers. They work for Di Maglio. They're good. One of his top teams. And they'll only have one mission. That'll be to kill. Either you or me, or both of us. So it's them or us."

"Claire, our only hope is to shoot out their tyres and make them crash. And there's a risk that this driver will crash if I do that. We'll have to take that risk. It's no use telling him in advance what we're doing. It'll only panic him."

She indicated her agreement and then gave him careful instructions.

"Wait till they drive alongside us. If they come on my side, then I'll duck out of your way and you can shoot through the window." She looked at him nervously, "You think you can manage that?"

"Do I have a choice?"

She shook her head and whispered, "Good luck."

The limousine pulled closer to them. He waited, leaning back in his seat ready to turn in either direction. The taxi was making it easy for them. The driver was speeding along in the central lane. He hoped they'd come on his side. That would make the shot that much easier. He saw that was not going to be the case. The long grey limousine pulled alongside them effortlessly. Its bonnet was alongside them and so was the driver.

He pulled the trigger as a burst of gunfire raked the side of their car. His bullet hit the car and its window shattered but did not break. They must have been bullet-proof. He lent over Claire who was lying forward to give him space and fired again. This time he aimed at the tyres and not the driver. There was a small explosion as a tyre burst.

The car swerved across the road and hit the central reservation. It bounced back into the path of another car. The two cars clashed together in an angry screeching of metal buckling against metal. They then bounded apart and swerved in opposite directions. The cab driver, his eyes wide open in abject terror, was babbling away in some obscure language. Charles yelled at him to brake and he must have heard. The tyres clung screaming to the road as they locked. He must have stamped on the foot brake with all his strength. They skidded from one side to another although, as Charles was flung from side to side, he caught a glimpse of the grey car well under control and speeding away ahead of them.

It was oblivious or indifferent to the turmoil in its wake. Its tyres were special as well. The bullets had done no immediate damage. The cab was slowing down now to a halt as they powered sideways up the road before ending up against a crash barrier. Cars behind them were stopping and a series of mini accidents littered the freeway.

"Get out," he called to Claire. There was a danger that someone would crash into them or that the taxi would start to burn. She didn't move. All of a sudden, he became conscious of a low groan. It sounded like an animal in pain. It was a soft, dull sound of anguish and fear. It came from Claire as she crouched forward, just as she had done some moments ago to make space for him to fire at the car.

But she should have got up by now. He stretched out his hand and touched her chest. He felt her body against his. It was cold where it had been warm. It was moist where it should have been dry. It was stained dark where it should have been white. She was covered in blood. Her breath was coming through in gasps.

He turned her round and looked her in the eyes. They were still soft and gentle, but the light had left them. There was a haze over them. He pulled open her shirt and saw the marks of the bullets that had hit her.

Her lips moved and he bent over her to hear what she had to say. At first he failed, he could not catch the words. Her voice was overpowered by the growing turmoil around him. There she lay, slumped on the seat of the wrecked taxi. Her clothes were covered in blood, her face was a pale shadow of its former self. The bullets had torn holes in her chest and her stomach.

"They killed my baby. They killed my baby. They killed me. I betrayed Di Maglio."

Charles shouted now. He was overcome with pain. "Don't leave. The farm. You forgot the farm. Riding the horse across the plain. Far away from anyone."

"It was a dream." And then her eyes stared lifelessly at him. The flow of blood slowed down. She was dead. She had been killed for betraying Di Maglio. Killed for helping Charles.

Charles looked around. He was crying. He cried for Claire. He cried for himself. He cried for what would happen. He cried for what could never be. The world was dark and cold. The people around him were lifeless as he sunk deeper into his anguish and grief.

He strode out of the car. He was furious. He brushed aside the people who had come to look and stare at the life that had gone. He sat at the side of the road and buried his head in his hands. He must have made a strange sight. He still had his gun in his hand. He was covered in Claire's blood. Tears were streaming down his face. They were tears of rage as well as remorse and sadness.

The spectators preferred to look at Claire. They must have felt there was something strange about him. They may have felt he was dangerous. He quickly slipped the gun back in his leg holster and thought up a story for the police. The whining of the sirens and the flashing blue lights in the distance told him that they were fast approaching.

They moved towards him in moments. One group went to the car and moved away the spectators. They were talking to the driver. He noticed that they, too, had problems understanding him. The combination of shock, his possible illegal status and a foreign language combined to make him even more difficult to comprehend than the average New York taxi driver.

The group moving towards Charles did so cautiously. They had their guns at the ready for they must have established that he was armed. They came to a few yards of him and ordered him to put his hands up. Covering him with their guns, they frisked him and removed the gun from its holster.

"The gun's quite legal." Charles told them. "I'm a British banker. There have been threats against my family and me. That's why I carry a gun. The dead girl was travelling with me by chance. We met at the airport and shared a cab. I'd forgotten to book a car. I usually have one laid on for me."

"I think you'd better come with us. We'll take you to the precinct. You'll need to talk to the captain. They'll need proof about what you are saying."

So the police stuck to the formalities of his name and address. He gave them all the details they needed about Claire. The body was now being loaded into an ambulance and they let him go over to her for one last time.

He stood on the hard concrete of the freeway. He pulled back the blanket that covered her. He looked at the lifeless features. The eyes looked back at him but they said nothing. The skin was white. The hair was remarkably neat. She didn't look like Claire any more. The face without emotions, the eyes without sparkle, the mouth shut in permanence. He said goodbye to her there in the desolation of crumpled metal and concrete barrenness that were so alien to her nature. He said "goodbye" to the child that she was and the child who would never be. He said "goodbye" to a girl he had loved.

He thought back to the sunny days in Barbados. He recalled the meetings in New York and London. The time they had all had together in the cottage and the laughter they had all shared. He remembered the chase across Europe and the night of love in the barn. He thought of the memory of the present that had already become the past. He reflected on the strangeness of her life and the futility of her death.

In that one fleeting moment, as he looked at the face he no longer recognised, it all came back to him. Claire had been a promising student. She had told him that she'd been good at sport and popular with her fellows. Claire, who had been a model and then headed at ease with herself, down the road that corrupted her mind but not her soul. Claire who had moved into a circle where evil was a way of life. Claire had been part of a system that knew no respect for life. And the callous ordering of her death by a man he knew as his father-in-law. Death used as a warning, death used as an example. Kill to make a point.

He mourned a girl who deserved her farm. He mourned a mother who deserved her child. He mourned a life that shouldn't have ended like that.

And he then swore to her memory that he would destroy the man who ordered her murder. He knew now that he wouldn't play his game. He wouldn't destroy him by gun or knife or fire. He would destroy him his way, stripping him of his power and wealth. Then he would leave him alone in his isolation. He knew now that he would make his plans. He knew now that family would have no meaning. He would be destroyed but he would leave him his life, leave him the desolation of death in living. He would give him the loneliness of exile in his home, he would strip him of his protection. He would strip him of his power. And without power he would be living in an endless impossible hell.

He bent over and kissed Claire's lifeless face. He waited that one moment for a response. He waited to hear that it had all been a mistake. But the thought left him quickly. This was not what dreams were made of. He turned away and left her for good.

They drove to the police precinct in silence. He was ushered into the bareness of an interview room and asked to call his lawyer. A phone was produced and he rang the number. It took minutes before he was released. One phone call from the right quarters ensured that. The police were not to know that he had used the Di Maglio local firm. Di Maglio himself wouldn't know. It was too trivial an issue to bring to his attention. Charles had no qualms about using Di Maglio resources for his purpose where needed and where he still could. Di Maglio, the man who was a major protagonist in the corruption which proliferated in New York. Di Maglio corrupted life in many countries. Charles and Jacqui knew how he operated and they would use that as they sought to destroy him.

Charles left the police station after changing. There was no way that he could go to the Pierre in the blood-stained clothes he had been wearing. He checked into the hotel and told the porter to take his case to his room.

He shut his eyes and worked to purge the events of the last hour or so from his mind. He then walked into the bar and over to the Honourable James. The world of business took over once again, as he went back to the web that would make them wealthy beyond their dreams.

Charles reeled the Honourable James further in by proposing that he could move his troublesome son to the States to work alongside the new chief executive. He jumped at the opportunity and comfort of distancing himself from his offspring. The boy was incompetent and Charles needed incompetent people to help him complete his work.

He thought through to the wives of the great and the good. They were signing documents as directors of special purpose companies without realising they were incriminating themselves. The more he wove this web, the more it was looking as if the very people he had been encouraged to retain in the company had duped him. The grey haired elite were going to take the biggest rap of them all when the crash came. He felt no remorse for them. They were all long past their sell by dates.

Charles left early and went to his room. He had the hard task of telling Jacqui and Maria about Claire. Jacqui would mourn her as a friend, and then would notch up another mark of hate against her father. He was less certain about Maria, for she and Claire had been close friends for too many years.

Yet, he had no choice and the calls needed to be made. He was right that Jacqui reacted with fury against her father. Maria strangled a sob and was ominously quiet. He told them to do nothing. He said they had to leave Di Maglio to him. He told Maria to be careful. Di Maglio would guess how she could react. Any false move now would be dangerous. And neither of them protested when he explained that, once the scam was in place, he planned to hit Di Maglio and hit him hard. He would leave him alive but, ominously, Di Maglio would wish he were dead.

CHAPTER THIRTEEN

In the end, he spent the whole week in New York. The good thing was that they finalised the deal for the Di Maglio banks. They set the take-over date for the end of the following week. At that point the new CEO, McGarth, would assume control with the dubious benefit of support from the Honourable James' dim-witted son.

Di Maglio had called Charles on the Tuesday. "Jacqui won't return my calls. Why?"

"Perhaps she thinks that you're a total slime."

"What the fuck's this all about?"

"Claire."

"There has to be discipline. She disobeyed orders. I told her to report everything to me. She didn't. She worked with you to double-cross me."

Charles was astounded that Di Maglio so openly admitted he had had her killed. But he didn't want to rise to any bait, so he ignored the comment.

"I guess also we're not that happy that you kidnapped Juliet and got your people to shoot Jacqui."

"Jacqui was an accident. She got in the way. That happens when you carry guns. The kidnap was necessary. You need to work with me on the rest of the Empire. Once the financial side is completed, then we'll talk about the rest."

"I don't want to see you, let alone work with you."

He laughed. It was a cold and malevolent sound. Charles felt uneasy as he sensed the hatred and contempt of that evil man. He knew the final battle was starting. He knew Di Maglio recognised that. He wanted them in his web and he'd play hard to get them there.

Charles saw Giovanni more often. It was evident that he was concerned at the antagonism between them. He thought it unhealthy. He saw them pushing each other to the brink, and he sensed that they would not stop before one of them had been destroyed. But there was nothing he could do and his first loyalty was always with his boss.

Between the formal meetings, Charles was working on another secure document. It was structured to run for exactly one page, and it was important that it fitted into the sale and purchase agreement after it had been signed.

The one page addition was to be slotted in among the warranties being given by the vendor. It contained the personal and absolute guarantee to all clients of the sold enterprises of one Di Maglio. When the US banks went into default, Di Maglio would be standing there with all his personal wealth.

They had agreed at the signing that they would initial all pages. All Charles needed to do was to ensure that there was a missing number on the Di Maglio copy and a correct number on the two others. As he would take charge of the copy for them as buyer, as well as a second copy to lodge with the US government, the only incomplete copy would be with Di Maglio.

And who was going to believe a Mafia boss when he protested that he had been duped? What government would not pursue him and all his assets to the end of the earth? And without money he would lose all his power. Without power, he would lose his grip on them. They would be safe. And they would have got their revenge.

The days were an endless round of meetings in New York. Charles had to get back to London on one day for business and explained his plans to Jacqui. She agreed with them wholeheartedly. He wanted her to be with him in New York for the signing. She would need to find a way to distract Di Maglio and Giovanni, for they could not risk that they were too alert. One lingering glance at page 33 of the agreement and they were sunk.

They agreed that the signing would be private. Charles would be there with Jacqui and the Honourable James, as well as McGarth. Di Maglio would be with Giovanni. Charles would initial each page of all the documents, then he would sign the final page and the Honourable James would witness it. Di Maglio would do likewise and Giovanni would witness. Then they would take their respective copies, hand the authorities' copy to the lawyers who would file them and certify additional copies as needed by the bureaucracies around the world. Only the copy they would file with the authorities and Charles own copy would have the important 33rd page.

During that week he also ran through the status of their complex market manipulations. Stephens and Jack Ryder had created a series of trades on markets all over the world. The figures were impressive. It looked as if the bank were making a splendid profit on these. But, in reality, it was now losing one point three billion dollars. Nobody could trace the routing of these deals. They could only identify the point where the money disappeared into the ether. In every case, the signature at that point was that of one of the so-called respectable IBE nominated directors or their families. It looked as if the Honourable James and co. were up to their necks in it.

Jack Ryder had now also warehoused over two billion dollars of strange shares and was slowly pushing their prices up. It was working like a dream and soon they would have a sales drive of the US funds, which would use the cash from those sales to buy those stocks from them. It was clear that things were going better than they even planned. They were already over a billion up on the purchases. And, while they could never have sold out at that profit in a fair market, there were plenty of opportunities to do so with the cash held by the funds.

And the loans were progressing well. Just as with Stephens' trades, they had been washed through the different companies. The secret accounts that Charles and Jacqui had set up with his parents had swollen already by a further billion and a half-dollars as a result. Once again payments had been authorised by a family member of one of the 'great and the good.' It now looked as if they could create more faked loans than originally planned, as the gullibility of those around them was such that it seemed a shame to be too conservative.

The money had been lent by IBE and they had paid it a fee out of the loan. They had enough money retained in the shell companies to pay the interest for about a year and had effectively shipped the rest out through a variety of routes into their own deep pockets.

In total, they were close to four billion dollars to the good and the big game had not yet begun even.

Charles talked through their next steps with Jacqui, "I need to get the US acquisition done and dusted fast. We are getting it for a song. And in any case your father's shares are going to a trust for our children, although in a few months the rump of them is going to be almost worthless unless I can manage to engineer that second coup with Associated.

I also need to get rid of Stephens. He is becoming tedious. One day he'll blow his mouth. Soon he'll have delivered all we want and we'll waste him. We'll get Maria to do the necessary. We'll let his deputy handle things from then on. We can still use the same computer programme to value the assets at whatever we want. The new man won't understand it and we'll pay him enough to ensure his silence. That will incriminate him when all comes to light and the trades are shown to be loss making."

The day for signing came. Charles and Jacqui decided to be there early and were waiting well ahead of Di Maglio. Charles had bought three bulky red folders. One was embossed with the name of Di Maglio. One was embossed with the name of International Bank of Europe. And the third was embossed in the name of the US Administration. They all looked identical, but Di Maglio's was missing that one crucial page. The page where he gave the added warranties that would be his downfall.

Charles extracted a second slim document. This was the deed they had agreed with Giovanni to allow Di Maglio to pass his shares in the combined operation to his grandchildren. They had considered he might now refuse to do that. But there was no purpose. He had nothing to gain by such action and everything to lose. For the planned deed had already been made public to the US Administration as part of the proof that Di Maglio no longer would have a say in the US bank.

There was a third document. This covered the split of the profits. This was different from the original split. They were now going to give Di Maglio only thirty per cent against the forty they had promised. The balance of ten per cent was going to Juliet.

Charles had manipulated things carefully. They would be busy. All three documents had to be signed for the deal to be finalised. That allowed him to hurry the proceedings along, particularly the initialling of the forty odd pages on the three copies of the sale agreement. That was seen as just administrative at this point as each party had already scrutinised each word in a draft.

Di Maglio entered the room with Giovanni. The broad shoulders, the slightly hunched back and the dark brooding look spelt menace for everyone else in the room. He seemed to be darker than usual and his face was engulfed in the spectre of an afternoon shadow. He stared grimly at each of the others.

He looked the Honourable James up and down. His sneer grew as he took in the hand-stitched shoes, polished to an immaculate shine. He looked at the razor sharp crease of the pin-striped double-breasted suit from a well-known man in Jermyn Street. The white shirt and the old school tie were noted. And then the sneer grew to vicious animosity as he looked at the carefully manicured hands, the immaculately brushed grey hair and that disdainful look that is so unique to the English aristocracy.

He looked at McGarth in his dark blue suit with a button down shirt and matching blue tie. He must have sensed the emptiness of the smile, the boredom in the eyes and the eagerness for lunch. He must have approved secretly of their selection of a chief executive of the US interests. The blandness of the man shone through. This was a cypher, descended from a suitably aristocratic family. This was a unique opportunity to lead the charge to oblivion and default. This was the man who would undoubtedly be visiting a penitentiary soon. And the sneer on Di Maglio's lips turned to a thin smile. McGarth took that as a welcome and moved forward to shake his hand. The grip of iron that typified a Di Maglio handshake made him wince before he was ignored by the slow roving of their visitor's eyes.

He saw Charles and nodded. It looked like a curt nod of dismissal rather than greeting. He then noticed Jacqui and started. He had not expected her. Nor had Giovanni, who had been watching this play for a few minutes and had seen Jacqui moments before. He made a move towards her and she moved back.

Charles interrupted the proceedings, "Gentlemen, as this is a private deal and we have also family matters to attend to, I would like us to start the proceedings now."

Di Maglio sat down on one side with Giovanni on his right. Charles was opposite him and the Honourable James sat opposite Giovanni. Charles signalled McGarth to take a seat at the end of the table between the Honourable James and Giovanni. Jacqui approached her father and moved to the end of the table. He made to talk to her but Charles quickly interrupted him.

"Gentlemen, we have two documents to sign. The first is for the sale of PAF to International Bank of Europe. The agreement has been completed and vetted by our lawyers and a copy is in the folders here. Mr Di Maglio and I need to initial each page of each copy and then we need to sign the document, with Mr Petroni and the Honourable James as the witnesses.

There is also a second paper to sign as well and the lawyers have again vetted this. This relates to the transfer of shares in IBE, the shares resulting from this transaction, to a trust in favour of Miss Juliet Rossi and any brothers or sisters she may have.

I suggest we sign the first and then the second. We will need Mr Petroni as a witness for the second. Perhaps at that point Mr McGarth and the Honourable James can go for a cocktail before lunch. I am sure we all deserve one after this momentous deal.

The lawyers are outside and will take the relevant papers to the Federal Reserve and then others will issue the required press releases. Are there any questions?"

There were none and Charles produced the first two folders. They were the ones for Di Maglio and him. He suggested they initial all pages and then sign their own agreements first. This they did, with Giovanni checking the pages that Di Maglio signed. But he obviously failed to notice the gap in the numbering, concentrating as he was on the text of the agreement. He finished the initialling and Charles and he exchanged copies to countersign. Giovanni did not pay much attention to this one and they saw Di Maglio initial the critical page thirty-three without stopping. Two copies were signed. They now needed to go on to the US Administration document.

Charles had at one time considered forging the initials on the critical page 33, but he had felt that was too dangerous. There would be a challenge and he needed these documents to stand up to the closest scrutiny. Jacqui kept a close eye on the proceedings. Giovanni was looking again at the paperwork. This was more from boredom than anything else. He had checked out the first copy and had found no fault. He suspected nothing. He knew nothing. But they knew his first loyalty, if not all his sympathies, would rest with his boss and he would alert him to any irregularity. They needed to distract Di Maglio and Giovanni this time round. Charles caught Jacqui's eye and she nodded.

Charles had instructed the heating to be turned up in the room and it was warm. Jacqui waited till Di Maglio had signed page thirty and then she fumbled in her bag. As he signed the next page, he turned to her inquiringly; she stood up. She looked pale. How she managed that Charles would never know.

"I feel a bit wobbly," she announced. "Charles, I'll go and sit down outside for a moment."

Both Di Maglio and Charles had got up. The others looked on curiously. Di Maglio took her by the arm. She didn't resist and seemed to sway, "Sorry, it's just that I'm pregnant. I 'm not usually so pathetic."

Di Maglio looked stunned. "You never told me," he said.

"I wanted it to be a surprise for later today. Look, it's all right. I feel OK again. Let's carry on with the business."

Giovanni looked perplexed. The others mouthed congratulations and started to look at Jacqui strangely. It was as if she had done something freakish. It was all strange but it had served its purpose. The diversion had been planned if ever the new pages were being scrutinised closely by Di Maglio or Giovanni. It took everyone's mind off the papers. Charles sat down again and so did Di Maglio. The next page or two had been initialled before Giovanni started looking again. And by that time the pages were normal. They had got past the vital page thirty three.

They signed and countersigned before Charles produced the next set of papers.

"I think at this point we can excuse Mr McGarth and the Honourable James."

They needed no second invitation and headed to the adjacent private dining room for the first of their stiff lunchtime Martinis.

Once they had left, Charles produced the document moving the shares in IBE into the trust for Juliet and any brothers or sisters. Di Maglio looked at the document. He turned to Jacqui who had by now returned to the table.

"You didn't tell me you were pregnant even when you were in the Geneva compound with me. At that time you didn't know I was involved."

Charles interrupted. This was an ideal way of making him feel even more insecure. Now Claire was dead it didn't matter if he knew. "Wrong. We were aware that you were involved. We followed the kidnappers through to Geneva. It wasn't chance that we were there. It was just chance that we found Juliet like we did."

"Whom do you mean by "we"?"

"Claire and I tracked them. We followed them to Newhaven and then on through Dieppe. We actually thought that they were Russians. That's why Claire was helping. She was obeying your instructions to protect us.

We almost managed to grab Juliet when she was handed over. But it was too dangerous. So we followed on. We thought they'd head on to the Russian compound in Uzes. But then they branched off and went to Geneva. It was only at that point that we knew it was you.

Till then we'd suspected you. There were too many unusual events. You're too good to have made such mistakes. At least you're too good to make them on purpose. By trying to make it look like a load of ham-fisted Russians you gave your game away.

We thought Juliet was in the compound. Claire and Jacqui were there to find her. It was only then that Claire worked against you. She was disgusted that you would stoop as low as to betray your own granddaughter."

Di Maglio had turned pale at this and muttered something under his breath.

"Pass the papers."

He skim-read the document and signed it. Giovanni countersigned and they did the same with the two added copies. This time there were no false pages. All documents were identical. And they had agreed that one copy could be lodged with the US authorities so that they had clear knowledge of the new ownership structure.

Di Maglio looked at Jacqui. He looked sad and embarrassed. But the words that followed were brutal.

"You're just like that bitch of a mother of yours. You'd betray me at the drop of a hat, just like your mother. You're not my daughter other than in name. I don't know who your father really is. But I had some blood tests done years ago and it's not me. So you're a bastard and you act like one.

I've still signed the agreement to give your kids some of my money. So they get the bank. That's going to be worth a few billion. So they owe me. And perhaps they'll appreciate that. Perhaps they'll be happier to follow in my footsteps than you were."

Jacqui looked shocked and bit her bottom lip. Charles slipped his hand under the table and squeezed her knee. She read the message. Put it out of your mind. We need to get at him first. This could be a diversion. It sounded true. The bitterness would have been hard to fabricate. But you never knew with a man as evil as Di Maglio. There were no boundaries for him.

Charles picked up the last document and said, "There is another document. I have drawn up and that is an agreement on the split of any profits. This has just one copy. And I'm going to keep it."

Giovanni and Di Maglio looked surprised. But it was Giovanni who spoke first.

"What does it say?"

"It advises of the change in the split of any profits we make."

"We agreed that in London at the start of the deal. There will be no changes," snarled Di Maglio.

"And think what has happened since." Charles stood up and spat out the list of events, thumping the table with his fist each time but keeping his voice low.

"You tried to fake a mock assassination in New York. You organised a phoney explosion in California. You had us attacked on the freeway. You staged an abortive kidnap attempt in Los Angeles. You gave Juliet the head of a dead woman as a present. You tried to have me roughed up at the airport in LA. We were waylaid in Sussex. You kidnapped Juliet. Fuck you. The deal's been changed."

"Then it's off."

"Too late you've signed. And try to draw a gun and Jacqui will kill you first."

Di Maglio glanced down and saw that Jacqui had taken a gun from her bag. It was pointing at him. There was no sign of emotion in her face. It was set hard and cold. And the gun was a real one. This was for stopping and killing. This was not for warning and wounding.

Giovanni again tried to calm things down, "What changes are there?"

"To ensure that Juliet is recompensed for the kidnapping, she is in for ten per cent of the profit. The clause also allows Jacqui and I to split out that ten per cent with any other children we have together."

"What if you remarry? What if she comes to her senses and sees you for the piece of shit you are?" spat out Di Maglio viciously.

"I said children we had together. In any event, Jacqui is married to me and not to someone like you. We plan to stay together. But, once this deal is done, you're out of our lives."

"Who passes Juliet the ten per cent?" asked Giovanni although he had evidently already worked it out.

"He does," said Charles jerking his head towards Di Maglio. "His share was reduced from forty to thirty once he started playing dirty tricks. And there are two other clauses."

Charles paused but there was no response. At least nobody said anything. Giovanni just sat there quietly. Di Maglio glared at him with a hatred that was so intense that he started to feel uneasy. He steeled himself to repel that look. The hatred was blind. The malevolent feelings of a twisted man blended with the darkness of soul that only he could muster. And that communicated itself through a glare of such intense evil. It made Charles question if they were not better seeing him dead rather than defeated. He would need to keep that in mind.

"The two other clauses are simple. There is a survival clause. If any party dies or disappears before the deal is completed, then the split of profits they would have received is redistributed."

"Run that by me," said Giovanni. He did that on purpose. He wanted to gauge Di Maglio's reaction.

"If you, Maria or Mr Di Maglio were to die before the distribution date, then the clause would rule and your shares would be redistributed proportionately between the survivors."

"I'll see it through," snarled Di Maglio. "But I wouldn't be so sure of your chances."

"The second clause excludes you, Maria or Giovanni from benefiting from the death of Jacqui or me. The distribution would then be as indicated in our wills. Those are not part of this agreement."

"Do we have to agree to this shit?" Di Maglio asked in a hoarse voice.

Giovanni nodded. "He has us caught. There was no written agreement. And he can pull out of the bank sale, too, if he wants on the basis of the kidnapping. And then our banks will be worthless and we could be exposed to other scrutiny."

Di Maglio exploded in rage and Giovanni went as white as a sheet as the fury was directed against him. "Why the fuck did you let him do that? You screwed up badly there."

"It's not abnormal in this sort of agreement. I didn't know your plans. But there is a clause on mutual trust and openness during negotiations."

Di Maglio glared malevolently at Giovanni, "Who do I trust? Do I trust that conman over there? Would I ever allow that bitch who thinks she's my daughter into my inner circle? This better work or you'll regret it."

Di Maglio reached over and signed the document. Charles followed suit. After Giovanni countersigned with a trembling hand, Charles calmly picked up the document.

"I think we have finished. I hope you'll stay for lunch," said Charles with a sardonic smile.

Di Maglio looked at him and growled "no."

"And you, Giovanni?"

"I have to as we need to see the lawyers and then go to the New York Federal Reserve," he replied. He turned to Di Maglio, "I'll join you around five this evening. Can we have a moment together?"

Giovanni pulled Di Maglio to a corner and they talked sombrely for a few moments. They knew that he was working to calm him down. There was no way for Di Maglio to try to get even with them yet. He would best wait till after the scam. But then he would be broke. He'd have the odd few millions stashed away. But he'd have nothing else.

If he had no cash, his Empire would crumble. You don't buy goods like that on credit. And you need hundreds of millions of credit, and credit in the form of cash. He would be destroyed. Without wealth he wouldn't know whom to trust. Others could buy his people. They would want to survive. There would be other drug barons to help them on their way.

Giovanni returned, still pallid and perspiring. Di Maglio, his face etched into a furious glare, strode out of the door without a backward glance.

Charles picked up his folder and checked it had the right document. The sale agreement went from page thirty-two to thirty-four. He slipped the trust agreement in front of the sale agreement. He then tied the cover together and handed the flawed documents to the unsuspecting Giovanni.

He next opened the Federal Reserve folder and checked the documents. That contained page thirty-three. He added the Trust agreement behind it and tied it together.

He finally checked his own folder and added the trust agreement. Then with a smile he added the revised sale conditions.

Giovanni looked at Jacqui and then at Charles to whom he said, "This is dangerous. Be careful. He is your enemy. Nothing should happen until this deal is done. After all, at thirty per cent, he's in for good money. But you just screwed him out of a billion and he won't forgive you. I've seen him react badly for less."

"I'd worked that out. But we need to teach him a lesson. We'll have a family dinner once the deal is done. Is it true what he said about Jacqui?"

He looked at her. She seemed to be pleading with him. "Look, your mother screwed around. I know she did later in the marriage. But I think she loved him early on. So I doubt she did then. He had his doubts and there was a blood test. But he lied. It didn't show that he couldn't be your father. It didn't show he was either. The only way you could prove that is through DNA. And those sorts of tests weren't available at the time. Until today he never mentioned it. He could, though, try DNA if he wanted. You could too if you got a hair off him or something. That is, if it's important to you."

Jacqui went over and kissed him. The little man with the scrawny neck protruding bird-like from his over large collar smiled at her. Charles changed tack again, "Let's get the show on the road. We should call in the lawyers and have lunch. Then we have an appointment at half two with the New York Fed."

He called in the lawyers. They were the very lawyers who had drawn up page thirty-three for him. They could be trusted. They didn't know Di Maglio. He never used them. They had come to them from other sources. And they worked for a twenty million covert tax free annual retainer over and above fees. That bought worldwide coverage and a willingness to be flexible.

The twenty million would already reap Charles a huge profit on this deal alone. And there were others where they would prove useful. The firm, reputed as it was in international legal circles, was happy to be involved in organised crime for a fee of that size.

They took the Federal Reserve copy and placed it in a briefcase that one of the lawyers held with him as they all went into the dining room where the Honourable James and McGarth were happily ensconced into their third or fourth dry Martini. That seemed to affect neither of them, they benefited from a lifetime of training into the best way to hold down a large number of lunchtime drinks.

Charles picked up his document case and slid his papers into it. Giovanni did likewise with Di Maglio's. Charles apologised for the latter's absence. "He felt quite distraught," he explained. "I never realised that he had a soft spot for his banks. I thought he saw them just as an investment."

McGarth waxed lyrically about it being a great day for two great organisations, "The International Bank of Europe and PAF will show that the sum of the parts is worth more than the individual banks. Together, we make profits of just over five hundred million dollars. Tomorrow we will make more."

They sat down to lunch soon afterwards. The Honourable James and McGarth blabbed on endlessly until Charles stopped them by saying, "Jacqui will run you through some of the plans that we have for the combined banks. She has been working on strategies. These will obviously need board approval. They are just plans for the moment."

Both the Honourable James and McGarth looked astonished at the thought of being told what to do and especially by a mere woman. And that made it all the more pleasant for the others in the room.

Jacqui lent forward and expanded on some of the plans they had formulated in secret. Giovanni and Charles knew what to expect but the information was new to the others in the room.

"The optimum strategy is multi-faceted. The key on this side of the Atlantic is to maximise our sales to PAF's customer base. We are going to focus on investment funds for this purpose. With five million customers and the recent changes in pension arrangements, there is an incredible opportunity here. Especially since PAF has some good performing funds. With help from IBE, they can extend their investments into emerging markets and specialised sectors. We believe we can sell up to five billion dollars of funds this year alone if we market right. That would add around a hundred and fifty million dollars to our profits."

There were nods of agreement around the room. Jacqui had not mentioned that they planned to skim off a good chunk of that five billion in a classical share ramp and by fabricating phoney investments. Neither did she reveal to them that they suspected this combination would make them between two and three billion dollars if they off loaded the five billion of funds planned this year. That was way beyond the original forecasts but the markets had been kind to them. Everything had gone their way, so far.

She went on, "We have a second plan. PAF has no major stake in the business market. But IBE does. With the combined balance sheet we can increase our lending to some of the major customers of IBE. We have identified those with US interests or ambitions and PAF will lend to them. We believe it could lend another two billion to this sector. That would improve its profits by around another hundred million a year, plus an added hundred this year through front end fees paid from the borrowers."

She again failed to say that they would cream off the entire two billion less some of the fees. But that was not for their current audience.

Giovanni played interested, "That, and the sale of funds, ups the combined profits this year by three to four hundred million dollars. That's an excellent result."

The others all nodded in excitement as they calculated the value of that increase to their end of year bonuses. "Sod the regulators" was the unspoken collective comment. They all knew that they would now be withholding important information from the authorities. But they wanted the reward and not the words of caution their plan would undoubtedly promote.

Jacqui continued, "We are also planning to offer some of IBE's sophisticated financial products to the corporate market clients of PAF. We suspect that we could sell quite a lot of those. That's enough to add a further hundred or so million to our bottom line."

The Honourable James intervened, "That would mean that we could make over half a billion dollars on the US side and we'll make over five twenty in the UK. That means this year's profits could be as high as a billion dollars. That's incredible."

And Jacqui added, "And that leads me to the final part of the strategy. We will sell fifty one per cent of our shares to the public. We will do so after we announce this year's profits and make our forecast for next year. We expect them to be around a billion, perhaps a bit more, if all these initiatives take place. As a result, the market is likely to take a very positive view of us. We suspect we should be valued at around ten billion in total."

Giovanni noted, "The bank would be worth more than ten billion in total. I suspect that, at such a profit level, you could well raise six to seven billion plus dollars for a fifty percent stake." He had now realised the profit was more than they had planned earlier. That was true, for they had upped the amount they would lend to the different companies since their first forecast. They had found more targets and had lent more to the ones they had identified in the first place. That accounted for the welcome increase.

As planned, everyone was suitably impressed. They all knew they could expect share options and other benefits as a result of these plans. Greed dispelled any thoughts that they should reveal these details to the regulators. Avarice prevailed and they ignored the possibility that some of the new revenue flows were not sustainable, and thus they should be questioning the treatment of them. Questions of the propriety of the deals were forgotten. Nobody worried that the board hadn't been party to these plans.

They didn't care as long as they made money. This was their swan song. They would be richer than they planned. They needed money to spend in retirement. The golden rule was not to be caught. They waved goodbye to the last vestiges of their morality. Money was more pertinent than principles.

Lunch ended on a high note. McGarth downed a last drink and prepared himself for the "tough one" as he called their pending meeting with the authorities. It was far from tough. They presented the documents and advised of board changes, They shared the press release that would be public in a few hours. The regulators were content. Di Maglio had gone from their world. They were as blind to the dangers as McGarth and the Honourable James had been to the illegal basis and risks of the huge plans Jacqui had just explained.

That evening the papers splashed the news. 'British financial giant makes US acquisition.' The commentators waxed enthusiastically about the experience of McGarth. They were misled by the spin-doctors stories about the prowess and reputation of IBE. They were nourished with tales of the new management's expertise in securities. It all helped for their plans for the future.

The depositors would be convinced they were better than the earlier management. The staff would be persuaded they were going to expand their business. Everything was wonderful. They were secure. More jobs and more opportunities would be created for everyone.

But that was a big lie. The truth was their livelihoods were at risk. That wasn't Charles' or Jacqui's concern. All they needed to do was boost revenues and get the maximum from the sale of the bank before it collapsed.

Inevitably, the news was no news a day or so later. They needed to start to get things moving. The next night, after a round of interviews and meetings, they left for London. McGarth and the Honourable James went on a whirlwind tour of the major cities, where PAF was located. They were good at PR and their trip would confuse the picture more. They would stress to all that they really ran the show. They would want to boost their over-inflated sense of importance and power. They would proclaim their part in all decisions, past and present. And they would effectively condemn themselves.

Jacqui and Charles landed in London. Giovanni stayed in New York. Douglas met them at the airport and they headed happily to their house and the start of their multi-billion dollar disappearing act.

CHAPTER FOURTEEN

The next day, Charles arrived at the office early with Jacqui. Minutes after he had started to look through the papers in his office, the door burst open. He glanced up into the red and angry features of his fellow directors, Sir Brian Ffinch Farquar and Lord Dunkillin. To say that they looked apoplectic with rage was an understatement.

He smiled at them gently. Every time he saw the overblown features of their tame baronet he recalled his penchant for being whipped in Soho nightclubs by girls in gym slips. And each time he saw the venerable Lord Dunkillin, he thought of his sexual antics with the late Wendy.

"Gentlemen, Gentlemen," he called. "Please sit down. I have no idea what's wrong. But we can discuss it calmly."

"Wrong," shouted Sir Brian. His face was puce. His eyes were bulging. One could almost hear his heart pounding with fury inside his double breasted pin-striped suit. "Of course, things are wrong. There's no consultation with the board."

"True," Dunkillin added in a whining, complaining tone. "No consultation. We buy the chaps in America and the deal goes through with pretty well no discussion. And there is almost no involvement from many of the board."

"If you're unhappy, we should wait till the Honourable James returns. He's the Chairman. I am just the chief executive. But I had understood that the authorities do not like too many directors overseas at the same time. For that reason you two, who are well known to them, have been holding the fort here in London."

"Holding the fort," yelled Dunkillin. "Stephens says he takes no orders from us. Just from you. That woman in your office won't allow us to see your mail unless she has seen it first. We have no authority. You and James have usurped it all."

Charles thought of blasting off at them. He had no time for this stupidity. But he kept calm.

"Stephens was wrong. I'll have a word with him. He should follow your instructions. I don't instruct him. The man's an expert in foreign exchange and derivatives and things. I'm no expert there. I brought him in to make us money but to adopt a low risk strategy. What did you need to instruct him about? With all due respect, I thought you knew little more about his area than I did."

Sir Brian seemed flummoxed, "We felt we should see his deals each day and approve them."

"Both of you?" queried Charles. He was really perplexed.

"Yes. It's an important area of our business and we should understand what we do there."

Charles looked at them closely. Did they suspect the tricks that Stephens was up to? He thought not. They just felt sidelined. They had hurt egos. The cretins were playing into his hand.

"I'll tell Stephens that he needs to get approval each evening from both of you for all trades he's done that day. If one of you isn't there, the other will have to do the approvals alone. I'll get him to prepare a daily schedule and you should sign it off as approved each night. Is that all right with you?"

"What about you?"

"I have enough on my hands. I'm only too happy to give you that role. It takes a weight off my shoulders."

"What about that Maria girl?"

"Maria checks my mail to remove any personal correspondence. Then there are always a couple of issues that I want to follow me around the world. She connects to me on the Internet. My portable has a scrambler and so she sends me any papers in encrypted form."

"What's encrypted?" queried Dunkillin suspiciously.

"It's scrambled so nobody can read it unless they break the code. Anyway, she sends me that stuff and then passes out all the rest. I'll ask her to check who should get the other mail with you. That would make it all the more efficient. After all, some of the things you could just deal with there and then."

They nodded. They were satisfied. Yet again they'd played into Charles' hands. He could get their signatures on even more things than he had thought. His noble friends were getting more than they had bargained for. Perhaps they would get even a few more years inside.

Maria came in then. She was pale and her eyes looked a bit red.

"Are you all right?"

She nodded. "I went to Claire's funeral. I wish you had been there. I know you couldn't or it would have blown the cover story. I also saw the autopsy report. She was pregnant you know. She told me about the barn. Funny isn't it, how we both love you in our strange ways. "She smiled at him. "I know I should be staying in your house to give you protection but I can't. I am too involved. But I'll do my job. It's just I want to kill him before he kills me."

"He won't kill you if you stay out of America. It was OK for the funeral but do be careful otherwise. And don't go to Geneva. Let me explain our plans to you."

When he had finished, she hugged him. "You're incredible. Both of you are. You two are incredible. I'll wait. I know you'll find a way to bring him down. I'll wait to see him suffer. He will if he becomes poor. At least, relatively poor, then he'll suffer. Di Maglio without power is a broken man. That will be worse than death for him."

"But, in the meantime," interrupted Charles, "We do have a lot of work to do and I need your help."

"What work?"

"This week I need to work on the bank and help set up as much of the scam as we can. Then next week, I want to go to France. I need to know if Turpin is there and if he is really in command of the Russian Mafia. I also need to know if he is a front for Rastinov, or if Rastinov is dead. I need to make a deal on the Di Maglio Empire with them. But if Rastinov isn't dead, I need to kill him first."

Maria frowned. "I'm sure Rastinov is dead. But what deal do you want to make with Turpin?"

"I want to sell him the Di Maglio Empire."

"But he's not selling. And it's not yours to sell. At least it's not yet."

"I'll try to persuade Di Maglio to sell. At worst, I'd have to wait till we fleece him. That's plan B. In extremes, when Di Maglio has no money, he'll have to sell out. I'll take his Empire on as a commercial deal. That'll get him out of the way. My precondition will be that he leaves the business to me and Jacqui to run. I'll then sell it to Turpin for whatever I can get. I want to agree what we're selling and what I'll get."

"How much do you want?"

"I guess a couple of billion up front and then fifty per cent of the first year's revenues. It'll be a snip. But I want to get out fast."

"He'll rip you off even on that one."

"Perhaps, but he'll pay me another billion or so. And he won't pay that up front."

"What else do you want from Turpin?"

"Nothing much, other than I want a promise to put down any of the Di Maglio clan who may be a threat to us."

"He'll like that."

"I thought he might. But first we'll head out and check about Rastinov. We can use the sensor I took to Geneva. We get inside the Uzes compound and then run the sensor. If it identifies an exact fit with Rastinov, then it'll tell us. The fit will cover a whole combination of things. So it doesn't matter if he has changed his features."

"When do we leave?"

"I can't before the weekend. First, we need to get down to work here. I wanted to wait for this business to be completed before I hit Di Maglio, but we only have protection till we close out the scam. The agreement on the profit split gives us that. But once that's over, Di Maglio will be lethal if unchecked."

That week was spent putting down the markers for the big fraud. The loans were pumped out through PAF at a rate of knots. The ideas appeared to come from the Honourable James' weird son. As he spent the large part of his time in the seediest New York establishments, he hardly paid any attention to the files on his desk. His role as head of risk management in the US meant that all credits had to go through him. He definitely did not read the proposals. The same was the case for McGarth, who had to agree them too. As for the Honourable James, surprisingly, he believed his son's assurances and accepted that the loans were good.

The plan had been to lend out some two billion to two billion and a half by this time. So great was the enthusiasm of the stool pigeons that they had soon pumped out over three billion of new loans in the US alone. That meant that they could be lending almost five billion in total across the bank to phoney companies by year end, and all that was being washed into accounts owned by Charles in various parts of the world.

McGarth and the others wanted to take on these loans so that the bank could earn the associated fees; therefore, they became ever laxer in their judgements. Big deals meant a big bonus for them, irrespective of their abilities and the long term harm they would wreak on the bank.

As McGarth started the sales drive for their US funds, Charles and Jacqui quietly exited the existing funds' management. They put in their place some incompetents from within PAF and a couple of their own people. Salesmen were recruited with special incentives to sell to the client base.

There were five million financial illiterates out there, all clients of PAF, who would buy their funds. And there were four key incompetents within their US operations who would agree the investments of the new money flowing into the funds. And those investments would all be drawn from the holdings prepared by Jack Ryder himself.

The investments had cost them under a billion in total, but, through careful market manipulation, now had an apparent value of over four billion already. And. as the market was rising all the time, so was their value. If they sold the shares at current prices to the funds, they would have skimmed off at least three billion.

Their final act was to appoint a specialised trader in PAF. He was one of Stephens' people. He was not that good but knew the basics. He would accept their valuations of the different products he was given and, once again, could push them to their selected clients. They got McGarth to give him a contract with a sales related target. The trader would make money on the amount of deals he did. It didn't matter if they made losses or profits. That was both outrageous and totally unusual. And Lord Dunkillin and Sir Brian jointly signed off on this arrangement. The hole they were digging themselves grew deeper.

At the same time, Charles and Jacqui pushed a few more questionable deals through IBE in London. They all had several things in common. They made money. The bank lost money. And they were authorised by Dunkillin, Sir Brian or the Honourable James.

Stephens again walked into Charles' office. He started yelling at him about the pathetic amount of money he was making. He was unhappy that he was only in for two per cent of the scam. "That's peanuts relative to the amount of money I'm generating. I'm the one doing the trading. I'm there at all hours. I find the deals. I make the millions. I want a fair share or I quit." Charles calmed him down, reminded him he could not quit but said he understood his anger and would look into it.

"Perhaps you're right. Let me talk to the others. Leave it with me. After all the more you have the less they'll get. It's not my choice alone. But I think we've done better from your side than we thought. So I guess they'll sympathise."

The eyes lit up with greed. The man exuded self-confidence. He was blind to the dangers he was facing. He was consumed in the belief in his own invincibility. He had not noted that they had given him deputies whom they could trust to do as told. One had gone to America. The other could be depended on in London. They were far from rocket scientists; in fact one was a Dunkillin nephew who had inherited some of that family's unfortunate genes. They would not question the flawed computer programme. They would definitely not understand it. And yet they would continue to use it. Charles had no further use of Stephens. He had done his bit. The pieces were in place. He could be disposed of soon.

Charles summoned a board meeting and explained that he had a problem with Stephens. He had to make sure nobody was surprised when he disappeared. He mentioned that Stephens wanted a bigger share of the bonus pool. He intimated it was an outrageous quarter of all dealing profits.

"The man wants us to pay him around a hundred million a year. But that's ridiculous. We have a sound deputy in your nephew, Lord Dunkillin. He will be able to run the department and he would do it at Stephens' existing salary. That's just a million a year plus bonus."

Dunkillin nodded. Ffinch-Farquar nodded. The Honourable James nodded. They acquiesced because they liked the ideas of the promotion of one of their own, even if he was not up to the job. And they nodded because the bonus pool applied to them as well. Every penny given to Stephens would have been one less for them to grasp.

Giovanni agreed from his video link up, sensing that Charles was going to dispose of an awkward partner now that his role was done. The investments had been created, the computer programmes had been set up to produce the answers they wanted. The scam was running. They no longer needed the inventor. Jacqui also agreed.

"Who will tell him?"

"I'll talk to him tonight. I had anticipated needing to talk to him and have suggested a meeting this evening. I suspect it might be better to see him alone."

Everybody was quick to acquiesce. Nobody wanted to handle a situation like that. In any case, tomorrow was an important day in the hunting, shooting and fishing calendars that featured so prominently in many of their lives.

"I will offer him up to five million as a break clause. I'll tell him there isn't a penny more, and, if I can make it, a few pennies less."

Everyone laughed. The sums they were talking about were astronomical, but not in the world of high finance. This was a cheap option to rid them of a problem. Charles knew that the money would never get to an account of Stephens except to pass through it. It would end up back in one of the secret accounts, with a good bit as a bonus for Maria who would help them in the disposal.

And the meeting took place with Stephens, ostensibly to agree his price for staying. He was told that the agreement had to be kept secret to avoid others asking for more. "One mention of this in or out of the office and the deal will be off. I don't want a stream of requests for similar treatment," noted Charles. Stephens would be seen in public over the next day or so. And indeed he was, celebrating his apparent good luck. Charles had had to ensure they were not the last people to be seen with him.

That Sunday, Charles and Maria laid watch on Stephen's flat in Bayswater. He wandered out and headed to his local pub at lunchtime. They let him go in. Maria, in careful disguise, walked in calmly.

A scruffy looking student type in that locality is a good disguise and nobody even gave her a second glance. She didn't look terribly wholesome or attractive. Everyone assumed she was one of the students, mainly from Australia, who lived in one of the vans, parked nearby and which plied their way around Europe with their unwashed and dishevelled cargo.

While at the bar, next to Stephens who ignored her, she slipped a few drops of liquid into his glass. In an hour or so, when he was likely to be out of the pub and heading for a small flutter in one of the Mayfair casinos, he was going to feel under the weather. They would then pick him up for disposal.

The drug would make it look as if he was drunk. He wouldn't be falling over though; just meandering from one side of the pavement to the other and feeling rather heady. The British, with their dislike of scenes, would ignore him. That would help make them invisible as they snatched him.

This would be away from his home. It would be out of sight of friends. It would be unnoticed by all. He owned his flat. His bills were all paid. His time of disappearance would be unknown. And once the scam was found, several months later, it would be evident to all that London had got too hot for him. He had done a flyer.

Luckily, Stephens was a man of habit. On the Saturday he had gone to the nightclubs he frequented. He had picked up a girl there and spent the night with her. But she had left the flat, looking angry, the next morning. Now was his lunchtime drink. Then he would gamble, before ending the weekend with some cocaine to help him through the following week. The futility of his existence had always amazed them. His life had no meaning.

They watched him exit the pub unsteadily. For one who frequented it on a daily basis, he was remarkably unpopular. Hardly anyone seemed to talk to him. The barmaid ignored him and left him to the landlord. He seemed to sit in isolation, eyeing up the occasional girl and leering at the chance sight of a thigh.

He walked along the side streets and Charles followed on foot. Maria jumped into the van and followed in their direction. There were too many one way streets and dead ends in that part of the world to tail someone on foot from a van. When Stephens stopped wearily at a bench by one of the small streets that run up from Hyde Park, Charles called Maria to come for a pick up.

The street was empty. The houses were quiet. It was ideal. The van was turning into the street. Charles walked to the bench and sat next to Stephens. He ignored him. He just sat there with his head in his hands. Charles jabbed the hypodermic needle into his thigh. In his semi-drugged state, he was too slow in his reactions. Charles pulled out the needle and slipped it back into his specially prepared boot.

He put his arm around Stephens and walked him to the kerb, pushing him quickly into the van through the sliding door on its side.

The van protected them from the view of houses opposite. There were no CCTV cameras in the vicinity. There were still no people around. There was a vague chance that someone had seen them, but the odds were low and nobody reacted. Maria shoved the van into gear and pulled off again, driving up towards Paddington and the wastelands of London beyond.

Charles looked at the unconscious form of Stephens and bound him and gagged him for safety. He then climbed through to the front and sat next to Maria.

"We pumped him with enough stuff to keep him asleep for a good few hours. Let's head down to Beachy Head."

Two hours later they were at the Sussex Beauty spot. It was a high cliff overlooking the sea. The cliff overhung the full tide, eroded at its base by the sea and up its sides by the wind and the spray from storms over the years. In the back of the van, they tended to Stephens. He was still out for the count, but they topped up the injection as a precaution.

They bundled him into a car Douglas had parked in the cliff top car park earlier. The timing was perfect. It was five in the evening. Nobody else was around at that time of year. They had changed from their scruffy clothes. Charles was in slacks and a blazer with an open necked shirt. Maria was in trousers and a sweater.

She slipped into the van and adjusted the engine. They had attached to it a neat device that would automatically start the engine in ten minutes time, switch on the headlights and put it into gear. The handbrake was off. The van would roll forward and crash into the sea below. Thirty seconds after the engine started, the device would blow up. And with it would go the van. Nobody would find it. And nobody was going to examine carefully a half-derelict hippie van with nobody in it. They would assume that it had been dumped. It was an annoying pastime of people in that area who used Beachy Head as a dustbin for unwanted or stolen goods.

They headed round the coast to the boat. It was simple putting Stephens on board. Again, there was nobody there at this time of the year. The mooring was deserted. The boat owners were far away. They knew that as they knew the owners. Indeed, they had the keys to the boat. Neighbours in London had asked Charles and Jacqui to keep an eye on it from time to time when they were down in Sussex. And they were free to use it.

Stephens was down below as Charles started the engines. The noise reverberated round the shore but nobody lived near enough to take any interest. In minutes they were slipping out to sea. By now Stephens was coming round. They had kept him alive till then as it is easier to move a drugged man than a dead one. But he was no use to them now. Maria drew her stiletto and ended him there and then. They pulled the body on deck, tying up the fine wound to avoid any blood spilling. There was surprisingly little.

The cement was there in the two large tubs they had prepared earlier that weekend. All it needed was water and they added that quickly. It was cold. Charles was in shirtsleeves. Maria had her sweater. But they both shivered in the cold breeze as the automatic control took them further out to sea.

The cement was quick setting and strong. They covered the deck with an old tarpaulin and placed the dead man's feet and thighs on it. Two large blocks of cement were soon around his legs. There was some left over and they placed that around his chest. It fitted tightly. They picked up the tubs, almost empty now but quite heavy. In a moment, one after another, they tossed them overboard.

Later, having put the boat into a wide ark, they checked the cement. It was firm and solid. Charles indicated to Maria and together they heaved the body to the side. It was incredibly heavy. It was no easy task. They scanned the horizon. There was no light in sight.

With one more heave they lifted him and dropped him over the side. He fell to the depths of the English Channel. He sank straight down to the bottom, some ten miles off the coast. He would lie there for some time, sinking into the sand and stone at the base of the sea. His chances of being found were remote.

They took off the gloves they had used and collected the tarpaulin and other implements. They checked for any odd lumps of cement. Everything went into a plastic bag. It was weighted with stones and after leaving Stephen's grave some ten minutes behind at full throttle, they also tossed that into the sea. They checked out the boat with a torch. There was no blood. No evidence of any struggle.

They had dumped him well away from London. And there, where nobody would look and he was unlikely to be found, he would lie. Once he had lain there for a few more months and the scam was over, even if found and identified they had no concerns. It would be assumed that he met his end because he dealt with the world of crime. There was no reason for anyone to suspect them.

They went below. Maria checked Charles out. She removed some cement from his shirt cuff. There was nothing else. He checked her out. The short crop of black hair was still neat and tidy despite having been teased by the wind. The eyes were soft and calm despite the killing. The skin was rosy rather than red from the biting wind outside. The dark sweater was spotless, falling smoothly down her body and moving gently with the rise and fall of her breasts. The trousers still bore their creases, but nothing else.

Charles put his arms around her shoulders and turned her towards him. They both knew what they needed to do. They both realised what they wanted to happen. He walked over to the motor at the front of the lower deck. There was one above deck and one at cabin level. He switched it off and allowed the boat to drift. They would come to no harm here.

They shut the door and he moved to Maria. She moved to him. He kissed her on the back of the neck and felt her lips move over his throat and then her face was buried into his chest. Her face was cold even against the coldness of his body. The wind and the sea had chilled her just as it had chilled him.

His hands moved up her back and he eased her sweater up. He felt her breasts taut and desirable against his half-opened shirt. The sweater came off without resistance as she raised her arms to help him.

He fumbled at the fastening of her clothes. She had no such trouble with his and carefully moved apart to pull them down in one eager movement.

He sensed the growing heat of her body as they moved together in that tight cabin. Its windows steamed up and the new-found warmth quickly dispelled all memory of the icy breeze up on deck. He felt excitement as he waited for her. He felt anguish as he fought for control. He felt then the surge of pleasure in her, which acted as an immediate release for him. They came almost brutally, driving their bodies together with all the force they could muster, pushing themselves together with all the strength that they had and crushing each other with a passion that frightened yet pleased.

They lay there for ten or fifteen minutes. They kissed each other gently. They stroked each other's faces. They kissed each other on the neck, the ear, and the eyes. They felt peace come over them. Then it was over. Then it ended. They drew apart and knew they would return to normal. Time goes on and there was no end to a relationship such as the one they had. But there was also no beginning, no middle and no reality. It was a relationship that existed in its fleeting moments. It never died. But it never survived. It had its memories but it had no past. It had few expectations and no future.

They were half-dressed when they heard someone hail us. "Ahoy there, is there anyone on board?"

Charles grabbed his gun and pulled open the cabin door. He saw the uniform and the coastguard immediately. He slipped the gun back although Maria still held hers behind him. That was a good precaution. The tall ruddy man on the coastguard vessel looked at Charles, "What are you doing here? Has your engine failed? You were spotted on a random radar search floating here with your engines switched off. Is everything all right?"

Then Maria came out and he grinned.

Charles said, "We were resting below. We'll head back to shore now. We felt like a spin on the boat to get some sea air."

That was a stupid explanation and the coastguard definitely did not believe it. He jumped immediately to the conclusion that they had been making love. He had been curious as to why they were there. He had not been suspicious. Charles breathed a sigh of relief. The coastguard said they would follow them back to see they returned safely.

So Charles went up to the deck and started the boat up. She purred into full speed and they headed inland. The coast became clearer, lit by the full moon as it edged itself from between the clouds. Then they came to the cove and turned in. The coastguard vessel gave them a cheery wave and headed off. It must have checked the boat's home port and now saw that they were returning to it. They had not questioned if they were entitled to be out in it, but Charles wondered if there would be a reception committee for them when they returned.

"I guess an affair is the best cover," he said to Maria. "We can use the usual story. We are concerned the wife will get to know. Keep our identities. They know me in this area. They'll be discreet."

They turned in to the shore and edged against the jetty. They tied up the boat and made everything secure. Charles saw they were being watched from a police car by the road. It was parked just behind theirs.

"Excuse me, sir. I wander if you could identify yourself," said a voice with a distinct Sussex burr.

"Of course, I'm Charles Rossi and live the other side of Newhaven."

"Ah yes, Mr Rossi. I've heard of you."

"This is my assistant, Maria. We have permission to use this boat while the owners are away. We went for lunch and then decided to come down here for a ride."

He smiled the smile of a man who thought he should act like a man of the world. "Bit dangerous what you did sir. The coastguard picked you up on radar and saw that you weren't moving. I realise it was a false alarm. It was a bit stupid, if I may say so, sir."

"Look, I'm very sorry. It was a mistake. But I would ask for discretion. It was stupid but no crime. The last thing we want is for this to be in the papers."

"Sir, it's a closed case. We know you were authorised to take the boat. And it's not a crime to have stopped out at sea. The fact won't even be reported at the station. That would be unnecessary. I would ask that you remember the consequences next time, sir."

Charles breathed a sight of relief. The last thing he wanted was a record at the police station. There would be a record at the coastguards' office but that was unavoidable. Still they were seen several miles away from the place they dumped the body. There was a bigger risk than they liked but nothing could be done about it. It was stupid as they had selected the sea as the all concealing hiding place. Still, the police were not suspicious and wouldn't be sending divers down. That was why they had gone so far out. Onshore there is always the chance that an amateur diver could see something. Way out there and, at that depth, there was little chance.

Maria and Charles got back in the car and, with a wave to the police, headed off to London. She was the first to speak.

"They fell for the secretary and boss story hook, line and sinker," she said with a laugh. "The younger one kept eyeing me up and down. He would have liked a go as well."

"I don't like getting stopped like that. If the cement fails and he comes loose we would be remembered."

"Look, the cement is going to hold firm for twenty years. That wasn't run of the mill stuff. That's the sort of high-grade produce they use for containers for radioactive waste. The main danger would be if someone found the cement in a couple of decades and discovered the feet in them. Or they could find pieces of the rib cage for that reason as we encased that too. We're safe. They won't keep the records that long. And nobody will put a date to the remains. So nobody is going to recall a couple playing naughty games at sea some time in the past."

She was right and Charles relaxed as they joined the motorway and sped up to London. They drew up in front of his house. It was gone eleven.

"Tell Jacqui about the police and their suspicions anyway. There's always a chance that she will need to know. Otherwise, say that everything went smoothly. The boat was stationary because we were cleaning up."

Tomorrow, they would depart to see the Russians. It would be just Maria and Charles. Jacqui would hold the fort.

Charles' plan was simple. He would buy the evil empire from Di Maglio for a billion dollars cash plus a share of future profits. That was a pittance but Di Maglio would have no choice. And he would have the satisfaction of believing he had ensnared them. But Charles would sell on the business to the Russians. And Di Maglio would have a hard time getting his share of profits from them.

Charles had also plans to ensure that the billion dollars could be traced and seized. They knew that a billion dollars was far too much money for a man like Di Maglio to own, for now he was their enemy.

CHAPTER FIFTEEN

The next morning they flew to Paris and then on to Nimes. They used the executive jet to avoid customs and security. When you are carrying everything the good terrorist needs, other than guns, you have to take such precautions. The guns would be delivered to them at the airport. Charles felt they were too bulky to have with them, especially as he wanted sub machine guns and not just pistols.

Maria and he were both dressed in office clothes. Once in Nimes, they would head to the Pont du Gard near the Russian compound in Uzes. The hotel there, a modest tourist place, would be their base. It was somewhere they would never be recognised, far from the normal luxury hotels they frequented in that part of the world.

They hired a car in Nimes. It was a simple saloon, a Renault. They had no need for a fast car. They were not trying to escape from anyone, they were trying to establish who was running the Russian Mafia and whether they could do business with them. They found a quiet spot to change into less conspicuous clothes. Two business people left Nimes airport but two tourists showed up at the Pont du Gard.

They arrived at the hotel in the early afternoon and made a big show of affection in the lobby. They kept their arms around each other and kissed regularly. Charles felt gently aroused as he always did when he felt the slim body of Maria pressing against him. But the show was not a prelude to any lovemaking. It was a cover to allow them to disappear for the rest of the afternoon and get some sleep. They would be up around two a.m. That was the best time to get into the Russian compound and check out Rastinov.

Once in the room, they closed the shutters and drew the curtains. Soon they slept. The training of years on the field had taught Maria to grab sleep at any time. Charles found it more difficult, but the quietness of the place and the regular soft sound of Maria's gentle breathing next to him in the bed soon lulled him to sleep. He woke up later and saw it was just after midnight. They had slept for around eight hours. Yet Maria slept on undisturbed.

It was a warm night and he looked at her. She was lying on the bed with a sheet partly draped over her. It ran across her waist and over her thighs. She lay on her back, her face at peace. Her dark hair was tousled but still kept its shape. The short bob never looked untidy, even after the wildest of exertions. There was a faint sheen of perspiration on her face, but it seemed to place a gloss on it. The long dark eyelashes didn't move. The small shapely nose flared slightly with each breath. The lips were red and moist and, from time to time, her tongue seemed to dart out and lick them lovingly.

He groaned quietly to himself. The excitement ahead always aroused him. Yet he knew that he had to put that all out of his mind. The venture was going to be dangerous enough. Maria was sleeping to be on maximum form in the morning. He needed to do the same. Reason triumphed over desire and soon he fell back into a deep sleep.

Maria was dressed when she woke him. She smiled down at him, as he lay there, naked as she had been. He was half covered by the sheet. She absent-mindedly licked her lips. Her eyes sparkled and she smiled almost to herself. He got out of bed and went to the bathroom. The shower hissed and then let out a slow dribble of coldish water. He fiddled randomly with the knobs and managed to change it into a flow of slightly warmer water. The plumbing protested at the early start and rumbled loudly.

Refreshed, he towelled himself dry. He shaved and walked outside again. Maria passed him a mug of coffee. The hotel did not offer that service but she had packed the necessary. It had the acrid taste of instant coffee but the warmth and the caffeine served their purpose. They were now fully awake and focussed on the task ahead.

Like Maria, Charles pulled on a pair of black jeans and a black shirt over a similar hue T-shirt. Dark trainers completed the look. He took a body belt and tied it to his waist. That had a couple of make-up jars with a solution that would enable them to camouflage their faces and hands. It also contained all they needed to set up plastic explosive that would make a blast out of all proportion to its size.

They each carried a bag with the guns. Each of them would have an Uzi with several rounds of spare ammunition. Then they had a second gun, a handgun that would go in the leg holster that they both preferred. Finally, they had an evil looking knife with a two-sided blade and heavy handle.

Their room was on the ground floor and they left it through the window. That, in turn, they left ajar to allow an easy return. They could not be certain when they would return and in what state. The 'do not disturb' sign would hopefully keep out any maid. In any case, they had signed in under a false name and Maria was now expertly going round the room eliminating any evidence of their presence. Their few belongings were left but they were all recently bought from popular stores and couldn't be traced back to them. Their travel papers were with them. They had all they needed for any possible retreat.

The car had been carefully parked away from the hotel. That avoided anyone identifying it and had allowed them to pretend their arrival had been by train or taxi. Covering their tracks and confusing any pursuer was second nature at times like this.

They drove along the dark, winding roads of the French countryside. The morning had not yet announced its arrival. They had another two or three hours before dawn. The car contained the sensors that would allow them to scan the house and establish the presence, or otherwise, of Rastinov or Turpin. If Rastinov were there, their objective would be to kill him. If Turpin were there, they would see if they could start to negotiate a deal.

The car purred round the deserted corners and along the quiet roads of that rocky corner of France. They skirted Uzes itself, sleeping, in the absence of its transient summer population, in all the calm of its recently acquired bourgeois tranquillity. They headed along roads that were familiar to Charles. Years earlier, he had been there in more desperate times when Jacqui had been captured and tortured by the inhabitants of the Russian compound. Then they had attacked in force and left behind a trail of destruction and death. This time their mission was more secretive. They had to ensure they were not seen before they had established whom they would be seeing themselves.

They left the car about a mile from the compound, in bushes just off the road. They would be able to make a fast getaway from that point, over the rocky, rough ground and onto the straight section of the road. But the car would not be seen, at least while it was still dark.

They walked the rest of the way to the compound and came to the high wall. They reconnoitred from afar, saw that the security cameras did not cover all areas. They identified an unsupervised part. The wall at that point was well over two metres high. Charles held his hands together and Maria used that as a foothold. His arms were down and she climbed up, her thighs pressing warmly against his face. He called for her to tell him when she wanted him to hoist her up. On her call, he lifted his hands, still joined together, to chest and then head high. Once she was that high, and had let her hold go from him, she turned and then pulled herself to the top of the wall. He passed up a rope and they both took one end. She eased herself over the ledge and he felt her weight tighten on it.

He moved the rope still taut, closer to the wall. Then he jumped to the wall, just as he had been trained, and climbed vertically up it using the rope as a lever. He knew that Maria was moving away from the wall on the other side to ensure that it was still taut. Then, as he saw he was a metre or so up the wall in just three strides, he pulled himself forward and grabbed the top. From there, it was no effort to pull himself up and over. He joined Maria who was already tying up the rope.

Out of sight, they unpacked their bags. He took the make-up from the body belt and they darkened their skins. They each grabbed a holster, knife and handgun and fastened them securely. Then the Uzis were attached to their straps and placed over their shoulders. They fell to the right height for them to shoot them one handed, if needed, keeping them taut by their straps against their bodies. Charles assembled the scanner and, having placed the spare ammunition in his body belt, they advanced.

They went quietly and slowly, checking out for hidden surveillance equipment and trip wires or other traps. They identified some and avoided them. The night was cool but not chilly. There was a quiet and gentle breeze but it was refreshing rather than unpleasant. The clouds could not hold out the moon but they reduced its brightness and that of the stars. It was dark enough for their purpose, although they would have preferred a thicker screen of cloud.

It was only a mile from the road to the house but they took around an hour to go across the wooded wilderness that led them to the more manicured gardens of the main building. There they would have to use cover from the clumps of bushes and conifers that spread around the perimeter of the cultivated area and marked out the different paths that criss-crossed the lawn.

They approached carefully. Maria tugged his arm and indicated a box on the front of the house. He looked and picked out another one. Then another. They circled the house. These would be alarms or sensors that would bathe the lawn and its surrounds with light from the powerful lamps that topped the house itself. Maria signalled that they should stop.

Charles hid behind the cover of a bush and pushed the sensor in front of it. That allowed it a free range to the house and improved its response time to objects. He set up the machine and focussed on the screen. He started down in the cellars, searching methodically over the whole area for people. There was a wine cellar. There was an armoury full of a variety of weapons, he also identified a storeroom. From the size of the packages, he would have said that there could be over a hundred million dollars of heroin. But there were no signs of life.

He scanned the next two floors and identified several people. They all seemed to be asleep or at least in bed. Then he saw a red light flash on the monitor. That indicated a target had been identified. He checked out as they zoomed into a sleeping form and established that Turpin was in the building. Turpin was an interesting man as he was only Russian by ancestry. His parents had emigrated from St Petersburg to Pittsburgh. Perhaps they felt that the similar names would make them less homesick. Turpin had run a few gangs in his hometown before striking the big time with the emergence of the Russian Mafia. He had worked as one of Rastinov's deputies and, after the sacking of this same Uzes compound by Di Maglio and his men, had assumed control of the whole Mafia itself.

He was not a crude and brutal man like Rastinov. He was a schemer. And he would be ruthless. The fact that he had managed to maintain his position of supremacy in the Mafia showed that. He was also, or so they believed, a man who would see the benefits of cutting a deal. It was better to negotiate a take-over of Di Maglio's world. That avoided a battle and endless bloodshed. Then it was better for him to be friendly with Charles, who owned banks and could be used to launder large sums. Turpin was not to know that their plans did not see them owning the banks for long. But there was no need for him to know that for the moment. In any event, even without the banks, the deal would be valuable for him.

Charles carried on examining the building. He now moved to the outhouses. In the old days, when he had hit the building to snatch Jacqui from Rastinov and before they subsequently attacked it and sought to raze it to the ground, these were unconnected other than by underground passages. These days they were all adjoining. It was in a small such outhouse that further trouble was detected. Charles' heart sank. He watched carefully as it analysed what seemed to be a sleeping figure. Then the answer came. The figure was that of the dreaded Rastinov.

He turned to Maria and mentioned what he had found to her. She bit her lip in concentration as he sent the sensors over the building itself. It consisted of three rooms. The one where Rastinov was located was some sort of cell. Next door was a room that contained a kitchen and an office. The third was a small bedroom where there was someone in bed.

He zoomed onto the figure again and noticed that the person was a woman.

He switched the sensor over to find guns. The sensor checked out the three rooms and found nothing. It identified several knives in the kitchen area but they were all standard household ones. Then it stopped by a unit on the wall of the second room. It identified scalpels and other surgical equipment. Charles checked out a table. It seemed high. He identified an operating table. The place seemed to contain a mini hospital. It seemed unguarded. And most ominously, it appeared to contain their old enemy, Rastinov.

He turned to Maria, "What the hell is he doing there? It's some sort of private area with a medical bay."

"Perhaps he's ill. They may be treating him there."

"I need to see. If Jacqui thinks he's alive, she'll be petrified. He caused us enough pain last time we met. I thought we'd killed him."

"Let's do it now?" said Maria. So they moved forward and slowly made their way to the outhouse. Inch by inch they crossed the intervening fifty yards or so.

They were careful not to activate the sensors around the building. External sensors have to be less sensitive than internal ones or they'll be set off by wild animals and birds. They slid up against the wall and approached the door. Maria gently turned the doorknob. It made no noise but it turned and she pushed the door gently. It opened. Still there was no sound.

Charles looked through the widening gap into a small hallway he had identified on the scanner. There were no cameras and apparently no alarms. Cautiously, they eased their way in. Maria shut the door carefully. In front of them were two doors. From the scanner, they knew that one led to the medical room and one to the woman's bedroom. They wondered now if she were a nurse.

Again, Maria opened the door slowly. Charles motioned her to go to the left-hand door. This was the one that led to the medical room. They needed to check out the cell before they did anything. The door opened silently again and they eased in. Maria indicated the sensors. They could not tell their range.

Charles recalled a small cupboard in the hall and nodded at Maria to stay. He slipped back the way they had come and opened the cupboard. The control panel was there. A key operated the alarm and it was in the lock. He hoped he would not activate the whole thing by switching it off.

He turned the key. The light indicated the alarm was deactivated.

He returned. Maria whispered, "We have two minutes maximum. The alarm could be linked to a control back at the main house. They would wonder who had switched it off at five in the morning. Go quickly."

They moved to the cell. The light fell on the face of the sleeping man. It was Rastinov. It was the face Charles recalled on his one and only meeting. This was a face he would never forget. He looked at the drip above the bed. He stared at the machines.

"Dialysis of some sort" whispered Maria. "The brute must be ill. This is really some sort of sick bay. But he actually is alive."

"That means he rules. We kill him."

Before he could move, Maria had drawn her knife and slit his throat. She did it without hesitation. Remorse wasn't needed.

Charles' one slight fear always, when he saw Maria at work, was that she never knew remorse. It didn't matter who the victim was. If she were ordered to kill, she obeyed blindly.

Charles loved Maria in a strange way. It was not like the love he felt for Jacqui. It was born out of the excitement from the chase and the kill. It was almost like a throwback to a previous life. One that he felt, one day, he would need to discard for good. Those thoughts flashed through his mind as he prepared the plastic explosive and attached it to the cell and then to the room beyond.

"It's going to be hard for anyone recognise him after this," said Maria who was attaching explosive to the body itself. They set the whole thing for one minute. And they moved back to the hall. They listened carefully by the nurse's room, but all was quiet. They crept to the door. This time they were not worried about sensors. If you are close to a major explosion, that's the least of your worries. Especially if you only have thirty seconds or so to go before the whole show starts.

They ran from the building. The lights were activated. Then a siren sounded. Lights went on in the house. But, by that time, they were well into the grounds. Both of them were running steadily, hands on the machine guns that hung from their shoulders. They had covered several hundred yards, perhaps less, when the explosion tore through the air.

There was an enormous blast. Then there was a rush of air. It was followed by the sound of frightened birds, leaving their nests for the safety of the skies and calling anxiously to each other. Then they heard the voices. Orders were shouted. But there was panic in the voices. That would give them a bit more time.

They ran on. They knew they had a mile of rough terrain to cover. But they would head in the same direction. For the wall on the inside was only a couple of metres off the ground. Outside the drop was more. That meant they could scale it without ropes. Maria would need Charles to climb it first and then give her a helping hand.

They then heard the dogs. They would be able to run faster than they ever could. They had run over a minute by then, perhaps two. They had estimated they needed six or seven. They ploughed on. The barking became louder. Maria ran faster than Charles and called for him to go on. "When the dogs get closer, I'll shoot them. Go ahead and then give me cover if more appear."

He ran on. He felt lonely without Maria next to him. The trees looked larger. The whole of the grounds took on a more ominous feeling. There was something about fleeing on your own that is so much more menacing than doing so together. He heard the crack of the sub machine gun. He stopped and turned. Maria was some hundred yards back and he could see a dog jumping towards her. The crack of the gun seemed to come after the moment when it was stopped in its track and fell back in the air.

Maria ran on towards him. She was alone. Then he heard more barking and a large black dog came bounding towards her. It looked ominous in the pale light morning. Its jaws were open and seemingly waiting to get hold of her flesh.

Charles straightened his gun. Maria was running towards him and the dog was coming in from the left to grab her. That allowed him to have a clean line of fire. The dog closed on Maria. She approached Charles. He waited. The closer they were, the more likely he was to kill the beast. Maria was now twenty yards from him. She must have known what he was doing. Her face though was a deathly white. Her breath was coming in gasps. He opened fire and the bullets sliced into the dog. They slowed him, and then he stumbled to his knees and fell.

All was quiet other than Maria's breathing. Charles turned and led the way again. This time they were running faster. She gasped at him, "I killed two dogs. I didn't see the third till it was too late." He signalled her to carry on running. They must have covered half the distance. They ran on. There was no sign of others pursuing them but they pushed on as fast as they could.

He looked over to Maria. She was running, her mouth open as she gulped in air. Her chest heaved up and down with the exertion as she ran and stumbled over the uneven ground. Charles could feel sweat pouring down his face as he struggled to keep up with her. He was pushing himself to run faster than before. He kept the image of the fangs of the dog he had killed in his mind. It served as a reminder of what could happen if he fell or flagged.

In the distance they saw the wall. Just a couple of hundred yards of scrubland separated them. They ran on. They could hear shouts again but they seemed quite a way off. Maria made the wall seconds before him. He carried on running and jumped, pulling himself up to get to the top. His arms felt weak but somehow he managed. He sat astride, leant over and held out an arm. As Maria grabbed it and seemingly ran up the wall, the voices approached. Some men ran out of the trees.

He loosed his gun and fired a round towards the pursuers. They threw themselves onto the ground. He saw Maria had one leg over the wall and then the other. He fired off another round and dropped over the wall himself. As he disappeared out of view, the wall reverberated with the sound of bullets tearing into it and then over it. Maria grabbed his arm. "Move," she called as they headed down the road, skirting the perimeter.

They continued until they heard the car. Both threw themselves into the long grass and shallow ditch they had noticed before by the side of the road. Charles rolled on his back, as did Maria, in anticipation of a battle. The Uzis were in their hands and ready to blast anyone who approached. But the car disappeared into the distance. Maria lifted her head carefully in case there was another. But there was no trap. They got up again and jogged along the road. All was peaceful as they came to the curve where they had parked their car.

They approached it carefully. It was there just as they had left it.

Maria suddenly muttered, "Shit," and pulled Charles away and down on the ground. They had walked into open view of a jeep. It was parked just over the brow of the hill with three men scouring the countryside. They were parked at an angle. He realised they would not be able to see the car. They couldn't have seen them either yet or they would have fired. But they were not well covered and if the jeep kept on the scrubland and off the road on the way back, they would be totally visible.

They waited and held their breath. There was no noise, no movement. Then they heard a low murmur. The jeep engine started and seemed to approach them. Then it turned away, and they could hear it moving along the tarmac in the distance. They waited a few minutes. Nobody seemed to be around.

They eased their way to the car and checked again. All seemed to be clear. Charles jumped into the driving seat and Maria got in beside him. He threw the car into gear and drove off. He jammed his foot down and drove at top speed down the quiet road and back through Uzes into the area around the Pont du Gard.

"Hotel," said Maria. "Let's get in through the window. Park in the street. If all's clear, we duck into the grounds."

All was clear. Charles slammed the car shut and they ran to the window of their room. Maria pulled it open and they got back inside. The bed was still unmade, and all seemed as they'd left it. Maria checked the door.

"We can't head off now. Someone could check out unusual movements. Tomorrow looks like being a nice day. We should move out with the weekenders who'll come here for lunch. That means we kill time till three or four in the afternoon."

"The best thing is to check out late morning," said Maria. "Then we can grab lunch. But it better be at one of the tourist restaurants. Not one of your normal Michelin starred joints. That would be too noticeable. We blend with the crowd and then head off. We're not going to make the plane from Nimes. We'd do better driving to Valence and jumping on the TGV."

Charles thought through her plan. The TGV would get them into Paris around seven or eight in the evening. And they should be able to make either a late flight to London or a train from the Gard du Nord through the Channel tunnel. They would be back in London, where the time was an hour behind Paris, by midnight.

He looked at his watch. It was just before six. "That means we have three or four hours to kill."

"And so we can have a decent breakfast. I'm hungry. We've had nothing to eat since lunchtime yesterday other than the odd bar of chocolate."

"Maria, breakfast won't be on offer for an hour or more."

"We better clean up then."

"But we'll wake the neighbours. And it's Sunday. You heard the plumbing earlier."

"What do you suggest then?" she asked in an amused voice.

He looked around the room. "There isn't that much we can do here. But there is one thing and it just happens that I couldn't think of anything better even if there were enormous choice."

And with that he stepped forward and took her in his arms. He felt again the warmth of her body. He sensed once more her softness. He breathed in again the bitter sweat smell of her perfume. He shivered as their bodies clung to each other in memory of the excitement and the chaos of the previous hour or so.

The crash of splintering wood shook him out of that reverie. He dived to his right to the gun on the bed where he had thrown it. Out of the corner of his eye, he could see Maria grabbing for hers. The door flew into the room, or at least pieces of it did. At the same time, the shattering of glass was accompanied by a shower of splinters and jagged pieces of window.

Charles had the gun in his hand and blasted it towards the window, raking the area from left to right. One hand held the gun and the other ripped open his body belt. He got ready to reload the gun the moment it stopped firing.

Maria had let off a round at the door in a similar way. Somehow, by instinct they had realised what the other would do. It was logical as an afterthought. Charles was closer to the window. She was nearer the door. A man half stumbled through the hole that used to be a door. Maria held her handgun in one hand, the Uzi, now strapped over her shoulder, in the other. The handgun blasted the already injured intruder, punching holes into his chest as he took one step and then another before he crashed, lifeless, to the floor.

Once Charles gun stopped firing, he ejected the spent clip and slammed in a new one. He waited but there was silence. It was strange. There were no cries, no movement. There was nothing. It was as if the hotel were dead to the world. It seemed as if nothing had happened. Where were the other guests? Where were the attackers? Where were the night staff? They couldn't have slept through that din. They just seemed to be stunned into a ghastly ghostly silence.

Charles felt blood drip from his head onto his hand. He suspected it was a cut from the flying glass but ignored it. He concentrated on the window. His finger curled round the Uzi ready to push it into its deadly action once again. The curtains were still half drawn. Otherwise they would have been showered with more glass. But he knew that they might have protected him initially. Now they were a danger. He had no idea who could be hiding there, all he knew was that they had won the first round and the second would allow their attackers to act first unless they moved quickly.

Maria must have sensed the same thing. The dead man on the floor must have destroyed the door. As she fired at it he must have been hit. When he fell through the door, wounded, perhaps even fatally, she finished him off. There would be more behind him. That much was certain.

Charles exchanged looks with Maria and moved to the curtains. He grabbed one from the side and pulled it open. Maria loosed off more shots at the clear space but nobody was there. Charles pulled out another clip and threw it to her. She reloaded and covered the open doorway with her gun.

Now there was noise. There was frightened shouting and screams. There was movement but it was far away. But there was no attack. They waited and still there was no movement.

"We're going to have some explaining to do if we stay here," Charles muttered to Maria. "It must have been the Russians. They want us in the open. They know we can't wait here. It'll blow our cover. We have no choice. I'll cover. Clean the room."

Maria quickly wiped the room clean and grabbed the guns, knives and papers they would need. They slipped the papers in their shirts and prepared for the battle. They both still had blackened faces, although that would not help them in the coming dawn light. Maria still held her sub machine gun across her body and in the other hand had a revolver. Charles was holding a sub machine gun by his side with a spare ammunition clip in his other hand.

He took the last piece of plastic explosive and set it up in the room. It would cause a fair deal of damage without too much outside. He waited for Maria to signal she was ready and mouthed "fifteen seconds" to her. That would allow them to escape and find maximum cover from the blast. It would also mean nobody was likely to get to the room before the blast. They had enough problems on their hands without another murder charge.

They had two options. They could leave by the door or the window. The window was too dangerous. They could get no cover. So they selected the door. Maria went first and then Charles. They moved down the corridor at a trot and turned the corner towards the lobby. The blast from the room seemed to rock the hotel. They heard the crash of falling glass and more screams of terror from the frightened occupants. Still they saw none of their attackers.

They moved through the deserted lobby and into the entrance.

Charles flung himself on the ground seconds after Maria as a volley of bullets brushed over their heads. Maria fired in their general direction but they knew that such random fire was unlikely to find its target.

They moved outside and took cover from the cars parked in front of the hotel. "We need a getaway car," called Maria. "Cover me as I try to get one."

She looked around and saw a sleek sports car. It would have power and that was what they needed. She drew her knife and manoeuvred it into the lock. The door swung open. She had opened the passenger side. Charles realised she would jump start the engine and then allow him to get in next to her as she drove away. He also realised that the light bodywork would offer little resistance to bullets and so they needed to ensure that no shots hit their mark.

He saw movement in the bushes and stood up with the gun roaring. The stream of fire that spat out of the muzzle pointed to his target, who came crashing down into the bush to his left. There was further movement and again he fired, drowning out the sound of the car engine.

He could see Maria crouched down and ready to go. He slammed another clip into the machine gun. He realised they were almost out of ammunition. Holding onto the open door, now half sitting in the car, he fired into the area where the movement had occurred. Maria pushed the car into gear and they screeched over the car park's rough surface.

At the main gate of the hotel, Charles pulled himself fully into the car. Wrestling with the force of the wind against the open door, he slammed it shut. Opening the window, he looked around the grounds. By the bush he had first fired at, a man emerged. He fired two or three shots at him but had little chance of hitting him from the moving car.

Maria swung into the road and accelerated away. "Make for the motorway as quickly as possible. We need to put distance between us and them."

"We're being followed," she called. "It's a blue BMW with two or three occupants."

"Open the roof. It's automatic. Then let them get closer and I'll try to take them out."

Maria pushed a button and the roof started to open. The slow opening seemed to go on forever. The BMW closed in on them as they inevitably slowed down against the heightened wind resistance on the canvas top. Then they seemed to surge ahead again.

Charles turned round and jammed himself against the dashboard to monitor the following car. They were increasing their distance from them with every minute. Maria was also an excellent driver, taking the bends smoothly.

"Ahead, look ahead," she shouted. He turned and saw that a large truck blocked the road. And he saw the guns that were pointed towards them.

"Left," he yelled. "Go down the slope."

She obeyed immediately and swung off the road and down the hillside. They bounced dangerously on the rocky surface, glancing a rock side on and then bouncing back. The car hit the road again and Maria struggled with the steering wheel.

She realised she wasn't going to make it and pointed the car down the next slope beyond the next bend in the road. This one was less steep but more bumpy. It was rocky and she forced the steering wheel right and then left again and again. Somehow, she steered them back onto the road.

Once again, her foot went to the accelerator and they gathered speed. "Keep an eye up above. They may still be able to target us," she shouted.

"The BMW is following. It's about three bends behind. Keep up this speed. Keep an eye on the warning light. You could have done some damage as we drove down the slopes."

They headed for the motorway. "We need to lose the BMW. Soon we'll have to dump this car. It's too dangerous to take it far. The police will be searching for it."

"Stop here." Moments later she had pulled in on a bend. They both got out. He crossed the road and hid behind a bush. She did the same.

"Fire at the wheels," she called. "I'll try the occupants."

They waited for a few moments and heard the roar of the BMW as it ploughed round the corner towards them. They opened fire together and the blast took the car and its occupants by surprise. The tyres ripped to shreds and they heard the ear-shattering scream of metal on tarmac. The windscreen seemed to implode and the men in the car screamed before the bullets ended their terror. The car veered off the road into the scrubland and, suddenly, all was ominously quiet.

They made their way carefully towards the car. It was wrecked. Three men were dead. There was no need to linger and they headed back to the sports car and drove on. There was going to be no further pursuit..

Charles took some wipes and cleaned the black camouflage from his face and hands. He took off his shirt, and turning it inside out, completed the task. He looked into the mirror. His face was cut just above the eye.

He felt the cut. There seemed to be no signs of a splinter. The bleeding had stopped but there was still blood on his shirt.

He looked over at Maria. Her face was tense. Her lips were pursed as she pushed the car to the limit. Her face and hands were still black from the camouflage but otherwise she seemed unmarked. She would be able to provide cover for the two things they would need a change of clothes and transport.

She pulled in just off the motorway and they changed seats. She was cleaning up just as he had done as he drove them along the still empty motorway that Sunday morning.

She wiped her face carefully and then took off her shirt to remove the last vestiges of the black. She delved into her pocket and surprised him by bringing out a lipstick and carefully applying it. Then she produced some eye shadow and carefully, but lightly, made up her eyes. Turning the shirt back to its right side, she brushed it clean and pulled it back on.

She looked at the signposts. "Let's get to Valence and then dump the car. We can get the train from there. I prefer that to hiring a car as long as one comes through soon after we get there."

"Shouldn't we go to ground somewhere? Dumping the car in Valence and getting on the train is dangerous. It's a long journey to Paris. So let's get a train for Paris but get out along the line. It'll be safer. We can go to ground overnight. Then we get new clothes on Monday. We can hire a car and be back in London by evening. We need to warn Jacqui. We may have been recognised. We were definitely followed to the hotel."

She agreed and they sped on, without hindrance, until they entered Valence. They left the car in a side street and walked to the station. It was just after eight. The church bells peeled and disturbed the peaceful calm of the provincial dawn. Picking up their earlier cover of two lovers on a romantic weekend, they made their way to the station and sought out the best options for their return home.

CHAPTER SIXTEEN

They walked through the deserted streets of Valence and entered the empty station hall. There was no train for Paris but there was one for Lyon leaving in a few minutes time.

Maria said, "We go to Lyon and then cross to Geneva. I know we've a problem with Di Maglio but we need him now. We need to know how he knew that Rastinov was alive."

Charles' instinct told him that she was right. In any case they had no time to discuss the matter. He walked to the ticket office and took tickets for the Lyon train. Minutes later they were on the platform and then in a half empty compartment speeding away from the town.

The French countryside at that time of the year is far from enchanting. The craggy scenery and the despondent, empty vines looked back morosely as they journeyed through them.

They didn't discuss the day's events. They sat there quietly and hardly exchanged a word. They were out of sight of the other passengers except when they walked down the central corridor. Their aim was to blend into the background. They needed to be forgotten. They could not afford being remembered.

Late that morning they pulled into Lyon station. They let the other passengers disembark and then followed the stragglers. As always, these pulled their over heavy cases and were too preoccupied by the thought of the long and painful walk ahead of them to notice others in the small crowd.

Opposite the station, they walked down a narrow street and found one of those gloomy hotels that are based in such locations throughout the world. They asked for a room and booked it.

"We'll be back later with our luggage. We left our stuff in the station." With that, they walked out and through the streets until they found a telephone. They called London and Jacqui answered. Charles spoke quickly and cautiously for he was conscious of the risk of being bugged.

"I don't want to be traced. It could be dangerous. Rastinov has been killed. We're on the run. We were close by when it happened and could be suspected. Don't tell your father what we've told you. He doesn't need to know. But we may need to get in touch with him. We may need to sort some things out. He could be the only one who can help. Unfortunate as that is, we'll have to work with him if necessary. We'll call you tomorrow."

With that, Charles put down the phone. Jacqui would understand. They couldn't risk anyone tracing them and, these days, modern equipment could do so in minutes. If she'd had problems, she would have alerted him. She would double the guard for, if they were on the run, it spelled danger. She knew they would only call Di Maglio if things were really grim. She also knew that she had to cover for Charles on Monday. If he planned to call her then, he wouldn't be in the office

They walked through the streets and found a luggage shop. They each bought a bag. They found a supermarket and bought toiletries. They then found a shop and stocked up on clothes.

They wanted to get out of their black outfits and into something less sombre. Charles found a blue sweatshirt and Maria got herself a similar one. They picked up some sneakers. Maria even managed to find some jeans but Charles had no such luck.

Sunday was not the best time to go shopping.

They grabbed a coffee and loaded their purchases into their bags before heading back to the hotel.

The room was as grim as the outside. The wallpaper was dark and dirty. The bed was high and covered by a dark coverlet. It seemed clean enough but one couldn't be sure.

Charles walked into the bathroom. The bath was stained. The basin was chipped. The bidet was uninviting. The toilet was cracked. The white tiles were greyish and only vaguely reflected the dim light from the ceiling bulb. There was a rotten smell of dank carpet and decaying wood mingling with the acrid reminder of the half-washed bodies of past occupants.

Feeling sickened, he went to the window and looked at the wall of another unimpressive building. He winced. She laughed.

"At least we're not overlooked," said Maria. "We can leave the blinds open all night. Mind you, I can't think of anything else going for this place other than the fact that we won't be traced."

Charles sat down on the bed. "Maria, this all doesn't make sense. Di Maglio said that Rastinov was alive. He was. Di Maglio alleged that Rastinov was behind the attacks. Yet, we know that Di Maglio was the cause himself. The evidence is overwhelming, and in cases like the kidnapping, absolute. We thought we killed Rastinov. I saw him dead myself all those years ago. I knew him. I recognised him. Then we had all the indications that Rastinov was dead. Turpin took control of the Russians. Their behaviour changed. I find it confusing."

Maria sat next to him. "Let's be logical. You saw a dead man years ago. He was Rastinov or he looked very like him. He could have been a double in effect. We know the Russians changed their behaviour those years ago but they had little choice. Their only alternative was to continue a vendetta and be totally destroyed.

"Di Maglio played clever and left them with a role. They could have taken that with Rastinov at their head. The man was no genius but he wasn't a total moron either. So he could have been alive. There was always a possibility that Turpin was just a front. Then we see Rastinov today. And those thoughts don't stack up. He's ill and in some sort of cell in a sanatorium. He's isolated. Why?"

Charles took up her theme, "Let's assume that the dead man was a double. Let's assume that the real Rastinov did acquiesce to Di Maglio's offer. If he was dying why was the sanatorium in an outhouse and why was he in a cell? And would that have started the Russians making a play for Di Maglio's Empire?"

"It could be that he was trying to attack Di Maglio and had faced opposition. He was a prisoner. That was certain. The fact he was ill could have been incidental. But why would Di Maglio then pretend to be under attack from him?" Maria agreed. It didn't make sense. They needed to see Di Maglio to check it out.

"What about the plan to sell off Di Maglio's business to the Russians?" she asked.

"We can't do that now. It would be no use tackling them until we know who's in charge. If Turpin has been in charge as a front for Rastinov, then he may not be now. On the other hand, he could be. Perhaps he overthrew Rastinov when he saw he was dying. But why do that? He would have waited for the inevitable." Then a thought struck him. "It could mean that Rastinov was the boss and there was a palace revolution by opponents once they realised he was dying. That would mean that Turpin doesn't run things but some new man."

"Why would they chase us if they were waiting for Rastinov to die? That hardly makes sense."

"Perhaps there is a group opposing Rastinov and a pro Rastinov group. Perhaps they didn't know who we were but assumed we were part of the pro Rastinov group. Then the antis would have attacked us. They could have thought we were trying to free him. They came after us immediately. They may not have known he was dead."

But they couldn't be sure. Charles and Maria knew they were going round in circles. They failed to come up with a solution. There was definitely turmoil in the Russian camp. They needed Di Maglio to help sort it out. After all, he had business links with them despite the battles they were fighting. They had enough information he wouldn't have to allow them to discover the truth.

"We'll have to wait till tomorrow," concluded Maria. "Should we hire a car and move out of here?"

"Better wait till tomorrow. But we should hire a car tonight and head out early. That way we can get to Geneva early and see Di Maglio in the morning. I have to get back to London by Tuesday. I need to concentrate on business there."

Maria looked at her watch. She went over to the TV and switched it on. They got a French television station and waited for the news. Perhaps it would cover the events at the Pont du Gard. Perhaps it would help clarify things.

The bulletin started with the ominous words, "Four policemen were killed and three seriously wounded in a gun battle at the Pont du Gard in the early hours of the morning."

Maria and Charles looked at each other in horror. The attackers had been police. Yet they had never identified themselves. They both went pale. The cameras went over to the hotel. The presenter gave the story.

"It appears that a couple who booked in yesterday were suspected by police to be part of a terrorist gang. The two, believed to be Iranian or Libyan, left the hotel in the early hours. The police trailed them but lost them. Then several hours later, they were seen returning to the hotel. They were armed and in combat gear. Police stormed their hotel room.

It was here that the first policeman was killed as an attempt to force the door was met with a hail of bullets from a sub machine gun. The couple escaped from the hotel as the police attempted to regroup, mainly by diverting attention through an explosion that totally destroyed their room.

There was a further gun battle, during which another policeman was seriously injured. After this, the terrorists fled in a stolen car. The car evaded a roadblock and later the terrorists, joined, it is believed, by accomplices, ambushed a pursuing car, killing all three occupants.

The car has not been found and the terrorists have disappeared. Police suspect they may have headed towards Marseilles and road blocks have been erected on all major roads around the area."

There was then a sketch of them. Maria looked quite Arabic. They had her height wrong as well. Charles looked quite thuggish, with black hair rather than light brown, and again his height was wrong. He was described as heavy build. Unless the pictures were intentionally misleading, the images did not look at all like them.

"That explains the pursuit. It still doesn't explain why Rastinov was being locked up," said Maria.

The only realistic solution they could find was the one they had put forward before. There must have been a palace revolution in the Russian camp. Rastinov had been ill and he was sidelined. But they still needed Di Maglio, for they had to find out exactly what was happening.

"Let's change plans," Charles said. "Hiring a car is too dangerous, even if we used false papers in Nimes on the way down. We should take a train to Geneva. That will allow us to remain anonymous for a bit longer. We may get searched. I'm glad we left the guns in the car at Valence. At least they can't be traced."

The guns had been delivered to a locker at the airport and they had collected them there. Charles was allowed to carry one with him on planes as he had a special permit, but they had taken the precaution of using a false name on the way out. Mr and Mrs Green would hardly be associated with them. They had, as part of their preparations, destroyed those papers long ago.

"What do we do now?" said Maria

"Let's find out about trains and then act like tourists. This fleapit is a tourist hotel. So we'd better see the sights and get some food. We have to act the part."

So Maria and Charles wandered around Lyon. They checked out the early train to Geneva. They ate in a café in the centre and then took in a film. Tourists don't go to bed too early, but they thought that they should wait around till around ten. At that time hotels are casual. In any case, they had paid the hotel in advance and in cash. So they didn't have to check out formally. They would just expect them out by the morning. There couldn't be extras, as the phone had not been switched through. They didn't do that for cash accounts. And there was nothing else on sale in the room.

So they watched a film, but only half-heartedly. Charles had his arm around the back of Maria's seat and she rested her head on his shoulder.

Both of them were quite shaken at the thought that they had inadvertently killed four policemen. That had been so unexpected. And it was highly dangerous. But, as they allowed the film to drift on in front of them, they took comfort from each other's presence. They calmed down in the strange silence of the cinema.

The movie ended and they returned to the hotel. At night it looked even gloomier than before. A sad faced man barely greeted them as he handed over their key. The message he conveyed was one of total indifference to them and to the world around.

Upstairs, Charles turned on the TV again and caught the start of the news. Television and radio had been a good means of tracking reactions to some of their more public escapades in the past. Sometimes they were big news, like now. At other times their news suppression machine triumphed and they failed to make the smallest of headlines. The newscasters focused again on terrorist activities. There was no mention of the Russian Mafia. There was no mention of Rastinov's assassination.

The story line was about the Middle East. They had to question the reason for this. Was it true? Or was it a useful scapegoat for the government? Would it allow them to make some moves against a domestic problem with the support of the population? Did they really believe the story? Charles found it hard to imagine people seeing Maria and him as Arabs. They just didn't look the part. But the South of France has its fair share of myopic bigots, willing to deceive themselves into believing anything that supports their prejudices.

Maria commented that the story served their purpose. If the police had been on their trail, the story would be different. There would be no point in putting out such misleading information in that case.

They discussed how they would approach Di Maglio. He must not know about their escapade with the police for that would give him leverage over them and make him more dangerous. He definitely had a file on them already that could put them away for years. They had one on him as well, and on many of his people, that would do the same.

Charles disliked this episode, as it was too valuable potential ammunition for Di Maglio. It weakened them, he still needed to destroy Di Maglio. And he would have preferred to deal with the Russians for that. He needed to know who was in charge. Was it the brutes, who had supported Rastinov and would stick to crime alone? Or was it the diplomats like Turpin, who would seek to diversify into legitimate businesses as well as operating their own version of the evil Empire?

They would have to wait. There was no purpose in planning further. They needed more pieces to the jigsaw. He stripped off. Maria looked up and moved over to him. She put her arms on his shoulders and lay her dark hair against his chest. She was fully dressed. For the first time since he had known Maria, she sought him out not for sexual excitement but for comfort.

He held her to him, gently. He felt her relax. His hands moved up and down her back and the tension left her. Her clothes slipped off without protest. They moved towards the bed and threw off the blankets and covers. They made love, slowly and peacefully, on that high bed with a pale, watery moon sending the odd oblique ray through the open shutters.

Then they fell asleep. They felt a peace descend. The horror was outside. The threats were far off.

Next day's morning light was faint and forbidding. Through the angle of the window, they could see the clouds. There was no blue sky. Charles glanced at Maria lying next to him. She had half curled up in a foetal position. She lay there, trusting and calm. She, who had been a protector for so long, now had one herself. For the first time, a killing had shocked her. Charles knew it meant that she was coming to the end of the road in her job. Once one developed a conscience, it was impossible to continue.

Maria would leave when the scam was complete. Meanwhile, she would be supportive, but not totally dependable. The future was going to depend on him much more than the past had. Jacqui was pregnant. Claire was dead. Maria was exhausted. His female entourage was slowly becoming dependent on him.

The need to finish this next stage of their road to fortune was becoming more urgent. The first stages had made them billionaires. This would make them powerful beyond their dreams. An island or a mountainside, the retreat Jacqui and he had discussed for many years now, was fast beckoning. Or it would never happen.

With that in mind, he woke up Maria. She came once more into his arms. Once again she sought comfort. Then she shook herself, or shivered, he couldn't be sure. Then, she got up and went into the bathroom, he heard the shower gurgling before she returned to dress. He followed suit and soon they were both ready to leave in the anonymity of the early morning. They dropped their keys off to the same sullen man who had been there the night before, then headed for the train to Geneva and Di Maglio.

The border was as casually supervised, as usual. Nobody even checked their passport. Soon they were in Geneva. There they took a taxi to the Di Maglio compound. They walked up the steps, clad in jeans and sweatshirts, and were ushered into an office. Di Maglio and Giovanni were there. Di Maglio greeted them curtly, "What's the matter?"

"You tell me," Charles snapped back. "Is Rastinov dead or alive?"

"He's dead. He was killed two days ago. Two Arabs are said to have killed him. I thought it was you and Maria, but I have the internal police report and it's clear it was Arabs. We don't know why. We've been contacted by the Russians. They want an assurance it wasn't us. We've given it to them. And it's true."

"Why would the Arabs kill him?"

"They supply drugs. Perhaps the Russians tricked them. I can't say I am sorry. Although I have to admit that I have no love for Burganov."

"Who is he?"

"He's been the leader of the Mafia in all but name for the last two years. He overthrew Rastinov in reality, but found it useful to keep him prisoner. At first it allowed him to use him as a hostage to avoid internal strife. Then he killed off most of his opponents at a gang meeting. That was about a year ago. At that time they diagnosed Rastinov with kidney problems. As they were incurable, they just carried on holding him. He was going to die soon. The killers were fools."

"Why did you tell us that Rastinov was after us?"

"You didn't know Burganov although he's as bad. I needed to shake you up. I know you say you won't do it at the moment. But you'll take on the business in time. It will be your next game after the bank scam is over. You need the excitement, the challenges and the ability to make money. You won't be able to resist."

"You're kidding yourself, old man."

"Who are you calling an old man? OK, OK. I know. But don't. I don't mind you hating me. But respect me. I'm Jacqui's father." He sneered, "At least in name." He turned to Maria, "What was the problem. Why do you need me?"

"We thought Rastinov was alive. We went to kill him. But when we got to their place, there was chaos. We were worried we might have been spotted. From what you say that's no problem."

"Why do you think you may have been seen?"

"We saw a man and woman run from the Russians' place. There was more shooting and we took cover. When they left, we decided we'd better lie low until we found out what happened. Then while we were driving back, we came across a car. It had been shot up. Later we found it was the police. That shook us."

"Well," interrupted Di Maglio with a look of contempt, "You weren't seen. So you're OK. You've gone soft, Maria. You used to be better. Don't come back for a job with me. You're unemployable in any decent set up."

He turned on his heel and left them. Giovanni was alone. He took Charles by the arm and led him outside. They went for a walk in the garden. He still held on to his arm.

"Are you all right? Was Maria telling the truth?"

Charles was not ready to trust Giovanni. He was too close to Di Maglio. He could even be wired.

"It was a mix up. We nearly walked into a problem. It shook us. Maria has been in an office for too long. It was stupid to take her along. Di Maglio's a bastard but he saw it. I didn't. It worries me. Claire's dead. Maria's gone soft. I distrust Di Maglio. Giovanni, we live too dangerous a life to be away from protection. It worries me."

"Then make up with Di Maglio."

"I don't think we can. We can't run his Empire; definitely not with him around. Jacqui couldn't. I wouldn't. If we ever did take it over, it would have to be on our terms and with our own people in charge. And even then, I doubt we would want it. It's not our scene."

"Think about it. You could change your mind." Giovanni could hardly suppress his smile. Charles continued to pretend to look worried. He had given the right message. This would throw them. They would think he was moving to them. They would think he was coming round.

Perhaps they thought he needed the safety of Mafia protection. They would not know that he had his own family protection. They didn't realise that Maria was still good. Less good than in the past, but she could still beat the best of them.

But he wanted to communicate insecurity. It reinforced their view that they had messed up in France. And it would dispel any suspicion that they may have as to their future plans for the Empire if they were to take it on. It laid the seed also for Di Maglio to move out and anoint Charles and Jacqui as his chosen successors.

Charles knew, even if he couldn't deal with the Russians, it was important that he brought Di Maglio down. And the mention of the Arabs had given him an idea. Years ago, Jacqui and he had dealt with a man called Ali. He lived near Monte Carlo. He was a middleman. And there were many reasons why they trusted each other. He would help. Perhaps the Arabs would be perfect buyers of the Di Maglio franchise?

They headed back to the house and were joined by Maria. "We're on a flight in three hours. When do you want to leave?"

They didn't have to wait. Giovanni said they could have his driver. The car appeared and they headed off within an hour of arriving. The car dropped them at the airport. They had a two-hour wait. They checked out for bugs. Charles then recounted to Maria his conversation with Giovanni.

"You know, Di Maglio was right. I'm past my peak. I knew that. I'm still good, but retirement beckons. As long as this all succeeds, it's time for dreams. Even if it doesn't work out as planned, there'll be enough for some of them."

Charles agreed. "It's the same for Jacqui, Juliet and me too. And then there's the new baby. We'll win this round. But then we need a break. At least we need one for a few years. My father will carry on with the investment side. But we need to recharge for a year or so at least. We need to get away from it all. Perhaps this is the last big play."

He smiled wryly. "Or perhaps it's not. Much depends." He half knew what it depended on. It depended on Jacqui, on Di Maglio's reaction and on a lot of other factors. One thing was certain, after a scam of this proportion, they would have to lay low for some time as far as the world of finance was concerned. But, if one's a few billion richer, one can tolerate that.

The plane landed in London and they hurried through customs and passport control. Douglas was waiting and they climbed thankfully into the back of the car. As it sped them to London, Charles started to dial.

His first call was to Jacqui, "I'm back. How are you?"

"I'm fine. Are you coming to the office, or shall I meet you at home?"

"Meet me at home. I have some calls."

He rang his father in France. Everything was going ahead perfectly in the opaque world of international banking. Things had taken off faster than they had expected. He was already starting to offload some of the investments he had fabricated and some he had ramped.

The figures were impressive. He now had holdings worth four and a half billion but they had cost him just over a billion. Some of the investments were totally fraudulent. They looked genuine but they were empty shells with no substance. Others were real but he had ramped up their prices by cornering the market in them. He had run them up by selling and buying them between his different funds and then making sure the market saw all the activity.

With carefully placed rumours, by using indiscreet brokers and by talking to bankers keen for a quick buck on their own account, he had ensured a lively interest in his chosen shares. Having them mentioned in the press as tips of the day and on the top performers list gave them credibility without substance and made for eager buyers among the ill-informed. And was there anyone more ill-informed than the incompetents they had put in charge of the PAF funds? He had already offloaded two and a half billion. And he was sure that he would soon be able to dump the rest. In the end, he would realise around three and a half billion profit from the funds.

"Even after we've sold, Charles, I'll carry on manipulating the prices so that the funds look as if they are doing well. At least until we pull the rug. We'll make money on that as well but not that much by comparison."

"How are we on Stephens' positions? Are you getting your report?"

"Yes Jacqui's passing me the data and I'm reworking it using the right prices. All in all, the books say that we're three fifty million to the good in the bank. In reality, there are about two billion of losses. We're about one point five up as a result on our own account. And we have more to go there yet."

"Excellent. I checked out the loan book. We're still pushing out money like there's no tomorrow. It looks as if we're three and a half billion in the clear. They all seem great loans and the chumps in the States think they are geniuses. But all the loans are fraudulent; all are fictitious."

"That's a bit over plan even, isn't it? You must still have loans to roll out. You're not being too greedy, Charles, are you?"

"No problem; we have some of the world's dumbest bankers on our books in the States. We'll get the figures up. We'll lend some more. "My overall estimate is that we'll clear close on fifteen billion of profit for us after we sell the stake in the bank. The trading side is running close to plan but everything else is way ahead of the targets we set. But we were being conservative then, anyway. So we may make fifteen after all."

"But, Charles, then your mother and I need to get out. You can just pay us a pension and use me as an adviser. This is pretty nerve wracking and exhausting. We'll find a quiet spot for a couple of years."

"We might join you. We can run our money from anywhere. All we need is telecommunications and a standard hands off legal system."

"There are plenty of those and some in really good locations!" he laughed. "See you soon."

Charles turned to Maria, "The finances are better than I ever expected. The scam is on the road and moving ahead with a momentum of its own. On the basis of those figures, we'll easily sell to the public on the back of a billion two or a billion three dollar of profits. With such a growth rate we could value the company at twelve billion. We'd clear at least six on the flotation. But we've got a few months to go yet. We need to be vigilant. We also need to sort out Di Maglio. I want to get Jacqui's thoughts on the Arab connection."

By the time they'd got home, he'd made several other calls. Douglas dropped him off. He noticed the security around the house. Nobody asked him anything. They knew who he was. Douglas drove on with Maria in the back. She would stay at her flat. There was no need for her to stand guard on them. At the house Charles continued making phone calls.

In America all was progressing well. The banks were further boosting their loans. They confirmed the investment products were going well. Their operations appeared to be running at record profits. The gossip around the banks was that the UK take-over had brought them luck. The greedy executives were looking forward to their unearned bonuses. The staff expected their pay rise. Nobody realised their companies had only a few more months to go. But how could they? They were just pawns in the game.

Jacqui returned early. She whispered to him to tell her all that had happened. He recounted the episode in France and she shivered. "I saw it all on the television. How did they confuse you and Maria with a load of Arab terrorists? It's so improbable."

"No idea. But they did. And that's a relief. Anyway, we holed up in Lyon and then got to Geneva. Your father didn't exactly welcome us. And Giovanni was pretty unhelpful. But we bluffed it. The annoying thing is that I doubt we can deal with the Russians. They talked of an Arab group. Could you do a deal with Ali?"

"No," said Jacqui. "Ali's all right when it comes to petty crime and money laundering. But I wouldn't trust him with several billion dollars. The evil Empire must be worth that much. We have to find another solution. My father won't let us go until he sorts that out. He wants you to run it. He called me at the bank this morning. He repeated what he said before. He wants us to take the show over for him. But how?"

"I don't really know. We have two options. We destroy it from outside or from within. If we destroy it from outside, that can only mean through your father's enemies or through the police."

She shook her head, "The police are no good. They're too corrupt.

They wouldn't do it. Gang warfare is not the answer, it will just mean lots of casualties. The Empire will live on."

"That means we can only scupper it from inside."

"But how would you do that?"

"What if we ran it into the ground?"

"You mean we take it on and then destroy it through incompetence?" she queried.

"Isn't that a possibility? Once we have control, we could leak information and start being raided by other gangs. The police could get more tip-offs and pick up some real shipments. Then the people in the gang would lose confidence. We could arrange a few ambushes, a few key killings. I could accuse some of the bosses of incompetence and worse. That would destroy morale. I could pretend I thought they're ripping me off. Then we can watch them all destroy themselves."

"How will we persuade my father that we changed our minds and get him to sell to us? You can't do anything till we've finished with the scam. And he isn't going to trust us if we have just ripped him off with the hidden page in the bank agreement."

"No we just tell him we did that to ensure we came out clean. I wanted to be able to go back into the world of finance. He has enough wealth through the Empire. I'll say it was him or us. He will be furious that he lost. He'll still try to get his revenge. But he'll understand. It's the sort of thing he'd like to have done. He'll know he can't trust us. And I'll actually pay him a couple of billion and offer an annual share of profits for the future. He'll need that."

"And the couple of billion will be discovered?"

"You bet. He'll think it's safe, but that won't be the case. Just as everything goes down the pan, his chances of a pension go with it. The Empire will be destroyed. His future payback will be eliminated. And the authorities will be on his back; we'll give them enough information to allow them to bring racketeering and other charges, and leave enough trails around that even the FBI will be able to find all his cash."

Jacqui still looked worried, "I think you underestimate his reaction. I'm not sure you'd get him to agree anything with you. I would think he'd want to kill you rather than deal with you. You may have to kill him."

Charles was surprised how much she hated all that her father stood for. But that was a fact. Her father had now destroyed all feelings she had for him. He had attacked her. He had attacked her family. He had threatened her child. He wanted to corrupt them even more. That had been too much already. And then he had revealed that he was probably not her father after all. That had been the final betrayal. Jacqui was even more certain than Charles. She wanted revenge. She wanted Di Maglio destroyed even more than he did.

Jacqui thought for a moment and then shook her head, "That's one hell of a risk strategy, you have proposed. I want to think about it a bit more. But we'd have to kill him if it went wrong. Or he'd kill us."

"Hey. You're talking about patricide."

"He's not my father. Or he claims he's not. He's lost all hope of any reconciliation. He tried to screw up my life by getting me to marry one of his thugs. He tried to destroy you. He tried to destroy our relationship. He kidnapped Juliet. He threatens us without hesitating. We'll use him. But we'll never trust him. And if the choice is him or us, he'll take the fall. He'd do the same. Don't kid yourself."

"There's one reason why he may not see we're heading to destroy him."

"What's that?"

"He thinks I'm a financial terrorist. He doesn't see us as competent in his world. That's why he was so willing to accept the story that Maria and I were stupid and almost stumbled on the shoot-out with the police. It was a crazy explanation. Yet he jumped at it. It re-enforced his views about me. It also confirmed his expectation that Maria was going fast downhill."

"We still need to be careful. Giovanni is clever. He sees through things like that."

"I considered that too. Giovanni wants to retire though. He's older than your father. He's older than your Uncle Aldo who's pretty well fully retired in Florida, although your father says he's still part of the inner circle. No, he'll tell him facts but he'll keep quiet on suspicions.

He needs our cash and I could stop him getting that. If we clear five to ten billion on the shared pot and he gets his two and a half percent, then that makes him one fifty to two fifty million. That's amazing money for him. Your father pays well but he's only a multi-millionaire."

"So you reckon we have everything tied up?"

"It's as tied up as I can make it. The only big loose link is the Empire. I can only think to run it into the ground. But we can't do that till next year. It has to be after we've completed the take-over. We're well down the road in the scam. We sell the bank to the public in April or May. Then we allow the shit to hit the fan in August at the latest. And, hopefully, we'll be taken out in September. Then I work on the Empire and try to destroy it in three months. That should be feasible but it's tight."

"And don't forget the baby is due?"

"I wouldn't. Nor will I forget you and Juliet in between times. It's going to be tough but we'll get there. And we need that island retreat so that we can spend the whole of the next year together."

She poured him another glass of champagne, "I'll drink to that."

And one thing led to another. What idiot said that pregnant women weren't inviting and exciting?

CHAPTER SEVENTEEN

Next morning the ringing phone woke them. Charles picked it up. It was five in the morning.

"It's Maria. I need you here. I've had visitors."

"Are you all right?"

"I'm hurt. But I'm not hurt badly. My visitors are in worse shape. They're dead."

"Should I come alone?"

"I think that's best."

"I'm on my way."

He got up and pulled on his black combat clothes. He slipped a gun into his leg holster and some spare ammunition into his pocket. He had another identical gun in his waistband, covered by a jacket.

"Be careful," pleaded Jacqui. "First, there was Claire. Now Maria's attacked. I bet it's my father. Be careful. You may be wrong about his opinion of Maria and his suspicions about you."

"I'll be careful. I'll see you in the office if I don't get back before you leave. You be careful as well and make sure Juliet has enough security."

She nodded. She knew better than him what to do. She'd been born into this lifestyle, he'd only grown into it. He got into the car. The security guards wordlessly opened the gates. He drove through the streets of Kensington and down to Chelsea. He had the key to her flat and let himself in, gun in hand. He thought she would be alone but you could never tell.

The light was on in the kitchen and he moved carefully towards it. If there were someone there, they would have heard him open the door. In those old mansion flats it was impossible to remain silent. If the doors do not creak, the floorboards do.

He pushed open the door, and slowly the kitchen came to view. Then he saw Maria, sitting on a stool at the breakfast bar. There was blood on the breakfast bar and on her clothes. She was wearing a short nightdress, but it was torn.

She turned round to face him. She was white. He saw the blood coming from her shoulder and arm. She had been stabbed and cut badly. She was holding a cloth against the wounds. The cloth was soaked with blood. The blood dripped slowly through her fingers.

He moved towards her and shut the kitchen door behind him. There was nobody else there. He asked her to let him look at the cut, it was deep but not life threatening. She needed a doctor. He was sure that she would have called for one already. At least once she knew that Charles was on his way.

"Tell me what happened."

"I stayed in last night. I was sleeping when I heard something. I went to look. It was two men. They were in the lounge. I shot one and then had a struggle with the other. He had a knife. He slashed at me and I managed to half avoid it. Then he slashed again and got me. He went to finish me off. I had fallen and pretended to be half-conscious only. The idiot took that for fact. As he approached, I managed to knock the knife from his hand. I grabbed it and stuck it into him three or four times. He just moaned. But he's dead."

"So I have to get rid of two bodies."

"Yes. And you can't use the normal disposal channels. They're Di Maglio men. But what's strange is that they're not the types he'd send if he wanted me to be killed. These were second rate thugs. One got lucky and managed to knife me. I think this was a warning. Perhaps it was to me. And perhaps it was also for you."

There was a lot of truth in what she said. Di Maglio was getting dangerously close to them. Charles needed him though for the moment. He could do nothing to stop him. He would remain all-powerful for some time. So they would need to live in a protective cocoon. And they would have to include Maria.

"What doctor did you call?"

"It's the one who saw to Jacqui the other week in the country. He'll be here soon."

Charles looked in the lounge and checked the men. They were dead. There was blood on the floor. The place bore all the signs of the struggle that had taken place. He saw Maria's gun under the table and picked it up. He slipped it into his pocket.

He called home. Jacqui answered and he brought her up to date. He asked for Douglas. A minute or so passed before he came to the phone. He could find a small van and he could bring some large refuse bags and sealing tape. Charles in turn would empty out a cupboard in the spare bedroom. It was just the right size for his purpose.

They would bring it downstairs and they would place the bodies in it. That way they could get them out of the house. All that was left then was to dispose of the men. That would not be difficult. He could depend on Douglas for that. He was an expert in that particular field

He went downstairs. Maria was still sitting in the kitchen. He explained what he had done, "I'll take you to our house after the doctor's seen you and we've got rid of the evidence. Douglas will tidy up your place tomorrow. You'll be all right."

"I can wait for Di Maglio's call."

"What makes you think he'll call you?"

"He'll call me. He'll want me to know that he let me off with a warning. I've not betrayed him He thought Claire did. Charles, we need to kill him. Or it'll be us. Perhaps it won't be the next time. That may be a warning again. But he never warns more than twice, and usually not even that often."

"I know. We'll talk about that tonight with Jacqui."

The discussion stopped as there was a knock on the door. It was the doctor. He came in and examined Maria.

"You should have this seen to in hospital. I know you won't agree to go, so I'll have to do as best I can."

He looked at Charles and obviously did not recognise him. Charles explained he was a friend and had been called over to help. He asked if anybody else had been hurt. Maria said not. He accepted that. He would be long gone by the time Douglas arrived with the fake delivery van.

The shoulder wound was patched up and the arm needed stitching. He gave Maria painkillers and explained how the dressings needed to be changed. The stitches would come out in a week or so. The slash on the arm may have bled a lot but it wasn't that serious. The shoulder wound was minor and Maria would be OK. Charles noted, though, that she was weakened and wondered if that may have been Di Maglio's main objective.

The doctor left, telling her to rest. So Charles made her a coffee and had one himself. It was not long before the ever reliable Douglas arrived. He glanced at the clock. It was just past seven. If they could move the cupboard quickly, they would miss the early morning rush hour.

They removed the clothes hanging in the cupboard and carried it to the lounge.

"Roomy for a double coffin," noted Douglas, lugubriously. "Glad they both look well under six foot, otherwise we might have had to shorten them somehow."

They quickly wrapped them in the bags and sealed them. They were then dumped unceremoniously in the cupboard. It was heavy. They made it appear light work. Nobody was in the street when they did the journey from the house, but you could never tell. They locked the van and returned indoors.

"Where will you dump it? Can you manage alone?"

"There's a building site I know down near the airport. I'll leave it there. I can drive up to wherever I want to dump it and just slide it out.

"They're in-filling the land on the site . But there's a strike on and so almost nobody's there at the moment. I'll put the cupboard in one of the pits and top it with rubble. They get the occasional casual labourer working. It won't be found. They have to cement over the rubble before they start building. Then they'll put the foundations over the cement."

"How much rubble will be over the cupboard?" Maria queried.

"I'll be there most of the day. Some of the pits are about ten by ten. The main one is almost filled. Then there were a series of small pits around the place. I'll find one that's at least ten feet deep. That means nine feet of rubble. It'll be rock and crushed stone mainly. That's what they're using. I'll leave an acid bomb with each body."

"What's an acid bomb?"

"It's a delayed charge that will release concentrated acid. It will disfigure the bodies and most likely destroy them. I can't be sure as the wardrobe will corrode as well."

"Won't there be gas escaping?"

"A bit, but it'll have been dispelled by morning and I'll time it for the evening so nobody will be there."

"Could it move the rubble?"

"Not the gas. The acid could cause a bit of subsidence. But that'll be no problem. It won't cause more than the odd few inches of drop. And I'll allow for that."

"If it's a construction site, there'll be a lot of machinery around, what about their security?"

"A mate of mine runs that. But he's only nights. They don't do anything in the daytime but spot checks. And I'll look like a labourer. One of the casuals they employ to be around and keep things moving."

"Could there be others around?"

"Yes. If there's a problem, I'll abort and do something else. But I want to get off and be there by eight. The casual labour doesn't tend to start till later. And the night man goes off at seven."

"Douglas, how do you know all this?" queried Maria.

"I always know a dumping ground. Not usually for bodies. But I'm flexible," he said with a laugh. With that, he was gone and Maria and Charles were alone. They packed her case. He had parked in front of the house. They locked up and quickly went to the car. Nobody gave them a second look.

Maria turned to Charles, "I didn't know that Douglas managed body disposal."

"He'll do anything for us. I wouldn't call him for a Miss Wendy Dale. But he'll help against thugs like this without a second thought. And he's not going to be indiscreet, I can be certain of that."

"What will he do with the van?" she asked. "Could it be traced?"

"He'll dump it. He'll have stolen it. Don't worry. He's a true professional."

She smiled weakly. "I must be in shock. I'm fussing. I'm usually not like that."

Once inside the house, Jacqui took charge of Maria. She was put into a cosy guestroom. Charles came down and saw her just before he headed off to the office. It was just after eight and he was to drive them both in. Jacqui came down the stairs in a neat suit.

It was tight fitting but her pregnancy wasn't showing yet and so she could carry it well. Tall, dark and elegant, her olive skin and large, soft dark eyes were framed by her long black hair. Her body seemed to fit neatly into the curves of the suit, or perhaps it was the other way around. She walked with a gentle sway, which seemed to ripple all the way down her body, before easing herself into the car.

They pulled out into the traffic jam that would accompany them all the way to the City at that time.

"You know it was your father giving us another warning."

"I know. What's his game? Is he still trying to intimidate us to take on his business?" She looked at Charles for an answer.

"That's part of it. I think he wants us to be at his bidding. I suspect he feels he could rule the world if he combined our money and his."

"Let's take out his Empire sooner rather than later? We could destroy it at the same time as we run the scam. In fact, we have to. It's too risky to do it after we have taken my father for several billion. He would never buy anything we proposed. The plan you mentioned last night just wouldn't work"

"What do you mean?" said Charles with incredulity. "We could never manage simultaneously the bank scam and the destruction of the Empire. That's why I needed to do them one after another."

"We take on the Empire and ease him out. We agree to pay him the money for the business, but with payment only when we've done the bank deal. We stick to your idea of a couple of billion up front and a share of future profits. Then we screw him out of the money and destroy the value of the future profits. Everything goes down at the same time.

We find the right person to manage the outfit for us; insist on an outsider we can trust. They'll organise the raids by the police. We can get other gangs to raid the business. Loose talk will ensure that alone. It'll be easy."

"Who can I put into the Empire?" queried Charles.

"Why not use Maria?"

"No. I need her as a general spy and support at the bank. In any event, I suspect she may not be quite up to it. By the time we sell the bank to the public, you'll be eight months gone. And you'll not be around when the plan reaches fruition."

"What about Commander Delaney?"

Charles was puzzled. "What about him? He can't help us."

"Why not tell him that Di Maglio is looking to hand the operations to you. He knows you want to avoid that like hell. Ask for one of his key undercover men. You'll have to manufacture a past for him, and it will need to be good enough to stand up to scrutiny. Put him in as our general manager. That'll give you the way to the police."

"It's possible, but how do we get them to do it without letting the cat out of the bag? I can't tell Delaney about the bank and our plans. He'd bend the rules and break them to destroy a major drug Empire. But he wouldn't help out on a major fraud."

"Why do you need to tell him anything? Play hard ball. We need him to accept out timing for the fall. Can't you just say that you have other things to do, as well as destroy the Empire, if you are also to destroy my father, tell him he has to accept that and the timing; or there can be no deal. "

"Jacqui, that's brilliant. I'll call Delaney and see what he's willing to do."

Delaney could be trusted. He knew of their connection. He would have to clear the plan, but he would do this at the top. Charles doubted if it needed to be known by more than two or three people and they would all be used to being discreet.

Delaney would find a background for the new man. Logically, he would invent a double agent. It would be someone who worked inside the police and worked for the other side as well. He could have a background in organised crime, in any case.

Charles would be able to sell him to Di Maglio. The plant would need to work alongside him for two or three months before they could take out Di Maglio. Then the destruction would start; and things would move all the faster if they had help from their man at the top. It would work like a dream.

He turned to Jacqui as he drove into the bank, "I'll call Delaney. I might suggest he come round tonight. We should suggest this to him. I can think of ways of making it work and it looks good. That was a brilliant idea."

They both felt as if a weight were off their shoulders. The fall of his despicable father-in-law was approaching. And he would fall sooner than they had hoped.

The office day went much as expected. They ran through the figures and arranged more dodgy deals. They ensured they were all signed by their stool pigeons. The US duo were especially keen to sign off on anything with a lot of zeros. It was as if they felt that there was some enormous kudos in doing bigger and better deals. It was while happily pushing out the loans that another thought struck Charles.

They would wait for the year-end. Then they would do a few mega deals. The Honourable James' son and McGarth signed anything. Their understanding of the basic rules of banking was so poor that they could be persuaded to do anything.

Charles even thought up a scheme where they would suggest that a deal had to be signed on a Saturday in Hawaii. That would be in demand. And each deal just flowed through to their coffers. It was a joke how easy the whole process had become. And, still, no one suspected a thing.

Charles ran through his secret records. Sir Brian's wife figured prominently among the signatories on the stolen money. His brother and nephew did, too. Dunkillin's family was prolific in their hunger for directorships and their willingness to sign away at random anything one put in front of them.

And, in the US, they had their strange couple. On the one hand, there was the snobbish idiot of a banker, McGarth, and, on the other, the perverted son of their noble chairman. It was going to be amusing when the proverbial hit the fan. For starters, the prison aristocracy would certainly increase quite dramatically in number.

They had some standard banking to do and Charles did those tasks as efficiently as he could. He met regulators. He met other leading bankers. He saw real clients. He looked over committee papers. He mulled over the deals from the traders, all dutifully signed by his fellow directors and, to his amusement, certified by them as understood and well structured. It was, therefore, quite late in the day when he got hold of the Commander.

"Charles. It's a pleasure to hear from you. Carrie was asking about you the other day. She says you haven't been around for a long time. You should wander over and we can jaw about old times."

Carrie was one Charles' oldest friends. She had left her husband a couple of years back and now lived with her father and her six-year-old son. It would be nice for them to get together again, but this was not the right occasion for revisiting the past.

"Commander, this is business. I need to see you. I have a proposition that could interest you. Is there any chance of you popping over tonight for a drink? We could discuss it then."

"You intrigue me. What is it about? Should I bring anyone?"

"No Commander. Just bring yourself. How would seven suit you for a pre-dinner drink?"

He agreed and, once again, Charles returned to work.

He walked over to the dealing room. It operated as smoothly as before. They were happy doing deals they could not comprehend. They knew how to feed numbers into a computer and the numbers told them the answers they wanted to hear. The numbers always told them that they were making a profit. The programme on the computer wouldn't allow them to make losses. They would only uncover them later and then it would be too late.

He said "hello" to the younger Dunkillin who was brimming with enthusiasm for all the deals they were doing. He kept his door shut and let others do the messy trading.

All the same one couldn't fail to hear the juvenile traders shouting "buy a hundred" or "sell fifty" as they casually omitted the millions whilst gambling away with other people's money.

Charles was relaxed, his secret systems were good enough to detect anyone else's fraud or a run of bad luck that would lead to unacceptable loss. He had invested good money to guarantee that.

He looked into Sir Brian's office. The great man reeked of drink and was much further gone than usual. Charles picked up a chequebook. It was lying on his desk.

He asked for his signature on a blank cheque and the unsuspecting fool signed it there and then. He took it away. It was a company bank cheque and he would fill it in later to credit the poor fool's own account. An account he would open in Switzerland or somewhere. The money moved to them very soon after it was deposited, although it would never be traced. But it would tie Sir Brian even more into the fraud.

He moved on to the Honourable James. He, too, was brimming with confidence. The management accounts for the first nine months had just been produced. He said that it looked as if IBE in London alone would make well over an annualised four hundred million plus. And that was in sterling! In dollars it was nearer eight hundred million. He told Charles of the fortune that they were making in the trading room. Charles could hardly stop himself smiling as he thought of all those phoney deals that were the main targets of their intended fraud. And the amazing thing was that the Honourable James sensed nothing unusual about this incredible performance.

He went through the figures with Jacqui later that day. Their sales of the funds in the US had reached six billion already. Amazingly, the US sales force was good. They had been given enough incentives. But the six billion of sales added up to another two hundred million of commissions. Adding in the trading and lending earnings, it looked as if the Group would be running at close on 1.5 billion dollars before tax. On that growth rate, with an optimistic forecast, they would command a high price in the market.

They ran some new sums given the soaring stock markets, and came out with an estimate of a stock market value for the group of over twelve billion dollars. They would easily get more than six billion, and most likely much more, from the floatation of half their holdings. Hopefully, though, they were going to float their company at the top of the market on inflated profits. It was going to be so easy to con the public and make themselves another fortune.

That evening Commander Delaney came to see them. He was inquisitive. Delaney was a tall man. He was an ex rugby player. His grey hair was cut short in military style and his moustache was trimmed neatly. The pin striped suit, the white shirt with starched collar, the regimental tie and the gleaming black shoes all pointed to his military past.

But the man was far from a stereotypical Colonel Blimp. He had a keen mind and an evil sense of humour. The former was evident from his double first at Oxford and the latter from his ability to mimic his political masters at Westminster. But the latter he only did among select friends.

He had known Charles since he was a child. Charles had been an only child. Delaney had a daughter, Carrie, who was his only child. The two had become close friends, almost like brother and sister. And, as they grew up, they realised that the friendship was more important than any other relationship. So they remained friends.

Charles had been Carrie's protector. She was accident-prone and had got into all sorts of scrapes. He suspected the Commander knew of her abortion, he definitely knew of her earlier drug habit and one or two other skeletons in her cupboard. He also would have known of Charles' role in supporting her. And there was, therefore, a close bond between the two men.

He did not approve of Charles and his family's financial activity. He may have actually believed that they had more or less kept within the law as they built up their fortune. He knew also that the only reason that had been the case was because the law was unclear.

He would have realised that they would have taken every opportunity to skate as close to illegality as they could, and, at times, they would have crossed the line. But these transgressions were untraceable. Delaney knew of Jacqui's past. He was not aware of the murders. He was unaware of some of their wilder escapades. He would not have been aware of the French shooting. But he was aware of a lot. He looked at Charles quizzically over a gin and tonic and waited for him to speak.

"I want to destroy Di Maglio's Empire. But I need help. And I need to call the tune on how it is done and when it is done. Does that interest you?" asked Charles, almost casually.

Delaney didn't hesitate. He just raised his eyebrows and looked over at Jacqui. She looked back. He nodded. "Explain how and why," he asked crisply.

"Di Maglio wants us to run his set-up. We will ask him to sell it to us and, as a precondition, he retires. We still need to agree that and the terms. We haven't really started talking yet. But he wants us in place as his successors.

If we don't do what he wants, we're at risk. He sees this as a battle. And he wins if the Empire stays in the family. Otherwise, he loses. And if he loses he becomes even more dangerous than usual. That's why we're all at risk."

Delaney glanced again at Jacqui. He waited for her response. She smiled at him, arched her eyebrows and nodded. He did not react, but he must have noted her look. She was angry. She was sad. But, she was certain. She knew they had to win the battle. He then looked at Charles and waited for him to continue.

"I need one person I can trust absolutely. That man will run the business for me. I suspect he'll have to work alongside Di Maglio in the beginning, but I'll try to limit that period. Initially, he will run the business for profit. He will make it work. And you know what business it is. It's prostitution, blackmail, extortion and, above all, drugs, but if we destroy drugs, the rest will just crumble on its own.

The business has to be run well for two or three months. Perhaps it will need to be run well for longer. My belief is that we will need to run it profitably till March or June at the latest. Then things will start going wrong. I will arrange for drug shipments to be seized. My man there will organise large shipments and we will tell you about them. You will be the only one who knows the source. You will also ensure that others are unaware that you are the recipient of the information."

"Someone will need to know. I'll have to pass the information on. But I can limit that to someone in the UK or someone overseas." Delaney was already thinking ahead. He was trying to work out how he would run the busts. He knew that he would be a silent partner. He was considering using overseas agencies. That was sensible.

Charles smiled and continued, "We will also pass word of smaller shipments to other gangs. Effectively we will start gang warfare, especially as some rival gangs will be told of the same shipment. You will also be told of some of the gang action, but not all. They could happen in Europe or in the US."

Charles paused but Delaney did not interrupt. "Then, the Empire will get desperate. It will be short of supplies and be getting short of cash. We will organise a mammoth consignment. The timing is critical for a lot of reasons but I can't share them with you.

We will tell you of the mammoth shipment and you will seize it. You can do that with your people overseas. That will give you some glory. We would be talking of a half billion dollar shipment or more."

Delaney interrupted this time, "What is the reason for the timing? You said it was critical and you could not explain why."

"Rest assured. It would not put you in any risk. It's part of our need to ensure we are safe and Di Maglio is harmless. It's better you don't know exactly how we achieve that."

He looked Charles in the eyes. Charles returned the look. Delaney held his gaze. A smile seemed to float around his mouth. Then it was gone. He said nothing. They knew, then, though, that he'd agreed.

"Who's the man in charge? You depend on him?" he asked.

"That's where you come in. I need one of your men."

Charles ran him through the whole idea of the double agent. They talked of the temptation that the agent would face. They talked of the strengths they had to have. They discussed the weaknesses they must not show.

Then Delaney said, "I've got the person. She's just what you need."

"A woman," Charles exclaimed. He saw Jacqui start. "No disrespect, but this is about running the biggest and most deadly Mafia organisation of all times."

"The woman I have in mind meets your needs. I'll call her Miss X for the moment. She can handle herself as well as Maria. She shoots as well as her, too. But she's a secret service agent and not a Mafia protector."

Delaney grinned. He knew Charles was surprised. He had never talked to him about Maria. Her cover in the UK was that she was his personal assistant. Yet the fact he knew about her told Charles two things. The first was that they were being watched. The second was that nobody knew of their killings in this country. That was a relief in his case.

"What cover would you give her?" he queried.

"It'll have to be the double agent cover. The Mafia will know her. She heads up the money laundering operation in my shop. But she has spent time with organised crime. She will know the business. And a woman will be better than a man will. The Mafia respects them in a strange way. So there'll be no shenanigans. She's good. She'll do your job. And the cover's perfect. She works in your area; it's the financial world. You could have had contact for years. Initially, she was second in command there. She runs the show now. All you have to do is say she was always working with you as your person on the inside. She gains credibility through that. And she is valuable for them if she knows how law enforcement works. Your main challenge will be to get Di Maglio to accept a turned agent as the new boss."

"When can we meet her?"

"I'll organise it for next week. You better see her on your own. I better not see you more than necessary till this ends. But I'll be in touch. If you destroy the Di Maglio Empire, you'll still be at risk. He's a billionaire and, while he has money, he's going to be a big threat."

It was Jacqui who replied, "Charles said there were bits you must not know. We have everything arranged. There won't be a big risk once we've finished. But leave that bit to us. We'll come to you if we need you."

"Who will you have to tell?" Charles queried. "The more people who know, the more dangerous the whole thing becomes."

"I'll have to inform Miss X, of course, and the Prime Minister. Then we'll just tell the head of the secret services. Nobody else need know. That's the beauty of my position."

"If this leaks out, Miss X would die alongside Jacqui and me. And we would not be the only ones. There would be a bloodbath."

"I know. Trust me. I'll trust you." Delaney smiled at them. He walked over to Jacqui and put his arm around her shoulder. "I know it's hard for you. But you're good. Your father's evil. The two don't go together."

She looked at him, "It's not that, Commander. He's evil. It's not that I'm so good. It's that I'm a mother, I'm a wife, I'm going to be a mother again. And he's attacking my family and me. I'm defending my own."

"And Charles, what drives you?"

"I hate drugs. Carrie showed me what can happen if you get hooked. I'm not above criticism, but I have ground rules. And he wants me to break them. Add to that the fact that he's going to kill us if we don't do as he wants. That's a fairly good motivation."

"If you need help, call me," he said. He then stood up and somewhat formally shook them each by the hand. He left, walking in the upright manner that was his trademark. He seemed to march in and out of rooms, as if on parade. Yet, one could almost sense his mind ticking over all that they had discussed. Charles also knew one extra thing. He had bought the story. He had put another piece into play in their game.

The next week or so went by without any contact from Delaney. Charles didn't want to contact Di Maglio until he knew they had the right person. He concentrated on the bank and spent half his time in the US and half in the UK. All their special deals went smoothly. Life continued and, for once, it was pleasantly quiet.

They went to restaurants and to the theatre. They saw friends. Life was as it should be for a rich couple in London. They waited and started to get impatient. Yet they knew that they couldn't contact Delaney. They kept on thinking that they were already in November and they wanted to start moving. When would he contact them?

One Saturday, he took Juliet for a walk in Kensington Gardens. He was pushing the buggy and she trotted alongside him.

A tall girl with long blond hair jogged past them and called out a cheery good morning. He was surprised. People don't usually do that in that part of London. He subconsciously checked for his gun which, as usual, he was wearing in a leg holster. Was this another of Di Maglio's tricks?

He turned a corner of the path and saw the girl again. She was sitting on a bench. Clad in running shorts and a shirt, her long bronzed legs pushed out in front of her. She was slim and athletic but not in a chunky or over muscular sort of way. She looked nice, but Charles was still wary.

She called to him, "Let's talk."

Charles grabbed Juliet by the hand and walked to her. "I'm from Delaney. He said I should see you. Can we talk?" she asked.

"Do you live near here?" he asked.

"Yes, but let's walk and talk. The little girl looks tired. Does she want to go in her buggy?"

He asked Juliet and she agreed. And she sat in the buggy as he walked down the path with Miss X.

She smiled. Her eyes smiled as well as her mouth. Charles knew he liked her instantly. He waited for what she would say.

"My name is Madeleine. It's Maddy Brown. You know about my background. I understand quite a bit about your business, that is the legal side. I know a bit also about your father-in-law and his Empire. I gather you want me to run it for you."

Charles was amused by the casual nature of her approach. Of course he wanted her to run the business but he knew it was dangerous. So he explained his plans.

"I can buy everything you say bar the timing. It doesn't make sense," she said.

He responded firmly. "You have to trust me. You have to promise you won't try to find out the reason for that. It's not worth it, anyway. You're talking about a delay of around two or three months. It may seem strange to you but it's critical to me."

She still looked puzzled. The brow puckered slightly. The eyes seemed to stare at him more intently. The body then moved closer to him. He sensed her perfume. He felt her breath on his cheek.

He looked coldly at her. This had to be a business proposition. Otherwise it would all get too dangerous. She was a professional. But it was not in the way of Maria or Claire. They would not let a relationship come between them and their role. She would. She hadn't their training.

"We have two objectives. Yours is to help me destroy the Di Maglio

Empire. If you don't follow my timing, you'll be dead and you'll just hurt the Empire. I have a different objective. I need to destroy Di Maglio. And part of that task involves the destruction of his entire network. The two go hand in hand. There are things you are able to do. And there are things you can't. Just remember that and focus on what you can do."

"I just don't understand." She sounded worried. This was not the reaction she expected. She had obviously heard that he was rarely monogamous. She had thought she could use seduction to underpin the whole plot.

"Look, no hard feelings. I want you as the boss because Delaney says you can do it. He doesn't know everything. I'm finishing off something that started years ago. Some of the groundwork has already been done. The more you know, the more dangerous it is. I need you to run the set-up well. Then I need you to give me information. I will warn you of events that will break the Empire. We'll break it financially as it loses big bucks on drug raids. We'll break its image of invincibility by using it as the catalyst for inter-gang warfare. And we'll break its discipline because, once it gets on the skids, the thugs within it will fight each other to the end."

She still looked puzzled, "I get the financial bit. But I don't know if I get the invincible one or the discipline part. If the other gangs get done, won't everybody be in the same boat? Won't they all rally round?"

Charles shook his head. "You don't know them as well as I do. They have beaten me up. They have fought alongside me. They've tried to kill me. They've killed my friends. I understand their psychology. And so does my wife. She was born into the life. She knew, though, how to escape."

"Explain to me what will happen," she persisted.

"When the gang warfare begins, a lot of people will lose. But, for the first time, those people will include the Di Maglio Empire. It is far bigger than all the other gangs. There will be an opportunity to wrest the top dog slot from the Di Maglio Empire. The top dog makes the top profits. They all want to be boss. You need a top dog to stop the gangs fighting each other. It's not a question of respect. It's a question of fear. The top dog destroys them if they screw up. Without that, they'll self destruct till a new top dog appears."

She seemed to accept the logic of that explanation, "I see why you'd want internal warfare but how do you bring it about?"

"The Empire is a federation. You have four arms. There is the drugs arm. That's the cash cow. As boss, you'll run it. Everyone else is a soldier. You're the only officer.

Then you have prostitution. That's run by Giorgio Carapli. You have protection, extortion and embezzlement. That's run by Veranski, who is also in charge of the hotels and casinos. And you have the legitimate businesses, mainly hospitals and pharmaceuticals. That's run by Charles Renflem."

Charles had her full attention now. He ran her through the structure of the Empire. He explained to her the names and roles of the key men. Juliet had dozed off. They walked up and down the paths that criss-cross the lawns of the park.

"Renflem is very closely involved with the drugs. He provides the front for much of their activities. He's a businessman. No scruples but he has no backbone when it comes to violence. He's also fleeced the Empire over the last years, so he's rich enough. Di Maglio knows that but tolerates it. He makes enough money from the other activities. And Renflem is believed by all the others to be honest."

He laughed at her look of astonishment. "I suspect, including your records by the look on your face. I guess you've been through the archives since Delaney called you in last Friday night. You can pick up a lot over a week."

"Touché," she said with a smile. "But you expect me to be briefed."

"Of course," he replied. "But let me continue. Carapli will go for independence. They can disengage. There are links between their activities and the rest of the Empire, but just links. There are no dependencies. They'll either try to declare their independence and expropriate it all, or they'll seek to negotiate a buy out. Extortion has no assets.

"The net worth of the hotel and casino business is around one and a half billion. It's a separate corporation and the property is kept through offshore special purpose companies. So a buy out may not be that difficult.

"What about Petroni? He's on the board of the IBE Group as well."

"Petroni is a functionary. He'll just fade into the background. He'll go fishing. He's tired. He's in his late sixties already, he's too old for this caper. He's honourable in a funny sort of way. He'll want to save his skin. He's another who wants out.

"It's the same with Di Maglio really. The man's nearly sixty and can't muster up the energy for such an Empire for much longer. You'll have to work alongside Giovanni. Be careful. He'll be loyal to Di Maglio till the man's finished. Even then he'll bail him out if needed. He can bail him out but he won't be able to save him. I've seen to that."

She smiled. This time it was a warm smile. "You appear to have worked it out. I get the feeling it's well planned. How do I get briefed and when do we start?"

"You get briefed by me. I want everything agreed this week. I'm in the South of France on Monday. I have things to do in respect of our business interests. That's my family business."

She grinned broadly, "And how is your father?"

"That's none of your business. That bit is outside your role. I have to be in the US on Tuesday and Wednesday. My diary's full Friday. I'll free myself up on Thursday. We need to get away for the briefing. Meet me in Paris. I'll be in front of the opera house at 8 a.m. Dress in jeans. Be casual."

She agreed. She didn't question why she should be in Paris. The reason was simple. Di Maglio could be trailing him. He could follow him to Paris. Then he would slip him. The metro is an ideal place for that. And then they would have a day to get briefed. He could easily get a room at one of the hotels near the airport. They were used to guests who kept strange hours. And by booking on the spur of the moment, he would not be traced. There would be no bugs. And he would have all the documents he needed in his computer notebook.

She waved goodbye. The tall, lithe body, which appeared to move a bit more seductively than those of the other runners, disappeared into the distance. Charles smiled to himself and headed home.

CHAPTER EIGHTEEN

Back at the house, he told Jacqui of his meeting. He told her of the seduction attempt and she smiled contentedly at his reaction. He thought of his relationship with Maria, and the earlier one with Claire, and somehow felt ashamed. But he quickly put that out of his mind. They both ran through the plans again and again.

They did that often as together they carefully perfected the details of their future moves. The next step was to ensure that they could get Maddy Brown on board. Then they needed to persuade Di Maglio to sell out on their terms and accept Maddy in as the boss woman until Charles had tied up the financial deals. That had to be done, they now agreed, before they defrauded him. It was too dangerous for Di Maglio to be fleeced before he had given up control of the Empire, he would still have too much destructive power. And, in reality, he would wield it without a second thought about the consequences for others.

On the money side, they continued down their many dubious tracks. They bought shares through Charles' father, ramped up their price and then sold them at a profit to the funds, which they sold, in turn, to the public through the bank network in America.

They continued to run out incomprehensible and complex financial products to the different companies they had established. They would close out those deals later and the banks would suddenly realise that their apparent profits were major losses.

They lent money to these and other companies but, in reality, they were just siphoning the cash into their own accounts.

In February they would declare the bank's alleged super profits and sell at least half of it to the gullible public. They might even be able to sell sixty per cent of it according to the latest indications from their advisors.

Nobody understood the frailty of bank profits. Nobody understood how much was hope over reality. Nobody realised how a small number of mistakes could eradicate years of profitable activity. But, then, nobody had ever dealt with a plan that had been so well concealed and actually created by the owners with the purpose of destroying their own bank.

It was agreed that the sale to the public would take place in April.

Once they had sold out, they would allow a month or so before they started to announce the bank's problems. The financial deals, those in the so-called derivatives, would be called in first.

It now looked as if they would make at least two and a half billion to three billion dollars from those positions alone. As they had rolled them out, they had realised that they did not need to be as cautious as they had planned. It was just too easy to get others to sign off on the deals. As Sir Brian and Lord Dunkillin were confirming the fake values of the deals each day, with an assurance they understood the structures, they made that an easy exercise.

Then the fund prices would tumble as they stopped buying all their selected shares or allowed some of the phoney investments to collapse. They would even sell some shares to help them on their way down. And, as they fell, they would buy them back at a lower price to make a profit. They were used to such dealings.

Markets rise because of perception, hope, greed and ignorance. And they fall because of different perceptions, despair, fear and stupidity. They knew how to fuel all these feelings and nothing does it better than ramping up or pushing down the price of an investment.

The rising price of their shares and the strong performance of their funds made them saleable. The reverse would happen soon. The shares would fall like stones as their props were removed and bad news eked out. The funds would fall as the shares they owned fell and their losses materialised on their fake investments; then investors in the funds would try to bail out, the funds would need cash, they would need to sell investments and they would further fuel the panic. It was a dream world for the insiders, disaster for others.

Again, they now estimated they would make much more money from these deals than expected. The US clients' appetite for high performing funds had been much greater than hoped. Their sales force had been far more effective than they had ever planned. Their target profit was now five billion from these activities alone.

And as Charles and his father were creaming off some of the profits in any case, not all would accrue to the others. There was no reason to be too generous.

As for the loans, Charles had overlooked one possibility at the original meeting. That was to push out a mass of loans just before the banks went under. It now looked as if they could embezzle around a further five billion from this activity.

And they still had the precious bank to sell. It was valued, on their most recent assessment, at twelve billion. And they could count on that final billion or so from Sir Piers. Charles was sure he would take over IBE, once it was in serious trouble, if only to save his City pals.

Charles and Jacqui thought through the split of the profits. The profit from the sale of the bank to the public went to them and the trust Di Maglio had set up for their children; something he, no doubt, now really regretted.

They agreed they should skim two or three billion from the money they made on the rest of the fraud for themselves. After all, nobody knew the true figures as they alone knew how the money moved around.

The other ten billion or so would be split fifty per cent to Charles' parents and them, ten per cent to their children and thirty per cent to Di Maglio with the last ten percent being split equally between them, Di Maglio, Maria and Giovanni, now that the unfortunate Stephens was languishing somewhere at the bottom of the sea.

They added up new figures. Their family funds would get over fifteen billion from the fraud against an outlay of a billion for the original purchase of the bank. Not a bad return they agreed.

Di Maglio would make around three billion or so. But clients of the bank would lose more than that and the money Di Maglio received would be moved in a way to ensure it did not remain secret, even if its origins were impossible to trace.

Maria and Giovanni left with a quarter of a billion each. That would at least guarantee some loyalty. Perhaps even hope of a stake in something in the future.

Charles had already run expert and insider checks on the Di Maglio private fortune. They estimated it at three or four billion, excluding the billion they expected to pay him for the Empire. That was a bit more than the failure of the bank would take but there would be other claims. They could, if Maddy Brown were put in place, pass on quite a bit of information on Di Maglio's affairs to the authorities.

Charles and Jacqui knew the main banks Di Maglio used and the names on his accounts. During the PAF take-over, they had put experts into the banks with the sole task of tracing flows of cash to Di Maglio. The patterns had been simple to identify. They understood all the tricks and Di Maglio wasn't as good as them. With that information, the authorities could freeze his cash while they prepared their case or even confiscate it if the courts agreed.

Di Maglio would be wiped out; or at least almost wiped out. Giovanni and some associates could give him money but not enough to fund his current lifestyle, or to succeed in any vendetta against them. If he tried, there would be one last job for Maria; namely the elimination of the wounded Mafia overlord.

They put their workings through the shredder. Neither Jacqui nor Charles saw any point in allowing the evidence to be kept. The figures looked good. They were far in excess of their earlier plans. But then they had underestimated the greed and stupidity of their carefully selected employees and colleagues. Human weakness would allow them to grow their wealth far more than they had expected.

"Your main task is to find a bolt hole. We need it from September. So I guess the West Indies or Asia is the best option."

"I'll find it," she said. "Don't worry."

The next week went quickly. France, New York, then back to London and out to Paris. Charles stayed the night in the Crillon, and, with fifteen minutes to spare, walked up to the Opera. He stood in front of the steps, his briefcase holding the computer and all the data he needed. He waited patiently for the clock to strike eight and Maddy Brown to appear.

He saw her approaching before she saw him. She was not quite dressed as instructed. She wore a pair of Armani jeans and matching T-shirt. That was hardly what he would call casual. He told to her to follow him and headed down the subway. They both got into the same carriage and headed through the maze of tunnels.

The Paris metro is a strange system. The lines criss-cross Paris. The journeys between stations are shorter than in London. Charles eased over to the door. So did Maddy in front of him. They were facing each other. He stayed on the train at the first station. He did the same on the second.

Then, at the third, he jumped out at the last minute. Maddy did, too. They ran down the station platform and then she followed him onto a train that was just about to leave the station heading back the way they came.

The next interchange was the Roissy one and they waited a couple of minutes for the train to the airport. They got to the subway station and then caught a bus to the airport itself.

They met at the airport and went to the hotel courtesy desk. Charles had booked a day room at the closest hotel in the name of Brown. It was useful to have someone actually with a common name like that with him.

He guessed that Di Maglio would have got a photo of Maddy at the park and perhaps again at the opera. Charles was pretty sure that he was being watched. The delectable Ms Brown was getting unusual visibility for a backroom girl.

They hurried through the airport and checked into the room. She used her credit card without comment. It was his first experience of being in a hotel room with a girl on the government's account. He mentioned that it made taxation worth paying for.

They set up the computer and the whole day was taken up in a painstaking briefing session. She was good and had only to be told once. She gasped at the complex money laundering techniques of Di Maglio himself.

"No wonder we never catch the guys. We could never have done that trace. How on earth did you uncover it?" she queried in amazement.

"I don't think you are meant to know," he replied with a laugh. "We don't follow quite the same rules as you do. And perhaps we have more experience."

They discussed the timing. "You're ready. Well as ready as you are ever going to be. So I'll start on Di Maglio next week. I'll target the end of the year for the hand over," said Charles.

"How much will you have to pay him?"

"I aim to keep the front end down to a couple of billion. I can get away with a small upfront as he is a keen seller. The annual payment will be that much higher, though. I would suspect that we would need to offer up to fifty per cent of the adjusted gross, capped at around half a billion a year."

She gasped, this time with incredulity. "But that's an enormous sum."

"No. He currently makes about two billion before pay-offs. That's after the cost of purchase, transportation and the stuff they allow the police to get. But pay-offs and bribes are high; the police aren't that expensive but the politicians are really greedy. "

"What is his bottom line then?"

"I guess the adjusted gross is around one point five billion dollars a year, or thereabouts. So, he'll get about his half billion a year. That still allows the business to make about a billion after all the other costs. They'll need that to fund business growth. But, as volumes grow, we would earn more and so the deal is logical for us as well. He won't be suspicious. On the most likely basis, Di Maglio looks as if he gets around eight or nine billion, assuming he lives to 75."

"Should he assume that?" she asked inquisitively.

"Look, Maddy. If you want to survive in this business, know only what you need to know. Otherwise, you won't see next June. That's not me threatening. That's reality. Keep your focus on the business. Stick to instructions. Don't go native. Don't take any initiatives. Through to about March or April, run for maximum profit.

In May and June, you'll pass me details of large shipments and we'll see you get busted by the police and raided by the gangs.

In August or September, at the latest, it'll all blow up and we'll snatch you out; or, at least, Delaney will. That's when you get revealed as an undercover agent and not a double one who came over to their side any more."

She laughed, "And everyone will say that poor Charles blew it. This wasn't his world. He was a financier, a bit bent perhaps but not really crooked. That's what they'll think. They'll think you were conned. They'll curse Di Maglio for his stupidity in allowing me to be put in charge. But I'll know differently from my safe house. I'll have my new identity. In any event, Maddy Brown's not a real one. And you'll keep quiet, you'll just retire hurt and still rich on your side. I will have disappeared, there'll be the rumours about me being taken out by you, Di Maglio, the Russians and a load more. It's good."

She nodded. He then said curtly, "Let's go. I've a plane scheduled in half an hour. What about you?"

"I'm booked on Eurostar. I have no reservation. So I head back into Paris."

"Do you want to join me?"

"Sorry," she said. "I'm a government employee. We can't throw away rail tickets and just jump on planes. These things need authorisation."

"It's a private executive jet. Not a scheduled one. It won't cost you and you may be able to use your train ticket again. There you are, I'm trying to save the government money. That's unusual for me. But I am a top rate taxpayer."

"You do surprise me, but I know you are. I had a look at your tax records. I was impressed. You could almost support the whole of my division with your taxes."

"Glad to know you spend your time so effectively. So you enjoy chasing after the records of the honest citizen. But then you have so much trouble catching the dishonest ones."

"Don't be sarcastic," she replied tartly.

He arched his eyebrows and took her by the arm. With that they took the bus to the airport and headed for the plane. An hour or so later, they were taxiing into City Airport in the heart of London. Faithful Douglas was waiting.

"Do you want a lift?" he asked.

She smiled, "We don't live in the same locality. I'll hop on a tube. Government wages, you know."

"Call me on the number I gave last week. Either Jacqui or I will give you instructions. Otherwise keep a low profile. And be careful. You're in play already."

She nodded. She waved 'good-bye' and disappeared into the distance. Charles joined Douglas and was taken home, but on the way they picked up Jacqui at the office.

"How did it go?" she enquired.

"Well. The girl's good. She'll be up to it. Mind you, I would have been surprised if it were otherwise. She's one of Delaney's top operators. He's no amateur. She's not, either. But it's far tougher than anything she'll have done before."

"When do we start discussing with my father?"

"I thought about that. My idea was that I should talk to Giovanni and ask his advice. He'll recommend that we agree. He wants to bring peace. That'll reduce the price at the least."

"When will you talk to him?"

"He's coming over for the board meeting on Thursday. We can invite him over for dinner and tackle him then."

She agreed and said she'd sort it. She was now beginning to show slight signs of her pregnancy. Charles noticed her shirt was a bit tight. She saw him looking at her and laughed.

"It'll have to be a shopping spree this weekend. I need new clothes. It will have to be something a bit bigger than the current lot around the waist and a bit less body hugging. Otherwise, everybody's going to know. And that's not good for business."

Work took over again. The scams progressed on all fronts. The money was lent. The money was laundered. The transfers were approved. The wires buzzed. The cash moved in and out of accounts. Then, in the end, their accounts were credited.

The deals were done on stock markets, on futures market, in over the counter markets, on foreign exchanges and in the money market. The shares were ramped. The prices were falsified. The shares were sold. The fund boom continued. More money came to them. More losses were built up at the bank, and still there was no record of the pending problems.

On Thursday, the board meeting was a good-humoured affair. It looked as if the year's results would make everybody a millionaire and so everybody was happy. The US acquisition seemed like a miracle and all in the garden was rosy. The board was hoodwinked. The board was dumb. Giovanni, Jacqui and Charles sat in full control of the facts and marvelled at the incompetence of the others. They believed in fairy tales. They believed in miracles. They were unaware that if you make wonder profits in financial markets, it almost invariably spells speculation or fraud. In this case, it spelt both.

Giovanni came round to dinner as planned. They arranged for Maria to be present. She was still weak from her wounds, but Giovanni made no comment. That just meant that he knew. The four of them sat down to a meal. They were alone. The food had been placed on hot plates at their request. The room had been scanned for bugs and checked for eavesdroppers. It was clean.

Charles waited till Giovanni had started on his soup, a creamy Vichyssoise decked with fresh herbs and a dab of cream.

"Why did you set us up to kill Rastinov? It served no purpose."

He smiled, "It was at Di Maglio's request. He was dangerous alive. The Russians were getting too strong. We needed them to be divided. Even in his dying and powerless state, he affected the balance of power. Now he's gone, the Russians will crumble."

"Why did you use us? You could have taken him out. Security was lousy."

"You needed to be given the chance. It would have been known. You would have been fingered. The Russians would have made you their public enemy number one. You would have been forced into the family again for protection, if nothing else. The pretence that you were at risk would have become a reality."

"And why isn't it a reality?"

"That's because of those idiots from the French police. We tipped them off but they let another group through. The Arabs or whoever they were. The idea was that you would do it and the police would stop you being followed. Once we had told the police it was you and Maria, they would have passed that on to the Russians. They pay them well for protection. We thought of implicating you anyway. But when the Arabs blasted away the police, it was too dangerous. We couldn't take the risk."

They noticed he was clearly stating his allegiance to Di Maglio. He had associated himself with the decisions. That made him more dangerous than they had thought. They all realised that they needed to be careful about their friend Giovanni.

Charles calmly tackled his soup. Maria chewed absent-mindedly a bread roll. She was waiting to see what would happen. Jacqui picked up her spoon and was about to dip it into the soup when Charles turned to Giovanni. The look on his face was not friendly.

"If you double cross me again, I'll kill you," Charles said to him in a quiet voice. "And Di Maglio won't be able to save you. I don't mind you working for him. But don't double cross me, or even make me think you have."

Giovanni paled. Sweat glistened on his high forehead. He swallowed nervously, his Adam's apple bobbed up and down. The veins on his neck seemed to turn purple. His breath became irregular. His hand went to his chest. Giovanni never saw himself as a threatened species, he was the archetypal backroom boy. This was a new experience. Charles continued, this time in a quiet and unthreatening tone. But there was a chill in the air and it was reflected in his voice. He was unsmiling.

"I'll make a deal with Di Maglio. But he has to accept my terms."

He took another spoonful of soup and waited for someone to speak. Maria was sitting there with her mouth open. She knew nothing of the detail of their plans. Jacqui was looking pale and stared fixedly at him as if she was waiting for what he would say. Yet she knew. This was a great act on her part.

Giovanni, still with the air of a frightened and trapped animal, opened and shut his mouth as if he were drowning. In reality he was most likely trying to ask a question. It was just that the words did not come out. So Charles continued, having wiped his lips with the napkin and put down his spoon.

"I'll take on the Empire but get someone to manage it for me. I have someone. They're good. They're loyal to me. Di Maglio doesn't know them."

Giovanni asked who they were. Charles didn't want him to know about Maddy Brown yet. He didn't want him to know that his manager was a woman. The surprise would do them good.

"That's irrelevant until we agree. The deal is simple. A couple of billion front end. But then he gets thirty percent of the gross each year for life, capped at half a billion. No more. No less. I'll keep the Empire going until our kids are of age. I don't want it. Jacqui doesn't want it. We'll try to make sure our kids don't, either. If they don't, we'll get rid of it. That's the deal. It's not negotiable. What do you think?"

And with that question to the shocked Giovanni, Charles rang the bell for someone to remove their abandoned soup plates. Douglas himself acted the butler. There was silence in the room while he was there. Then Giovanni spoke, "That's a stupid bid. It won't fly. "

"Then it will have to be war," said Jacqui quietly.

Maria actually gasped. Giovanni looked at Jacqui in horror. She repeated her words,

"It will have to be war. And I mean outright war. There's no alternative. It's our army against his."

"Your army?" queried Giovanni.

"I said our army. Do you think we're stupid? We have one and it's well trained. They're ex SAS and similar organisations. We have people from Special Forces. It's a real army. These are loyal mercenaries. Not the thugs you use."

"So," said Giovanni with the look of a worried man, "that's your final offer."

"Yes. And Giovanni, don't forget what I said about being double-crossed. I rather like you on the board."

With that Charles got up and offered the main course. It was veal done Swiss style with rosti and salad. He served the portions and noticed how Giovanni found it difficult to eat. Maria and Jacqui had no such problem. And Charles was actually hungry. Nobody spoke during the meal. The silence was oppressive to start with, but then they seemed to get used to it. They let it remain.

Maria looked at Charles and then Jacqui and then Giovanni. Jacqui and Charles looked fixedly at Giovanni. He stared down at his plate. Then suddenly Giovanni broke the silence.

"I'll try to sell it to Di Maglio. But it's a poor deal for him. I mean thirty per cent? That's three hundred million a year. You'll have to offer more."

"There's nothing more on offer," said Charles, noting that the profits seemed less than they had estimated, "Except war. And that starts on Monday. It's a new week and a new month."

"We need to agree everything. It's complicated. We can't do that by Monday."

Jacqui and Charles exchanged glances. The offer was now being considered. It was time to carry on playing hardball. Charles ignored the comment, "Di Maglio agrees the sale terms by the weekend. The handover will be midnight on December 31st. My manager goes in situ on Monday week. You have the sale agreement drawn up this weekend and you can tell all your people the following week. And don't forget it's not negotiable."

Charles rang again. Once again, Douglas appeared. He took away their empty plates and the full one from Giovanni. He never had a great appetite, but today he had none. Douglas placed cheese and fruit on the table. He replenished their wine glasses. He left without a sign that he found the silence, that cold silence, in any way strange.

"If he wants to talk the details, not the substance, then we can meet in Paris on Saturday. Jacqui has some shopping to do. We'll be at the Crillon. I'll have my lawyers there on Sunday to go through the papers. We're free from four to seven on Saturday for discussion. Otherwise it will have to wait till Sunday. We have tickets for the opera on Saturday night."

Giovanni nodded. He sipped his wine. He looked so worried that Charles started to laugh.

"Giovanni, this is business. Don't look so miserable. It's just that you're a willing seller and I'm not a willing buyer. That's fucked up the price. It's tough but that's life. And we don't want to kill you. We'll only do it if you cheat us. I've no concern about you working for Di Maglio. But you tried to con me in America when the phoney attacks were taking place. That was your one chance. So be good."

Jacqui nodded at him, a grim look on her face. Maria said nothing. She just watched the drama unfold in front of her eyes. They ate the cheese in silence. They sipped at their wine. Charles offered coffee. Giovanni declined it. He wanted to leave, and leave quickly. Charles knew he had to get back to Di Maglio.

That night they had doubled the guard on the house and had told the guards to be visible to Giovanni, not when he arrived but when he left. They wanted to avoid a pre-emptive strike.

As soon as he could, Giovanni left. Charles saw him to the door. One of the bodyguards appeared and then two more. Their coats were open and, as they had agreed, the guns they carried were plainly visible. Giovanni was startled. In the distance he could make out more shadows, more men. The army was there. Then Douglas came in the car and drove him slowly away. Giovanni didn't look back. He hardly looked at Charles as he left.

But they knew that the next two or three hours would be decisive. If they were not under attack tonight, the chances were that they would have a deal. They would try to negotiate better terms, but no more. And Charles could play hardball on the terms. They had no other buyer but him.

"Do we wait for the attack? Or do we go to bed?" asked Maria.

"You think he'll attack?" asked Jacqui.

"Sixty-forty" said Maria, "The chances are that he will be seriously upset. And that usually means retribution."

"You're wrong" Charles replied. It's sixty-forty he'll accept. Especially when Giovanni tells him there's little chance of us improving the offer. And Giovanni will recommend it."

"How do you feel so sure?" asked Maria.

"Because, just now he's reading a paper that Douglas gave him. It contains information he'd rather we didn't have."

"What information is that?"

"Like his own bank account. It's a bit bigger than we expected. It's numbered. But it's his. And Giovanni has been a bit of a naughty boy. He's been creaming some money off his boss."

"And what will you do with your paper?"

"Show it to Di Maglio the day war breaks out. That should be fun, especially as Di Maglio could trace all the outflows. And that would be the end of poor Giovanni. He wasn't very good at laundering his own cash. But it's nice to know he has a couple of hundred million, even if it appears to be mainly money that ought to belong to his boss."

"So we go to sleep?" asked Maria.

"We go to sleep," said Jacqui.

And so the day ended. The night was peaceful. The next morning, the phone call came at the office, it was Giovanni.

"We meet you Saturday at four at the Georges Cinq."

They agreed and rang off quickly. There was no point in any discussion. If they were having a meeting, then they would be negotiating. Charles was happy to play at being indifferent.

That evening they headed off to Paris in the private jet. Douglas came with them and would chauffeur them in a hired car. There were two other cars parked nearby, carrying guards. One would drive in front. One would be behind. This was not a weekend where they would take chances. So they sped into Paris with their convoy.

But they didn't go to the Crillon. They headed towards the Arc de Triomphe and stopped off at the flat they owned. The security was better.

The guards and Douglas would share shifts while they waited for a response from Di Maglio. Charles wondered if he knew where they were. They had employed the normal evasive tactics, but these were always harder when you are in convoy. So he suspected he would have been followed. But one never knew.

On Saturday, they headed to the Faubourg Saint Honore where Jacqui shopped for her new clothes. The shops were all instructed to drop the clothes off at their room in the Crillon, which had been booked for them in any event. The guards would see that they were sent on to the flat. There was no point in making it too easy for anyone to learn their precise address. They lunched in a little restaurant near the Opera and then headed to the hotel for their meeting with Di Maglio.

Di Maglio was sitting in the lobby. There were some fairly nasty looking thugs at the next table. But nobody would say a word to them. The hotel knew who their guest was and realised that there was little they could do about his unsavoury entourage. And the thugs would keep the rest of the public out of earshot of the table where Di Maglio was seated.

He didn't greet them but came straight to the point, "That's a stupid offer."

"We agree," said Jacqui with a smile. "But it's not going to get better. In fact, at five it goes down by a per cent and then at six by another. And so on. I think you get my meaning."

He glared at her. He then looked at Charles. He was standing, as was Jacqui. He motioned for them to sit down. Charles shook his head.

"Look, I'd rather have tea without you. Have we a deal? Or should we go back to our place and leave you with your boys?"

He motioned them to sit down. Giovanni, seated next to him, pleaded with his eyes for them to do so. They ignored them both.

"Well, I'm waiting for an answer. This isn't a place for negotiating. So either you accept or you reject. What is it?"

He looked at them. For the first time he looked old to them, really old. The hair was still black but the face was grey. The hands were old man's hands. He was ill at ease. He looked at Charles and his eyes seemed to say different things from his face and his body. His eyes said he was beaten and knew it. He saw they were about to leave and knew they would not return. They would start the war because there would be no alternative. One can't make threats and then not keep them.

"I accept, but there are two conditions."

Charles said nothing but watched and waited.

"Tell me your manager. And one of my men becomes number two."

"I can agree to your first condition but not the second. These businesses need one boss. A number two from your side would be your man. It's a showstopper. We keep our nominee in charge of the business while they perform. But we don't keep them a moment longer if they fail. And we have full control. It's our business and not yours."

"You could destroy it."

"True," Jacqui said. "We considered that. But it wouldn't work. It would need to be destroyed by someone like the Russians and they're all as bad as you."

"What about the police? They could destroy the business."

"They're more corrupt than the criminals."

He smiled, or at least bared his teeth, at that comment, "So I have to trust you."

"You have no choice."

"Well who are you going to put in charge? What's his name?"

"It's a girl, not a man. She's worked for me for several years. She heads up the fraud side of the UK secret service. She was in organised crime before that. She worked as a gangbuster. It's a good spread. But she's quit them. It got too hot. Not her fault. But an agent like that only has a limited life. She's tough and she's good.

She's thirty something and wants to make some real money. I must have paid her a couple of million in the last years. She wants to get seriously rich and this is her big chance."

"What makes you certain about her?" queried Di Maglio.

"She's worked for me for some time. And she won't get a better offer from anyone else. And she wants to move to greater luxury. She needs real cash or she won't be able to disappear and enjoy life. Now, she has to pretend she has nothing but her salary at the secret service or they would be suspicious. In any case, she would get twenty to thirty years for what she's done for me already and that can only get worse when she works in the Empire."

"We meet tomorrow here at ten." That curt sentence was Di Maglio's only acknowledgement that he knew he'd lost. There was no point. He was not one to negotiate without a chance of winning. He wanted out. He wanted them in. He had a purpose in life again. He would seek to corrupt one of their children to try to get them to take over the Empire. He still did not realise that, by then, there would be no Empire to take over.

They left without sitting down. They didn't shake hands. There was no emotion between him and Jacqui. And they did not care. They had won the first round. There would be negotiations and he would try to retain some power. But he had no choice. He had the losing hand.

That evening they went to the opera. Don Juan was one of their favourites. The beauty of the music and the richness of the voices overpowered them and allowed them to forget the reality of the present. They held each others' hands as they enjoyed the scene before them. The words had less meaning than the sounds. The bodies talked. As it ended and Don Juan descended into hell, Charles thought of Di Maglio. He longed to destroy him and his Empire. He wanted revenge for all the lives he had destroyed.

He felt no remorse for the gunfights and the gang warfare. But he thought of people like Claire who had been tempted into prostitution and then worse. He thought of people like Carrie who had taken drugs and perhaps lacked the strength to stop. He thought of the murders and the punishments. He contemplated the deceit and the threats.

Did they differ from them? Perhaps they did. But he knew it was only because they destroyed through money. They killed but only with reason. They destroyed but only for a purpose. He knew he was trying to distinguish his world from that of Di Maglio. And he knew that the only real difference was in Di Maglio's casual disregard for the lives that he wasted through his world of drugs. Charles persuaded himself it was material but he had only half convinced himself of that fact as they left for home.

The contract was short and clear. The changes were only for clarification. The dates were set. The price was agreed. And they signed. It all seemed an anti-climax after the hours of anguish. He had agreed. This was the best deal. He now wanted to have it over.

They signed and this time they shook hands. Di Maglio's hands were cold as ice. They were rough to the touch. They were powerful and almost crushed Charles. Di Maglio looked him in the eyes. Was he pleading? Or was he threatening? Charles would never know but he spat the words out under his breath. He alone could hear.

"This has taken my whole life to build. We've been grossing two billion or so a year before bribes. Grow it or you'll regret it."

"I'll look after it as I said," Charles snarled back. "Let's hope your people are disciplined or they'll have trouble. From December you're out and an outsider. Make sure they know that. The rules you made about outsiders will continue. And those rules will have no exception."

Di Maglio muttered "bastard" at him under his breath and then took Jacqui's hands.

"You're something of family. Act with honour. Make sure he looks after it well." It was a plea. Jacqui looked coolly at him. She kissed his forehead, very briefly.

"You've done the right thing. You need to rest and then enjoy yourself." She quickly disengaged herself and joined Charles. With their lawyers in tow they walked out. They had the Empire. And on Monday, Maddy Brown would start to run it their way. And destroy what Di Maglio had dedicated his entire life to building.

CHAPTER NINETEEN

They returned that evening from Paris. And on Monday morning, Charles left again with Maddy Brown for Geneva.

She was wearing trousers and a tailored tweed jacket. She was also carrying a gun. He had not realised until he saw her take off her jacket.

She was keen to start and was trying to find out how to make her mark. It was going to have to be with Di Maglio. Any victory over him would be noted and give her the reputation for toughness. And she would need that reputation and the power of control that went with it if she were to nurse the Empire through to its final destruction.

Di Maglio was waiting for them at his compound. He looked at Maddy. At first glance, she did not seem to have the strength to run an Empire. He looked with ill disguised contempt at the long elegant legs, the slim waist and the long blond hair. They all seemed to indicate softness. The eyes continued that impression, as did the mouth with its tendency to crinkle into a smile.

Di Maglio ignored her outstretched hand and turned to Charles, "She's a kid. This is your idea of a manager? She'll be eaten alive."

Charles didn't have time to answer. Maddy interrupted in a soft and quiet voice, "By whom?"

"By my animals," snarled back Di Maglio. He gave her a look of total contempt. "They're hardly going to be keen to have a barbie doll as a boss."

Di Maglio had a couple of his sidekicks with him. Charles had seen them before but only knew they came from the prostitution and extortion end of his business. One of them laughed at this comment and, in a thick accent, offered to get the barbie doll a real job on his books. His laugh seemed to jerk to a halt as Maddy's foot streaked upwards and caught him neatly in the crotch. Then a slow and effortless arm crashed down on the back of his neck as he doubled over and then crashed down again as he started to fall.

The second man moved forward as Maddy drew her gun and calmly shot him in the knee. The gun had disappeared and the man had collapsed, bleeding, on the floor before the guards came through the door.

Di Maglio ignored the injured men. He turned on the guards and raged at them for having allowed someone to his presence still armed. Then he ordered the men to remove the casualties. He turned to Maddy and this time there was a smile on his lips.

"You're tough. You'll keep them in check. Now, let's see if you can run a business like this."

There followed a discussion about the intricacies of the business. Charles was amazed at how much Maddy knew. She was impressive. She looked good. She fought well. And she sounded good. She was getting more attractive by the moment. He now saw why Delaney had selected her. He wondered if she would cross over to his business after they had finished with Di Maglio. She had something of Claire about her. There was that fresh look of innocent fun, behind which stalked a ruthless killer instinct. Maddy played to win.

Three hours later, they were finished. Maddy asked Di Maglio when he would leave.

"As agreed, at the end of December," he said. "Till then I'm the boss and you work for me."

"No way," Charles said quietly. "Maddy works for me. You're the boss and you call the shots. But it's handover time. You can hand everything over on the last day or you can hand things over as time goes on. But you hand things over in whole chunks. I want one business at a time. No fuzzy handovers. No dependencies on areas under your control. We do this my way. You follow the line in clause eight."

Di Maglio turned to Giovanni who had come into the room at the time of the commotion over the shooting. "What the fuck's clause eight?"

"There shall be no joint running of any part of the business during the handover period," he replied. "Both parties have to agree before any area of activity is handed over."

"That's a crap clause."

"It's normal in this type of arrangement."

"Nothing's normal. I'm giving this jerk my business. The ungrateful sod doesn't even want it. And you're telling me he has me by the balls until the day I go. I only do what he agrees. You call that normal?"

"Wrong," said Charles. "You do what you want. You explain it to Maddy. She has no say in your decisions. When you want you hand over a part of your business. Or you hand it all over together on December 31st. If Maddy agrees the business stands alone, then she'll take it. If she doesn't believe that, she'll tell you. Maddy talks to me. She's your contact to me. I depend on her call. Call me and I'll still ask her. Those are my rules."

He mouthed "Fuck you" and walked away from them, talking in an agitated manner to Giovanni.

"Well, he really loves you," said Maddy sarcastically. Her mouth puckered again around the edges. Her eyes sparkled with fun. "This is not a good start. But you don't need a relationship with someone who's not going to be around in a month or so."

Charles cut her off sharply, "Don't kid yourself. He could have you killed in that month. He could set traps. He could do a lot of damage. Be careful and be alert. A couple of kicks and blows or a shot or two doesn't impress anyone. They've killed for less. You crucified two macho men's self esteem just now. That's the human equivalent of castration for them. And they won't forgive you."

She looked at him in a new light. She was serious. "You're tougher than I thought. You live this life. You've lived it for years. And it hasn't affected you."

He returned her stare. He knew his face betrayed no emotions. "That's what all this is about. It's about lifestyles that are sustainable. Just do as you're told and succeed. Otherwise, I'll kill you if Di Maglio doesn't."

She stared at him. Her face was quite white. Her nose flared out. Her eyes looked a bit frightened. "You mean it don't you," she whispered. They were standing, but their heads were close together.

"It'll be you or me and my family. I mean it. That doesn't mean I want it."

"Do you say that every time you kill anyone?" she queried. The colour was returning to her face but the eyes still looked worried.

"Look, I'm not new to this business. I've fucked and been fucked as he would say," he said jerking his head over towards Di Maglio. He was still in deep conversation with Giovanni. He was gesticulating angrily, ignoring their presence totally.

She looked at Charles. "And I thought you just hung around the periphery with the chosen few, with Claire and Maria, but nobody else."

"Forget that. By the way, noting the innuendo, my private life is taboo. It's outside your brief. Don't forget I'm the boss and the only boss. Otherwise I'll deliver you back."

"In a wooden box?" she queried.

He stared at her. Did she know more about him than he thought?

Maddy was getting dangerous. But then this was a dangerous game. And he was dealing with a tiger, not a pussycat. He noted to be careful nevertheless. Meanwhile Di Maglio returned to them with Giovanni by his side.

"I'll hand over the hotels next Monday, then extortion and prostitution the following week. The drug side will be last on the day that I leave."

"Fine," said Maddy crisply. "Where do I work from?"

"We head for New York this afternoon. Is your boss boy going to come with us?"

"I doubt it," she replied. "The boss man already said that he would leave me in charge. He's got more important fish to fry. Otherwise, he wouldn't have hired me. You have plenty of hit men, yes men and "I shall obey" men on your bankroll. He could have recruited one of them if he wanted just that. Don't you agree?"

The last question was delivered with a saccharine sweet smile. Di Maglio looked at her with loathing, but then also with a bit of respect. The lady did come over as having balls, definitely more than the vast majority of men employed by him.

Charles looked at them and smiled at Maddy. He went up to her and gave her a peck on the cheek. "Be good. And enjoy yourself. But don't enjoy yourself too much. Be on guard."

She laughed and said, "I'll keep you in touch. Don't get concerned, I'll look after your inheritance."

Charles said "goodbye" to Di Maglio. He still found it hard to be polite. Giovanni was more distant than usual, but then, the last time they had met, Charles had proposed to take him out if he double-crossed him, so that wasn't surprising. He looked at the two and then at Maddy. The girl was going to earn her keep this time.

Business back in London, New York and all the other places the bank took him led them up to Christmas. Maddy called him on schedule every day. The handover was going smoothly. She knew how to handle herself. She co-existed with Di Maglio. She believed his affection for the cesspool of a business he'd built up meant he would hand it to her in good shape.

The common gossip showed they had been right about his inner thoughts. He was gambling on the fact that Jacqui and Charles would have a son and that son would turn against them. Just like Jacqui had turned against him. That son would be the saviour of his business, taking it to new heights, or depths, depending on your viewpoint.

Christmas at the office was one round of endless parties. They appeared at the junior ones in time to be noticed and left before the under the table frolics became too embarrassing to watch. They attended the dinners that the chief executive is forced to attend. The select restaurant was the preferred venue for corporate finance. A rowdy funfair was taken over for the evening by the traders. A disco was the choice of the operations' people. And so the final weeks progressed in their alcoholic haze for the many, as compulsory jollity became an unnatural by-product of the season.

Christmas at home was limited to the family. On the day after they saw friends. But they spent most of the five-day weekend playing and going for walks with Juliet. The last day of the holiday was cool and crisp, in sharp contrast to the damp and dismal weather of the earlier part. With a pushchair as a precaution against tiredness, they walked through Kensington Gardens with Juliet. They carried the bread that she wanted for the ducks, although they suspected that the holiday would mean they'd be spoilt for choice.

And they were right. The ducks came up and looked in contempt at the soggy chunks of bread that floated at the side of the round pond. They had no doubt supped on finer produce earlier in the day. Their needs satisfied, they did not care if they disappointed the children. Their charity was transitory, and they would not come when it was cold and wet. That was the time when ducks really wanted feeding.

Luckily some pigeons swooped down and grabbed the floating morsels. That cheered up Juliet no end. She transferred her affections to them, indifferent to the fact they were grubby City dwellers. They needed her offerings and she now loved the bird kingdom's equivalent of the City vagrant.

They walked on. In the end Juliet got into the pushchair. Jacqui put a blanket over her. They guessed she would soon be tired and doze off. Jacqui hardly looked pregnant at three and a half months and she was happy to stroll on with him. They both didn't like round trips. They would walk on as far as they could and then head out of the park in search of a taxi to take them back home. They meandered through to Hyde Park and along its paths.

The crisp day had brought out many, keen to walk off some of the extra calories caused by the Christmas feeding frenzy. They walked slowly, Jacqui leaning on Charles' arm and Juliet fast asleep in her buggy. Everything was peaceful. The people around them were distant blurs as they gently talked to each other about friends and family.

Charles' parents had headed for the West Indies for a sunnier climate than the depressing bleakness of the Provence coastline. Many of their friends had gone skiing. Others had headed for the sun. Few seemed to have stayed in London. But that was no problem for them. They had had five days together and that was a rarity indeed.

"Our New Year's resolution should be to be together more," said Jacqui. "When we have broken the bank and destroyed the Empire, we'll be free. We'll be worth endless billions and we can sink back and relax in luxury. We haven't really done that for a long time, since we started on that money laundering in France all those years ago. Those were fun days. They were exciting. Things have changed. We've become too much part of an establishment to which we don't belong."

Charles agreed, "We're free spirits in reality. My parents are and so are we. We're too unconventional for the bank. But then we're doing unconventional things with it. I wish we could find that beach where we could have our house and our retreat."

"You carry on working," laughed Jacqui. "Perhaps I'll surprise you and find something."

Charles went to interrupt her, "Don't ask. We may be closer than you think. But I want to be sure first, then I'll surprise you."

"How will that be? Would you buy it without me seeing it?"

"Why shouldn't I? We could keep it as an investment and rent it out; or keep it for ourselves if we wanted. Or use it for part of the year. But I haven't done anything yet. I haven't even seen anything. But I'll step up the pace now. I want it soon. There are several options open. I'll fly out to some of them next month, then I'll tell you which one to see."

"You say which one? That makes it sound as if you'll decide without me."

"No," she laughed. "Don't worry. I'll not force you. I just know that we want something so special that I doubt there's more than one on the market at any time. If we can't find the right one, I'll get something for the short term. We can then find the permanent place later."

He looked at her and asked jokingly, "Permanent? Is there such a thing for us in terms of living space?"

"There could be. But we'll see."

It was at that moment that he saw the man. And he recognised him immediately. He was one of Di Maglio's people. He was the one Maddy had attacked in the house near Geneva. He didn't seem to realise that Charles had recognised him, or even noticed him. Charles eased Jacqui casually off the path and they headed across the grass. He could see the man out of the corner of his eye. There was now no doubt he was following them.

"We're being tracked by one of your father's men. But he seems to be on his own. Yes. He's definitely following us."

Jacqui frowned. "Unusual, they never use one man. Could he be here by chance?"

"Do you believe in chance? He's the man who Maddy beat up in Geneva. He could want revenge?"

"My father would kill him if he acted freelance. Why would he want revenge on us? Surely, he'd try to take out Maddy?"

"He's approaching. Be careful. Watch for others."

The man approached. He now realised they had seen him. He kept his hands in view and walked slowly. He wanted to talk, or at least that was the impression that he was giving. But why would that be? Why did he want to talk to them?

Charles reached inside his jacket. He was carrying a gun. He always did. Jacqui watched the man and Charles carefully. The man didn't react. He made no attempt to draw a gun. If he tried now he would be dead. Was he alone or with someone else? He could be just a decoy to keep them occupied.

Jacqui and Charles had worked together often. He kept his eye on the approaching man and she scoured the area beyond. Her hand was in her coat pocket. She would have a small gun in it.

The man came closer. They watched him carefully. But this was a lousy place for any ambush. There was too wide a space between the trees and them. Juliet slept on. The man approached. He was about two or three yards from them.

Charles called, "Stop. One step more and I shoot. If you have something to say to me say it now. There's nobody around. You'll not be overheard."

He stopped, "I have a deal. I still need to broker it to Carapli and Veranski, but that won't be a problem."

They waited for him to continue.

"We'll buy out our side of the business. That's the extortion and prostitution side. Your heart isn't in it. We'll pay top dollar."

"Talk to Miss Brown if you have any proposal. She's your boss."

"You're the boss."

"No. Maddy Brown is. And she's not going to be pleased when she hears what you've done. Nor will Di Maglio be. Nor will your bosses, unless you are telling lies about broking the deal to them and they really sent you. So think up some excuses. And get out of here."

The man made to say something, but Charles brushed him aside. He would have liked to know who his associates were, but he had no doubt Maddy would find out. She was already running his area. He wondered what she'd do to him. Di Maglio would have had him killed and he'd have been right. Discipline was important. He wondered if Maddy would do the same. She should. He, somehow, felt that she wouldn't have the stomach to make an example of him. He should help her. So he asked him if he was alone. He said he was and Charles felt he was most likely telling the truth.

"Do you have a gun?"

He looked surprised at the question but nodded.

"Then come with me, I have a job for you."

Charles took him by the arm and led him away. They got to some trees. They were hidden from view. Charles allowed the man to get slightly ahead and then grabbed the gun that he had seen in outline in the man's pocket. The man realised what was happening and struggled until the gun went off. The coat muffled the noise. The bullet passed downwards through his thigh and into his leg. At least he grabbed hold of his knee in agony as he fell sobbing to the ground.

"Don't try that stunt again. And remember it wasn't that I am soft. That wasn't why I didn't kill you. The reason was quite simple. I didn't want to take the risk of killing you here. I may have been caught. But, if I see you again without my permission or Maddy Brown's, you're dead. And tell your pals, the rackets are mine and the exit rules are the same as always."

The injured man groaned and grabbed his knee again. Charles laughed openly, "Remember one thing. I'll put you on the list. You know what that means. If anything happens to me or to my family, you'll be history."

With that Charles turned his back on him and walked away. But a few steps later, he spun round to see the man fumbling with his gun. He saw the finger as it eased onto the trigger and moved quickly towards Jacqui as he fired. In his pained and weakened state, the man missed by a mile. But Charles did not and the silencer on his gun made it almost soundless. The first bullet took the man in the chest and the second. He twitched and then lay still.

Jacqui and he fussed with the pushchair. They woke Juliet and comforted her as she cried. The only noise had been from the man's gun. Bystanders had looked in that direction to see where the gunshot came from and they now ran towards the man. Someone called out that he was a doctor. He was let through although they knew that it was too late. They made their way to the edge of the crowd and looked on. The doctor had a newspaper and covered the man's face with it. It looked comical for it was a tabloid with a panicky headline about the latest crime figures.

The police came across the lawn on motorbikes, sirens screaming. Some people hadn't seen anyone, others imagined they had and described strangers to the police. Charles and Jacqui said nothing. Their names were taken and that was all. They wondered how long it would be before Delaney called. They knew he would and that would be the end of the story.

He would understand why Charles had killed the man. He would understand, just as Jacqui did. And Di Maglio would approve. Ironically the man's death would be a great help. Delaney would be aware of the murder and cover it up, he would understand the danger that Maddy would have been in if the man had not been taken out. That made it dangerous for him in the future, as he became a co-conspirator. And Di Maglio would be pleased; he would feel Charles was reacting with the brutality he would have used and would, therefore, feel he could trust him that bit more.

They walked down to the road and called a cab. Jacqui shook her head, "One day we'll get away from it all. It really stinks. I'll be so pleased when we get rid of it."

"Then get our island. We need the clean air and the fresh breeze."

She nodded. She would do that. Somehow it was all getting closer. The scam was well underway. The bank results would be out in two months or so and then they would sell it to the public. There only remained their last big moves in the scam. And those were the most risky.

Maddy would be fully in charge in a week's time and then they would plan for the Empire's limited future. But between then and now, there would be incidents. They would have to be far more ruthless than they had ever been before. For this time they could not afford any laxness. This was the prelude to the big game. Their lives were in play from now on.

It took about an hour for Delaney to ring. "I am right that it was you? He was one of the Di Maglio team."

"Yes. The rot is starting already. He wanted to buy out the prostitution and extortion business. He needed to be treated as Di Maglio would have treated him. Otherwise, Maddy would have been at risk. They would have seen us as a soft target. I had to take him out. I was unsure if she could."

"Wouldn't Di Maglio have organised that?" queried Delaney.

"He would only have done it if Maddy failed. But it still would have weakened her. And I couldn't afford that."

"I thought you did it for Maddy?" he responded.

"Our needs happen to be the same. I only do things like this when it's imperative."

"How often have you killed, Charles?"

"Commander, I doubt as often as you. Perhaps I've killed just this once. Perhaps it's more than once. Who knows? And who cares? But I want to stop the risk of killing again. That's part of what this is about."

He phoned Maddy in New York, "You know the little shit you beat up in Geneva. He's dead. He got shot in Hyde Park of all places. They are dangerous things parks these days. He wanted us to sell the extortion and prostitution side.

He had partners. Find out who they are and warn them that you'll finish them off if they even think about it in the future. And warn them quickly. Get to them before they know of the shooting. Ask who's closest to our pal in the park. And then tell him to organise the funeral service. Carry a gun. You may need it in self defence. So cover your back as well. Tell me what happened."

"You killed him for me?" she asked.

"Yes."

"Thanks. I appreciate it."

"Be careful Maddy. I don't want you to get hurt."

"I'll be careful. Don't worry."

He knew she would check out with Delaney but he would only give the same message. So he calmly went back to their Christmas routine and watched a video with Juliet and Jacqui. As they watched the Disney film and heard the excited laughter of Juliet, he longed for the end game. He wanted to be with his family. He knew that it was now unlikely that he would be able to spend another five full days with them until the whole business was over. But then they would have their freedom.

The phone rang. It was Maddy. She sounded strained. "I did what you said. He had a brother. He drew a gun on me and I killed him. Then there was silence. All the men looked at me. They hate me."

"Good. That means you scare them. That's how it's got to be, Maddy.

The more they smile, the more dangerous it is. Watch Di Maglio. They hate him too. Not one of them loves the bastard. Mind you, he doesn't love them either. But they do as he says. And they wouldn't harm him. They know the price of disobedience, and you've shown that you intend to continue the penalties. That'll give you the power to run things your way."

She was still upset. He could hear it in her voice. "I know how to kill. But I never have before."

"Maddy, it was you or them. This is a dirty game. But the end justifies it. Pull yourself together and keep vigilant. Oh and tell Di Maglio what has happened and ask him to pass the same message onto the drugs arm."

"When should I do that?"

"Do it now. It's not Sunday. Mind you, Di Maglio doesn't exactly belong to the keep Sunday sacred brigade."

She laughed and he knew that she had recovered. The voice was then firmer. The joke, banal as it was, had broken the spell.

"I'll do it now."

"Good. Be careful, Maddy."

He rang off and waited for the next call. Di Maglio would get his people together for an incident like this. And he would also call him first. Sure enough the phone rang.

"You killed the fucker. Have you sorted it out at your end?"

"There was nothing to sort out. I left my name with the police. There were no witnesses. The killer disappeared into thin air. I look innocent. So does Jacqui. And we were with Juliet. She was asleep in her pushchair."

"You did well. It'll be a lesson."

"And Maddy killed the brother. That'll show she means discipline as well."

"Yeah, she did OK. Mind you I'd have preferred her to shoot as a punishment rather than in self defence. When she does that, I'll believe she's as good as you say."

"Happy Christmas," said Charles as he rang off, thinking uncharitably 'And may you rot in hell.'

The New Year came and went. January came and went. The auditors were hard at work on both sides of the Atlantic. They would publish results soon and their books were being vetted. Charles knew their profits would easily exceed a billion dollars. He also knew how much of that was phoney. But he had reckoned that they could produce a forecast of well over one and a half billion dollars for the next year ahead of the sale to the public. And the market was still going wild on bank shares and IBE was outperforming them all. The fact was that the scam was getting bigger and more profitable by the day.

It was on a cold wet, windy Sunday in February that they all sat down and once again reviewed their progress. They were not sitting in the same room as on that Sunday so many months ago. They were in a secret location in Liechtenstein, the little princedom stuck between Austria and Switzerland. They had some companies registered there, its rigid secrecy laws were like manna from heaven for them.

The location may have been different but the group was almost identical. There was Maria, Jack Ryder, Giovanni, Jacqui and Charles. Di Maglio had been invited but had declined. Stephens was presumably still reclining in the deep waters of the English Channel.

Charles banged on the table to draw their attention. "Gentlemen, ladies, I thought it important to run through where we are and also to tell you how we plan to progress. The good news is that all is running smoothly. And it's going better than we expected. Jack Ryder will give you details of where we are on our stock market and other dealings"

His father smiled broadly, "We have done better than I ever anticipated. We estimate we will make five point two billion on the investments we sold to the US funds. I have to say your sales people in the US were incredible; mind you so were the sales commissions you paid them. They had no qualms, any that they had were bought out by our generosity. They would have sold any junk we created for them.

We've stopped creating fake investments now, although we are still manipulating share prices. So the profit has stopped from this activity."

Our trading positions show a profit of just over two point eight billion; that's for us and not the bank by the way. We've slowed down there since Stephens left. It was getting difficult to push out too much more as there is always a risk that some bright young business graduate works it all out." He knew that was not quite true, they had actually made much more than this. They had skimmed off a large portion of the profit on the later deals for themselves.

Charles then talked of the loans they had written for the bank, "The loan position is going fantastically and we look as if we are going to make around five billion from that source. All that money has now been banked, obviously not with IBE!" Charles did not mention that he was about to complete the process with a jumbo loan. This would go to a Di Maglio company and would reach them by way of a Di Maglio bank account.

That loan would look like an in-house fraud by one of the known Di Maglio henchmen at the bank. That would bring yet more pressure on his father in law.

"That means we make around thirteen billion before the proceeds from selling off the bank to the public. And on the estimate of the bank's value, Jacqui has some good news"

"Indeed," said Jacqui. "I have been talking to our advisors and things have improved for us even further. On the basis of the rating the analysts expect for us now, especially given our apparent growth rate, we should have a market value of around fifteen billion.

We should also be able to reduce our stake further than originally planned. There are loads of so called ethical investors in the market these days. They want us to show we will not control the voting in the company meetings after we sell down to the public. We therefore need to sell about three quarters of the bank to satisfy them. That's no hardship as the rest is not going to be worth much once we've finished!

If I am right the share sale will personally gross us around eleven billion net of the exorbitant fees of our advisors. That, of course, is not of interest to most of you. But I want to be open about all our operations."

Jack Ryder interrupted her. "If you feel there are strange things happening to our shares after the sale to the public, you will be right as we plan to manipulate them."

He believed that they could make around a billion by this but saw no reason to admit it. He continued, "We shouldn't lose money on this exercise although it will be almost impossible to make anything. The aim is to hold up the price and help it rise; it would be dangerous if it lost ground in the very early days. Nobody else must touch the shares, for that would be too dangerous. Quite bluntly, we know how to keep insider dealing under wraps and you do not."

"The total profit from the scam so far is the thirteen billion I mentioned earlier," added Charles. "That gives a pot to share of one point three billion. It goes four ways, as agreed, and that means three hundred odd million for each of you. I hope you like that, Maria, and you too, Giovanni. Welcome to the world of the super rich."

Charles stopped. They all smiled at the news. After all it was twice as much as they had expected in their wildest dreams.

Charles' take, with that of his parents and Jacqui, was around twenty billion before allowing for the three billion or so they had creamed off the profit and the expected billion they would make on insider dealing.

They would have a family fortune of close to thirty billion dollars. Even if they just deposited the money, and there were better ways of dealing with it than that, they would make megabucks every minute of each day of the year. A pleasant thought.

They still also expected that they would sell the rump of IBE and, all the time, their other fund operations continued to make money, especially with all the opportunities they had for insider trading. They were well on track to being some of the wealthiest people on earth.

Charles, though, had to consider other things beyond the bank and those meant that they were still at risk. Everywhere they went now, they had guards. And those guards were armed and ready, hopefully ready enough.

From the plane he talked to Maddy, who reported all was going smoothly. The business was continuing to produce about four hundred million a month before expenses and around two hundred after them. Charles was amazed at how little the drugs cost to produce and prepare. It was the bribes to the authorities that really cost money. That web of corruption swept across government and law. It took in police and the judiciary as well as customs and border police. It included local and national figures, too. Indeed, some were even users.

And the corruption was the seed from which the extortion rackets grew. They monitored the bribes. The corrupt were then blackmailed. And then they had to take more bribes to pay the blackmailers. The money was paid out with one hand and then part of it was paid back with the other. It was a classical case of recycling, a typical Di Maglio ploy.

The next week marked another milestone. The auditors gave them their initial findings. Not surprisingly, they had failed to spot any problem. They complacently noted the large trading position without realising it was outrageously risky. They commented on the US profits growth without challenging how a bank can turn round its performance at the drop of a hat, simply because there is new management in place. They noted the loan book had soared. Yet, they still saw no warning signs.

And they congratulated the new management repeatedly on their performance, despite all the signs of over trading or excessive risk taking. Charles realised that there might be another group to lose out on the scam. The lack of attention of the auditors was going to cause them problems. They had not questioned the valuation of the open trading positions or the quality of the loans made. They had taken the lazy route and they had taken management's word for it. They were also on the wrong side of the law.

And, as they explained to them the profit outcome for the year, it was clear that they had fallen for trick after trick. It became clear that they were unable to understand the bank's books. They believed them. Charles placed the gentry on the board in front of the auditors, they were totally duped by them.

The landed gentry must be sound, the old school had to be trusted. Old money ran the firm even if new money owned it. The old school could be believed. Or, at least, that was the view of the establishment. It was a case of 'my word is my bond'; and it may have been in the old days but, in the modern world, it was more often a mere ruse to avoid the right level of scrutiny.

The end of February saw them declare their results. Fund sales had gone from strength to strength, although they were no longer loading the funds with fake stocks. The genuine business had boomed. The combined profit beat their forecast and they used every single accounting trick to claw in every penny of possible gain. The new enlarged Group had made one point five billion. They forecast, and the Honourable James stressed to all, on a very conservative basis, that they would make at least one point eight the next year.

And they announced their planned sale to the public. The papers for the offer for sale would be published in March. The sale would take place in April. That was earlier than foreseen. But there was no sense in delaying. And the sooner they closed out the scam, the less they risked. The quicker they came to the market, the lower the risk of a genuine market fall making life difficult for them all.

The press were wild with enthusiasm. The tabloids talked of Jacqui and Charles as a dream power couple. They were the golden couple. All they touched turned to gold. The press looked for better than forecast results. The City elite were wild about the shares and said profits would be far better than expected; they talked of two billion for the next year and even more. The great and the good did nothing to dent their enthusiasm; they even fuelled it as they were feted in their clubs. But Charles and Jacqui refused to comment in public or private, so nobody could say then that they had encouraged speculation.

But their very silence drove the speculation as society's elite continued to whisper the news to their friends in their clubs. Those friends in turn told their friends, who then talked to anyone who would listen. The roller coaster had started. The buyers were waiting for the offer to the public. Greed was all powerful, logic was disregarded and prudence was thrown to the wind. Everyone wanted a share of the action for the hottest deal in town.

The press and brokers conspired to create wave after wave of enthusiasm for the shares. In the US and UK, the support did not waver. It was good for the bank and good for them. The publicity generated some genuine business and the support would help them float at an even better price.

They announced the details of the sale at a joint press conference in London and New York. Charles made sure he and Jacqui kept in the background. The Honourable James made the announcement in London as Chairman of the bank. And Lord Dunkillin, whom they appointed as Deputy Chairman ahead of the sale, made the simultaneous announcement in New York. There he was accompanied by a voluble and enthusiastic McGarth, as the US chief executive, while Charles sat quietly next to the equally garrulous and over optimistic Honourable James in London.

Charles could see no point in being high profile, especially after all the publicity they had been given when they announced the sale. Now was the time for him to become a backroom boy. He wanted cash and not glory. Cash would buy them freedom, glory would bring disaster to the rest.

CHAPTER TWENTY

March was frenetic. The whole show roared forward in great style. The Empire was running well. Jacqui had to slow down as she approached her seventh month. Maria was fit again and kept a close eye on Charles' fellow directors, both in and out of the office.

Di Maglio called occasionally but it was always with ill grace. Jacqui and he had become all the more estranged since he had suggested he was not her father. It was as if the only link between them had been broken. Charles' relationship with him appeared better. Di Maglio was duly impressed by Maddy Brown who ran the Empire with the necessary iron fist.

Charles and Jack Ryder carefully monitored the complex web of transactions that would bring down IBE and make them the first part of their fortune. They had now completed the large part of the fund heist.

They had created and sold their phoney investments, shell companies backed by skilfully structured mirages of smoke and mirrors that blinded the experts and bamboozled the rest. And all that profit was already in their accounts. They had it in cash, well away from IBE and its associated banks.

But even more profit had come though the genuine shares they had sold to the US funds. The prices of these shares, though, were highly inflated. They were incredibly overvalued. They had kept the market in those shares short of supply and the prices soared all the time that the funds bought them from them. It had all been so simple, and it was much less risky than dealing solely in investments of their own creation.

The stock markets boomed. The fund prices soared to reflect their holdings. Investors poured more money in and the funds used that money to buy even more shares. And so it had continued with the funds fuelling the rise in the shares they owned as they bought more of them and pushed the price higher and higher. Demand was slowing down now and Jack Ryder was simply manipulating the market to stop the share prices from falling; at least until they wanted them to.

They had guessed that it would take the bank and their auditors some time to figure out something had gone seriously wrong in the trading room and with their lending. And they had the comfort of Lord Dunkillin and Sir Brian signing off on everything in the meantime. But time was their enemy. Sooner or later the hole would be found. It was just too big not to be noticed. They would act fast. The longer they waited, the greater the risk of discovery.

The loans would go into loss as their borrowers defaulted. They had ensured that the companies were able to meet financing costs through to the end of June. That was the date when the defaults would really start.

They still, of course, had the final billion-dollar loan scam to do, but that deal was being negotiated. Nobody could tell that they were behind it. Like any good fraud, they had kept it all so simple, using a Di Maglio shell company without his full knowledge. The money would just flow through it to allow, yet again, the finger of suspicion to point at Di Maglio. But where it flowed to, nobody would be able to trace. At least, it would not be traceable after the first payment into an account of one Di Maglio in Panama. But it stayed there for just one minute and then was routed away to secret accounts that could never be traced by taxman, government or just the inquisitive.

The bank was being built up to allow it to fall. And with the bank went Di Maglio, thanks to the generosity of the warranty in the elusive page thirty three of their agreement. Few would believe, when the claims were made, that the authorities had found all his money. But Charles was certain he could ensure that most of it was traceable, at least the parts he wanted to have traced.

And the losses of the bank and their investors would largely to be covered by the warranty from Di Maglio in that extra page thirty-three of the sale agreement they had signed the previous year. The page that stated that, for a period of twelve months after the sale of PAF to IBE, Di Maglio personally guaranteed the bank and its clients from any losses due to fraud, malpractice or wilful neglect by the previous or then current management And who was going to believe that Di Maglio hadn't removed it from his copy, especially as it went straight from page thirty two to thirty four. Innocence and Di Maglio would be deemed strange bedfellows. While many would applaud the foresight of Charles and the negotiating team in getting such protection, just as many would question why Di Maglio had signed his financial death warrant in that way. And they would ask how he had allowed his hidden wealth to be traced and seized. How had he allowed himself to be destroyed?

The sale of the bank to the public was helped by a continuation of the speculation on the likely level of the next year's profits. McGarth played his full part when he appeared on prime time TV. He enthused about the numbers of new accounts the US bank was opening. He marvelled at the outstanding investment performance of the bank's funds. He even did them a great favour by insisting that he and his local management, and not the bank owners, were the driving force behind the amazing performance. He boasted that it was due to the expertise of 'his boys in Wall Street' as he called them. He claimed so much credit for himself that he helped exonerate all others from blame. The man was certainly earning his keep.

Charles toyed with the idea of getting the Honourable James to do the same thing, but he felt even he was too bright for that job. So they managed to get Sir Brian on one of the money programmes and he excelled. Charles told him to play down his and Jacqui's role and play up that of himself, the Honourable James and Lord Dunkillin. He said that investors needed to believe in the solid state of the bank and that could only be achieved if Charles had a lower profile and the distinguished, well-known directors a higher one. Indeed, gullible Sir Brian lapped Charles' suggestion up with joy on a roller coaster of an ego trip and needed no further brief.

When interviewed, he proudly stressed his role as the wise man overseeing the key areas of credit and treasury. He stressed the role of the old guard. There was, according to him, a belief in experience on the board. He implied that Charles had the occasional good idea but suggested he focused on his outside interests rather than the bank. He failed to mention Jacqui's role at all and made her choke with laughter, and perhaps fury, when he said that, quite rightly, she was a mother and a mother first rather than an active director. The bank's success was all about himself, the Honourable James and Dunkillin.

He actually took it a bit far and they started to challenge him. He countered all by saying that Charles' role was to think strategically. He pointed out that Charles had engineered the PAF deal. But he stressed that did not mean he ran it. McGarth was credited with that, reporting to the board and not to Charles. It was outstanding. The media were manipulated. And that happened on both sides of the Atlantic.

April saw Charles again heading all over the world as they put together the prospectus and ran the interminable road shows that are meant to impress the big investors and give them the sight and feel of management. Or, at least, the sight and feel that they wished them to have.

They had little more to do inside the bank but wait for its losses and their profits to crystallise. So, always in the background, Charles kept busy on the sale of the bank to the public. He marvelled at the expressions of interest. And he laughed at all the hyperbole in the press.

They were getting enquiries from the Far East and the Middle East, as well as the US and Europe. They were desired by pension funds, sovereign wealth funds, insurance funds, mutual funds, the wealthy and the not so wealthy. The advisors agreed they would try to hit the high end of the range in price. In the end, they issued the prospectus.

They stuck to the one point eight billion-dollar forecast made at the time of results, despite the belief in the market that this was too low and the opportunity of raising the price if they raised the forecast profit. But Charles was concerned that any changes would have to be re-audited and could see no value in encouraging any added scrutiny of their books. There was always the outside chance that such an exercise could lead to someone sharp stumbling over one of their phoney or phantom deals.

So they revealed the price. They said that they would float at just over sixteen dollars a share. They announced that, to ensure that there was no dominant control of the company, they would sell seventy five per cent of the shares. The company would be valued at an incredible eighteen billion dollars and the sale would raise over thirteen billion dollars for them.

The markets boomed and the shares were in heavy demand. As the final day for applications arrived, the flood of requests rose. The banks had to take on extra staff to handle the flow of paper. In London, New York, Paris, Frankfurt, Hong Kong and the Gulf they clamoured for shares. Then the offer closed with television coverage showing near pandemonium as investors rushed to meet the last minute deadline for getting their applications in to the advisors. The next day, they announced that they had been oversubscribed a massive six times. The issue was a major success. The forecast was that the price would go to twenty dollars a share and that helped them keep on the front pages for the rest of the month.

The atmosphere in the bank was electric as everybody became a capitalist. The employees had privileged access to the pot of shares for sale. The bank lent them money to buy them. They were hungry to make their fortune. Charles knew many of them would sell at the first opportunity and, therefore, not lose money. Otherwise he would have felt awkward about it.

They didn't care what happened once the scams hit the world of big business. But they didn't want to have to face popular approbation. And they had engineered the famous page thirty-three of the agreement with the unlimited warranties from Di Maglio to ensure that the small depositors were protected. Some would lose, they couldn't afford to be purists. Not if they wanted to succeed. There would always be casualties.

The deal finally closed and the money was paid over. After all expenses, the shares had been sold for thirteen point four billion. The advisors and others had made two hundred million dollars from the deal. But that was not of concern to them. Top advisors were expensive. But they would also be hit by the eventual demise of the bank. Were they lax in their scrutiny? Did they give the company the benefit of the doubt? Were they swayed by the temptation of super millions for their fees? If there were losses, they could even be sued. And the more people in the dock, the less the spotlight fell on Charles and Jacqui.

For Charles and his family, the money joined the cash already banked from the frauds. Their expected cash kitty totalled well over twenty billion dollars. It was conservatively invested well away from IBE and in structures that only the very rich can afford. As one could guess, they were not paying much tax on those gains.

June approached its end and they put the final three phases of the scam into play. Jack Ryder and Charles worked night and day. They started calling in the trades through their different companies and structures, always using trusted intermediaries. And a trusted intermediary was one who was paid well, anonymously, and understood the meaning of discretion.

There was pandemonium the first day in the IBE trading room as they claimed their profits, lodged their claims and exercised their options. Charles sensed it as he passed the room and heard snatches of anguished conversation.

"What the fuck's happening. We owe them and the computer says we've made a bundle?"

"Who wrote this agreement? What's clause seven? What's meant by a fucking alternative algorithm?"

"What shit-head wrote a trade and guaranteed the price of the Zimbabwe dollar. It's worth just one percent of what it was last month!"

"What asshole did something called a reverse default swap? What is it and why's it costing us a hundred when the computer says we are making twenty on it.....of course I'm talking frigging millions. What did you think? I wasn't talking... oh, shit another bloody claim. We never shorted the euro at the bottom, did we? This company wants to close the deal out. Here it is; the buggers right. Who agreed this? Bloody hell, it was Dunkillin and nephew and it's one of their family companies. The auditors are really going to like that one."

"I've a loss here on a swap deal. It's madness and this sod of a computer still says we are making money on it. Something's wrong with the programme. We must have been legged over by that arsehole, Stephens. When I next see him, I'll kill the mother fucker."

"Of course we have to pay the claim. They'll put us in default if we don't."

"Shut up about your fucking bonus; if it carries on like this there won't be money for the bloody latte this afternoon."

Charles saw the worried faces of Sir Brian and Dunkillin. But he pretended not to and kept well away. He failed to see the Honourable James on the first day. But he knew, through Maria, that he spent a long time with McGarth. Apparently the US Chief Executive was hyperventilating on the phone.

They set the stage for the billion-dollar loan. The Honourable James' son grabbed all the credit as originator of the deal. That was just as well as the billion was going to be easy to trace as it went to a Di Maglio account, before passing into an account in New York in the name of the Honourable James' son himself and then onto a very secret account he appeared to hold in the Cayman Islands. That account was so secret that even he did not know about it. Unfortunately, there the trail ended and nobody could trace what had happened to the money. Charles was the master money-launderer.

And all the deals quickly completed. Funds flowed. Wires buzzed. Bank after bank eagerly grabbed its commission as the money winged round the world and then back again. It changed its name. It was split into a variety of different payments. They were regrouped. They transited every tax haven in the world. They caressed the shores of countries, that had strong banking secrecy laws. They washed here and there and lost themselves in the maze of payments that are made each day around the world. And all that happened within a day. Some banks rashly made payments away before they had received the funds in. Others waited. The e-world buzzed as the funds, like a helter-skelter swooped around the globe that day. And they did so the next day and the one after. Sometimes they were invested in the morning, only to be sold off later that day. Other times, they were used in complex stock market operations that were unwound in another centre. In yet more cases, they were united with payments waiting for their arrival. By the time it all ended, they had been washed, not just clean but whitewashed to perfection. No Maddy Brown would be able to trace one of the biggest and best money laundering acts in banking history. Charles felt proud of himself. They were the masters of the disappearing cash act.

They sold shares in IBE. Jacqui was expecting the baby any day but she had to come in especially to handle the forging of the share register. She had taken charge of that area; a tedious occupation that nobody else wanted but which was a rich pasture for fraudsters such as them. That was Jacqui's last role at this stage, as she manipulated the share register and hid the true source of the sales.

They had sold shares at twenty five dollars and raised about two billion. And the sale took place without anyone in the market smelling a rat. Even Jack Ryder was amazed at his own audacity. The shares in time risked being almost worthless. But they were in line for another couple of billion. The money making machine was on fast forward. The till was open and the cash was pouring in.

At the same time, Jack Ryder was also handling a series of transactions for their personal funds. They started to deal to anticipate the market slump that would automatically follow the announcement of losses, and, eventually the collapse, of the bank.

They placed around a hundred million on deposit into IBE. It helped increase the illusion they were innocent.

By the end of the week, they had called in around five hundred million of trades from the bank. Still, Charles had not been told anything. As he had given the control of that area to Sir Brian and Lord Dunkillin, he let things ride. He planned a few days off the next week as Jacqui was due to give birth on the Sunday.

They had a quiet dinner together that Saturday night. Juliet was asleep upstairs. Maria had long since returned home. They had arranged security for her and she felt safe. Indeed, they all did. Bathing in that security, they ate and waited for the baby. Then the phone rang. It was Maddy Brown.

Maddy announced her news, "Di Maglio has been attacked. It was the Russian Mafia. And they've delivered us an ultimatum. Hand over the Empire to them for payment of two billion dollars in the next forty-eight hours or you, Jacqui, Juliet and the new baby die. I'll also be a target. I think they mean business. They say they've already got the hit in place and they mentioned the Portland Hospital."

Charles froze. That was where Jacqui was to have the baby, but Maddy's next words hit home more, "They've also got Carrie's address and say she'll be blown away with all around her." Carrie had agreed to look after Juliet while Jacqui was in hospital. They had thought she would be happier with other children to distract her rather than be alone with nanny.

"How bad is Di Maglio?"

"He should pull through. Hit in the chest and the stomach but it doesn't look too complicated. Two bodyguards were killed. It all came out of the blue."

"Let me sort things out here and I'll come back to you. We need to act. And act fast."

Jacqui had been listening on the other extension so there was no need to tell her anything. Charles thought for a while. Then he looked at her. Her face was serious. She understood. This was the crunch. They had to move forward quickly. Charles thoughts turned to the bank. His father could sort out the open trading issues. The loans were done and dusted. The issue was off the ground. The news of Di Maglio would be known. It would surprise nobody if Charles were out of town.

Jacqui looked at him. She read his mind, "You'll have to be here for number three. It looks as if number two is going to be born without you there. You haven't a choice."

"What about security?"

"Delaney," she said. "You need Maria."

Charles didn't answer but picked up the phone and called Delaney. He listened carefully. "I'll step up security. We'll sweep the Portland anyway but we'll move Jacqui elsewhere. I'll be over in half an hour. Wait for me. I'll see to Carrie's place as well."

"Is it wise for you to come over? You could be recognised. I'm likely to be under surveillance."

"Don't worry. That's why I need the time. They won't recognise me. I doubt you will either."

Charles called Maria, "Get ready. There's a change of plan. I'll pick you up in around forty-five minutes. We're going abroad."

She didn't ask anything. She would know that he wouldn't leave Jacqui just before the baby was born unless it was vital. He could brief her in the car.

Jacqui was watching him. She was pale but calm. Her dark hair fell over her shoulders. Her eyes were bright but reflective. They seemed to mirror thoughts of the birth to come, the older man lying wounded and the dangers ahead. They could handle most things, but this could be gang warfare on a scale that they had never known before.

The last time she had been by his side. Memories of past dangers in France, California, Mexico City, Paris and Monte Carlo came to mind. She smiled at him, once again with that smile of sadness mixed with love. It was also a smile of hope mixed with trepidation. Charles would now be like the conductor of an orchestra, guiding the music to its finale and final silence. Alone on the rostrum, everything would depend on him. Di Maglio had him where he wanted him to be. He wanted him at the head of his Empire. And now he would have to be there, for that was the only way to triumph.

Delaney arrived. Or, at least, a vagrant shuffled down the street. Nobody would have guessed his identity. Moments later, four or five extra men appeared. They took up their positions silently as one of their number started to check the house. One of the duty guards was handed the lead to a dog that sniffed through the house in search of explosives.

Charles waited till the house and grounds had been searched, "That looks OK. Now, it's time for me to go."

Jacqui looked strained. She bit her lip. "Come back," she whispered. "I'll be waiting. So will Juliet and the baby. We'll be on the island. I'll see that the deals go through. I'll work with your father."

He kissed her quickly. There was no point in long goodbyes. He turned and, without looking back, headed to the car that was already waiting. Douglas asked no questions. He drove the mile or so to Maria's. They didn't go in. They waited, engine running, outside in the street. A minute later, Maria appeared and got into the car. She carried a small bag. That was all. They didn't need clothes. Those could always be bought.

"Where are we heading?"

"New York will be the second stop. But, first, it's Geneva. We need to pick up Maddy Brown. Di Maglio was hit. He may have lied about the Russians last year. But his concerns weren't totally ill founded. They want the Empire. It's the usual stuff. They'll kill us all or buy it for two billion. In reality, they most likely would double cross us whatever we did. But we'll sort it out. We need to talk strategies on the plane. I need to consider them now. Then we discuss them with Maddy. I want the US to be the battleground. It's our home territory for this type of activity and so easier for us than for the enemy."

She listened. She said nothing. She left him alone. The twenty minutes or so to the airport would give him opportunity for thought. He needed to work out both how to destroy the Russians and the Empire. In the end, the Russians had to be so weak that they posed no danger. And the Empire had to be destroyed so totally that it was impotent. The destruction of the Empire had to look accidental. Otherwise they would be faced with revenge killings and worse.

Charles needed everyone to think "poor guy". He lost his bank. He lost his Empire. He knew they would realise he was worth a few billion irrespective. But the untold riches that he could have expected would have slipped his grasp. He had to be seen as the one who could have been the most powerful businessman in the world.

They got on the plane. Alone in the lounge area of the private jet, Charles discussed his strategy with Maria.

"We need to run this as a threesome. It will be you, Maddy and me. There's nobody else we can trust with the whole deal. There'll be a fifty million dollar bonus for you if we succeed."

He looked at her and noted her look of surprise. "That's generous," she remarked.

He knew now he could depend on her one hundred percent. He was happy to trust her in the bank. But this was different. This was about the Empire. And previously she worked there. Previously, she had different loyalties.

"It'll be dangerous. You'll earn it," was his careful reply. There were thoughts one did not share. Especially as, if she double crossed him, he would have to kill her. But he didn't think that would happen.

"The plan will be simple. We'll destroy the Empire. It can only cause us problems. We'll bring it down with stealth. It will be worthless. At the same time we will destroy the Russians. We'll hit them like we did in Uzes those years back. But we won't do it in quite the same way. We'll set them up and allow the police to do the rest. The three of us can't fight battles like we did in the past. We no longer have the people for that sort of thing any more. Or, at least, people we can trust."

"How will you set them all up?"

"Maddy will become a double agent. She will negotiate with them. She'll persuade them that they need to weaken me. She'll pretend my heart isn't in the business and one big failure will push me into their arms. They'll be told to try to take us out on a big drug shipment. We'll organise one. And they'll be drawn into making a heist. Except that the FBI will have the whole plans leaked to them. That's the outline. We need to work the detail."

Maria thought through the plan, "How much will you need to use as bait?"

"It has to be big. I thought around a billion in street value. We'll get the Russians to believe we have protection and are bringing in six months' supply in two shipments. We can suggest that we are doing it because of uncertainty. One shipment should be into one of the private New Jersey airports we use. The other will be somewhere more remote, perhaps in Alabama where they have the secret drugs depot. There'll be no problem finding an airfield there but the communication lines are tough. That'll mean they'll need two full attack forces. That'll stretch them."

"Charles, Alabama is awful. The communication lines to us would be poor as well. You need to use somewhere in California."

She was right. And it would add to the story's credibility. It would appear they were warehousing for the New York area and also the San Francisco and Los Angeles strip. That counted for around sixty per cent of the entire US demand and about ninety per cent of their franchise.

Lake Geneva came into view and the plane landed at the main airport. Their two bags were put in the waiting car. Douglas replaced the driver and they headed to the compound. Three men on motorbikes surrounded them. Each had a pillion passenger. And as they drew out of the gates of the airport a four-wheel drive pulled in front and one slipped behind them.

"Maddy sees you as very important," remarked Maria. "I'm impressed. I've never met her. But the word is that she's tough. You kept your links to her very quiet."

He looked at her. "On the grounds of only telling people what they need to know, wouldn't you? She was useful, especially in the early days. I needed to ensure we didn't blow her cover."

The car made the compound without incident. They headed up the stairs to the house. The door opened and Maddy was there. Charles watched the two women closely. Maddy would know that his relationship with Maria was not always platonic. Maria would wonder whether it was not the same with Maddy. The cool leggy blonde with the ice blue eyes looked at the sultry brunette whose combat clothes hid the voluptuousness of her body and made her look surprisingly androgynous. The atmosphere between them was immediately cool, but not hostile.

They entered the study. It was just the three of them. Charles walked to the drinks cabinet and poured himself a beer. Maria took a malt whisky on the rocks. Maddy took nothing. Charles explained the plan to Maddy. She didn't question it. Her only comment was that she would need to organise a driver and guns in New York.

"No, Douglas will drive us. He's useful for a back up. But get me a bodyguard that you can trust. The important thing is when can you organise the drug shipment?"

"I take a large delivery, around six hundred million bucks on Thursday in Columbia. I could up it to the billion without problem. They'll deliver more for a premium."

"Stick to a billion. You have the funds?"

"No problem. We'll borrow from your banks in the US."

"Good," he said and laughed inwardly. It would be the final irony if they lost money on this deal. "Now, you two stop sizing each other up. No antagonism. Work together. If there's a problem, tell me."

Charles had noticed how the two women eyed each other up. There was competition there and he needed to ensure that it didn't get in the way." Maddy, you're on the same bonus as Maria. Fifty million if we succeed."

She looked as surprised as Maria had. Charles wondered if she'd claim the funds or if they'd go to her expense account at MI5. He didn't ask. If she'd grabbed them, that would give him useful future leverage, so he rather hoped she would. Charles dialled Delaney's number. He answered. It had gone midnight in London.

"How are things?" asked Charles

"There are no signs of explosives here at all. We can't identify a watch on the house. The Portland's OK. Carrie's place is OK as well. But we continue our watch. Jacqui went to sleep half an hour ago. She's fine. Is everything all right with you?"

"Yes. We have our plans sorted. We're off to the US tomorrow. Can you get me someone trustworthy to contact me? Use the usual codes for identification. I need two major hit squads. And I need a guarantee of a shoot to kill policy. One's likely to be in California and one's going to be in New York. We'll give the details to the contact. I prefer him to be one of yours. He should be the linkman. And I want a guarantee of immunity from prosecution in the US for anything we do. And I want it from the President."

"That may be tough to arrange."

"Then arrange it. I need it for Monday morning. The hit could be

Friday. And I need it for Maria, Maddy and me. Oh, and you better get it for Douglas in case he has to break the law. "

"How do you want it worded?"

"I want a full indemnity and total anonymity. On anything we do in the US between now and end August. That should be enough time."

Delaney muttered that he would see what he could do. Charles felt sure he would deliver. And the indemnity could be useful as further immunity for the scam, should he need to do anything in the intervening period.

It looked as if the banks would collapse during July or early August. It was difficult to gauge the exact timing. And, still, the great and the good had not told him anything about the trading losses. They must be hoping against hope to drag themselves out of their mess. That was crazy; it just appeared to compound their guilt and reinforce the notion that he had been duped. Charles hoped this was all the start of a month or so of good luck. He sensed that they would need it.

Maddy had, meanwhile, been on the phone. She had booked three first class seats on Swissair from Geneva for the next day. She had also arranged guns and transport in New York. She was now phoning the hospital where Di Maglio was being kept. She listened to the report from one of her men.

"He's rough," she advised him. "We thought it was simple but it appears there are complications. The next forty eight hours are critical."

"Can you arrange for his early demise?"

"Not with my boys. They'll retain their old loyalties."

Charles shrugged his shoulders. "It's an option, it would simplify things. But forget it."

He saw Maria's shocked look. She still felt loyalty in that direction. He had to remember that. Even though Di Maglio had threatened her and killed her best friend, she couldn't be relied on to kill him. It was worth knowing. Charles, surprised by this unexpected loyalty, only hoped she felt the same way about him.

They had nothing else to arrange and so all went to their separate rooms. Next morning they headed off to the airport and then onto New York. They landed in the early afternoon and drove into the city centre. The car was waiting, accompanied by the necessary outriders and escorts. This was not a time to take too many risks.

They travelled down the road where Claire had been killed. Charles could remember the exact spot and felt a strange urge to order the car to stop. He wanted to sit and reflect on the gentleness of Claire. To say a last goodbye to the girl who was and the child who didn't make it.

He thought back over the years and remembered the loss of Jacqui's first baby at Rastinov's hands. His torture had killed the unborn child. Now Rastinov was dead. He thought of Di Maglio and his hand in Claire's death. Now Di Maglio was critically wounded in a hospital here in New York. He thought of the children who had died as a result of the Empire's drug and crime riddled hell. The final stage of that game was coming to its conclusion.

Maria looked over as they passed the spot. She knew. She realised what he was thinking. Her hand took his with a gentleness that was not usual and she stroked it rather than squeezed it. Her body moved closer to his and he felt her calming warmth. The gentle swell of her breasts pressed against his arm. She woke him from his reverie as they sped down that fated highway.

Maddy, in front next to Douglas, was watching them keenly. She sensed something had happened here and they needed each other as companions rather than lovers. And she was sensitive enough not to want to intrude.

Moving into the city through the deep tunnel and into mid town Manhattan, Charles took the phone. Jacqui's mobile did not answer, but Delaney's did. She had gone to hospital. He had had her transferred to one in Paddington. It was easier to guard. Nobody had identified any sign of trouble but they were keeping a close guard on the house, Carrie and the hospital. Delaney called. His man would contact them at the hotel. They were gradually getting the final pieces into play.

Charles called the hospital number that Delaney had given him. The nurse said she could not pass him to Jacqui. She was in labour. They expected she would give birth soon. It all sounded so clinical. The nurse clearly disapproved of the husband whose business took him away at such a time. She told him he could ring in an hour or so and she would tell him how things were.

They pulled in at the Pierre. They had a suite and two rooms, which all interconnected. Maria and Charles took the bedrooms and Maddy the suite. It was a sort of present for someone who was on active service for the Empire for the first time. Charles' room adjoined her bedroom and Maria's her lounge. They would keep the doors unlocked in case they needed to move together in the event of attack.

They checked plans. In reality, there was little they could do until they had set up the shipments on Monday, so Charles called his father and ran through the actions needed to put the bank into play.

Loan proceeds were safe in their hands. Companies were waiting to be placed in default so that the banks took their hits.

The portfolio of overvalued shares and phoney investments had all been sold on to the funds. The cash from them had long since been washed around the world into their secret accounts.

They had sold shares in the bank, and then unloaded some more as the market and the shares continued to rise.

Jack Ryder was also selling other shares they did not own in the markets, in anticipation of the inevitable fall out that would occur when the bank went into default. But that was like their normal day to day activities. Taking advantage of insider information but ensuring they left trails good enough to avoid discovery by even the most expert forensic auditor.

Charles called the hospital. The news was unchanged. He got the frosty nurse again. Jacqui was in labour. She was fine. He could get a message to her but not talk. He sent her his love. He called Delaney. Everything checked out. There had been no suspicious action. All was quiet on all fronts. They had placed guards on Maria's house and put the bank's main office under surveillance. He told him that the contact was in play and would be known to Maddy under the code name of Galileo.

Charles told Maddy. She said he was good, an older agent, trustworthy but not too reliable if the action got over hot. That was the right man to act as go between for them with the US secret service. Charles needed to keep a careful barrier between them and him. There were too many friends of Di Maglio on the US side for his liking. Nor was he sure of the scale of the Di Maglio web of corruption.

He called the hospital where Di Maglio was being treated and Aldo came to the phone. He said the hit had been unexpected. It happened in a restaurant in Little Italy. Attackers had opened fire with sub machine guns. Two bodyguards had been killed. Di Maglio had been hit several times. He was still unconscious. The prognosis was not favourable. He could be wheelchair bound if he was unlucky. He was still at risk.

Charles hung around another hour or so. He called the London hospital again. He was father of another little girl. Jacqui and baby were fine. Jacqui was resting. He insisted that the mobile was given to her. Her voice sounded fine. He asked about the baby. She looked like Juliet at birth. Blond hair and grey blue eyes. She weighed eight pounds and was perfect. Jacqui had been in labour for six hours. She was tired. He told her about her father and said they would be acting this week. He promised to call the next morning to see how she and the baby were.

They talked on for a few minutes in that strange language of love spurred on by the birth of a child. They talked again of the island. They knew they needed it badly.

Charles walked into Maddy's room to tell her and Maria the good news. Maddy wasn't there but he heard her singing to herself in the bathroom. The door was open and she was lying under a sea of foam with just her face and her mop of hair visible above the water.

He told her about the baby and she blew him a kiss. She looked at him with a soft smile as he seemed to gaze at her body, hidden under the foam. "This calls for celebration," she announced. "We should at least have a dinner tonight. Let's go somewhere special. See if Maria is game."

Charles walked across the lounge area and through the connecting door into Maria's room. "Jacqui's had a girl. They're both fine. How about a small celebration tonight? Maddy is keen."

"I'm willing. But we can't go anywhere too visible. How about the Village? There's a little place I know there. It seats about thirty. It's easy to guard. It's down a small alley that ends in a cul-de-sac. It's only good for a suicide attack, so we should be safe."

He agreed. They needed to relax for an evening and he wanted to celebrate the baby. If he'd been in London, he would have left Jacqui by now. And he suspected he would have done the same thing, so the very idea made the day seem more normal again. They all wore dark jeans, part of their standard battle dress. He went downstairs and found an open news-stand. It sold I love New York T-shirts and he bought three. He took them upstairs and showed them to the girls.

"We don't want to wear full battle gear. And we need to do some shopping tomorrow before we start working. We'll need to get ourselves some work clothes. I think I'll need to get into the bank. I'd like to see if everything's OK."

Maria looked at him with a slightly mocking expression. Maddy did not react. For her, it must have seemed a fairly normal request. Maria knew better. She realised he wanted to give yet another example of the duplicity of his colleagues.

Then, quite calmly she pulled off her dark shirt, undid her bra and pulled on the T-shirt. Maddy took up the challenge and pulled off her shirt as well. Like Maria, she realised that the black bra would show through the light material of the T-shirt. So looking at him calmly straight in the eyes with the hint of a smile on her lips, she languidly undid her bra, eased it gently off her shoulders. Then, as if in slow motion, she pulled her new T-shirt on and pulled it tightly into her trousers. The outline of the breasts pressed against the taut material as if they wished to burst free.

Now there was a hint of a smile from Maria as well. She saw competition and enjoyed the thought. In a strange way, the tussle for attention, with Charles as the quarry, brought the two girls together.

Maria booked dinner for seven thirty. Dinner starts early in New York. It was already gone seven and so they called one of the drivers. Douglas had already been given a well-deserved break. The car sped through the empty streets of Manhattan and down into Greenwich Village. The restaurant that Maria had chosen was bright and airy. The clientele was relaxed and noisy. They would fit into this group with ease.

Maria ordered a drink. Charles heard her ask for champagne. She was right. That was the only drink to have at a time like this. The waiter returned and whispered something into her ear. He suspected that she was out to buy some of the best champagne they had. She smiled at the response and nodded her head. The man disappeared with alacrity, only to return a minute or so later with a magnum of vintage Bollinger. The bottle was opened with a satisfactory pop and the contents fizzed up to be caught neatly in a large goblet. The three glasses were filled and the bottle placed in a giant ice bucket.

"To baby Rossi," called Maria and emptied her goblet in one go. Maddy inevitably took up the challenge and did likewise. Charles had no choice. The waiter swooped back and replenished their glasses. The six glasses had accounted for well over half the magnum.

"To Jacqui," called Maria and again everyone's goblet was emptied as they drank her health. Once again the glasses were refilled. "To Charles," called Maria and the act was repeated again. This time Maddy giggled as she finished off her drink and spilt some down her chin. She caught it with her hand and then wiped her chin clean with a napkin. The waiter appeared with second magnum. He filled their glasses again and Charles raised his to the girls. "To our success," he said. They all drank the goblet dry.

He realised that this was becoming quite serious drinking. They hadn't been there long and were already on their second magnum and their fourth goblet. And each goblet looked as if it were a couple of normal glasses of champagne.

They ordered food. It was the sort that you get in those small smart restaurants. It had an artistic look; there were slightly spicy sauces to contrast with some quite bland, but perfectly cooked, food. They ate and they drank, moving on through their second magnum. Maria was drinking faster than Charles and Maddy was drinking almost as fast. Both girls were joking and making gentle fun of each other. There was no maliciousness in their fun. It was friendly to the extreme.

They moved to the main course and then onto ice cream with strange sauces. Charles was amazed that the girls remained sober. Maria, he knew from past experience, could drink most men under the table. But he had never realised that Maddy had the same ability.

Charles heard the noise first. There was the sharp rattle of a sub machine gun and the return of fire. He ducked down to table level. His hand grabbed the gun from his leg holster. He moved quickly to the door. If it opened he would have a good line of fire and an excellent chance of gunning down anybody before they ever caught sight of him.

Maddy had pulled her gun from her bag. He noticed it was a small one. It would be powerful enough to kill. Maria was moving to the other side of the door, taking cover behind the overloaded sweet trolley.

She called out, "Keep calm," with little effect to the other diners whose noisy enjoyment had ceased when they heard the sound of guns outside. The firing continued and Charles eased to the door, gently opening it as Maria carefully covered him. They saw that their two man escort was slowly retreating down the cul de sac, carefully keeping out of the line of fire, as they faced up to their attackers. The force that opposed them seemed to be seven or eight strong. Charles realised they had to intervene if only to balance the odds or the escort would simply be overcome by force of numbers. He eased himself out and crouched in the doorway. Maria joined him standing just behind him. Maddy was still inside.

Two men broke cover, their machine guns spitting out a hail of bullets at the escort. They ran closer to the restaurant and two others moved into their places firing all the time, ensuring the escort were pinned down behind a line of parked cars. They, in turn, ran forward and another group took their place. The four men at the front then moved towards the restaurant, obviously unaware of Charles and Maria's presence in the doorway.

They did not expect to be challenged then and were unaware of what hit them as they fell. Two more men jumped out of the cover and headed their way. But Maria and Charles had reloaded and were able to stop them.

Both they and the escort now moved forward. Maddy appeared and Charles signalled her to be careful. She knelt behind a car and watched the street. Then, suddenly, there was the roar of an engine. The gunfire seemed to move away in the distance and then there was quiet. It looked as if the survivors among the attackers had fled in their getaway car.

As the escort stood guard against any renewed attack from the road, Charles edged forward with Maria to check whether their attackers were dead or injured. Maddy covered them from behind. There was a sharp crack of a gun. Charles whirled round. It was Maddy, her mouth wide open in horror and her gun still smoking. One of the men lay on his back, his staring eyes bearing testimony to the accuracy of her aim.

"He waited till you passed and then moved to his knees with a gun pointing at you. He was shamming death." Maddy looked at him reproachfully, "Watch out. This isn't a game."

And then she lent back on the car next to her and started giggling uncontrollably. They knew that this was the affect of champagne and the excitement of the kill. Charles ignored it as Maria and he checked out the others. They were definitely history. The escort told them to leave. They would organise the restaurant and the police. It would only complicate things if they stayed.

And so, carnage behind them, they drove to the Pierre. And, thankfully, they got there without any further incident.

CHAPTER TWENTY-ONE

They all got into the lift. Maria started laughing. That was unlike her, she must have drunk more than Charles had realised. This put him on edge but he let it ride. He knew that it was wise always to overestimate the opposition, yet she derided them and said contemptuously, "They were so stupid. They must have realised we would have security. That was a suicide mission. The Russians couldn't run an Empire like Di Maglio's. They couldn't do it even if they had the best of managers."

"Let's wait till we get the report," warned Charles. "I have a suspicion that they've adopted a typical Di Maglio ruse. Hire a few stool pigeons as cannon fodder and make a botched attempt. That way they signal to us that they are serious. And they don't risk killing us and screwing the deal. If the dead guys were Russian it was stupidity. But if they were local hoods, we should be warned. The bastards are watching and tracking us."

Maddy asked, "When will you know?"

"I'll call our contacts tomorrow morning. They'll give me the police reports. But I bet they were local hoods."

Maria laughed. She sensed something in the tone of his voice. She realised she had overstepped the mark. And she was sufficiently scared of him to correct her mistakes quickly, "Well, that shows they've learnt one thing. I guess we should be careful. Lock our doors tonight and be doubly vigilant"

Maddy giggled. "Yes, and everyone is gated. Nobody is allowed to leave their room, unless there is an attack."

"That's a stupid rule," replied Maria. "I want another celebratory drink. We left half a magnum in the restaurant. We need to finish on a high note."

Charles glanced over at her and noticed the look in her eyes. She knew he wanted her even if her earlier attitude had annoyed him. He knew she wanted him. It had always been like that when they faced danger. And it was especially like that if that danger involved any killings. Charles wondered if Maddy felt that need as well. She had killed today. However, he hoped they all realised that today was not such a day. Despite the killings, he wanted to be alone. And he only wanted to be with Jacqui.

They entered the suite with their guns drawn and checked it over room by room. Maria looked through the fridge and rejected all the drinks there. She called for room service and ordered yet another bottle of Bollinger. She had obviously decided that another magnum would be a bit excessive, even if there were three of them. Charles had definitely drunk less than both the girls. At times, they appeared quite sober. At others, they appeared less so. In any case the bottle arrived and they told the waiter to leave it unopened.

Charles opened the bottle with a gentle pop and poured them each a glass. He raised the question of their plans for the morning. They agreed that Maddy would work with Maria and arrange the multi-million dollar shipment. They would meet again in the afternoon to go over the plans. Meanwhile, Charles would head to the office and catch up on work out of London. He was still debating if anyone would warn him about the bank's problems. He definitely would not prompt them.

His glass empty, he decided to make a move. He stood up, kissed each girl on the cheek and headed off to bed. He suspected, given how much they had drunk, that there could be fireworks later. He knew that Maria would be an eager participant, although he was not sure of Maddy. He wondered how he would deter them.

He stripped off and went to bed, lying there thinking through the events of the day. A baby had been born on the other side of the Atlantic. A botched murder attack, yet again, on this side. An evil old man, perhaps dying in a hospital, was not that far away.

And suddenly, he felt lonely. He felt isolated. He was lost in the muted silence of the hotel. The pipes talked. The corridors echoed briefly with distant voices. A door creaked somewhere in the distance. A phone rang. Then there was silence again. He thought again of Jacqui. Again he cursed Di Maglio and his world for keeping him away from her at a time like this. He shut his eyes and he slept.

The next day, Charles left before either of the girls were up. He had plenty to do, and some of it was not going to be done in the office. From the lobby downstairs he called Delaney.

He explained he could not depend on Galileo for all his needs. He had to ensure that Di Maglio didn't leave the hospital. He had nobody to trust. He needed someone better and more dependable than the FBI.

Delaney didn't react to Charles' desire to see his father-in-law have an accident. He would be indifferent to the fact that he was a relative. For him, the man was one of those evil people he worked to destroy.

"As you're going down to Wall Street, you need a contact place nearby. That's quite easy as nobody watching is likely to be surprised at a chance meeting there. You know people and so, even if you were recognised, it wouldn't matter. Where could you meet?" asked Delaney.

"There's a hotel, just opposite the old World Trade Centre. It's called the Millennium. It has a popular bar the yuppies like. I'll be there at noon and wait till twelve thirty. The password should be your granddaughter's second name."

"You'll be met. Ask them to show you their ID as well. It'll impress you and you'll realise why. Always better to be doubly sure."

With that, Charles rang off and headed out of the hotel. Douglas was waiting with the car. They headed south.

"Is there any chance of us being attacked? I gather you had trouble last night."

Charles was surprised. "How do you know?"

"The driver left me a message. Said it was better to have a gun. I had one already but he passed me another. There's no reason for him to know anything about me, other than the fact that I drive you. They must think you're pretty green if they believe that your driver is a mere chauffeur."

"That's true, but to them I'm just a money man. They may have heard about the fights before I married Jacqui, but I was more of an amateur then. I really was; even more than I am now. I only do the gangster bit when it is needed. It's not my career."

Douglas laughed. "You'd have been better than your father-in-law if it had been. But drugs and prostitution are out of fashion. Money is the best weapon now. And you know how to handle that."

"Douglas, don't think too much about what I do. It's not healthy."

Douglas said nothing. Charles thought about his words. He thought back to Maria's comments the previous night. He had to be careful. This was dangerous territory and amateurs, however well meaning, had limited life expectancy.

The weeks ahead were going to be more fraught than he had hoped. It was with this in mind that, after having stopping off at Saks to buy a suit, he arrived at the New York office. He walked in. Nobody was expecting him. Nobody recognised him, at first.

Then McGarth's secretary came in and took over. Charles was whisked up to the boardroom. He asked where McGarth was. He would be in later, he had a breakfast meeting and would only be in at ten thirty. The Honourable James' son was also away from his desk. It was confirmed that was not unusual. It hardly surprised Charles, as his nocturnal habits had been one reason for their selection of him as the second fall guy in the Americas.

Charles called his father and was updated on the different positions. He carefully used his mobile to avoid being recorded on the tapes that were linked to the in-house phone system.

They had almost closed out all the trading positions. The banks had crystallised a huge number of losses and yet he had not been informed. Irrespective of their real innocence on any charge of having instigated the trades or manipulated the books, they were guilty of withholding information. Charles could hardly fail to feel pleased about that; this was their undoing rather than something he could have foreseen. The Honourable James and his revolting son; Dunkillen, Sir Brian and McGarth were heading for the big dipper in serious downward mode.

He called Jacqui. She was fine. The birth hadn't been difficult. The baby was sleeping and feeding well. They would tell the world her name when he returned, hopefully at the weekend. He said he would look up Di Maglio that evening. He hinted that he didn't like the prognosis. She didn't react. She still felt bitter towards him and appeared to have shut him out of her life. Little Claire Jacqueline Di Maglio Rossi cried for attention and food in the background. Charles smiled as he heard his daughter's voice for the first time. Jacqui told him he was soppy and she had to go back on shift.

He talked to the office, carefully using the office phone. The recording would be useful. He talked to the Honourable James and even asked him for a first cut of the last quarter's results. He expected them any day but hadn't had them yet. He queried if the Honourable James thought they'd beat the budget. Charles was assured they were hopeful. Charles said he was impressed at the results in America and hinted that the Honourable James' son seemed to have buckled down to his new role. He couldn't get a reaction, which was unfortunate but not unexpected. There was no real love lost between the pair.

He asked to be transferred to Lord Dunkillin and asked him specifically how things were on the trading side. He enthused. He believed they would produce record results. Charles allowed him to prattle on and then finally talked to Sir Brian. He heard all was well and was assured that the business was booming. They all obviously knew the truth but were hoping against hope for a miracle. They were petrified of being forced off the gravy train and, in reality, out of the City, for they were in it too deep not to be deemed undesirable even by the low standards of many of their old chums.

Soon afterwards, McGarth walked in. He was full of his successes. Once again there was no mention of the trading losses. He showed Charles a pack he had prepared for the board the next week. Financial product sales outside of the dealing room were up. Investment funds were growing. New accounts were at a record. Charles asked to keep the paper. It was wonderful evidence of the man's dishonesty and incompetence. McGarth happily left it with him, especially as Charles implied that he expected the remuneration committee to ensure that this result was reflected in the end of year bonus awards. Then having ensured that greed blossomed even more, he left for his lunchtime meeting. The last thing he wanted was for the bank to implode before he had sorted out Di Maglio and his erstwhile operations.

And if the fools he employed talked to their friends in similar vein, the share price would soar and that would allow his father to sell even more shares at even higher prices. Everything was going their way at the moment. More time meant just that they made more money. It was no issue if they waited the month they needed to rid them of the corrupt Di Maglio legacy.

Charles walked up Wall Street and across Broadway, then down to the glass fronted Millenium and up to its bar. Wall Street is not a place of lunchtime drinkers. In London the place would have been packed. Here it was half-empty. He sat and waited for the contact to appear. A tall man, with steel rimmed glances approached him. His thin face was topped with thinning slicked-back blond hair. He had a lop-sided smile and a quiet voice that said in a Southern burr, "Clarissa said you'd be here."

"I guess you have a badge to show me."

He calmly passed the black wallet over. In it was the presidential insignia; he was part of the President's bodyguard. His unmistakable face was younger in his photo. But it was the same smile and the same gaunt appearance. A small, yellow piece of paper was stuck to the edge of the photo and it said in minuscule writing "I owe my life to Delaney."

The waitress took their order for two sodas. "I need Di Maglio to pass away. Can you arrange it?" asked Charles.

"Why?" The voice was inquisitive but not shocked.

"You know our long game plan. Originally, we were to fabricate gang warfare. Now we can't. It's real. And there's danger in that. I need to get rid of Di Maglio. Whatever his state, his presence threatens us. He could cause trouble. I always knew that. There's a solution now. I need you to finish him. I'd have it done myself but I have no people I can trust for such a job. Just do it."

"We're not going to lose any sleep if he's dead. We'll do it tomorrow. His people want him moved back to his house. It'll look like natural causes. Nobody will think he died of any cause other than from a cardiac arrest. You can trust us. We have drugs that nobody even knows about. And they won't leave any traces."

Charles looked at him suspiciously, "Are you wired?"

He smiled that lop-sided smile again, "Don't you trust me?"

"I don't trust many people. I trust Delaney. But I've no reason to trust you."

He opened his jacket. There was a wire. A tape of everything they'd said.

"Bastard," Charles muttered fiercely. "Just do your job and keep out of my way."

With that, Charles got up and strode over to the lift. He punched the button angrily. He stalked into the lift, paced it up and down. Then, with a face that looked like thunder, he left the hotel. He walked back to the office. He stopped and looked at the kiosks in Wall Street. He didn't think that he'd been followed but couldn't be sure.

He rode up to the executive floor in the office. He walked to the washroom. Nobody was there. He went into a cubicle. Then he took out his miniature recorder and played it back. He heard every word he had said. He heard the agent speak. He heard him confirm he was wired. He had him on tape. This was his insurance. It was strange that the agent hadn't asked him if he was wired. Either he had slipped up or had assumed he would be anyway.

Charles walked over to the office and called Delaney, "I saw your friend. He can exit Di Maglio as he is my only option. But tell his superiors that the bust is off. He was wired. I don't trust them any more."

"I'll call," Delaney replied. "They said they wouldn't. Is the bust really off?"

"It is for them. Stay on stand-by. I may find another place to do it, but only if they deliver on Di Maglio."

Charles then called Maria and told her to come over. She arrived half an hour later. He came straight to the point.

"We have a change of plan. We need to divert the plane with the drug consignment. I don't want it to land in the US. There's a danger that they'll set us up. We'll land it in Canada. What airfield should we use?"

She hesitated, "There used to be a strip just north of Buffalo near Niagara. We used it a few times. It almost straddles the border. It should be OK now. It's unusable in winter because of the weather. I can check if it's still operative, I assume it will be. It was mainly used as a flying club's place."

"Good. And change the planes. We'll split the cargo in two and put it on executive jets. We land them at the strip within a few minutes of each other. But, first of all, get me the exact location. And find out what the border control is like while you're at it."

She nodded, "Do I tell Maddy?"

"Once we're organised and if I agree. There's no need to tell her yet. She may tell Delaney and I want him to know as late as possible. The fewer who know, and the shorter they know for, the better."

"What do we do tonight?" she asked.

"I have no plans. I want an early night. Best to get as much sleep as possible before the pace steps up. Tomorrow we head off for California. Maddy can stay here. But we're visiting the bank there. I don't want to be too close when the heist takes place. The further away we are the more credible it appears."

He didn't want to tell her that he also wanted to be out of New York when Di Maglio died. And it was for the same reason. But there was no way that he was going to admit that one to Maria.

The rest of the day was spent on the phone as they planned the bank's demise. His father had sold more shares in IBE. Jacqui would spend a couple of hours at the office on Friday and adjust the share register by reshuffling certain holdings.

Jacqui would just move the stock out of the names of the big institutions to the new owners. Later, once Jack Ryder had bought back their stock at rock bottom prices, she would move the stock back in again.

None of the staff knew that she was also able to hack into the system, change records and then cover her tracks. The beauty of it all was that, in the end, the programme would eliminate all records of what had actually happened and then self-destruct. An expert would know there was a problem. But there would be no link with Jacqui, her terminal would have reverted to its normal view only. That meant that, officially, she could look at the records but not change them.

Charles called Jacqui but they kept the discussions down to family matters. She would leave the hospital that afternoon. Everything was arranged. They did not talk about the job needed on Friday for he was on the office phone. He had used his mobile for the discussion with his father. It was important that they completed their illicit sales of IBE shares quickly, it was impossible that the good or bad news about the bank, depending on who you were, would not break over the next week or so.

The losses on all their trades had crystallised and been paid away into the money launderer's maze known as the international banking payment systems. And some of the larger loans would default at the end of the following week and start a roller coaster of failed loans for the bank.

The end game was now in play. The next two weeks would see the collapse of the Di Maglio Empire and of IBE. Meanwhile, the Empire carried on making its money and the IBE share price soared on to reach twenty-six dollars, more than fifty per cent up on the price at its launch.

Charles had some business calls and even accompanied McGarth to the New York Federal Reserve. McGarth painted the regulators the rosy picture that had become his trade mark. His patrician jowls quivered with excitement as he vouched that all was well in the bank. All the ratios were moving in the right direction. Their capital was strong. Their investment funds were performing well. Loan losses were negligible. In short, business was exceptional.

McGarth's blindness to the danger of their situation was staggering. He was already aware that they had been burnt badly on the trading desks with hits of well into two billion for the US end alone.

And Charles knew that, within a week, their investment funds would also slump, as his father stopped manipulating the prices of the worthless shares they had bought; then worried clients would start to panic as their fund prices crashed.

Then the loans would start defaulting. And IBE stock would slump as the market absorbed one bad news announcement after another. The darling of the market had risen to a staggering price, and would now plummet to unknown depths as it edged close to bankruptcy amid a public display of incompetence and apparently fraud by its top management.

Charles just built up the image of his total innocence. He commented on his dependence on McGarth and his experienced management team. He noted that he would be doing a courtesy call to California. He stressed the shortness of his visit to New York. They were duped and there was no way that they could be surprised that he was too.

That was the last meeting and Charles declined the offer of a drink from McGarth. He needed to get up early for the West Coast the next morning. He wanted a quiet evening to go through papers from the family businesses. And with that he headed back to the hotel. Maria was there.

She told him what she had arranged, "I've established the landing strip is still operative. It's not manned normally. We've booked two slots on it for Friday and arranged our own ground crew. We have two of the latest executive jets. The locals in Canada think that they are arriving from Chicago, according to the manifest. The cover is that they're bringing executives to see the Niagara Falls.

We've also rescheduled the South American flights and already had the cargo split. That wasn't difficult, as it hadn't been loaded anyway. We're all set for Friday. I haven't told Maddy. She won't be happy not knowing but won't make a fuss of it."

She gave him the co-ordinates and expected timings. All was ready. They knew the room was clean of bugs but couldn't be certain about the phone. Since the meeting with the US agent, Charles was not in the mood to take chances. The rooms had been empty at times during the day and phones could be tapped. He was comfortable about using the mobile with its scrambling device from the office but less so from the room. So he and Maria headed off down street and went over to Trump Tower. He called Delaney.

"Change of plan. First, you'll need the Canadian police. I suspect they'll need the US to help them as they are unlikely to have the right resources. But the hit will need to be early evening on Friday, New York time – that's around six in the evening there. They'll be told the co-ordinates around two that afternoon. You'll need teams standing by in Toronto. They need all to be ready to scramble and fast."

Delaney was angry at the lack of information but Charles cut him off, "Don't preach at me. You had your chance and you blew it. Or at least your agent did. You're playing it my way. This is for all of our protection. If anything else doesn't go to plan, the whole deal is off and not just relocated."

Delaney didn't say another word. "I'm off to California tomorrow. I'll call you from there," said Charles. There was no answer. Charles sensed his anger but he knew that Delaney would control it. Delaney wanted the Empire dead even more than he did.

They called Maddy to join them and told her to set up the Russians between Toronto and Niagara. That gave little away as that area was littered with airstrips. She called a contact she had in the Russian camp "I have a big shipment. I want a hundred million for the location. I want fifty up front. It's a big one. Two executive jets. It will be around a billion in value. That's a few weeks supply for the US of A."

There were voices on the other side and then she replied, "I'll give the general area once the money's in the account and the exact co-ordinates in time for you to make it there. You have a few days but I want the cash there by Thursday, or I'll call off the planes."

With that she cut them off. She turned to Charles and grinned. She sensed the Russians had fallen for it. Once the fifty million was in her account they would definitely have been duped. The Russians would believe her story of being unhappy with the cut she was getting. They understood greed and respected it.

She dialled again. This time she would be calling another Mafia syndicate. The story was similar. The code name was different. The other side agreed to pay. This time it was fifty million with twenty-five up front. The Italian Mafia were always tighter than the Russians. It came with their long traditions.

She smiled, "That's all arranged then. It was so simple. I can't believe it."

Charles turned to Maddy, "I'm heading back from California to London. I need to be there on Thursday. Are you staying in New York after Thursday?"

"No. I'll head back to Geneva once I give the green light to the Russians and Italians. I'll arrive there on Friday morning and wait for the call with the exact location. Then I'll contact you and we'll have to see what's left to be done."

"Hopefully we can just stand back and watch the whole thing self destruct. The Empire will have lost a billion. The non-drug side will revolt. After all, they already tried to split off a few months ago."

They walked back up to the hotel. The evening was peaceful and they all had plenty on their minds. There was something awesome about the events that were about to unravel. There was the death of Di Maglio. Then there was the fall of the Empire. Then there would be the spectacular collapse of the bank.

And then Charles would go into exile until they managed to find a way to make a comeback. But an exile helped by their tens of billions.

They all had everything to play for. And, still, they had to be careful. Everything was not won yet.

Charles sent Douglas back to England with key papers. The main one was the indemnity from prosecution in the US. He also took a copy of the tape Charles had made of the talk with the US agent. He would give both to Jacqui who would keep them safely with some other useful mementoes they had. They were all incriminating and all would be useful, later, for blackmail or worse. In time he would put the originals in their Swiss bank vault and only keep copies in London. It always paid to keep these in duplicate and he trusted the Swiss for one thing above all; their commitment to banking secrecy and security.

They went to the coffee shop and had a light meal. They talked through what would happen once they had finished the scam. Maria knew she would be worth several hundred million. Charles asked Maddy what she'd do. She couldn't say if she would go back to her old job because Maria didn't know that she was a double agent in more senses than one. So she spun a yarn about always wanting a ranch and loving South America. She talked of Buenos Aires and yearned for its splendour. She reminisced about the restaurants she knew there. She remembered the late night dancing and the singing in the Tango district. She talked of the plains and riding on fiery horses.

Charles thought she was serious and wondered if Delaney knew of the millions she had transferred to her accounts in bribes and wondered if they would stay there. He was amazed at her innocence. She had always seemed oblivious to the dangers facing her when the Mafia knew her true identity. She seemed unaware of the risk of letting him have a hold on her through any embezzlement on her part.

Money corrupts; her millions were big money. Charles had a feeling that Miss Maddy Brown would never be a government employee again. He even wondered if she had salted away some money from the Empire. After all, she was a money laundering expert. Perhaps their gamekeeper had turned her hand to a bit of discreet poaching too?

They turned in early and they stayed apart for another night. Charles and Maria knew the game was coming to an end. Their paths would soon diverge and there was no going back. There would be no reminiscences. They had had their pleasure and now they would have to find other opportunities to satisfy their needs. Charles knew that he would never love Maria. He had not really loved Claire. Claire was for a fleeting moment when their lives were in unison. Those women needed him as a man rather than as a person. They served each other. That was all.

It was with these thoughts in mind that they headed for California. Maria dressed in her office outfit sat demurely beside him in the first class cabin of the plane. They breakfasted from paper bags and drank coffee from plastic cups as their carrier fought to prove it could cut costs and price more than the next man could. It was difficult to understand the selling of airline seats. A nation in love with the oil guzzling stretched limousine offered the most cramped flying conditions. And nobody complained. The plane equalled the bus and the bus didn't have to be comfortable. So people accepted the tedium of discomfort.

In California, they did the official visit and saw the regulators once again. As they went back to the hotel in the evening, they saw the office had booked them rooms that were well apart. This did not worry them. They doubted they were in any danger there.

Charles called home and Jacqui told him the news he had waited for, "My father's had a massive heart attack. He died a couple of hours ago."

"How do you feel? Can you handle it all?"

"I've asked the lawyers to find the will. Aldo will organise the funeral with the family. It'll be early next week. We'll have to go to New York for it. I'll tell you when. There should be quite a bit of money in the estate. I wonder who he left it to. I hope there's not going to be a family row."

Charles knew that was shorthand for her concern that the eventual loss of all the estate as it bailed out the bank in America could cause problems. For that reason, he hoped she was the beneficiary. But he could not be sure. In any event, it was ironic, if that were the case, they would themselves bail out the bank. That hadn't been the aim in the beginning, but the bail-out would cost them much less than the gains they had made.

Jacqui seemed quite calm and assured him that she was well, "I suppose the attack tripped it off. He lived a pretty rough life. He drank too much. He was always stressed. He whored around. His body must have been in pretty bad shape. I can't feel too sorry for him. I'm sad we rowed, but that was inevitable. We need to finish the job and make sure that the Empire doesn't exist for any of our children. It caused enough misery for me."

She then changed the subject and surprised him when she said, "I've bought our beach. It's in the Maldives. It's close to the main island and therefore easily accessible. It's not a place for all-year. But it's beautiful. I bought it unseen. If we don't like it we can sell it. But we have a place for later in the year. It has a small airstrip that will take our plane. It has one house with a cottage in the grounds. I'll send Douglas and his wife over once you're back to look at it. Then we'll get an interior designer in. We could spend a week or so there in September if we want."

Charles understood the shorthand again. The place would be ready by then. He couldn't see them getting away before then. But it meant that, at long last, they had a place. They would get a boat there, so they could sail as well as spend time on the beach. The Maldives would be humid in the summer months but would be an ideal winter location. They could spend several months there and then, perhaps, get a place in California for the summer. At least he hoped they could, as long as they did not become persona non grata in the US.

Charles rang Aldo and Giovanni. He couldn't say he was sorry but he asked how it happened. They explained. If they felt any suspicion, they didn't say a word. He then called Maria and told her. She seemed to accept it as normal, even ironic.

"I suspect that saves you from wondering whether to kill him," she commented. "I always thought you had that truly on your mind. Get rid of the Empire and get rid of Di Maglio as an insurance policy."

That insight surprised him, but he had the presence to laugh, "You know me too well. But it looks as if Mother Nature has let me off that decision. I wonder who'll inherit. It would be ironic if it were Jacqui."

Maria savoured the irony, "You can pull back even now you know."

"No. We go ahead. Just relax and soon you'll be seriously rich. I'm going to crash out early tonight. I'll have a meal in my room. We have a busy day till we get the flight home tomorrow evening. So let's take it quietly. I'll see you in the morning."

The next day went smoothly and by evening they were heading back to London. Then on Friday they would really put the Empire into play. They had the centre seats in the first class cabin.

They drank champagne and ate their evening meal. They looked at each other nervously. For the first time, Maria seemed unsure, "Will it all work?" she whispered over to him.

He laughed away her doubts, "It'll work. You'll see. The money side is already in play. That's just a matter of time. The Empire had to go. And the beginning of the end is Friday. I just don't know how fast or slow it will be."

She shook her head, "It'll be fast. You can bet your bottom dollar that they'll jump at the opportunity. The boss is gone. The bimbo is in command. The major hit happens. The Empire is bust. The Di Maglio private money is not there to fuel it. You'll be seen as an unwilling owner when you don't put up more cash. No, it'll go and quickly."

"What'll happen, in your opinion?" Charles queried.

"The other rats will all seek to leave the sinking ship. They may even offer you money to get out. It will be either something front end or a share over the years. That's the usual stuff. There will be new alliances. There will be new deals. Another Empire will arise from the ashes of the old."

She was mocking him as well as answering the question. They might have purged themselves of guilt but not the world of evil. Charles knew that well enough. He had no regrets about the Empire. He disliked the people who ran large parts of it. He hated the death and destruction that it bought. He didn't want it as part of Jacqui's inheritance. He knew that it was now theirs, but he wanted to be rid of it.

Yet, others would sell the drugs to the addicts on the streets. Others would tempt new candidates through soft and into hard drugs. First, they would drag on some cannabis. Then they would sniff cocaine. And then, before they knew it, they would be hooked on heroin. They would look to finance their ugly habit and prostitution or crime would beckon for those who were pretty or tough enough; at least for as long as they were still pretty or able. The others would be destroyed by it all. Destroyed; other than the few who would break their habit before their habit broke them.

"But you will be far away," he said to her.

"And so will you. We'll have our memories. Mine start well. Then I stray. But then you saved me. You're like a missionary. You plucked me from a life of sin and showed me a life of pretty rampant crime. And you showed me more. But soon I'm going to be a model citizen. As model as someone who is filthy rich can be." She grinned, "And I'm looking forward to it."

He lent over and whispered to her, "Will I have your address? I'd want to send you the odd Christmas card."

She laughed, "Not just a Christmas card."

"Maybe there will be more. But I'll have to see who you're living with. I wouldn't want to cause trouble."

Charles then called Jacqui on the phone. She had news. "Giovanni called. He knows all about the will. He believes that my father has left his entire estate to my mother. Apparently I get nothing. That doesn't bother me. But it's amusing that he left all to my mother. She'll be overjoyed. Funny, isn't it?"

Charles laughed. They had never had contact with Jacqui's mother. Indeed, she had had no contact with her former husband. Now she would think that she had inherited billions. She would undoubtedly be at the funeral. She would never see a penny of the inheritance and she didn't deserve to. Charles thought long live page thirty-three as he reminded himself of the added page to the sale agreement. Undoubtedly, their salvation would be her mother's misfortune.

They slept through the flight and soon landed at Heathrow. Douglas was there. He whisked them to the house where, for the first time, Charles saw the new baby. Little Claire Jacqueline was asleep and looking peaceful in her pink crib. He held Jacqui's hand as he got the first sight of his second daughter. They then walked over to the other bedroom and kissed the sleeping Juliet. They then kissed until a little voice said "What are you doing?" and they saw Juliet sitting up in her bed.

Charles picked her up again and kissed her on her forehead. "I was just saying hello, to you, the baby and your mother. Now sleep little one. It's late."

They left the room as their daughter fell asleep. On Friday they would need to be in the office. Jacqui had some final work to do on the share register for the last part of the big scam and Charles had to put everything into play.

CHAPTER TWENTY-TWO

Late that Friday morning, Maddy called. Her voice was breathless, "The Russians and the Italian Group have both bought it. I have the seventy five million in the account and it is moving through the web I set up. It'll be in my Cayman account by this evening."

"Don't give details over the phone unless it's needed," Charles snapped back. "They have the area and are just waiting for the co-ordinates and the time?"

"Yes," she replied. She sounded abashed at the reprimand.

"Have you got your exit route?"

"I'm flying to London tonight."

"OK, you know the routine. See you then." Charles said curtly.

Charles called Delaney, "Put your Toronto men on standby. I'll give you the co-ordinates in a few hours. If I'm late, then it's because we're delaying the flight. You'll be facing twenty people on my side and at least fifty or sixty other attackers plus a billion dollars of drugs at cost."

"I'll be waiting," he said. "And, Charles, we owe you if we pull this off. The US owes you also. They're sorry. The tape was not authorised."

"Nor was mine of their agent, but, if they do anything, they'll hear it on CNN. And it makes fun listening."

"You taped the conversation. I can't believe it," he gasped. "He didn't frisk you?"

"They were amateurs. Only amateurs would have tried to pull that stunt. That's why I'm being secretive. But don't worry, with a jet you'll be able to make it with an hour or so to spare. Just keep everyone on standby."

Once he had finished with Delaney, he joined Jacqui. She looked incredible for someone who had given birth just six days ago. She had organised the childcare. They had two nannies now. And, although they didn't know it, both had been vetted by the British Secret Service as well. Charles explained what he had done.

"I'll tell Delaney the co-ordinates about an hour or two before they land. He has jets and helicopters standing by and expects he will have to parachute his people into the region. In reality, he's close enough to bus them in from Toronto. And it may be safer if he does."

Jacqui agreed, "But what are you doing about Maddy? She'll be in danger after the attack."

"Yes. I'd realised that from the start. But she seemed unaware until the other day. Delaney has realised that, though. He has a safe house and will make arrangements for an identity change. She'll meet us tonight."

Charles had an operations centre in the basement. It had full international radio and satellite communications and sleeping quarters for three or four people. At the moment it would only house Maddy and Maria. He could need them both to be there 24/7. Charles couldn't afford to be cut off from the office that long in case something went wrong there.

"You think Maddy will tell all to Delaney?" asked Jacqui.

"I doubt it. She'll hold back on the payments; it's her one chance. They'll have a huddle and he'll authorise an official payment and give her a new ID. At least, once we have finished. He knows I need her with me, if only to brief me on the men I'll have to deal with from your father's operation. I think they'll contact me soon after the hit. The funeral will be the ideal place to complete the deal."

Douglas drove them to the office. In the car, Charles explained their plans for the island. Then he added, "Douglas, we'd like you to work for us as long as you want. And I'll give you a half a million-dollar bonus for each year you work. That starts today and is in addition to the rest of your salary. It's joint with your wife."

They were at the top of Fleet Street when that announcement was made. Douglas swerved, then quickly corrected, "You often surprise me Mr Charles. What's that for?"

"It's your pension fund. You'll need it one day. You earn it. Both of you do."

"Thank you sir, I appreciate that. If I may say so, you're a gentleman. A bit like Raffles."

"Thanks Douglas, I like the analogy."

He then looked over at Jacqui who had an enigmatic smile on her lips. She was wearing a loose black dress. Without a hair out of place and perfect make-up on her flawless skin, she looked desirable in the extreme. She saw his look and laughed happily.

She leant over and whispered, "I'm not superwoman you know. You'll have to wait a few weeks. But I'll make it worth your while."

Charles grinned at her and muttered, "A few weeks, I don't believe it. And you haven't organised a stand-in?"

She looked at him; eyes flashing. "She'd make the mistake of her life. One she'd regret. After all, I'm a gangster's moll."

"But you're not a gangster's moll. You're his daughter."

"Wrong. You're as much as a gangster as he was. You're just a zillion times more gorgeous. And a billion times smarter. And a million times nicer. And several times richer. Almost perfect you know."

"You deal in big numbers. I've trained you well."

She laughed. Douglas opened the door and showed them out. They both walked into the office, greeting some of the staff as they went in. They noticed a sign at the entrance. It was the share price in neon lights. He noticed the price was twenty-seven dollars, which was a couple of dollars up on their average sale price. But he was hardly worried. He knew it couldn't last. They had sold more shares as the market had risen. And Jacqui was to rig the records during that morning. She planned to leave after lunch in the office.

Charles called Maddy's number as planned. The office told him she had not been in that morning. He knew she was either in London or on her way. But he left a message all the same, "Tell her I called, and I'll be in the office till after lunch." Once again this was part of the plan to cover up his knowledge of Maddy's impending disappearance.

He saw his fellow directors. He noticed that the Honourable James looked pale. He had shadows under his eyes. His face looked gaunt. He had lost his usual sleek look. He knew the gravity of the banks' financial position. At last.

Charles pretended to be concerned and asked if he was well.

"Feel a bit under the weather. Nothing else is wrong. I've a touch of flu. I should be all right after the weekend," he said quickly, casting a guilty look in Charles' direction. In front of his office, Charles outlined the report he had been given by McGarth.

"He was as optimistic as you are. He told the regulators about our US performance. It's booming on all fronts. We really have a great team. I only wish we could find something in Europe. I spend all my time looking at possible acquisitions. Feel a bit guilty as you and the others just make us more and more money. And the share price is responding well."

James' secretary looked at him and then at her boss. She was old school and adored him. She looked at Charles condescendingly. You could see her think that the Honourable James ran things while he played around. That was what she would tell people afterwards and that would help exonerate Charles further from any culpability.

Charles smiled and headed back to his office. The rest of the morning he checked out their accounts, both personal and official. He reinforced his apparent innocence by asking for the management accounts and checking that the trading desks were not reflecting their losses. He wrote notes on the accounts and put notes at one or two of the points. There would soon be a board meeting and his notes were for questions to raise then. The reason was not to ask questions, but to have a reason to get his secretary to file the accounts. The paper was just another part of part of his cover-up. He couldn't believe the news could be suppressed for another week. The board meeting would surely not take place. But the secretary would think he spent an hour on the accounts in preparation for the board meeting. He would have acted just as he normally did.

The morning passed and Jacqui and he lunched in the office. She then headed home while he worked on. He found it easy to clear all the papers and soon his desk was empty. He had pushed decisions out to other areas. He had made others. It all looked as if he had spent another normal day at work. He even had another take-over candidate passed to him and promised to look over it at the weekend. The office would note that he had spent time looking to the future. And it would appear that he did that while his associates lied to him and put the bank into bankruptcy.

He headed home to meet Maddy, but not before calling the office again and asking for her. She was not there, of course, but he was the only one who knew why. He pretended to be annoyed. He questioned if she often skipped off. He insisted he needed to talk to her a soon as possible. He even told her assistant that the reason was his concern at feedback that he was getting on the size of some shipments. They had not known him angry before. In reality he was enjoying his role, he knew he was fooling them into believing he was sincere.

Once home, he headed to the operations centre. Maria was organising things there. She now knew the truth about Maddy. She looked up as he entered, "Maddy will be here in about ten minutes. And she said that Delaney would also come along. She has realised she's a marked woman now. The reality of it all has hit her. It's as if she were playing a game that wasn't real until now. She wants out quick with a new identity. You really think that'll help her? She'll be target number one and that's on the Mafia hit list."

Charles shrugged his shoulders. They would see what was to be done. Meanwhile, he checked timings and details of their coming operations.

This was the time for work and not speculation about Maddy. In any event, she had finished her job. She was not part of the future.

Maddy and Delaney entered. Charles greeted them and carried on looking through the papers. Ten minutes later he had finished. He looked at each of them. He then looked at his watch. It was 6.30 in the UK and five hours earlier in the eastern part of the United States.

Maddy was looking pale. It was as if the reality of her situation had just hit home. She would be a fugitive for life. Delaney would have told her that announcing she was a double agent would just make her a target for another reason, so there was no value in that. It made it harder for others he might want to place. Charles looked at her. The sheen had gone from her hair. The colour had left her cheeks. Maddy had burnt out.

Maria was her normal dark, sleek self; efficient and ready. Her job had been defined. Her price had been agreed. The mercenary was at work. Tell her what you want her to be. A whore, a lover, a seducer; she could be all three. A murderer, a bomber or a thief; again she would have no problem. Her morals were set aside when she joined them. Her scruples were eradicated at birth. It didn't matter if a few more were to die. She would cope with a bit more treachery. Di Maglio was dead. The Empire was dying. Charles would soon back out of her life. Her view was simple. Get to the end. Get there in one piece. And collect the few hundred million or so before finding a personal nirvana.

Delaney was edgy. For the first time, he was riled. He needed to know what was happening. This was a master who was being treated like a pawn. His eyes were dark with fury. His florid neck sat astride the white collar and regimental tie. He perspired as he looked impatiently at the screens in the centre of the table.

Then, finally, the message came through. It was 7.30 in the UK and 2.30 in the US. It read, "DM1 and DM2 in position. The cargo is fine. ETA as agreed. Location as agreed. Destination is clear with good visibility. Forecast no change. We are awaiting final co-ordinates."

Charles pressed the button and the scrambled message with the final co-ordinates was released. Seconds later, the response came, "Message received and co-ordinates accepted."

Charles turned to Delaney and passed him a piece of paper. "These are the co-ordinates. The airfield is fifty miles from Toronto. You have three and a half hours. The planes are en route. Their estimated time of arrival is now 6pm US time, when it will be dusk and fairly poor visibility. There are two planes. The reception committee is not in place. Allow the

Russians to take the airport. Allow the Italians to counter attack. Then swoop in. The cover is that there was a leak from the Italian Mafia, that's why the forces are there. Shoot to kill. They will."

He turned to Maddy, "Pull yourself together. Give out these co-ordinates to the Russians and then in an hour's time to the Italians."

Delaney picked up the phone and called through to his office. His office must have patched him in and scrambled the line down to their phone. When Charles played the recording later, he got high pitched sounds and nothing else. Delaney waited a minute or so and then gave the instructions.

Maddy told the Russians. Her voice was strained but credible. An hour later she repeated the task with the Italians. They waited in silence until Maddy finally spoke, her voice still anxious, "What do we do now?"

Maria laughed contemptuously, "We wait, unless you want to go out to the cinema or something."

Charles looked again at Maddy. She was finished. He realised Maria had written her off as too weak.

"Maddy, we need to agree your cover. Is it my problem or Delaney's?"

Delaney glared over at him. "It's mine," he said gruffly.

"OK. What about the seventy five million. Is it for her, me or the government purse?"

"What seventy five million?" he queried.

"I mean the bribes that they gave Maddy. I thought you knew about them."

Delaney looked at Maddy. He was shocked. He didn't know. Miss Brown, as Charles had suspected, had taken all the money for herself and not for the government.

Charles stepped in, "Maddy can have them. I'm indifferent. I'll set off the fee I told her I'd pay her against it. That puts her twenty five million up."

Delaney again looked horrified. Maddy was close to tears. She had stepped over the line. He would withdraw his protection. She had gone native. She'd gone freelance. She'd believed Charles would keep silent and now he had blown it. He was her only hope. She looked pleadingly at him. He needed her for today, he knew he had to re-assure her.

"I thought he knew; you should have told him what you were doing. Or you should have told me that you had gone solo. That was stupid. But we'll sort things out. If he thinks you went too far, you can work just for me. But don't forget it. If that's the case, you've left his service."

Maria glanced over at him. Her face was motionless. Her eyes flickered. He flashed back a look at her. Maddy would need to be disposed of. She was dangerous. It would be easy to kill her. She needed a bullet in the head before she talked. You can disappear from the authorities, but not from the Mafia. And she would talk and incriminate them all. Her reactions now made that almost a certainty. She didn't know it, but she would soon be history. They needed to survive more than her life was worth.

Delaney didn't notice the exchange. He was examining the table. Charles had annoyed him more than he would admit, but Maddy had betrayed him. And that was worse. Maddy was beyond realising anything. Charles wanted to keep her under scrutiny or he would have told her to go. She was not going to be any use to them as the evening wore on.

Maria stood up and got herself a coffee. Charles switched on the camera. The airfield came onto the giant screen. They could see the peripheral road and the two runways from the hidden cameras. There were no signs of life. It was just an empty airfield. There was one small building. Inside there were people; these would be the locals who managed the strip.

He turned to Maddy, if only to give her something to think about, "Anyone coming in will leave lookouts. Where would you place them?" Before she answered he turned to Maria. "And where did you place the remote cameras and other electronic tracking equipment?"

Maddy looked blank. She didn't know. Maria chipped in, "We have camera and electronic equipment about a mile from the site and then on the site itself; as for them, it's unlikely they'll leave lookouts away from the periphery of the airfield. It'll be safe for us to bring our forces in to a two mile radius."

Delaney nodded, "OK. I'll bring them in to about ten miles till we've identified the attackers are there. Then I'll move to two or three miles. We'll be using infantry. I can cover two miles in around three or four minutes depending on the terrain. We'll hit from all sides so we operate a pincer. They'll be pretty busy killing each other by then."

Charles turned to Maddy, "You said the other day that the Russians would come overland. The Italians would come by helicopter from near New York. Are you sure?"

She looked blank still but nodded.

He asked Delaney if satellite would track any helicopter and if they could have a feed from that as well. Delaney nodded. There was another series of instructions over the phone. They sat there and waited. The door opened and Jacqui appeared. She sat next to Charles and watched the airfield.

"I need to see this," she said. "This is my way of purifying our name. The last connection of the Di Maglio name with organised crime."

"You're an optimist," muttered Delaney. "I am glad you trust Charles. I sometimes think he'd deal with the devil if it made him money."

"Let's not get personal," Charles snapped. "We may yet need to work together. And this could go wrong. In that case, there'll be some hides to save."

He looked at his watch; it was 9.30. That was 4.30 in the US. They had an hour and half to go. The Russians should be approaching.

Suddenly, Maria called out, "One of the sensors has picked up movement."

They glanced at the location map and then at the video. There they saw the convoy of eight vans and two huge articulated trucks. Charles looked at the map. He turned to Delaney.

"Where are your men now? Make sure they keep clear of this area."

Charles studied the map again. "They'll go down this road and then take this turning to the airport. That lets them park the articulated trucks here in that siding. That's close to the hangers. It would be useful for loading."

Maria looked at the map area, "There won't be enough of them to make a two pronged attack. They'll cut a gap in the fence and advance under cover of the buildings."

Delaney barked some instructions down the phone. They switched to the camera near the hangars. They watched carefully. Then the vans came in view. The articulated trucks were nowhere to be seen. The cameras did not pick up the area where they would have parked. They watched the vans. They pulled up. Maria counted the men getting out the one nearest to the camera. There were eight of them. There were six vans, that made forty plus men. Delaney passed the information on to his people.

They watched as the men crept up to the perimeter fence. They saw one of them cut a gap in the wire. They then crept in and moved to the far side of the hangars. They were out of view. Maria broke the silence.

"They must be attacking the ground staff."

"I counted forty two of them in all. They will have some more in the trucks. Could be fifty plus in all."

Delaney had been on the phone. "We'll approach from the other side.

I am also throwing a cordon round the whole area from the moment the attack begins. We have two hundred men approaching by road. And we have a further group in ten helicopters. They'll cut off any who try to escape. The helicopters have all the equipment. They can even pick out the people escaping through the trees. I have four planes that will disable their helicopters. We'll get them on the ground before they can be used for an escape."

Charles looked at him, "It'd be better to shoot them out of the sky. That way you eliminate survivors."

"We're not murderers," he snapped back as Charles knew he would. "We're the law. Not one of your run of the mill hoodlums."

"Charles," called Jacqui with a frown. "Stop winding up Mr Delaney. Act your age. Don't let the tension get to you."

Charles grinned back. "Sorry, but I was only half joking."

Maddy looked at him, "How can you joke at a time like this?" she cried. "It's awful."

Charles had no ideas why. But he played along. "If we don't take it like this, we'd go mad. You'll find it easier next time."

Poor Maddy looked even sicker than before at the idea of a next time. But she said nothing. They reverted to the screen. It was 5pm in the US. One hour to go. Maria checked the screen. "The planes are on schedule. No sign of the helicopters anywhere on radar." She turned to Delaney. "That still could mean that they are close by. Be careful how you bring in your men. Be careful they are not visible to the people on the ground or the air until we have action."

Then she called out, "There's a group of helicopters forty miles north, north west of the field."

Delaney watched the radar. There were seven dots. That meant seven helicopters. They came closer to the ground. Delaney read the co-ordinates and again called them down the phone.

Charles traced them on the map and minutes later called, "They'll be heading here. It's a clearing in the trees. There's about half a square mile of open ground. Well away from the roads. It's totally hidden from view. It's the best landing spot for them."

"I'll get my people closer," said Delaney. "Everybody is there and I can't see them placing look-outs. The helicopters didn't even look around. They suspect nothing. So we'll come in from the east and north. That way we avoid the Russians on the ground. Our own helicopters can always mop up anyone who escapes."

It was 5.15 US time. Three quarters of an hour to go. They monitored the radar and could see helicopters on the ground. They monitored cameras near the hangars and could see no movement. Maria and Charles exchanged glances as the moments ticked by. Delaney checked his phone as his men approached.

"Split the screen into three. Half screen on the hangar and the others east and north to pick up Delaney's people," Charles called to Maria.

The screen split. It was void of movement. The radar was also motionless. They sat and watched. The room was silent. Maria seemed to breather faster than before. Delaney looked more and more impatient. Only Maddy seemed indifferent to it all and untouched by the tension. Then, suddenly, she turned to Charles.

"Are you going to have me killed?" she asked in a whisper.

He looked at her coldly, "No. But I'm going to find it hard to offer you protection. You don't obey orders. You think you know better."

"Please help me. I 'm sorry."

"I said before; if Delaney can't help you, I can. I'm not annoyed by what you did other than moving money from the Empire through to your secret accounts. He, on the other hand, thinks you betrayed the country."

Maddy gasped. "How do you know about the other twenty million?"

Charles snarled back at her, knowing that there could be no way she would only take such a sum. "It wasn't twenty. Even I can identify more."

She buried her head in her hands and seemed to sob, "You knew. You are a bastard. You knew before America."

He looked over at her, "I didn't know until you told me. I then played poker to get you to tell me what you'd done. Maddy, we're professionals. More professional than you'll ever be. You have to remember that."

She looked at him, "I took two hundred and fifty. And then I got the seventy-five. "

He hardly gave her a look. "Put two hundred back to my account. And send fifty to Maria as a special bonus. Keep the rest. Use the computer over there and do it now."

Delaney glared at Maddy. He realised Charles wanted her to be occupied whilst he focused on the action at the field. "Do as he says. I'll still help you though," he grunted.

The colour came back to her face. She breathed more easily, "I'll do all you say."

Maria monitored the radar and Jacqui was watching the screens. They saw movement. "It's more helicopters," called Maria. "Two are coming in. Who the hell are they? The Italians are in the field. The Russians are by the hanger. No other movement."

"Is it your people?" Charles asked Delaney. He was already on the phone and checking out.

"Negative," he called. "We've picked them up. There are two people movers. We believe they are Chinooks or something. They're big helicopters. We don't read them."

The helicopters moved over towards the Italian Mafia's landing ground. The helicopters on the ground started to move. Then the large helicopters opened fire. The whole area was under attack. And whoever was in the attacking helicopters was making sure that nobody escaped alive. This was a fight till the death. The Italians stood no chance. Not one of their helicopters seemed to make it. There were explosions. They could see bullets tracing through the open ground.

They glanced at the cameras near the hangers. No movement. No reaction. They must have expected the attack. That could only mean that it was the Russians in the helicopters. Somehow, they'd known about the Italians. Charles looked at Delaney. He had come to the same conclusion.

He muttered, "It's the Russians. That means that either there was a leak from the Italians or someone close to Maddy knew about their presence and leaked it to the other side."

Jacqui said sombrely, "And, if it's Maddy's people are responsible, there's been a bad breach of security. That could even mean there's an outside chance they know about her role and Delaney's men."

They waited and watched. The helicopters had landed. There was an occasional blast of fire and then silence. The helicopters took off and then headed to the hangers. They landed near them. Some ten men jumped out. Two men came from the hangar and there was a discussion. Delaney was the first to speak.

"They've got two gun-ships. They could outshoot us. We'd be decimated if they attack us from the air. I've only small transport helicopters. We didn't bring heavy artillery."

Maria looked at the clock. Just eighteen minutes to go. "Can you bring some in? Can you get in some heavy artillery?"

He shook his head, "I can't send the men in to be killed. We'll be decimated."

"Have you got any commandos?" snapped Maria.

He nodded.

"Couldn't you use them and attack first?" she asked.

Charles shook his head, "The planes won't land if there's a battle out there. We'd only be able to strike once the planes had landed and taxied in. Otherwise, they'll abort the landing and we'll find it hard to set it up again."

Delaney was talking on the phone. He was getting more agitated. Then he snapped orders. He turned to them.

"We'll put commandos near the hanger. They're advancing already. As soon as the plane lands, they'll advance through the fence. Then they'll get as close as they can to the helicopters. They'll either plant plastic explosive or blast them with a small rocket launcher. It'll ground them if they're accurate. The plastic's better. It's like semtex, just more powerful."

"What if they put guards on the helicopters?" asked Jacqui.

"We have to kill them," he said. "If they know we're around, they'll have the pilot and gunners in the things. If not, they could be empty."

"If they are empty, the leak is from the Italians and not Maddy's people," interrupted Maria.

"Those helicopters could be to help take out the merchandise. They may prefer that to risking all on the road."

"Let's hope," said Delaney.

Charles glanced again at the clock. Seven minutes to go. The area around the hangars was quiet. The big machines would be hidden from the view of the incoming planes. There was no movement on the field at all. He peered at the screens but it was impossible to tell if there was anyone in the machines. It was just too dark.

"We're five hundred yards from the airfield. We are still going in from the North and East. The commandos are just by the perimeter fence. There are seven. We'll hear nothing from them. They're going in under radio silence."

They waited. Still silence. The area around the hangar was still. The helicopters were in one corner of the frame and they could see no movement. The radar around the location where the Italians had been was motionless. There would be war if the underworld ever heard what had happened.

The Mafia would be at war and would tear its heart out until they were all dead. Or until a powerful enough Godfather arose to call for peace. Charles glanced automatically at Maddy. He wondered if perhaps they could let her live. She would be a target and she knew so much. Too much.

He looked up and noticed Maria and Jacqui watching him closely. They communicated their views clearly. Maddy was too dangerous despite the charade that had just taken place. Maddy was already dead, although she may have thought she had saved herself. And nobody would be able to pin the evidence on them. She had lived too dangerously.

Once again, he shot a glance at the clock. Four minutes to go. The whole place was silent. Nobody was talking. The world seemed to be sleeping. But they knew this was the calm before the storm. Then Maria called out, "We've picked up the planes coming in from the south. They're flying in close formation and approaching fast. We have an estimated time of arrival of two minutes."

Jacqui spoke quietly; "There's movement around the hangars. The men are outside now but most are keeping in the shadows. Two are advancing near the runway."

They watched the cameras at the airfield. Suddenly, the lights went on along the runway. They could see two men near the hangars. Then they saw the plane. It came in from the south and seemed to float down onto the runway. They saw it coming towards the camera as if motionless. It was hard to know if the camera was moving or the plane. Then, behind it, they saw the second plane. It mimicked the first plane and was soon approaching the hangars. The first plane had stopped and they identified the steps that were being moved up towards it. The second plane was taxiing in, its flaps down as it slowly moved to the hangar area.

"Men moving towards the helicopters," whispered Delaney. "Those are our men."

The figures approached the parked helicopters. They then seemed to move away without doing anything. They knew better. They would have attached the explosives. That took moments. They withdrew out of sight of the cameras. The area around the helicopters was silent.

They waited. The first plane had stopped. The second was just turning into the hangar area. The door of the first plane opened. The video camera picked up the flash and the results of an explosion. Then there was another flash. More debris flew across the screen. The helicopters were destroyed. Men were now rushing out of the hangar. They were confused. Then all hell broke loose.

Soldiers poured into the field. They could see the flashes of the guns. They could see the tracing of the bullets. The second plane moved to return to the runway, but more men poured into the field and it stopped dead in its tracks. They suspected that the tyres had been shot out. Then they saw explosions as men threw grenades. It was strange watching the explosions. They could see the figures running around. They could sense the noise but couldn't identify it. Confusion reigned.

Men were swarming everywhere. There were explosions all around. Then they spotted planes on the radar. They saw the rockets streak from them and then picked up the explosions again.

Delaney said grimly, "That'll be the trucks they had in the woods. The planes would have hit them. Our friends have nowhere to go. And our second group are still waiting in our helicopters."

The fighting went on. Delaney picked up his mobile. "No contact unless by your secure land line," Charles snapped. "There would be radio monitoring of the area now. Maddy is right. The Russians would have had their information from the Italians. The Russian bosses will assume that there was another leak from the Italians to the authorities and that got to the FBI and others. That makes things easier for Maddy. They'll look for her. But not with as much purpose as if they thought she were the source of the leaks to the authorities."

More helicopters landed and more men streamed across the airfield. There was no more shooting. They could see men being herded into a pen. The battle was over. Once again the screen was tranquil. The movements were more measured. The guns were silent. The explosions had ended.

Delaney was on a landline, checking out with his office. He took notes and then he turned to them.

"We've taken eleven prisoners. We have five wounded on their side, two seriously. We had four injured, none seriously. We destroyed their trucks with our planes. Any men there were killed in the explosions. We wiped out the helicopters. We don't believe there was anyone in them. We are approaching the planes. The first one had the merchandise. It is being checked out to see if it all tallies with your manifest."

"What'll happen to the prisoners?" asked Maddy.

"They'll be taken to Toronto. They'll be handed over to the Canadian authorities. Depending on what we find on them, there could be an extradition attempt by the US. But, for the moment, they're involved in drug running, at the minimum, involvement in homicide and armed resistance. That's enough to keep them out of circulation for some time."

Charles walked over to the drinks cabinet and poured three juices. He passed one to Maria and one to Jacqui. "Take what you want," he told the others. "Your game is over. Ours is just starting." And they left Maddy and Delaney together.

They walked upstairs into the house. Jacqui kissed Charles by a small door in the hallway. He headed through it and Maria followed. It led to a stairway that took them down some steps into a wine cellar. They calmly walked between the wine racks and came to the end one. It was a floor-to-ceiling rack, full of bottles of wine. Charles pressed a brick on the left-hand side. He pushed the one below it twice. Then he pressed the first brick again. The racks split in two and swivelled round about thirty degrees. There was now a gap between them and in the gap was a door.

They walked through. Charles pressed a button on the other side and knew that behind them the wine rack would move back into place. He and Maria followed the path for about two hundred yards. They came to some stairs and climbed them. At the top there was a door. It opened into a shed at the bottom of their garden. They checked out the area. It was clear. Quickly, they walked through a door in the garden wall into the street. Opposite was a parked car and they both climbed in. They pulled away to the end of the road, turned left and left again and then along another tree-lined road. At the end, they turned left. They now parked near the junction. The house and the front door were visible. They sat and waited.

Then Delaney appeared. And with him was Maddy Brown. Delaney got into his car with Maddy. He pulled away. They waited for his escort to do likewise and then followed at a distance. Delaney's car stopped outside the hotel. He and Maddy went in. Minutes later he came out alone. Maria slipped out of the car as they drove up a side road. Moments later she returned.

"What room's she in?" he asked.

"Three seven five," said Maria calmly. "It has to be. There's a guard on it. They arrived when I did. You can tell British Intelligence from a mile off."

"So Delaney has given her protection," he said. "Let's get out before we're picked up on CCTV."

He drove a short distance away and parked in a residential street.

"Dress as a tart and return," Charles said to Maria as he stopped the vehicle. She nodded and headed to the main road. He saw her hail a taxi and waited. She returned half an hour later. She now looked the part. She wore lipstick, high heels, short skirt and low cut top. A blond wig covered her dark hair, while a large pair of dark glasses shaded her eyes. While she'd been away, Charles had changed and put on a dark sweater. They returned to the hotel.

He entered the lobby and went to the lift, keeping his face away from the cameras. He headed up to the fourth floor. He walked down a flight and waited at the top of the stairs. He held the door half-ajar. He could see he was close to room three fifty. He waited. He knew Maria would come through a side entrance and join him there. Soon enough she walked along the corridor.

Charles slipped out of the door and they walked arm-in-arm along the corridor. They approached three seventy five and saw the two agents guarding the door. They glanced at them and one looked keenly at Maria's legs. They approached them and passed the agents. Then, the knives flashed. Maria's target dropped dead, with her trained precision the stiletto pierced through his heart. Charles' target struggled for a moment and then was still. They searched the victims, found a key card and placed it in the slot. The green light flashed and they pushed the door open.

He covered the interior and found himself staring at Maddy. And Maddy was holding a gun. The silencer on Charles' worked perfectly but hers had none. There was a roar and a bullet streaked past him. It wedged itself into the wall.

Maria pulled the two men into the room with his help. They waited carefully. Nobody seemed to take any notice of the gunshot. They looked at each other, breathed a sigh of relief and turned to the tasks they had still to do.

They first checked the three bodies. They were all dead. They'd never doubted that but one had to be careful and eliminate any evidence. They placed the explosive and set the timer for two minutes later. And then they headed back out of the room. They made their way to a service lift, where Maria clipped the cable of the CCTV as they rode down to the basement. They left the hotel by a side door, avoiding any other cameras.

The explosion was muffled and they saw no smoke. They returned unseen to the car and drove off silently. Ten minutes later they were back in their street. They got back into the house by their earlier route. Maria stripped off and put on the clothes she was wearing before. He pulled off his sweater and put it into a bag with her outfit. They would collect it later and get rid of the incriminating clothes.

They walked into the office. Jacqui was there. She smiled at them. "Welcome back. You've just made a call to Douglas at the island. He's been telling you of the changes he is going to suggest at the house. You also made that call to Maddy's number two. I played that tape as well. It sounds good. You ordered them to be careful and not to make too many large shipments. And said that you suspect Maddy may have gone AWOL, as she hasn't contacted anyone for so long. Nice touch to ask them to put an alert around the place."

They waited a few minutes and the phone rang. It was Delaney. "Maddy was killed. And they also killed two of my agents. Be careful. You must be under surveillance. Otherwise they couldn't have found her."

"Where did it happen?" Charles gasped in mock horror.

"Her hotel, Park Lane" he said.

"But she stayed there always when she came to London. She used to use false names. But everyone knew. They'd have watched the place. Why on earth did you choose it?"

"She wanted to stay there. It was her choice," he said. It was as if he knew she would be killed and had decided that was the best way out.

"Were there any witnesses?"

"No. Not yet. We're going through the CCTV tapes. We suspect they'll be disguised. They knew what to do and how to do it."

"Watch yourself Delaney. They may know you are involved. The Mafia is hardly forgiving. And don't forget we're likely to be heading for a prolonged period of gang warfare. Things are going to get worse before they get better."

And with that Charles put down the phone. He turned to the others. "So far, it's worked. I suspect Delaney knows who killed her. But he has chosen to keep it quiet. Perhaps even the ultra correct Delaney has a price. And he may have access to Maddy's account. We'll monitor it. That could be useful in the future.

Now, all we have to do is encourage the gangs to destroy each other. But let's focus first on the bank. Phase two is about to begin."

CHAPTER TWENTY-THREE

Maria gave him a strange look as she left. She knew what was going through his mind. They had been through this before, but somehow this was worse. One of the victims had been Maddy Brown. He had employed her. And now he had killed her.

Jacqui put her arm round him and they walked to the children's room. He kissed Juliet and she smiled in her sleep. He walked over to the baby. Claire was asleep and he kissed her on the hand. He thought of the other Claire and then of Maddy. There would be no little Maddy. They would have no memento of her. She would join the others in oblivion. The people he had killed, or had had killed, in Europe or America. She was one of those people who had no future in their plans. They were people who had got in their way. One had to be ruthless to succeed and the world they inhabited had little sympathy for losers. He thought of Wendy, Jefferson, Rastinov, Stephens, Di Maglio, the detectives and now Maddy. The list was getting too long, but at least this stage was coming to an end.

They walked into the bedroom and slipped into the bed. Jacqui stroked his face. He burned with desire for her. He wanted her body to clear the painful pictures from his mind. But it wasn't to be. He fell asleep in the end but it was not a restful sleep. He kept on seeing Maddy's face. She would have shot him but he had got her first. He saw the flash of hatred and fear, then the moment of her anguish before the eternity of nothingness.

He got up the next morning well before Jacqui awoke. He washed and dressed, still feeling the weight of the events of the previous night. He drove through the early Saturday morning traffic, looking at the people he passed. He drove into the City and was at his desk before seven. He took a coffee from the machine and glanced at the papers that were on the desk. He found it hard to concentrate. Then Maria walked in.

She gave him the same strange look she had given him the night before. She produced a key from her bag and locked the door from the inside. She walked over to him. He pushed his chair back and watched her approach. Maria was dressed in a dark short skirt and white, open necked blouse. Her face was flushed, her lips were moist. Her eyes were bright, her breath was hurried

They kissed passionately. He slowly undid the buttons of her blouse one by one. She loosened his tie and then took it off. The buttons of his shirt were undone much more quickly as if there was a race. He took off her blouse and then they quickly tore off the rest of their clothes. Maria's eyes sparkled even brighter. Her breath became more laboured and her face became more flushed. He was panting excitably too as he pressed his mouth against hers.

His hands moved to her thighs. The desire for closeness was more acute than ever. This was the way that they expurgated the horror of the killing. And this time they needed that purification more than ever. Maria looked at him.

She came closer to him. They came together. She was close to him. She came yet closer to him. They were as close as they could ever be. Physically they were close. Mentally they were united in a common purpose. They reached a new sense of arousal as the horrors of the night were expelled by the joys of the morning.

Then it was over. Then it was quiet. Then it was peaceful. Now it was over. Now it had never been. It had maybe happened. But it had not mattered. They sat there for a moment. Then Maria kissed him one last time and moved away. He felt the cool air against his nakedness. Then he pulled his clothes back on. Maria did likewise.

"I thought of you last night" she said. "I knew you would be in turmoil and would need me today. I knew you'd be in early."

She smiled and then looked serious again. "She would have killed you if you hadn't shot first. As it was she almost did. Your bullet must have hit her just as she pulled the trigger. She missed you by inches. You had no choice. Is there anything in the papers or did Delaney do a cover up?"

Charles walked to his desk and picked up a tabloid. "Delaney did a spin on the story. It says that there was a gangland attack on a female crime boss. It names Maddy and calls her the head of a drug gang. No mention of the guards. They must have been spirited away."

She looked at him sadly. "It's all coming to an end. Soon we'll all say goodbye. I'll miss you. Will you miss me?"

"I'll miss you. I miss Claire. There are bits of my life that are yours and yours alone. I'll always miss you. But we need to end this and you need to have a life away from it all."

Maria walked over to the door and opened it quietly, "I'll see you later. It's work time now."

Charles sat back at his desk. He felt refreshed and alert. He saw the pad on which he had written "reschedule Tuesday" when Jacqui and he would have to go to New York for her father's funeral. He had died just the previous week and now his Empire was fully in play. Charles worked through the rest of the papers and looked at the notes for his secretary. He thought to check out the position with his father. His hand moved to the phone, he realised someone was at the door.

Three people were there. The Honourable James, flanked by Sir Brian and Lord Dunkillin. They all looked as if they had had a terrible night. Pale and tense, they looked at him with some trepidation.

"What on earth's wrong?" Charles asked innocently. "What are you doing here?"

Charles was genuinely surprised. They were too. "Didn't Jacqui call you?" asked the Honourable James. "She said you were here when I said I needed to speak to you."

"I've been working here," he said. "My phone must have been on the answerphone. But what is it that's so important? Why don't you come in?"

Just at that moment Maria returned. She had noticed them too late. She covered herself quickly. "What's happening? I wasn't expecting anyone here? I've just come over to pick up my spare house keys. I've a friend coming and she'll need them. I left them in my desk."

"We have a meeting. Maria, you can go. We won't need you. Unless you think otherwise, gentlemen," Charles said with a courteous smile.

The Honourable James shook his head.

"Well, gentlemen, I wasn't expecting you. Now you're here, why don't you sit down? Maria, have a good weekend. See you on Monday," said Charles.

Maria left and they were all alone. He looked at the three pale, nervous faces and waited with interest.

"Well, gentlemen," he repeated. "What is it that you want me to hear?"

The Honourable James stood up. He placed his hands behind his back. He took a deep breath and then spoke in an emotional voice.

"The bank has lost a substantial, ahem, a very substantial, sum of money on the derivatives market."

Charles looked at him. His voice was cold, "How much have we lost? When? And how?"

"Most of the trades," he said miserably "were done by Stephens. The valuation model was a fake. We were losing money all the time we thought we were making it. We've lost in London and in the US."

"How much have we lost?" Charles repeated menacingly.

"We've dropped about two point seven billion." Dunkillin looked at the carpet. Sir Brian went redder and redder.

"Pounds?" Charles exclaimed.

"No, dollars," he responded, as if hopeful that Charles would find some comfort from that explanation.

"That'll put us in a loss," added Dunkillin weakly.

"I'd worked that out for myself." Charles snarled at him. "Is that the sum total of the bad news?"

"Of course," said the Honourable James quickly. "We've been through the books with a fine tooth-comb. Nothing else has gone wrong. We can guarantee that."

Charles looked at him angrily. "We need to tell the Bank of England. And we need to tell the Stock Exchange. We'll have to do that before the market opens. There could be a run on the shares. And we could have trouble in the markets. Have you got the figures? Let's work through them?"

Charles turned into a man of action, "Get the company lawyers here. They need to draft a statement. We'll release it late Sunday. Get the number for the Bank of England. They must run a duty desk. We'll reconvene in an hour and I expect the lawyers to be here by then."

Charles dismissed them contemptuously and picked up the phone. He called Jacqui and recounted what had happened. She played along. The call would be recorded and would show how surprised and shocked they were. This was part of their carefully crafted cover up.

The hour passed and the lawyers arrived. Charles briefed them and told them to prepare the announcements. He then got the Bank of England number from the Honourable James. He dismissed everybody and called it. He knew he would get a junior official at the Bank. He answered crisply.

"This is Charles Rossi, Chief Executive of IBE. I need to talk to someone in authority. Now. We will be putting out a statement on Sunday. It could cause problems."

"Have you told the FSA, Sir?" asked the minion. He was referring to the bank regulators.

"No, I felt it more appropriate to talk to you first."

"Can I have a number?"

Charles gave it and he rang off. He thought for a moment. He got up and walked into the Honourable James' office. Dunkillin was there, slumped in a chair. Sir Brian was standing by the window.

He addressed the Honourable James. "We need a report on the dealings, both here and in New York. As Lord Dunkillin and Sir Brian had joint responsibility for the treasury area because of their alleged expertise, they could write the report. It may, though, be better if they co-operate with the auditors and we get them to do the work. Do you have an emergency number?"

The Honourable James shook his head, "But I know their senior partner. I have his home number."

"Then call him." The Honourable James did not react to the evident contempt in the tone. He did not complain about the instructions he was given. He just called. He spoke for a moment and then handed the phone to Charles.

"I need a team of people around. I need experts in treasury and especially derivatives. We have a problem. In fact, we have a dreadful problem. I need an initial report by Sunday night and a full report as soon as possible thereafter."

The auditor knew better than to ask more questions. His people would soon take over. He would be there too. He agreed that the Honourable James would instruct him. Charles suspected he himself would have to be with the Bank of England. Then another thought struck him. He decided to step up the pressure. He knew they hadn't told him everything. Some of the bad debts had already come home. But they had said nothing about them.

"Oh, and by the way, I want a special extra audit of the whole treasury and credit area to be undertaken from next Monday. The remit will be simple. I want a full report on all exposures of the bank. And I want it fast. And I want it to be for me, personally. "

The auditor agreed. Charles left and returned to his office. The phone rang. A meeting between the bank and one of the regulators was scheduled for midday. Charles would present himself at the front door. They would be waiting for him.

At noon, he stood outside the heavy metal door of the Bank of England. The door opened and he was ushered into a small gap between the outer door and an inner one. The outer door closed with a clang. Immediately after the inner one opened and he was standing in the spacious lobby of the elegant old building. Ahead of him was the green strip of garden.

A young man in a crumpled suit approached him. "Mr Rossi, please would you come this way. One of our assistant directors will see you now."

They walked upstairs and the young man ushered Charles unctuously into the office. It was a cross between a railway waiting room and an academic's study. Books were untidily piled into a cabinet at one end. The table was old and highly polished. The heavy wood desk was covered in stained leather, contrasting with the plastic PC that stood there, unblinking and unloved.

Once again, Charles was received with extreme courtesy. But the look was apprehensive. A bank chief executive only calls on the central bank on a Saturday if he is the bearer of some pretty dire news. Charles didn't wait for the question.

"Let me put you in the picture. Before the Far East opens at nine p.m. tomorrow, IBE has to make an announcement. We have incurred material losses as a result of illicit trading. I was only advised this morning. I would also note, for your ears only, that I suspect my Chairman and two of the executive directors have been withholding vital information from me."

Charles stopped and let the devastating words take their effect. The Bank official looked at him, still apprehensive, and then asked, "Can you quantify the loss?"

"I am told that it's two point seven billion dollars. I called the auditors in this morning. They will also audit the credit and other key risk areas. I have to say our Chairman assures me that the loss is no greater than this. Lord Dunkillin and Sir Brian have joint line responsibility for the treasury area. They assure me nothing else has gone wrong."

"But," said the central banker thoughtfully, "You have no confidence in their judgement?"

Charles looked at him and raised his eyebrows, "Would you in my place?"

He didn't answer. He was not one of the old school-tie brigade. Charles suspected he was worried of the effect of the announcement.

"We can withstand the likely loss of liquidity through to Wednesday. Then we could have a credit crunch. We have a lot of short dated loans up for renewal. If we find people won't renew, we'll be in a liquidity crisis. On Monday and Tuesday we're all right. We have lots of cash coming back to us," explained Charles.

"What about the US?"

"I thought it better to talk to you. I can get our US chief executive to talk to the Fed. Or would you prefer to?"

"He'll have to talk to them. But let us get in touch first. I'll need to talk to the Governor."

Charles was surprised. So, in cases like this, even the Governor had to work weekends. And he would not realise that, by next weekend, things were bound to get worse. Once the auditors found all the bad debts, the real fireworks would start.

"I've called in the lawyers. They'll draft a statement. We need to advise the Stock Exchange, too."

The central banker nodded, "Can we see the statement before it's released?"

"Certainly, I'll make sure you do."

"Are you in charge?"

"I will be calling a board meeting later today. I'll speak to the US based directors around one. They should be at home."

This time, the central banker grinned for the first time, "Yes, they're a bit long in the tooth to play away from home."

Charles grinned back. It was useful to have soul mates at this time. "I guess so. They're hardly spring chickens."

"All right," the central banker said. "I'll put my people in the picture. Then we should talk again. We need to use a landline. Where can I catch you?"

"I'll be in the office for the moment. The direct line's on the card." Charles wrote another number. "That's the one at home. We'll be in."

"What will you do?" he queried.

"We would be solvent on a hit of two point seven billion. We are heading for a two billion-dollar profit this year. I only hope that I have all the bad news. In that case, other than with help in the short term, this will be a two or three week wonder. Not on the stock market, but definitely on the money markets."

"What if you discover more problems?" the central banker asked, as his training clicked in and he thought of the worst possible scenarios.

Charles could hardly tell him that he knew there would be many more problems. So he adopted the high ground. "If there is an issue of needing more capital, I can manage it. We can inject money. Short term, I would need help. If there is more bad news and nobody wants to lend to us, there's nothing I can do. We'd hit the rocks. But I am assured this is not the case and we'll have a first cut from the auditors over the next week."

The official looked at him with relief. Charles was obviously on the side of the angels as far as he was concerned. Charles couldn't tell him that he knew the Di Maglio guarantee would bail out the bank and stop it becoming insolvent, although its value would be severely weakened as a result of the frauds.

And why should they worry in any event? They had made their billions when they had sold the bank at an inflated price and when they had initiated their different frauds. As for the bit of the bank they still held, they were not going to lose money on that, irrespective of what happened, thanks to his father's expert trading and Jacqui's fraudulent manipulation of their share register.

Charles and the central banker talked a bit more but about nothing of consequence. He gave Charles his card and said that he would act as his contact point for the weekend. "I'll be here all the time," he said ruefully. "I can hardly leave in the circumstances."

Charles left the same way he arrived. He walked to the bank and headed up to the top floor. The Honourable James rushed out to him. "How did it go?" he asked nervously.

Charles looked at him coldly. "I hardly sung your praises. I told them of the problem. I'm in charge. I'll talk to them from now on."

"Do you want my resignation?" he asked, as if that was what a gentleman would do.

"Fuck you. No. I need you, Dunkillin and Sir Brian here. Not today. You can bugger off now as far as I'm concerned. But you'll be here till we sort this out. And don't try to be too clever."

"I don't like your tone," he said pompously. "I could resign."

Charles looked at him with contempt. "Get this in your thick skull. And make sure that your pals understand it too. You do as I say. We get IBE out of this shit. And if we don't you could be in it up to your precious aristocratic necks.

I don't care if you end up in prison. Eton, the Guards and some high security jail may worry you as a CV but it doesn't me. This is my company. This is my money. And you've screwed me. You've done it either through incompetence or through something worse. You're all out, but when I say so.

And I wouldn't try anything. Your names are shit now. Your reputations are worthless. The only thing between you and prison is my money. If I bail out the bank, you lot should be OK. If not, say goodbye to the grouse moors and all the other crap that turns you on."

With that Charles turned away from him and went into his office. This would put them all on edge and that was what he wanted. They were already close to panic and could even top themselves. That would compound their guilt. Charles, though, didn't need that. Either way they were in deep trouble. And he was happy to allow them to decide how they wanted the future to be.

The rest of the day was spent monitoring the auditors' work and sorting out issues with the lawyers. He also called his father and put him in the picture. In reality, he was alerting him so that he could start to buy back the shares once markets opened on Monday.

At 1pm, he called New York. McGarth, of course, knew all about the losses. He had the bulk of them on his own balance sheet. Charles recounted the meeting at the Bank of England. He told him to stand by to call the Fed.

His last call was to Giovanni. He was not surprised as he had been party to the whole plan, but he was concerned over the timing. He wondered if they would be in New York for the funeral. Charles confirmed they would. He planned to fly out on Tuesday morning and then back again overnight for Wednesday. Giovanni said that he would stand by for the inevitable board meeting that night or on Sunday.

Charles returned to his desk and waited for more news. The Bank of England called. They agreed to meet on Sunday morning at 10am. By then Charles would have a draft of the lawyers' paper. The auditors would be unlikely to give any information by then. McGarth would have seen the Fed.

Charles was alone in the office. He called Jacqui and said he would be coming home. There was no point in staying any longer. The die was cast. The final act had begun.

Once back home, they took stock. They did it in the war room where they had watched the set up at the airfield. It was Jacqui who recapped the position, while Charles sought to put it into a sort of schedule.

"The bank is now in play," she said. "The auditors will uncover some of the phoney loans next week. It'll take them a bit of time to sort out the exact position. But the bank will go downhill now."

"Yes. But at some time I'll call Sir Piers at Associated and make them bid for the company. It will be child's play to get them to bid for the bank. We still have the whip hand there and they're hardly going to want us to leak the dirt we have on them to the public. After all, the market in bank stocks is going to be nervous; any tainted bank would be at risk. And boy would they be tainted if we leaked all the dirt we have and the stuff we have fabricated about them!"

Jacqui laughed mockingly, "But most of what we have on them is phoney."

"I know. But some is true. And they will be scared witless about the bits that are true. They'll believe the rest and think they were ill-informed or unaware."

Jacqui nodded, "Stupid of them to do those insider trades. That would put them in prison. But the falsification of the letters and all that rubbish about murder and blackmail is hard to believe." Then she looked pensive, "The Brits here are so crazy. They make lousy criminals. And they are so easy to manipulate. At least the old guard is. The new lot are more professional. They'll be tougher."

"Perhaps," laughed Charles. "But so will we be. That's if we head back this way."

"The gang warfare is going to start soon. The funeral could be a problem," said Jacqui reflectively. "I guess that the prostitution and extortion boys will try to make a deal. They'll realise that the drug's side is in for a tough time. We could sell to them but the price will be bad."

Charles shrugged his shoulders. "Who cares? We just need to get out. In any event we will be using any money we get from the drug side to bail out the bank. So it won't really be ours."

Don't assume your father has left the money to your mother without strings attached. He thought that you would be annoyed and hurt by her getting the money, but I bet it's in trust or something and that the kids are also beneficiaries. Still, there won't be anything left after the bank is bailed out through his guarantee."

Jacqui was not overly concerned, "Once the guarantee comes to light, and that'll be soon enough, we'll get ourselves named as executors to help the bank. What'll your father do?" she asked.

"He'll buy back the shares he sold and he'll manage to keep out of sight of the surveillance guys in the markets. There'll be so much activity that his will be lost in the sheer volume. All the hedge funds will seek to make a play. Don't forget that you will need to adjust the register. But the details won't be available before Friday or the following week. So we need to make sure that nobody tries to take a print out of the register. Go into the programmes as we planned and stop that happening."

She nodded, "Do we have anything else to do?"

"Not that I can think of. We need to keep alert. The next weeks are going to be tough. We need to see that nothing goes wrong."

"And then we head out for the island. Douglas will have sorted that all out. It isn't long now? Nothing can go wrong, can it?" she asked nervously.

"Everything could go wrong. That's why we have to be careful. We've set your father's mob up against two of the vilest Mafia bosses in the world. Delaney will have it in for us. The establishment will look to protect their own. The Fed and the Bank of England will write their own agenda. They're in it up to their necks, too, and they are going to have to come out smelling of roses. And then we have our fall guys. They'll try to find someone to blame."

"We stay together. We'll get through. But just let's be careful."

The next day went to plan. The auditors were working and couldn't really tell them anything new. They knew they were up to their necks in it. They would have to alert their insurers that there could be a huge claim on them. They were gloomy, even by their normal standards.

The lawyers prepared the announcement. They talked to the Fed in New York and the Bank of England. The board meeting was strained. Giovanni grabbed the high moral ground and made sure that the establishment figures on the board knew what he apparently thought of them. And his language was more fitting of a mafia man than a banker. The targets of his apparent wrath just sat in shock as they saw their worlds crumble before them. Jacqui wore a pained look and didn't even greet them on their arrival. This was not a happy team. But Charles got what he wanted. They even found that there was no humble pie to eat. They were lost in a vacuum that marked the end of their lives, as they knew them.

They released the announcement in time for the evening news bulletins. They stressed the soundness of the company. They stressed this appeared to be a one off. Charles liked the announcement. It left the door open to the next one they would undoubtedly make, the one that would announce a further five billion of losses. They had agreed with the Stock Exchange that their shares would continue to trade the next Monday. There was no point in suspending them. In any event, they wanted to be able to buy back the ones they had sold.

On the Monday the share price crumbled. Everybody was a seller. It fell from twenty seven to eighteen dollars. From eighteen dollars it fell to ten and then to six. The volumes were incredible. Jack Ryder passed the message that he'd bought back half his position at a twelve-dollar a share profit. He would alert them as he bought more.

The next morning they flew to America and prepared for the funeral. Jacqui's fears were ill founded. The funeral was a quiet affair. Mind you, few would have wanted to have dinner with many of the guests. Police photographers updated their records outside the church. Thuggish looking old men vied with each other to show grief. The church was dignified. The priests talked of heaven. But the congregation thought of the hellish battles to come. They were as close to mourning as night is to day. The service was an excuse for forging alliances as they all prepared themselves for the gang warfare to come.

After the service, Charles and Jacqui met at the lawyers. They had a will. Di Maglio had re-written it just two months back. He had re-made it after they had taken the Empire from him. He left all his wealth to his nephews and not Jacqui's mother. Charles found that amusing and somewhat ironic. There was even an element of poetic justice in it all. There were seven nephews. They included his brother, Aldo's, son. But they also included some nephews from two brothers-in-law, in whose deaths Di Maglio had allegedly played a part. The poor guys would think themselves rich. Charles only hoped they didn't start spending the money before it was taken away.

That evening, it was back to England. Charles and Jacqui stretched out side by side in their beds, as the plane winged its way back to Heathrow and its sombre early morning welcome. Wednesday and Thursday went more quietly. The share price recovered to ten dollars. Then the auditors came to see Charles. They looked grim, but then auditors often do. He waited for them to tell him their tale of woe and wondered how much they would have uncovered.

He looked at the senior man. He would be the one who led the way. He was incredibly grey. His hair was grey. His suit was charcoal grey. His tie was blue grey. And his pallid face was tinged with grey.

"We believe," said the senior man, "that the losses from derivatives in your treasury area are as you have been advised. It was simple. The prices made were wrong and the valuations used were wrong. It was a computer error. It was as simple as that."

"Rubbish," Charles exclaimed sharply, for he didn't want the great and the good to get off. "There was gross negligence on the part of my senior colleagues. They should have checked out why we always won the business against the competition. Everyone knows that's a danger sign."

The auditors said nothing. "I want your professional opinion on that issue and formally in writing as part of your report," Charles added. The auditors were caught. They could hardly exonerate Dunkillin and Sir Brian. And that was Charles' aim. And it also begged the question of their failure to spot the strange pattern of trading during their audits. Their report would make interesting reading, for it could boomerang back on them.

"But we have more bad news, I'm afraid," said the grey auditor. "There appears to have been a series of bad loans made. They are very bad ones. There's a hint of fraud too. We need to examine more. But it looks bad."

"Will we need to make more provisions?" asked Charles. He wondered what they would reveal.

"No doubt," replied the grey one wringing his hands in concern.

"What level of bad debt do you expect?"

"It will be at least three billion, possibly five or more. We need another week or so to be certain."

Charles played astonished, "Is it all a write off?"

"We know three billion is a bad debt. One loan especially worries us. It was for a billion and it looks like a fraud involving the Honourable James' son."

"A billion," Charles exclaimed in mock horror.

The grey auditor nodded miserably, "Here's the schedule of known bad loans. Here's another schedule of suspicious loans that we need to investigate further. They make another two billion."

Charles buried his face in his hands as if in despair. He then looked up, "I need to call a board meeting and I need to talk to the lawyers. I need you there to explain your findings. The rest had better get back to work. I leave it to you to bring in more people if that will accelerate things."

Charles called Maria to his office and told her to get the US on line and ready for a board meeting. He knew that the great and the good were unaware of these latest events. It would be interesting announcing it to them. He then called the Bank of England and told them the news. He also informed the Fed. The regulators were in a state of near panic now. They could foresee a run on banks. This was their worse nightmares coming true.

"Can you guarantee that you can keep the bank afloat?" asked the Fed.

"Not till I know the extent of the losses. But we should be helped by the guarantee that Di Maglio gave in the sale document. I have to assume that his estate will not be pillaged in the meantime. I'll ask our lawyers if we can do anything to protect us against such an event."

"What do you mean?" asked the regulator. He had had no involvement in the sale arrangements and, therefore, knew nothing about the dreaded page thirty-three.

"Di Maglio gave a guarantee. His estate will ensure that no US depositor loses out."

Charles could almost hear the whoop of delight from the Fed regulator. He could almost visualise him scurrying from his office to unearth the wonder document. Of course, they did not know yet that they would hit further problems on the fund side. But that was a problem still to come.

The board meeting was brief. Charles advised the Honourable James, Lord Dunkillin and Sir Brian that he expected their undated resignations on his desk within ten minutes. They would be suspended, pending clarification of their role in the different fiascos. In the US, he did the same with McGarth and the Honourable James' son. Giovanni took over the reins in the US. Charles became acting chairman in the UK and he brought the senior partners of their legal advisers and auditors onto the board as a temporary emergency measure.

The lawyers talked to the Stock Exchange. They would issue a statement and Charles agreed that he would be willing to loan up to five billion to the bank, although he knew that would, in reality, never need to happen. That promise would allow them to carry on trading, but it hardly solved their problems. The shares could only fall.

They made the announcement at the close of business in New York. The following day, their shares hit six dollars again in panic trading. Jack Ryder called and told him he had closed out all the sales. His average price had been ten dollars. That meant twelve to thirteen dollars a share profit after expenses. On this sideline, alone, they had made a cool billion and a half profit.

And Charles knew his father would have been taking advantage of his insider knowledge to trade in other shares. And, better still, the stock markets were crumbling on the news of the losses and frauds. Charles would have been surprised if they hadn't made another few hundred million through that route.

The weekend was a time to draw breath. But, on Sunday, the news of the poor investments of the US funds broke. The bank had lent money to companies without substance. The investment managers had bought shares in those companies. The companies had defaulted as the money they had borrowed was spirited out of them. The shares were worthless. They said lightning never struck twice. But they had had three major strikes. They had been hit with scandals around derivatives, the loans and now the US funds. Their share price was at half the issue price. The newspapers were all questioning whether they would survive. A run on the bank was inevitable.

Once again Charles found himself in the hallowed portals of the Bank of England. This time they had an open line with the Fed in New York. They had established that Di Maglio's accounts held just five billion dollars in all. That was a bit less than they had expected. But, at least, it was almost all readily available in cash, deposits or federal funds. Paradoxically, his investments had been as conservative as his business was unorthodox.

The Fed would seize the funds on their behalf the next day and use them to bail out the US bank. The terms of the guarantee Charles had written were so all-embracing that they could use it for anything. They agreed the money would buy back some of the funds. The prices would be depressed, as the defaulting companies held were valued at zero. That way the investors would get at least some money back. Their confidence was important as most investors were also depositors. And if the depositors withdrew their money, all hell would break loose.

It was agreed that they would pay two billion to investors as compensation for some of their losses. That would buy them some gratitude from their richest clients in any case. But the bulk of the money had to go to shore up the bank. They would explain the guarantee to the world at large. That would help confidence but not re-establish it.

And the Di Maglio estate would never see the proceeds of the scam. Indeed the beneficiaries would never know of it. The shares in IBE had all been placed in trust; most had since been sold to the public and the rest would be worth whatever they got from Associated. All in all, a tidy sum. Juliet and baby Claire were already billionaires.

As for Di Maglio's share in the proceeds of the frauds, the estate also got precisely nothing. As the money had not been distributed at the time of his death, under the agreement, Charles and the other conspirators shared his take. And that meant the bulk went to Jacqui, Charles and his family, with a small balance to Giovanni and Maria. Those two would be seriously rich and neither, not even Giovanni, would want to do anything to alter that.

The UK side could still bring them down. So they came to an agreement after a long night of haggling. Charles stretched out the negotiations on purpose. He was not concerned, he planned to snare his white knight the next day. And that white knight, a company that would really bail out IBE, would be Associated.

So he agreed to deposit five billion dollars next day in the Bank of England to support the UK end of the bank. They all felt this would calm the market. Charles also told them that he would discuss a merger with different people in the City. He left them at 4am. They saw him as a man of integrity. Little did they know how far from the truth that actually was.

The next day the press coverage was universally kind to him. Little was said of the suspended directors for fear of legal action. But the innuendoes were in all the reporting. The rumours spread like wildfire over the City. Their reputations were in tatters. Their guilt was proven before their crimes were known. Charles and Jacqui were the honest victims. They had ploughed their proceeds from the share sale back into the bank to protect the depositors. The press, the politicians and all the pseudo-experts who were wheeled out at times like this, were totally fooled. They all pronounced if more people behaved like them, the City would be a far better place.

One person who despised the deification of Charles and Jacqui was Sir Piers Rupert Jones. He was the head of Associated. He did not know that Jack Ryder was Charles' father, but he knew him as one of his associates. And there was a history of animosity between them. They had forced him to pay over the odds when he acquired United Bank of Europe some years back, and there had been several other reasons for his antipathy towards Charles. But at 8am Charles was back in the office and on the phone to Sir Piers. He was his usual curt self but agreed to see him. They would meet later that day.

It was 11am when Charles appeared at the door of Associated. Its gleaming tower was just a three-minute walk from their office. Maria accompanied him in her role as his personal assistant. He had brought her along to make Sir Piers feel awkward. Women in business suits always made him uneasy.

The morning had been better than he expected. The run at the bank had been manageable. They had lost around a quarter of a billion of deposits. The share price had been volatile and was now stuck at a miserable eight dollars. The auditors had also advised that they would complete their work by the end of the week. Charles would have a definitive report on all loans by the weekend.

Sir Piers walked in. He didn't offer to shake hands. He nodded at Charles without moving a facial muscle. He ignored Maria. She promptly sat back and crossed her legs. This served to make him more anxious.

Charles looked at him with amusement. He saw a patrician figure. He saw the arrogance of power, the absence of intellect, the overwhelming and misplaced self-confidence.

"Sir Piers, I would like you to bid for IBE. At eight dollars a share, it's a snip."

He looked at Charles as if he were barking mad, "I wouldn't touch that Mafia riddled money shop with a barge pole. I can't even think of it as a bank."

"That's unfortunate," Charles said. "We'll just have to adopt plan B then."

Maria opened her mouth in delight. She seemed overjoyed, "I told you he'd say that. Plan B it is then."

"And what is Plan B?" asked Sir Piers haughtily.

Charles looked at him, "Plan B is summarised on this piece of paper."

He passed the paper to him. It was a schedule. It read like a death sentence to Sir Piers. The papers to be issued were damning to the extreme. They were copies of statements relating to insider trading by him and associates. They were documents alleging his involvement in a murder a year or so back. And there were others showing his bank had been used for major money laundering exercises. The first was a genuine set of documents. The second set was all-fake. But it was impossible to prove that. And the third was genuine, although nobody would ever know the provenance of the money laundering. How could Sir Piers realise that he was sitting opposite one of the world's experts at such corrupt games?

"This will destroy us," he gasped. He knew about some of the documents. Others were unknown to him. "The market's nervous already after your problems. This will be a killer blow."

"Your choice," Charles responded brutally. Maria grinned.

"Is it to be an agreed bid?"

"It'll be an agreed one. The Di Maglio guarantees remain but my undertakings to the Bank of England and my support is released."

"Your board?" he queried.

"No problem. What about yours?"

"I can persuade them. Eight dollars a share as long as the bad debt position is clarified by the auditors."

"That'll be done at the end of the week."

"But I don't bid for your shares. They are just cancelled."

Charles laughed, "Good try, but not accepted. You pay us too."

"How much will it cost us and what capital injection is needed?"

"At eight dollars a share, the company is valued at ten billion dollars. The US will be recapitalised through the Di Maglio guarantee but the UK side will need a capital injection of around two billion. But, once you are in the driving seat, the companies should be able to generate over a billion a year. So it would be money well spent."

"I'll decide that," he retorted. "We get in touch at the weekend. Bring your auditors and other advisers."

"I agree."

"And the originals of the papers," he added hastily.

"No. They will go to a mutually acceptable trusted third party and be given to you when the deal completes. I don't trust your type. Not after all I have had to take from your trio of pals at IBE."

He shrugged his shoulders, "I'll get someone to tell you where to meet."

"Will you tell the regulators?" Charles asked.

"Not till it's agreed."

"We'll keep quiet as well."

With that they left. "Is it in the bag?" asked Maria.

"Definitely. He'll buy. First, it's not a bad deal. Not a snip, but it appears reasonable. And second, he knows we'll release the papers. And that scares him witless."

The week continued. The depositors were calm. Some withdrew funds but there was no need for any panic. It was unreal. Everything was so quiet. It was almost business as usual. That was just as well, as it was now the turn of the evil Empire to grab their attention.

CHAPTER TWENTY-FOUR

Santa Barbara, California, is a strange place for the start of a Mafia war but there it started. Giorgio Baroneli, nicknamed George the Baron, had been Maddy's second in command. As the news of Maddy's death filtered through, Charles sent a message to make him the new boss of the drugs Empire. The prostitution and extortion side would report to Paul Castell. Both were in the classical tradition of Di Maglio's people, but they were new and untested. It was wise to have new hands in charge of an Empire that was about to collapse.

Baroneli had worked for Di Maglio all his life. He had been a killer, an enforcer, and a drug runner and, latterly, as one of the chiefs of the drugs' division. He had boasted to Maddy that his speciality was garrotting. Apparently, he took great pleasure and pride in his ability to cause pain to his victims. He deserved to die.

Castell had lost an eye in a fight and wore a black patch over the vacant socket. He thought it made him look attractive. He was a twice-accused rapist. And his boast, apparently, was that it would have been more often, but the victims usually ended up dead. He had neither a wife nor a family but a series of girls, sometimes under age runaways, who stayed with him before he put them out to work in one of his streets or hotels.

The charming duo were in Santa Barbara, mingling with the holidaymakers. They were there because Castell's latest conquest, a sixteen-year-old called Jancie, came from Chicago. This was her first trip to California and she had longed to see the Pacific. Baroneli had a third wife and two children aged eleven and twelve. He was holidaying. Baroneli wanted to talk to Castell about the hit in Canada. The loss of trusted men in that fight had been a problem. Castell saw it as an opportunity to infiltrate Baroneli's area with his own men. He was now the stronger. It was perhaps the first time that this had been the case. For drugs had always been the money-spinner.

Both men had been at the funeral on Tuesday, but this weekend was their first chance to make a deal. When Charles heard of the meeting, he was sure that the deal involved him. They would have seen the death of

Di Maglio and Charles' reputed indifference towards the Empire as a wonderful chance to take over the operation. Unfortunately, neither, quite rightly, would really trust the other, and that hardly bode well for any agreement.

So suspicion ruled on both sides. But, to any spectator, all seemed sweetness and light as the two men walked along the street. It was 10am and not even the shops were open. They had decided to walk along to the seafront to talk, well away from inquisitive ears and possible bugs in the walls. They strolled up the broad esplanade with their bodyguards, relaxed as Santa Barbara was seen as a safe haven.

He was tall and dark, with wild Slavonic features. From the description, he must have been one of the Russians. As he walked up towards the two men, he drew a gun and calmly shot Baroneli in the head.

Castell used his split second of opportunity to save himself, ducking away and pushing his girlfriend at the gunmen. Once again, the gun blasted and the girl fell backwards. For a moment, she seemed to look at the red stain spreading over her dress. Then her face contorted into shock and she screamed. It was a sharp piercing scream that continued as she fell onto the pavement. But that scream shook the gunman, and his hesitation was his downfall. Castell fired three times. The man fell dead as the bullets punched into his stomach and his chest.

The scene was pandemonium. Baroneli's wife and kids started to scream as the girl collapsed into her final paroxysms of torment and died. The bodyguards joined Castell. They ignored the screaming woman and the terrified kids. A few passers-by approached but scattered as the men drew their guns and fired into the air. A man with a surfboard ran up to the scene. One of the guards shot in his direction. He stopped, but a large track suited woman, behind him, fell down clutching her stomach. She would be the first totally innocent victim in the vicious war that had now started. And she wouldn't be the last.

"We get the fuck out of here," called Castell. "Let's move before the cops get hold of us."

They hurried down the street. The bodyguards had their guns drawn. One man tried to secretly video them as they passed. The guard closest to him pulled the camera from his grasp and threw it to the ground. A well-delivered kick smashed it open. Another caught the man on his shins, the third in his stomach. He crumpled to the ground in agony. Nobody else tried to video them after that

They had no need to run to the car park. Two cars crashed through the sea front car park barriers and approached them at speed, ignoring shouts to stop. The back-up, as usual, was in place. They screeched to a halt. Castell jumped into the first. The guards jumped into the second and the mini convoy sped away towards the freeway. Their lawyers would argue the case and ensure that Castell was not troubled by the problems that they had left behind.

As the news came through, Charles ordered a meeting of the heads of the drugs business. He also ordered one later that night for prostitution and extortion. He would link into both remotely from London by videophone. They needed action. And the action he was planning was totally different from the action they would expect.

Charles called Delaney and told him where the first meeting would be. In four hours time, seven of the remaining top ten Drugs executives would be in the Westin St Frances in San Francisco. The video conference call would be set up there in one of the meeting rooms. It was deemed safer and more private. Charles had said he didn't want the authorities to see the men gathering. They could achieve anonymity in the Westin with groups of sales and other executives on their training or other indoctrination courses.

Delaney was given the time and did the necessary. They waited for news. 7pm came in London and Charles sat in front of the camera and waited. Out of sight but close to the monitor was Maria. Moments later she was joined by Jacqui. The seven men entered the room. They congregated around the table.

Guards would be outside but they would not be able to prevent what would happen next. At 7pm precisely, Charles called the meeting to order. The video camera in San Francisco wheeled round the table, activated the link with London and detonated the explosives. The blast tore through the room killing and maiming. Moments later the doors burst open as men swarmed around. Their drawn guns were pointless. The FBI had left long before.

Charles played the game and called for information. One of the men who had been round the table called back. "There are three or four dead. Two are badly injured. The rest of us are OK. Boss, who could have done this? Who knew?"

Charles looked worried, "Castell knew. I wanted him to pull his men together for a similar meeting later. The idea was to ensure everything was under control and decide strategy."

But it was clear that strategy was now never going to be on the agenda. The murders began that evening. By nightfall, there had been attack after attack. The drugs boys attacked the prostitution chiefs. Then they in turn counter-attacked. Other Mafia bosses joined in as they sensed the Empire was disintegrating.

The authorities were active. They added to the chaos and the death toll. In the twenty four hours that were known as the end of the Di Maglios, seventy two people were killed, of whom sixty one were known Mafia. America's gangland was being torn apart. It destroyed itself, helped by the FBI. Nobody knew where the intelligence came from. In reality, it came from Charles, via Delaney. But he was careful that it could never be traced back to him.

Charles flew out to New York to see the lawyers. Jacqui came too. This was a calculated risk as it was an ideal opportunity for a Mafia hit. As it was, they were safe. They kept out of the city and took a helicopter to the meetings.

Jacqui was cool and calm. She wondered if she should not mourn her father, but she didn't. That wasn't out of cruelty. He had destroyed her affection for him over years. He was only useful now for the help he would give them in death.

In the US, they appointed a new head for the casinos and the hotels, and added the legitimate drug and pharmacy operations to that. He was new to the whole organisation but they had been tracking him already for some time. The short-term package and the golden handshake on its successful completion dispelled his concerns and he signed up immediately. Lawyers helped him. For his role would be to sell the cocktail of businesses and help add to the amount available for the bank depositors, the investment fund holders and others.

They told the different Di Maglio criminal groups they could take over their operations; Charles and Jacqui said they just wanted out. There was a lull in the violence but then it broke out with renewed viciousness. The freedom given to gang members to seize their operations led to another outbreak of fighting. This time it spread from internal battles to outright warfare among the different Mafia groups.

They fought in New York in the East, San Francisco in the West and most major cities in between. They all espoused violence as gang attacked gang. Greed, old scores, traditional enmity all came to the fore. The fighting was vicious. The Mafia was weakened. Their old order was coming to an end. They awaited the inevitable new order that would take charge of the disorder and run the remnants of their orgy of destruction back to profit and greater glory. Drug shortages on the streets would mean higher prices. Higher prices would mean higher profits.

Charles and Jacqui knew they would have done little but cause a blip in the level of power exercised by the evil men of the global underworld. They hadn't taken charge of the Empire. They had abandoned the world of real evil. But the world of evil did not know that they were behind all its problems.

If the evil men of crime ever sought to attribute blame to them, then it was for their amateurism. They would see Charles and Jacqui as having been incapable of following in the footsteps of the great Di Maglio. They thought they were too honest. They had, in their mind, too many scruples. They would blame Di Maglio for failing to have the right successor.

But Charles and Jacqui were part of another world. They had managed to exit from the world of crime that Di Maglio had created. Maria also watched its demise with a lack of concern that surprised them. She seemed now to have reconciled herself to the end of her association with that evil world. She would pick up her fortune and find a new life.

Charles was astounded at the speed of destruction. By the end of the week it was apparent they need have no further role in it. A few days after Di Maglio's funeral, his Empire had moved almost totally to self-destruct. Now it was well and truly in the final throes of that process. It had taken Di Maglio a lifetime to build. It took them a lot of planning, a mass of intrigue, but then only a week or so to destroy.

If destroy was the right word for something that would automatically come back from the brink in a moderately different form. Evil destroyed would be metamorphosed into a new order of evil reformed. Di Maglio was dead. The Don had gone. Long live the Don. Would it take a week, a month or a year? The FBI struck for as long as they could but, by the end of that week, their information was no longer reliable. At the end of the second, they were spectators rather than agitators.

And as the weekend approached, Charles and Jacqui waited for the meeting with the auditors and the announcements they would make about IBE. Giovanni called, he suspected, perhaps he knew, but he was wise. He was an outsider and needed to close the IBE episode. Then he would retire a wealthy man. And a silent one, he would see no value in sharing his fears. One word and he was dead. He would be dead either by the hand of the FBI or Charles. And Giovanni would only do things for money. That was their insurance.

The day of reckoning came. The auditors gathered and made their presentation. All foreign exchange and derivative positions had been closed out. The loss was two point eight billion. Bad and non-performing loans for a total value of five point eight billion had been identified. They had also pinpointed a common feature on most of the bad loans. And that common feature was three noble directors and their families.

"Quite simply," said the solemn grey auditor, "you appear to have been fleeced by the very people meant to engender confidence in the company. It is apparent that Sir Brian, Lord Dunkillin and the Honourable James have been involved in some of the lamentable losses the bank has incurred. McGarth also appears to have been brought into a systematic campaign of embezzlement. Other members of their families were involved. Half the capital of the company has been lost. In order to continue operations the bank needs another six to eight billion dollars."

Later, the auditor would remark on Charles' coolness. He would marvel at his commitment to save the bank. And that was reality, for they still had a few billion tied up in it. Charles responded to the auditor's analysis, "The Di Maglio cash or bonds are worth around five billion and will cover much of that. We still, though, need the money we want to pay to investors in our funds. There remain businesses in Di Maglio's estate worth between three and four billion dollars and that gives us eight to nine billion in total. How much of the losses are attributable to the US?"

"Your total loss is eight point six. Six point four are out of the US banks. They were being fleeced before you acquired them. One suspects by Mr Di Maglio. That made some of the tracking difficult."

"Well, the cash is immediately available," Charles reminded him.

"You need at least the six billion plus of cash in the US or the bank fails. There will be a run on it. It needs to have the strong capital base."

Charles thought. Then he suggested, "I could make a bid for all the Di Maglio businesses. The estimated value of the companies for sale is three to four billion. I'll bid three point five for the companies and take a risk on selling out. That will give you the six point five billion for the US bank and another two billion for investors."

The grey auditor nodded approvingly, "When can you arrange the sale?"

The auditor was eager. That was no wonder. He had a vested interest. If the sale went ahead and the losses could be covered by the guarantee, then his firm would not have to make a claim under their insurance. He almost breathed a sigh of relief. He looked as if he were praying quietly to whatever God his noble profession supported.

Meanwhile Charles turned to the lawyers.

The US one said sombrely, "We need to get a judgement. I could arrange an emergency session. But the court will want a guarantee against conflicting claims on the estate."

Charles doubted that anyone else had priority. He knew Di Maglio never took credit outside his banks. And the guarantee in their sale agreement had been tightly worded. Nobody could contest it.

"Can I get the IBE Group banks to waive any further claims on the Di Maglio guarantee?"

They nodded.

Charles told them to go ahead, "Then get the judges to rule whatever you need. Get the bank to sign the affidavit. And I'll give a personal guarantee to buy out the businesses at three billion five. But this should extinguish also the need for the deposits I made earlier."

"You could reduce them to two billion and restrict them to the UK based businesses," said the grey auditor. "But the bad debts there mean that it will be needed at that level. And we need the money fast, both in the US and in London."

"If I can get the agreements, I can put up the cash Monday morning. I can authorise the transfer start of business in Europe. So they'll be waiting well before New York opens."

The auditors and lawyers conferred. They then agreed. Charles would stand by. But the die was set. The legal hearings would be started. They had a weekend deadline. Charles was unconcerned by the money he would have to put up. That would put him in good light once again. The sanctification of Charles Rossi would continue. The US banks would not have claims on them. And he knew enough about the Di Maglio world to know that his nephews would not fight any court battle, for fear of what could be discovered about the rest of their nefarious activities.

Charles knew they would get their money back. He was sure that the businesses he would acquire from the Di Maglio estate would be worth four or five billion on a relaxed sale timetable. The three to four billion was an estimate on the base of a fire sale. Jacqui would get some inheritance from her father's estate after all.

As for his deposits in IBE, they would revert to him once Associated took over the bank.

Against the grim background of gang warfare, they waited that weekend for the courts to decide. The banks all set up their paperwork. The money was pinpointed. They waited for the two key judgements. The court in the US, considering their purchase of the Di Maglio businesses, would be the first judgement. The Fed and Bank of England would then judge on the solvency of the banks after the cash infusions. If they got positive judgements, they would be able to announce the saving of the IBE on Sunday, well before any possible run on its operations. And Charles had a meeting with Sir Piers on Monday afternoon. It was scheduled for after his board meeting. He was confident that the bid would take place.

Charles ran over the arrangements with his father. He agreed all the actions and the logic of the decisions. Charles explained them to Jacqui. She arranged a meeting of the survivors of the London board-room meeting of the previous year.

There was Charles, Jacqui, his father, Giovanni and Maria. Di Maglio was out of the picture. Stephens was long dead. A few others had died. But the winnings were far greater than they had ever planned. Charles suspected they would make in excess of thirty billion. Their total family wealth was going to hit thirty five billion plus. And that would be mainly in cash. That cash would fund their next campaign for they were too young to retire. But before then they needed to take care and complete the deals.

They had distanced themselves from the collapse of the Empire. They had manipulated that collapse. They had distanced themselves from the criminality associated with the collapse of the bank. Now they would distance themselves from the banks that they had created, as they were absorbed into Associated.

Charles would go with the lawyers to the Bank of England. They were expecting him. They would then hand over some of the papers to the authorities and they would need to decide what action to take against the allegedly dishonest directors. That would constitute an amusing revenge for their arrogance. Charles regretted the Honourable James' fate, but not the others. But it had to be all of them.

Charles started the meeting. Giovanni, on a video link, was charm personified. Charles' father looked proudly at him. They all had played their roles to perfection. They knew the meeting could well be bugged. In fact Charles was betting on that. And he felt that, if it wasn't being monitored, then Delaney was not the man he reckoned. And he had little doubt about that judgement. Charles called the meeting to order and advised that he had taken over the acting Chair in the UK and the US. He continued, "I have asked Jack Ryder to sit in as an observer on this special board meeting and help us on any issues relating to stock markets. I have also asked our auditors and lawyers to attend as well as their board nominees. Maria Carter is also here. I take it there are no objections.

Tonight, we will advise the end of the intense examination into the affairs of the bank. We will advise that we have been systematically fleeced. Over and above derivative losses that we have crystallised at two point eight billion dollars, we have an enormous bad debt mountain. It stands at five point eight billion dollars.

The bulk is through the US banks in a series of embezzlements, many of which go back to before our acquisition of the US operations. The balance is in the UK. As you are aware our investment funds took stakes in many of the companies to which we were lending money. That was, of course, totally unethical and I am absolutely horrified that management condoned it or lacked the controls to identify the misdemeanours. The fact is that the funds have lost substantial sums. Those fund holders are our depositors. Their losses put the banks in the US at risk. We plan to give guarantees to fund holders, to limit their losses, and these are likely to cost us two billion dollars"

Giovanni interrupted, "There'll be panic and a run. There'll be a massive run. Where do the funds come from?"

Charles replied quickly, amazing him with the news, "No, we can cover a run. I have taken steps. Di Maglio's guarantee will be exercised."

"I heard that mentioned. What is this guarantee? What have you fabricated? I thought it was from Rossi and Di Maglio Holdings, not Di Maglio himself. Anyway, he's dead."

"It's from Di Maglio. I am talking about the one in the sale document."

"There wasn't one," he retorted.

"There was. I have a copy here. The Fed has an identical copy. You must have forgotten about it. Could the auditors fax Giovanni a certified copy of the appropriate pages of the document and highlight the relevant text?"

Moments later, Giovanni looked at it. He looked at Charles, over the video link, with amazement, "You son of a fucking bitch," he exclaimed.

"Hey watch your language. That's my mother-in-law you're maligning," interrupted Jacqui with a mischievous grin. She was relaxed now. For the most costly game in financial history had been won.

Giovanni shook his head, "Aldo's kid will kill you. He thinks he's a billionaire."

"I think we should avoid personal issues. The reality is that we have to use two billion dollars of the money identified in the Di Maglio accounts to support investors in the funds. The balance of six billion or so will be used to counter some of the other losses in the US. The balance sheet can manage the difference."

"There's around five billion cash only in Di Maglio's accounts. I know that. I have the audited figures," interrupted Giovanni.

"There is five billion in cash. As I said two billion goes to the investment funds. That leaves three billion plus three point five I have bid for the balance of the assets. These are the hotels, casinos, pharmaceuticals and so on."

"They're worth more," growled Giovanni.

"Then bid more. But we need the money from the guarantee by Monday and I am bidding on that basis."

He shook his head again, "Aldo's kid will murder you. The other nephews will too."

"So be it. The last I heard they were in the thick of gang warfare. We'll come across that hurdle when we get there. But they should be aware they would be the first suspects. I hope they have more sense."

"What about the UK end?" It was Jack Ryder who planted the question.

"I have agreed to continue a guarantee of two billion. With that the balance sheet ratios stack up. It is also important to note that I am seeking a purchaser for the bank. I hope to be able to enter into negotiations with a major financial institution. I take it I have board approval?"

Everyone nodded. The board meeting ended. Everyone left the big boardroom, but Charles. Jacqui, Jack Ryder and Maria reassembled in Charles' office. This time there was no link with Giovanni, other than over a very special scrambled telephone line. The room had been swept for bugs. All was secure. Charles was certain that even Delaney would not be able to penetrate this security.

Charles spoke, "I will be frank and tell you what we have made and what everyone's share is."

Charles knew that this was not entirely true, as he would be silent about their share dealings in IBE itself and also their insider trading activity. That had raised around one and a half billion for them. And they had creamed off a further three billion during the scam. But he continued. "Let me run you through the final figures on the private balance sheet. In all, we made thirteen billion from the sale of seventy five per cent of IBE. The bad debts made us five billion, as some were genuine. The trading made us two point three billion, a bit less than planned as the idiots in the trading room actually lost some money on official positions. The scam we pulled on the investment funds made us five point two billion.

We take the proceeds of the share sale and 60% of the scams and frauds. Mr Di Maglio's thirty per cent share is redistributed proportionately among us survivors. Allowing for that and the fact that Stephens is no longer with us to share the pot we agreed, there's over half a billion dollars each for Giovanni and Maria. That's a hell of a lot more than we ever expected."

Maria looked at Charles, her eyes sparkling as she contemplated the scale of her wealth. "That's so much more than we planned."

"When we planned, we acted conservatively and we thought there would be more of us around the table. And the scams became bigger and bigger. We underestimated the greed and stupidity of the great and the good. The frauds were larger. And we also underestimated the American love affair with strong performing investment funds. That helped too," said Jack Ryder.

"So," added Charles, "I'll make your shares available as soon as you give me account details at a bank in one of the countries on a list I will send you. You can guess these are ones that don't ask many questions; especially of the super rich. The payment will come to you from a multitude of banks around the world, in different amounts, and will not be traceable back to us, however many forensic accountants are set the task.

He continued, "We need still to sell off the Di Maglio businesses but that doesn't affect your payment. I also have to see the Bank of England again and the police. That's going to be interesting, but pretty tough for some of our former board whose resignation letters I have in my hand. And they are further confessions of guilt."

As they split, Charles prepared himself for the inevitable discussions with the authorities. They went as expected, focussed on solutions and not root causes. Finally, the courts agreed to their requests. They then made the announcement they needed to make. It was 8pm, Sunday.

It read, 'IBE advises that, as a result of a series of unauthorised and apparently fraudulent loans, it has incurred, primarily in the US, bad and doubtful debts of five point eight billion dollars. The frauds date back to a period preceding the date of acquisition of the US interests of the bank. However, a substantial proportion was initiated in recent months.

Mr and Mrs Charles Rossi, who own 25% of IBE, have successfully petitioned US courts to activate a post sale guarantee of the late Mr Giorgio Di Maglio. As a result, a sum, in excess of six billion dollars, has been injected into the US interests. Mr and Mrs Charles Rossi have acquired for cash the hotel, casino and pharmaceutical interests from the estate of the late Mr Giorgio Di Maglio to enable part of this cash injection.

The Courts have also approved the allocation of two billion dollars from the estate of the late Mr Di Maglio to be assigned to investment funds sold to investors in the US. It is clear that there were fraudulent activities being undertaken by the management of those funds. This contribution will cover a good part of the shortfall resulting from these activities.

Mr and Mrs Rossi have also converted two billion dollars of their earlier guarantees into loans to the bank in the UK to reinstate the required capital ratios for the UK.

The auditors are willing to confirm that there is no loan with past due capital or interest on the books of the bank, except those fully provided for. They are also confident that there are no other significant at risk positions in the trading and derivative areas.

The Bank of England and the Federal Reserve Bank of New York confirm that they are content that the capital positions of the affiliated banks of the IBE Group are adequate and that the interests of all depositors are protected to the extent required under US and UK law. Insurance of depositors continues in force to a hundred thousand dollars in the US for each depositor and fifty thousand pounds in the UK.

The company also advises that the Honourable James Johnson-St John-James, Sir Brian Ffinch-Farquar, Lord Dunkillin and Hector McGarth, all former directors of the Bank, are helping police with enquiries. Mr Percival Johnson-St John-James, the son of the Honourable James, and a former senior executive of the bank is also assisting the police. Other investigations may lead to further arrests.

We would also note that the US authorities have stated that there may be residual monies in the estate of the late Mr Giorgio de Maglio and that they are taking action to seize these under racketeering laws in the US. They have agreed, though, that all their claims can be subordinated to those of the bank and that they have no recourse to it for any shortfalls."

That brought the press to an ecstatic crescendo of vilification of the great and the good. It brought self-righteous articles about crime not paying as the Di Maglio wealth was seized in retribution for his decades of crime. And it brought a glorious and obsequious adulation of Charles and Jacqui.

Delaney called, "You expect us to believe all this. You have to be joking, Charles. We'll be watching you."

Charles laughed, "Don't forget you owe me and I have enough information to sink you."

The poor man was not amused. But he knew Charles was telling the truth. There would be no trouble from Delaney's quarter, especially as Maddy's secret accounts had never been declared.

Giovanni called. "You screwed Di Maglio's estate for the cash he had. You screwed it for the assets in the hotels and other things. You screwed it for its stake in the scam. You set up the authorities to claim any balance on the estate. Someone's going to cotton on and they'll be after you. You double-crossed us all."

Charles laughed, "Giovanni, I didn't double-cross you. You have your share. You have the money you stole from Di Maglio. Other than Maria, nobody knows of the split. And Maria knows we changed it but is not sure how. She'll keep quiet. You'll keep quiet too. You both know what's good for you. Go off and enjoy being rich beyond your wildest dreams. After all, with what you skimmed off Di Maglio, you must be pretty well a billionaire."

He was quiet. He would remain so. At least he would remain so for as long as he didn't tire of life. And Giovanni loved living more than revenge, especially, if the revenge in question brought him no gain.

Then the markets in Asia opened. The share price trembled but held up. The depositors did not desert in droves. The other banks cut back their lines of credit but to no great extent.

They held their breath as London opened. The same situation continued.

Then, in the afternoon, they anxiously watched New York and followed events round America through into California. It continued. The bank remained solid.

And that caused the phone call he had been waiting for. It was Sir Piers.

"We'll buy. It will be at eight dollars a share in our stock. It'll be done and quickly; I don't even want your personal business in any bank I run. We'll buy your shares for cash. And we'll repay your loan. That means you get your two billion back and a further two and a half billion for your shares. There'll be papers to sign. But they're not significant."

Charles didn't trust him one bit, "What papers?"

"There'll be an agreement to keep out of the business. Things like that."

Charles shook his head, "You get your papers back and that's all. You get the originals."

"Then the deal's off."

"I think I'm going to enjoy this. I'll sell a few of your shares and then release the papers that incriminate you. And the financial press will know all about it for tomorrow morning. Come on you don't have a choice. Your board has agreed. You won't have told them about the papers. So you better call them back and tell them. Or agree and keep quiet. And do it now."

Sir Piers crumbled. The poor fool agreed to do everything on trust. As if he could trust Charles. The thought of joining the long list of friends under investigation was too much for him. They met the next morning and agreed the sale with the lawyers present. Charles already had his board approval from the earlier meeting.

That evening their shares were transferred as the funds flowed in. The link with the bank was over. All that was left was to sell off the Di Maglio holdings. And that happened sooner than they envisaged. The phone call came from one of the large private equity funds in New York. They wanted to buy the entire Di Maglio package. They haggled for a couple of hours. Then they were joined again by the lawyers as Charles sold out for four point five billion, with completion to take place in the next two weeks.

The family kitty had risen to close to forty billion dollars. And Jack Ryder called to say he had liquidated all their investments. They drew up the accounts. It was all in cash waiting for the next opportunity. But this time round, the game was approaching its end. The only open issue was for the courts to decide. The great and the good would be sentenced, but that would take years.

Charles' parents headed back to the South of France. They felt they needed a break but, at the same time, Charles knew his father was already monitoring the stocks he had identified. Maria had done one last covert job. She had raided the offices of Associated. And that raid had produced copies of their entire target takeover list. That list was with Jack Ryder, who was researching their performances and their every stock market move. So, as Jacqui and Charles drank champagne at home that night, Jacqui looked and said, "It's all over for now, isn't it?"

Charles nodded, "Maria is heading for America. She wants to buy a ranch. My parents will stay in the South of France. Giovanni will retire to California. There are some people who hate us out there. The British Secret Service is unhappy with our role and the cards we hold. The Di Maglio nephews cannot feel good about us. And we need to set things straight."

They did and quickly. Two months later, there was no need for them to be in London. Somehow everything seemed quiet. The guarantees were all extinguished. His father would advise them of investments from the luxury villa near St Tropez. Giovanni retired to La Jolla in Southern California and told them bitterly he never wanted to see them again. Maria had bought her ranch in Colorado and called them occasionally as if she wanted to be around if they re-launched their business. Douglas and his wife ran their place in the Maldives and also the summer retreat in the hills of Northern California. And he arranged their safety as only he knew how.

Many had been killed. Some deserved it. Others had to die to allow them to meet their objectives. Some had been charged and jailed with frauds they committed without knowing. Life had been good for some and cruel to others. That was their fate.

It was now time to relax with Jacqui, Juliet and little Claire. They were on the bay beneath the house. The sand was golden. The sky was blue with little puffs of white as the clouds made their occasional incursion onto the horizon. The water was warm and clear. There was a landing strip about a mile from the house for supplies to be flown in. The yacht was moored a few hundred yards on the left.

Jacqui and Charles walked along, Juliet trotting alongside them. He was carrying little Claire. They all sat on the sand. The water lapped around them. The sand was warm beneath them. A gentle breeze came in from the sea. All was peaceful.

"We made it in the end," said Jacqui.

"We made it, but it was more dangerous than I thought," he replied.

"But next time we can do it without the Mafia snapping at our heels," she said.

"Will there be a next time?" he mused.

"Well yes, we'll not stop now. We'll never stop. We'll need to think about the future. Not today, not tomorrow. Not even next month. We'll spend the winter here in the Maldives. We're safe on our private island. In summer we'll head over to California. Then some time, once the immediate past has been forgotten, we'll be back. You know that."

He smiled. "The Rossi team will be back. One day, the cult of the equity will be challenged. There will be the inevitable crisis. And then cash will be king. And we have cash. We've ridden one global crisis in Asia and one market boom with IBE.

Next time, we'll take out Associated and create the biggest financial institution in the world. The fools who run the financial markets will not be able to withstand our pressure or our tactics. We know their weaknesses. We know their strategy. One day Sir Piers and the others will finally learn never to trust us for one moment."

Jacqui lent over and kissed him. Juliet paddled in the warm water in front of them. Baby Claire crawled towards her. "Then we will really call the shots; and globally. More powerful than governments, one step ahead of the so-called professionals, deeper pockets than anyone else in the market, we will be the ultimate insiders."

Charles smiled contentedly, "Live. Enjoy. Love. Enjoy. And then, if we need that bit extra, we'll take over the world. "

A gull swooped down and squawked at him. Did it agree? Did it object? Who would ever know? Its comment was as indecipherable as the trails they had never left behind. He took Jacqui in his arms and they rolled over in the sand and into the shallows where Claire and Juliet joined them. They played on through the late afternoon and then headed back to the house.

There, amid the high tech electronics of his sea view study, Charles plugged into his father's analyses of the target banks. The records were being set up. The process was already under way. It was evening in the Far East but morning in New York. The stage was already chosen. The timing was not clear. But when the time came, then the world would see again the return of the ultimate insiders, Rossi and Di Maglio. Only the world would never suspect wrongdoing. Money scares. Few knew with certainty the truth about the financial terrorist. And, for those who did know, the price of indiscretion could be death. And so it would prove to be for anyone who had the temerity to cross them.